Language History

Language History

from *Language*

(1933 Edition)

By LEONARD BLOOMFIELD

Edited by Harry Hoijer

UNIVERSITY OF CALIFORNIA, LOS ANGELES

HOLT, RINEHART and WINSTON, INC.

NEW YORK   CHICAGO   SAN FRANCISCO   TORONTO

EDITOR'S PREFACE

Language History is a reprint of Chapters 17–27 of Leonard Bloomfield's *Language* (1933) made from the original plates without any editorial revision or renumbering of pages. Bloomfield's notes to each chapter and his extensive bibliography have been replaced by a new set of Notes and a Bibliography prepared by the editor, primarily for the purpose of explaining the many cross-references in Chapters 17–27 to chapters not reprinted and to supply the reader with references to material published since 1933. Most of these references are to current textbooks in general linguistics where materials supplementary to those contained in Bloomfield may be found. The index of the original edition has also been revised by the elimination of references to pages not included in the reprint.

Leonard Bloomfield's *Language* summarized and clarified the main achievements of the science of language up to that time. Approximately half of the book is devoted to descriptive or synchronic linguistics, the remainder to historical linguistics. The first part was for its time revolutionary and provoked discussion and controversy that went on for many years. Investigations stimulated by Bloomfield's novel approach to descriptive linguistics brought about many new discoveries and formulations, particularly in respect to methodology, that as time went on out-distanced or replaced Bloomfield's formulations in *Language*. As a result the book is no longer the satisfactory introduction to descriptive linguistics that it was in 1933 and for several years thereafter.

The second part of *Language*, an introduction to historical linguistics, has not suffered the same degree of obsolescence as the first. Although it lacks, understandably, discussion of recently developed methods (for example, internal reconstruction, glottochronology) and is not up-to-date on investigations (for example, in dialect geography) published after 1933, Bloomfield's chapters on historical linguistics nevertheless provide an excellent introduction to the fundamental theory and methodology of historical

v

research. Moreover, his presentation is designed for the student who is beginning his studies in linguistics and who often does not have the background in Indo-European languages that will enable him to understand texts that present methodology very largely in terms of concrete problems drawn from the older Indo-European languages. It may be noted too that Bloomfield does not take his illustrative material from the Indo-European languages alone, but employs as well examples from such little known language families as Malayo-Polynesian and Central Algonquian. In all of his examples he provides enough background on the languages cited to make the principle he is illustrating clearly understandable and so avoids the difficulties that arise from an inadequate linguistic education.

In reprinting a portion of a book, one question inevitably arises: is the reprinted portion sufficiently independent of the chapters omitted to be understandable when torn from the total context? The answer, in the case of Bloomfield's *Language*, is clearly yes. It is true, of course, that Bloomfield employs in Chapters 17–27 a terminology he has defined and explained in previous chapters. Surprisingly, however, this fact offers no serious obstacles to the reader since Bloomfield's procedure, in nearly all instances, is to make such terms understandable from the context in which they are employed. In the few instances where this is not the case, or, more often, when Bloomfield's terminology is antiquated in terms of modern descriptive linguistics, the editor has provided clarification in the Notes. It is assumed also that the student who uses the reprinted portion will have had some introductory work in linguistics and will therefore have some knowledge, however elementary, of the terms commonly employed in descriptive linguistics.

HARRY HOIJER

Los Angeles, California,
September, 1965

CONTENTS

CHAPTER 17

WRITTEN RECORDS

17. 1. The language of any speech-community appears to an observer as a complicated signaling-system, of the kind that has occupied us in the preceding chapters of this book. A language presents itself to us, at any one moment, as a stable structure of lexical and grammatical habits.

This, however, is an illusion. Every language is undergoing, at all times, a slow but unceasing process of *linguistic change*. We have direct evidence of this change in the case of communities which possess written records of their earlier speech. The English of the King James Bible or of Shakspere is unlike the English of today. The fourteenth-century English of Chaucer is intelligible to us only if we use a glossary. The ninth-century English of King Alfred the Great, of which we have contemporary manuscript records, seems to us like a foreign language; if we could meet English-speakers of that time, we should not understand their speech, or they ours.

The speed of linguistic change cannot be stated in absolute terms. A speaker has no difficulty, in youth, in conversing with his grandparents, or, in age, in conversing with his grandchildren, yet a thousand years — say, thirty to forty generations — have sufficed to change the English language to the extent we have just indicated. During these generations, it must have seemed to each London-English mother that her children were learning to speak the same kind of English as she had learned in her infancy. Linguistic change is far more rapid than biological change, but probably slower than the changes in other human institutions.

Linguistic change interests us especially because it offers the only possibility of explaining the phenomena of language. Speakers acquire their habits from earlier speakers; the only explanation of their habits lies in the habits of these earlier speakers. If we ask, for instance, why present-day speakers use the form *dog* for the animal 'canis domesticus,' or, let us say, why they add the suffix [-ez, -z, -s] to derive plural from singular nouns, the obvious

281

answer is that they acquired these habits, in infancy, from the older people round them; if we then ask the same questions about the habits of these older people, we are referred to the habits of still older people, and so on, back into time, without limit. If we could realize our diagram of density of communication (§ 3.4), in which every speaker was represented by a dot and every utterance by an arrow from the dot that represented the speaker to the dot or dots that represented the hearer or hearers, we should find that the network reached indefinitely back into time.

In the normal case, then, the explanation for a speech-habit is simply the existence of the same habit at an earlier time. Where linguistic change has been at work, however, the explanation will be the existence of some other habit at an earlier time, plus the occurrence of the change. Our lexical habit, for instance, of using the word *meat* 'edible flesh,' is not very old; a few centuries ago, the word *flesh* was used in this meaning, and the word *meat* meant 'food.' The explanation of our present-day habit, in this case, consists in (1) the earlier habit, and (2) the intervening change. Since linguistic change never stops, it sooner or later affects every habit in a language; if we know enough of the speech of the past, the second type of explanation will apply to every present-day speech-form.

Since written records give us direct information about the speech-habits of the past, the first step in the study of linguistic change, wherever we have written records, is the study of these records.

We today are so used to reading and writing that we often confuse these activities with language itself (§ 2.1). Writing is a relatively recent invention. It has been in use for any considerable length of time in only a few speech-communities, and even in these its use has been confined, until quite recently, to a very few persons. A speech-utterance is the same, whether it receives a written record or not, and, in principle, a language is the same, regardless of the extent to which speech-utterances of this language are recorded in writing. For the linguist, writing is, except for certain matters of detail, merely an external device, like the use of the phonograph, which happens to preserve for our observation some features of the speech of past times.

17. 2. Writing is an outgrowth of drawing. Probably all peoples make pictures by painting, drawing, scratching, or carving. These

pictures, aside from other uses (§ 2.9), sometimes serve as messages or reminders — that is, they modify the conduct of the
beholder — and they may be persistently used in this way. The
Indians of North America are skilful draftsmen, and in older
times made extensive practical use of pictures. Thus, we are told
of an Ojibwa Indian who owned a long strip of birch-bark with a
series of pictures, which he used to remind himself of the succession
of verses in a sacred song. The third picture, for instance, represents a fox, because the third verse of the song says something
about a fox, and the sixth picture represents an owl, because the
sixth verse says, "It is an ill omen." A Mandan Indian sent the
following picture to a fur-trader: in the center are two crossed
lines; at one side of these lines are outline drawings of a gun and of
a beaver, with twenty-nine parallel strokes above the picture of the
beaver; at the other side of the crossed lines are drawings of a
fisher, an otter, and a buffalo. This means: "I am ready to trade
a fisher-skin, an otter-skin, and a buffalo-hide for a gun and thirty
beaver-pelts."

Records and messages of this sort are usually spoken of as
"picture-writing," but this term is misleading. The records and
messages, like writing, have the advantage of being permanent
and transportable, but they fall short of writing in accuracy, since
they bear no fixed relation to linguistic forms and accordingly do
not share in the delicate adjustment of the latter.

We have no record of any people's progress from this use of
pictures to the use of real writing, and can only guess at the
steps. In the use of pictures we can often see the beginnings of
the transition, and traces of it remain in the actual systems of
writing.

Real writing uses a limited number of conventional symbols.
We must suppose, therefore, that in the transition the pictures
became conventionalized. The way of outlining each animal, for
instance, becomes so fixed that even a very imperfect sketch leaves
no doubt as to the species of animal. To some degree this is true
of the pictures of American Indians. In actual systems of writing
we often find symbols which still betray this origin. In the so-called
hieroglyphic writing of ancient Egypt, most of the symbols are
conventional but realistic pictures, and many of them actually
denote the name of the object which they represent; thus, the
picture of a goose (drawn always in the same way) denotes the

word [sɪ̆] [1] which means 'goose.' In Chinese writing, some of the symbols, such as, for instance, the symbol for the word [ma³] 'horse,' still resemble a picture of the meaning of the word, and this is sometimes true of the older shapes of characters whose modern form shows no such resemblance.

When the picture has become rigidly conventionalized, we may call it a *character*. A character is a uniform mark or set of marks which people produce under certain conditions and to which, accordingly, they respond in a certain way. Once this habit is established, the resemblance of the character to any particular object is of secondary importance, and may be obliterated by changes in the convention of forming the character. These changes are often due to the nature of the writing-materials. Some of the characters of the *cuneiform* writing of the ancient Mesopotamian peoples still betray their origin in pictures, but for the most part this is not the case: the characters consist of longer and shorter wedge-shaped strokes in various arrangements, and evidently got this shape because they were scratched into tough clay. In the hieroglyphic writing of ancient Egypt the characters were carefully painted, but for rapid writing with a reed brush on papyrus the Egyptians developed a simplified and rounded version (known as *hieratic* writing) whose characters have lost all resemblance to pictures. Our own writing is ultimately derived from the ancient Egyptian, but no one could recognize pictures in our letters; as a matter of fact, our letter F still has the two horns of the snail which was pictured in the hieroglyphic ancestor of this letter.

The other, more important phase of the transition from the use of pictures to real writing, is the association of the characters with linguistic forms. Most situations contain features that do not lend themselves to picturing; the picture-user resorts to all sorts of devices that will elicit the proper response. Thus, we saw the Indian drawing twenty-nine strokes above his beaver to represent the number of beaver-pelts. Instead of depicting the process of exchange by a series of pictures, he represented it by two crossed lines with the sets of traded objects at either side. The Ojibwa represented "ill omen" by an owl, in accordance, no doubt, with some tribal belief.

When the picture-user was confronted by a problem of this kind, we may suppose that he actually spoke to himself, and tried out

[1] We do not know the vowel sounds of ancient Egyptian.

various wordings of the troublesome message. Language, after all, is our one way of communicating the kind of things that do not lend themselves to drawing. If we make this supposition, we can understand that the picture-users might, in time, arrange the characters in the order of the spoken words of their language, and that they might develop a convention of representing every part — say, every word — of the spoken utterance by some character. We can only guess at the steps of this transition: real *writing* presupposes it.

In real writing, some characters have a twofold value, for they represent both a picturable object and a phonetic or linguistic form; other characters, having lost their pictorial value, represent only a phonetic or linguistic form; purely pictorial characters that are not associated with speech-forms sink into subsidiary use. The linguistic value predominates more and more, especially as the characters become conventionalized in shape, losing their resemblance to pictured objects. The characters become *symbols* — that is marks or groups of marks that conventionally represent some linguistic form. A symbol "represents" a linguistic form in the sense that people write the symbol in situations where they utter the linguistic form, and respond to the symbol as they respond to the hearing of the linguistic form. Actually, the writer utters the speech-form before or during the act of writing and the hearer utters it in the act of reading; only after considerable practice do we succeed in making these speech-movements inaudible and inconspicuous.

17. 3. Apparently, *words* are the linguistic units that are first symbolized in writing. Systems of writing which use a symbol for each word of the spoken utterance, are known by the misleading name of *ideographic* writing. The important thing about writing is precisely this, that the characters represent not features of the practical world ("ideas"), but features of the writers' language; a better name, accordingly, would be *word-writing* or *logographic writing*.

The main difficulty about logographic writing is the providing of symbols for words whose meaning does not lend itself to pictorial representation. Thus, the Egyptians used a character that represented a tadpole, to symbolize a word that meant 'one-hundred thousand,' presumably because tadpoles were very numerous in the swamps. The Chinese symbol for the word 'good' is a combination of the symbols for 'woman' and for 'child.'

The most important device of this sort is to use the symbol of some phonetically similar word whose meaning is picturable. Thus, the ancient Egyptians used the character that depicted a goose, not only for the word [sỉ] 'goose,' but also for the word [sỉ] 'son,' and they used the character that depicted a conventionalized checkerboard, not only for [mn] 'checkers,' but also for [mn] 'remain.' Chinese writing used the conventionalized character depicting a wheat-plant not only for a word that meant 'wheat,' but also for the homonymous word that meant 'come' — in present-day North Chinese, [laj²]. The ambiguity that arises in this way, leads to a further development: one adds some character that shows which of the similar words is to be read; these additional characters are called *classifiers* or *determinants*. In Chinese writing, which carries the logographic system to perfection, the *phonetic* (as the basic symbol is called) and the classifier are united into a single compound character. Thus, the symbol for [ma³] 'horse' and the symbol for [ny³] 'woman' are united into a compound character, which serves as the symbol for the word [ma¹] 'mother.' The symbol for [faŋ¹] 'square' combines with the symbol for [thu²] 'earth' into a compound symbol for [faŋ¹] 'district'; with the symbol for [sr¹] 'silk,' it forms a compound symbol representing the word [faŋ³] 'spin.' The phonetic part of the compound symbol, as these examples show, does not always accurately represent the sound of the word; we have to suppose, however, that at the time and in the dialect where this development took place, the compound symbols (that is, such as were there and then created) were phonetically accurate.

The logographic system, as we see it in Chinese writing, has the disadvantage that one has to learn a symbol for every word of the language. The compound symbols of Chinese writing can all be analyzed into 214 constituents ("radicals"), but, even so, the labor of learning to read and write is enormous. On the other hand, this system has a great advantage in that the symbols are non-committal as to the phonetic shape of the words. The Chinese speak a number of mutually unintelligible dialects, but in writing and printing they adhere to certain conventions of lexicon and word-order and are thus able to read each others' writings and, with some training, also the writings of their ancient literature.

Our numerals (derived from ancient India) are examples of logographic writing. A symbol like 4 is intelligible to many nations, although we read it as [fowr], the Germans as [fi:r], the French as [katr], and so on. Moreover, since we arrange the numerals according to a fixed convention, we can read each others' numeral phrases even though our languages differ as to the structure of these phrases: 91, for instance, is everywhere intelligible, although we say not ['najn 'won] but ['najntij 'won], and the Germans say, in opposite order, ['ajn unt 'nojntsik] 'one and ninety,' and the French [katrə ve^n $o^n z$] 'four twenties eleven,' and the Danes ['eɪ'n ɔ hal 'fɛmɪ's] 'one and half five-times.'

17. 4. In the device of representing unpicturable words by phonetically similar picturable words, we see the emergence of the phonetic factor in writing. Once a symbol is associated with a particular word, the phonetic features of this word may suffice to bring about the writing of the symbol. In Chinese, where the words are of uniform structure, this transference has been made only from word to word, and the compound characters, in accordance with this structure, are written as units and held down to uniform size. In the writing of other languages, where words are of various lengths, we find word-symbols used for phonetically similar parts of longer words. Thus, the Egyptians wrote the symbol for [mn] 'checkerboard' twice over to represent the word [mnmn] 'move.' By a succession of the symbols for [mç] 'duster' and [ɒr] 'basket,' they wrote the word [mɪçɒr] 'car.' In accordance with the structural variety, they represented words not always by one symbol, but also by various arrangements of logograms, phonetics, and classifiers. Similarly, in Aztec writing, the place-name *Teocaltitlan*, literally 'god-house-people,' was represented by the symbols for *tentli* 'lips,' *otli* 'path,' *calli* 'house,' and *tlantli* 'teeth'; this is the more intelligible as the -*tli* in these words is an inflectional suffix.

The symbols in this way may take on a more and more constant *phonographic* value: they become *phonograms* — that is, symbols not for linguistic forms, but for phonetic forms. The commonest result seems to be a set of *syllabic* symbols, each one of which denotes one syllabic sound with (or without) preceding and following non-syllabics. The cuneiform writing of the ancient Mesopotamians reached this stage; it had characters for such syllables as [ma, mi, mu, am, im, um, muk, mut, nam, tim]. Throughout its use, as it passed from nation to nation, it carried along logographic features. For instance, the ancient Sumerian word for 'god' was [an]; when the Babylonians learned the use of writing, they took over the Sumerian symbol as a logogram for the Babylonian word [ilu] 'god,' and as a classifier which they placed before the names of gods. This kind of retention often occurs when a system of writing is adapted to a new language; thus, we retain Latin abbreviations, such as & (Latin *et*) for *and; etc.* (Latin *et cetera* 'and other things') for *and so forth; i.e.* (Latin *id est*) for *that is; e.g.* (Latin *exempli gratia* 'for the sake of an example') for *for instance; lb.* (Latin *libra*) for *pound,* and so on.

In Babylonian writing the syllabic principle was never fully carried out; thus, a single symbol (a vertical wedge with two small wedges aslant at the left) represented the syllables [ud, ut, ʊᴛ, tam, par, pir, lax, xiš] and, logographically, the words [u:mu] 'day,' [šamšu] 'sun,' and [piçu] 'white.' In its Old Persian form, cuneiform writing had developed into a genuine syllabary, with a relatively small number of symbols, each representative of some one syllable. In general, syllabic systems of writing are widespread and seem to be easily devised. The ancient Greeks on the island of Cyprus used a syllabary of some sixty-five symbols. The Japanese largely use Chinese logographs, but supplement them with two syllabaries, both of which are derived from Chinese characters. The Vai, in Guinea, are said to have a system of 226 syllabic signs. When persons acquainted with modern writing devise a system for an illiterate people, they sometimes find it easiest to teach syllabic writing. Thus, Sikwaya, a Cherokee, devised a set of eighty-five syllabic symbols for his language; the Fox Indians have several syllabaries, all based on English script forms; and the Cree have a syllabary consisting of simple geometrical characters.

17. 5. It seems that only once in the history of writing there has been any advance beyond the syllabic principle. Some of the Egyptian hieroglyphic and hieratic symbols were used for syllables containing only one consonant; in the use of these, differences of the accompanying vowel were disregarded, and the resultant ambiguities were removed by the use of classifiers and logograms. In all, there were twenty-four of these symbols for one-consonant syllables. At an early date — certainly before 1500 B.C. — Semitic-speaking people became acquainted with Egyptian writing, and hit upon the idea of setting down words of their language by means of the twenty-four simplest Egyptian symbols. This was feasible because the structure of Semitic identifies each root by its consonant-scheme (§ 14.8); the non-indication of vowels could leave a reader in doubt only as to some features of word-derivation which he might, in most instances, guess from the context.

Our oldest examples of this Semitic writing are the Sinai Inscriptions, which date from somewhere round 1800 to 1500 B.C. One later style of writing these characters is known as the South Semitic; it is represented by old inscriptions and, in modern times, by the Ethiopian alphabet. The other, North Semitic, style, was used by the Phoenicians, the Hebrews, and the Arameans. The Aramaic varieties include the style which we see in the modern "Hebrew" type, the Syrian style, and the writing of modern Arabic. It is the North Semitic character, in its Phoenician and its Aramaic varieties, that has spread, with many changes, over Asia and Europe.

The syllabaries used in India seem to be derived in part from Aramaic, and mostly from Phoenician writing. For the languages of India, indication of the vowel phonemes was necessary. The Indians used each Semitic character for the syllable of consonant plus [a] and then devised additional marks (*diacritical signs*) which they added to the symbol to designate the combination of the consonant with some other vowel. Thus, a simple sign means [ba], and the same sign with various marks means [ba:, bi, bi:, bu, bu:) and so on. Further, the Indians devised a mark which meant that the consonant was followed by no vowel at all, and a set of symbols for vowels without any consonant. At the same time, they increased the number of basic symbols until they had one for each consonant phoneme. In this way they arrived at a system which recorded their speech-forms with entire phonetic accuracy.

17. 6. Of all the offshoots, immediate and other, of Semitic writing, we need trace only the one which includes our own system of writing. The ancient Greeks took over the Phoenician system and made a decisive change. Some of the Phoenician symbols represented syllables containing consonants that were foreign to Greek; thus, A represented glottal stop plus vowel, O a laryngal spirant plus vowel, and I the consonant [j] plus vowel. The Greeks used these superfluous symbols to indicate vowel values, combining two symbols, such as TA or TO or TI, to represent a single syllable. In this way they arrived at the principle of *phonemic* or *alphabetic* writing — the principle of using a symbol for each phoneme. They fell short of complete accuracy only because they failed to invent enough symbols for vowels: they never distinguished between the long and short quantities, distinctive in their language, of the vowels [a, i, u]. They did later devise diacritical marks to indicate the position and the two qualities of their word-accent, and some signs of punctuation to indicate sentence-modulation.

From the Greeks the alphabet spread to other Mediterranean peoples. The Romans received it apparently through the mediation of the Etruscans. In the Middle Ages it passed from the Greeks to the Bulgarians, Serbians, and Russians, and from the Romans, directly or indirectly, to the other nations of Europe.

The transfer of writing to a new language occurs, apparently, in this way, that some bilingual person who knows writing in one language, hits upon the notion of using the alphabet also for his other language. He may retain whatever defects the alphabet had in the first language and he may retain letters that are necessary in the first language but superfluous in the new one, and he may fail to devise new letters for additional phonemes of the new language. On the other hand, he or his successors may be clever enough to mend these defects, either by inventing new characters or by putting superfluous characters to good use, or by semi-phonetic devices, such as using combinations of letters for a single phoneme.

The phonetic pattern of Latin was such that the Greek alphabet, as the Romans got it (probably from the Etruscans), was almost sufficient. One defect, the use of the symbol C for both [k] and [g], they mended by inventing the modified symbol G for [g]. A more serious matter was the lack of symbols to distinguish long and short vowels; the practice of placing a stroke over the letter or of writing the letter twice to indicate length, never gained much ground. There was no need for indicating the word-accent, since this in Latin was automatically regulated according to the primary phonemes.

The Germanic-speaking peoples took over the Graeco-Roman alphabet, we do not know when or where, in a shape somewhat different from the ordinary Greek or Latin styles. This form of the alphabet, known as the *runes*, was used for short inscriptions, chiefly of magic or religious character, such as epitaphs. The runes were not used skilfully, but they did include letters for some typically Germanic phonemes, [θ, w, j]. The customary order of the alphabet, too, was different from that of the Graeco-Roman prototype; it ran: [f u θ a r k g w h n i j p ɛ z s t b e m l ŋ o d]. For this reason the runic alphabet is sometimes called the *futhark*. The oldest runic inscriptions date from round 300 A.D. Later, as the Germanic-speaking peoples were christianized by Romance and Irish missionaries, they gave up the runes in favor of the Latin alphabet. However, the Gothic bishop Ulfila, who in the fourth century devised an alphabet for his Bible-translation, retained several runic letters, and the Old English priests, in the eighth century, when they took to writing English, retained the runic characters for [θ] and [w], since the Latin alphabet provided none. It was only after the Norman Conquest that English writers gave up these letters in favor of the combinations *th* and *vv* (whence our *w*). The five Latin vowel letters have never sufficed for English; on the other hand, we retain the superfluous letters *c*, *q*, and *x*. The writing of present-day English lacks symbols for the phonemes [a, ɛ, ɔ, θ, ð, š, ž, č, ŋ] and for the stress-accent. This lack is only partially repaired by the use of digraphs, such as *th, sh, ch, ng*.

Occasionally we find our alphabet fully adapted to the phonetic system of some language. In the ninth century, the apostles Cyril and Method added enough extra letters to the Greek alphabet to make it cover the primary phonemes of the Old Bulgarian language. This Slavic alphabet, in its modern form, is well suited to the Slavic languages; for Serbian, some extra characters have been added. Several modern languages have adequate forms of the Latin alphabet; in the case of Bohemian and of Finnish, this result has been reached by the use of diacritical marks, and in the case of Polish by the use also of digraphs, such as *cz* for [č] and *sz* for [š].

17. 7. The principle of alphabetic writing — one symbol for each phoneme — is applicable, of course, to any language. The inadequacy of the actual systems is due largely to the conservatism of the people who write. The writer does not analyze the phonetic system of his speech, but merely writes each word as he has seen it in the writings of his predecessors. When the art of writing becomes well established in a community, not only the spellings of words, but even lexical and grammatical forms become conventional for written records. In this way, a *literary dialect* may become established and obligatory for written records, regardless of the writer's actual dialect.

This conservatism, as time goes on, works also in another way: the conventions of writing remain unaltered even though the speech-forms have undergone linguistic change. For instance, in Latin writing the letter C represented the phoneme [k]. When the Irish and the English took over the Latin alphabet, they used this letter for their [k]-phonemes; in Old English, *cu* spelled [ku:] 'cow,' *cinn* spelled [*k*inn] 'chin,' and *scip* spelled [s*k*ip] 'ship.' Later on, the phoneme [k] underwent certain changes in the various dialects of Latin. In Italy, [k] before front vowels became [č]; Latin ['ken-tum] 'hundred,' for instance, became Italian ['čɛnto]. The Romans wrote their word as *centum;* the Italians still write *cento*. In France, the Latin [k] before front vowels has become [s], as in [sɑ^n] 'hundred,' but the French still write this word as *cent*. In English, we have taken our foreign-learned words from French, with the [s] pronunciation, but also with the traditional spelling with C, as in the word *cent* [sent]. In Latin, the letters A, E, I, O, U were used for the phonemic types [a, e, i, o, u], and they were taken into English writing in these values. Thus, in medieval English writing, a graph like *name* represented a form like ['na:me] 'name.' In the fifteenth century, English spelling became conventionally fixed in much its present shape. Since that time, however, our vowel phonemes have undergone a great deal of change. The result has been that we use the Latin vowel-letters not only in entirely new values — this, after all, would do no harm — but in inconsistent ways. We have kept on using the letter A in graphs like *name, hat, all, far,* although these words have now entirely different syllabic phonemes. Sounds which existed when our spelling became habitual, but have since been lost by linguistic change, are still represented in our writing by silent letters, as in *name, know, gnat, bought, would*.

Once a system of spelling has become antiquated in its relation to the spoken sounds, learned scribes are likely to invent pseudo-archaic spellings. The words *debt, doubt, subtle* contained no [b]-sound in Old French, whence English received them, and were written both in French and in English as *dette, doute, sutil;* the present-day spellings with *b* were invented by scribes who knew the far-off Latin antecedents of the French words, *debitum, dubito, subtilis*. The letter *s* in *isle* reflects the Old French spelling *isle* (from Latin *insula*); at the time when the word was taken into English it no longer had an [s] (compare modern French *île* [i:l]) and was appropriately spelled *ile*. The scribes not only favored the spelling with *s*, but even introduced the letter *s* into two similar words which had never contained any [s]-sound, namely the native English *island* (from Old English *iglond*) and the French loan-word *aisle* (French *aile*, from Latin *āla*). People who saw the runic letter þ in ancient English writings but did not know its value [θ], took it to be a form of the letter *y* and arrived at the notion that the article *the* was in older English *ye*.

17. 8. It is evident, from all this, that written records give us only an imperfect and often distorted picture of past speech, which has to be deciphered and interpreted, often at the cost of great labor. To begin with, the values, logographic or phonographic, of the written signs may be unknown. In this case, the problem of decipherment is sometimes desperate. The best help is a bilingual inscription, in which by the side of the undeciphered text there is a version in some known language; other aids are some knowledge of the language or of the contents of the inscription. In 1802 Georg Friedrich Grotefend succeeded in deciphering cuneiform inscriptions in Old Persian, and round the middle of the nineteenth century a succession of workers (E. Hincks, Rawlinson, Oppert) deciphered those in Babylonian-Assyrian; in both instances the decipherers made ingenious use of their knowledge of related languages. The cuneiform texts in other languages (Sumerian, the language of Van, and Hittite) were deciphered thanks to bilingual texts, such as dictionary-like tablets of word-lists in Sumerian, Assyrian, and Hittite. In 1821 Jean François Champollion began the decipherment of ancient Egyptian writings by using the famous Rosetta Stone (found by the French in 1799; now in the British Museum), which bears parallel inscriptions in hieroglyphics, in a later form of Egyptian writing, and in Greek. In 1893 Vilhelm Thomsen deciphered the Old Turkish Orkhon inscriptions; Thomsen saw that the writing was alphabetical and the language of the Turk family. The hieroglyph-like inscriptions of the Hittites and those of the ancient Cretans have never been deciphered; of the Maya picture-writing in Central America only some characters. denoting months, days, numbers, and colors, have been interpreted.

If the system of writing is known, but the language is not, the situation is little better. The most famous instance of this is the

Etruscan language in ancient Italy; we have extensive texts in
a form of the Greek alphabet, but cannot interpret them, beyond
reading personal names and a few other words. We have dice
with the first six numbers written on the faces, but cannot determine the order of these numbers. The Lydian inscriptions in Asia
Minor are intelligible, thanks to a bilingual text in Lydian and
Aramaic; the alphabet is Greek, and the language apparently
related to Etruscan.

17. 9. When both the system of writing and the language are
intelligible, we aim, of course, to learn from the texts all we can
get as to phonetics, grammar, and lexicon. The phonetic values
of the characters in ancient writings can never be surely known;
thus, the actual sounds represented even by the alphabetic symbols of languages like Ancient Greek, Latin, Gothic, or Old English, are in part uncertain. When the writing has become conventional and unphonetic, the lapses of scribes or the way they write
uncommon words, may betray the real phonetic values. Our
Old English manuscripts show the same inflectional system from
the ninth century until well into the eleventh century, distin-
guishing the vowels of unstressed syllables and the presence of
final *m* and *n;* but occasional lapses of the scribes betray the fact
that already in the tenth century most of these vowels had changed
to [e] and the final [m] and [n] had been lost; such lapses are, for
instance, spellings like *worde* for usual *worda* 'of words,' *fremme*
for normal *fremman* 'to make,' *gode* for *godum* 'to good ones.'
When an English writer in the fifteenth century spells *behalf*
without an *l*, we infer that he no longer pronounced the [l] in this
word, although the tradition of writing insists upon the symbol
to this day. So-called *inverse* spellings tell the same story. Old
English had a sound [x] in words like *light, bought, eight,* which
is still reflected in our spelling with *gh.* When we find the word
deleite (a loan from Old French *deleiter*), which never contained
the sound [x], spelled *delight,* then we may be sure that the [x]
was no longer spoken in words like *light:* for the writers, the *gh*
was now a mere silent graph, indicative only of vowel-quantity.

A serious factor in the linguistic interpretation of written documents is their transmission. Inscriptions, chiefly on stone or metal
or, as in the cuneiform texts, on clay, are generally original notations; we need reckon only with one scribe's errors of spelling or
dictation. Most writing, however, is made on perishable material.

and has come to our time through successive copyings. Our manuscripts of Greek and Latin writings date from the Middle Ages, often from the later Middle Ages or from the early modern period; only fragments have been preserved on papyrus in the sands of Egypt. It is rare good fortune when we have a contemporary manuscript of an ancient text, like the Hatton manuscript of Alfred the Great's translation of Pope Gregory's *Pastoral Care*. The scribes not only made mistakes in copying, especially where they did not understand the text, but they even tampered with it, by way of improving the language or falsifying the content. The study of ancient writing, *paleography*, and the technique of reconstructing ancient texts from one or more imperfect copies, *textual criticism*, have developed into separate branches of science. Unfortunately, textual critics have sometimes lacked linguistic knowledge; our printed editions of ancient texts may fail to report linguistically valuable forms that appear in the manuscripts.

Sometimes the text which appears in our written records has undergone re-spelling into a new alphabet or a new system of orthography. This is the case with our text of the ancient Greek Homeric poems, and with our texts of the Avesta. We try, in such cases, to reconstruct the original spellings and to detect misleading or erroneous features in the traditional text.

17. 10. There are a few side-issues which sometimes help us in the linguistic interpretation of written records. In the forms of composition which we group together under the name of *verse*, the author binds himself to observe certain phonetic patterns. In modern English verse, for instance, the author shapes his wording so that stress-phonemes come at certain intervals, and that words of like ending, from the stressed syllabic to the end, occur in pairs or larger sets, again at certain intervals. Thus, if we know that a poet composed under a convention of exact rimes, we can gather from his rime-words a great deal of information that may not appear in the spellings. Chaucer rimed — to quote the words in their present-day spellings — *mean* with *clean*, but not with *keen, queen, green:* he evidently spoke different vowels in these two sets of words. On the other hand, inconsistencies are equally illuminating. When the Alsatian poet Brant, at the end of the fifteenth century, rimes the word for 'not' both in the Alsatian form [nit], as, for instance, with *Bitt* [bit] 'request,' and in the present-day standard German form [nixt], as, for instance, with

Geschicht [ge'šixt] 'story,' we know that in his day the modern standard form, *nicht* [nixt] 'not' had already gained currency alongside the provincial form of the word. Even when rimes are used traditionally after they cease to be phonetically true, as, in modern English poetry, rimes like *move : love* or *scant : want*, a study of the tradition may be of interest.

Other types of verse lead to similar deductions. In old Germanic poetry, high-stressed words occurred in alliterative sets with the same initial consonant, as in *house and home, kith and kin*. Accordingly when in ancient Icelandic verses of the Eddic poems we find ['wega, 'vega] 'strike' alliterating with [rejðr] 'wroth,' we conclude that the men who coined this alliteration still pronounced the latter word with an initial [wr-], although the spelling of our manuscripts, in accordance with the later language, no longer shows the [w]. In Greek and Latin verse the succession of long and short syllables was regulated; a syllable containing a long vowel or a diphthong, or any vowel followed by more than one consonant, counted as long; the position of words in verse thus often informs us as to vowel-quantities, which are only in part shown by Greek orthography and not at all by Latin.

Another occasional help toward the interpretation of written records is the transcription of speech-forms from one language into another. At the beginning of the Christian era we find the name of *Caesar* written in Greek texts as *kaisar:* since the Greek language has not undergone a change of [k] to [č] or the like, and the Greek *k*, accordingly, represented always a phoneme of the [k] type, this transcription makes it likely that Latin at that time still preserved the [k-]. The old Chinese transcriptions of Indo-Aryan names in Buddhist texts give information about the sounds which were attached to Chinese logographic symbols.

Finally, written records may contain statements of a linguistic nature, as in the case of Sanskrit grammar and lexicon (§ 1.6); the Hindus, moreover, were excellent phoneticians and interpreted the written symbols in physiologic terms. Often enough, however, we have to distrust the information in our texts. The Latin grammarians give us little help as to speech-sounds; the English phoneticians of the early modern period, likewise, confused sounds with spellings and give very poor guidance as to the actual pronunciation of their time.

CHAPTER 18

THE COMPARATIVE METHOD

18. 1. We saw in Chapter 1 that some languages resemble each other to a degree that can be explained only by historical connection. Some resemblance, to be sure, may result from universal factors. Such features as phonemes, morphemes, words, sentences, constructions, and substitution-types, appear in every language; they are inherent in the nature of human speech. Other features, such as noun-like and verb-like form-classes, categories of number, person, case, and tense, or grammatical positions of actor, verbal goal, and possessor, are not universal, but still so widespread that better knowledge will doubtless some day connect them with universal characteristics of mankind. Many features that are not widespread — among them some very specific and even minute ones — are found in distant and wholly unrelated languages; these features, too, may be expected some day to throw light on human psychology.

Other resemblances between languages bear no significance whatever. Modern Greek ['mati] means 'eye,' and so does the Malay word [mata]. If we knew nothing of the history of these languages, we should have to work through their lexicons and grammars in search of other resemblances, and then weigh the probabilities of historical connection, taking into account both the number of resemblances and their structural position. Actually, our knowledge of the past forms both of Greek and of Malay shows us that the resemblance of the two words for 'eye' is accidental. Modern Greek ['mati] is a relatively recent development from an ancient Greek [om'mation] 'little eye,' and this word was in ancient Greek connected, as a secondary derivative, with an underlying word ['omma] 'eye.' The Malay word [mata], on the other hand, had in ancient times much the same phonetic shape as today. Even if, against all present seeming, it should turn out, some day, that these two languages are related, the relationship would lie far back of Primitive Indo-European and Primitive Malayo-Polynesian time, and the resemblance of the modern words for 'eye' would have nothing to do with this relationship.

Still other resemblances are due to the borrowing of speech-forms. In modern Finnish there are many words like *abstraktinen* 'abstract,' *almanakka* 'almanac,' *arkkitehti* 'architect,' *ballaadi* 'ballad,' and so on through the dictionary — cultural words of general European distribution, which have been borrowed, in the last centuries, from one European language into the other, and evidence nothing about kinship. To be sure, we cannot always distinguish between this sort of transmission and the normal handing on of linguistic habits within a speech-community, but for the most part the two processes are very different. If the Finno-Ugrian languages should be related to the Indo-European, then the kinship dates from a time when the words *abstract, almanac,* etc., were not yet in use.

18. 2. When we say, in contrast with these cases, that a resemblance between languages is due to *relationship*, we mean that these languages are later forms of a single earlier language. In the case of the Romance languages, we have written records of this parent language, namely, Latin. After the Latin language had spread over a large area, it underwent different linguistic changes in different parts of this area, so that today these different parts differ greatly in speech, and we call the divergent speech-forms "Italian," "French," "Spanish," and so on. If we could follow the speech, say of Italy, through the last two-thousand years, we could not pick out any hour or year or century when "Latin" gave way to "Italian"; these names are entirely arbitrary. By and large, any feature that is common to all the modern territorial forms of Latin, was present in the Latin of two-thousand years ago; on the other hand, when the modern forms of Latin disagree as to any feature, then some or all of them have, in this feature, undergone some change during the last two-thousand years. The resemblances appear especially in features that are common in everyday speech — in the commonest constructions and form-classes and in the intimate basic vocabulary. The features of difference, moreover, appear in systematic groups, with each territorial form diverging in its own characteristic way.

In most cases we are less favorably situated, in that we possess no written records of the uniform parent speech. The Germanic languages, for instance, resemble each other much as do the Romance, but we have no records from a time when the differences had not yet arisen. The *comparative method*, however, makes the same inferences in both cases. In the latter case we merely lack the confirmation of the written record. We assume the existence, at some time in the past, of a *Primitive Germanic* parent language, but the speech-forms of this language are known to us only by inference. When we write them down, we indicate this by placing an asterisk before them.

18. 3. Compare, for instance, the following words in present-day standard English, Dutch, German, Danish, and Swedish:

	ENGLISH	DUTCH	GERMAN	DANISH	SWEDISH
'man'	mɛn	man	man	manʔ	man
'hand'	hɛnd	hant	hant	hɔnʔ	hand
'foot'	fut	vu:t	fu:s	fo:ʔð	fo:t
'finger'	'fiŋgr̩	'viŋer	'fiŋer	'feŋʔər	'fiŋer
'house'	haws	høys	haws	hu:ʔs	hu:s
'winter'	'wintr̩	'winter	'vinter	'venʔdər	'vinter
'summer'	'sɔmr̩	'zo:mer	'zomer	'sɔmər	˅sɔmar
'drink'	driŋk	'driŋke	'triŋken	'dregə	˅drika
'bring'	briŋ	'breŋe	'briŋen	'breŋə	˅briŋa
'lived'	livd	'le:vde	'le:pte	'le:vəðə	˅le:vde

This list could be extended almost indefinitely; the resemblances are so many and they so thoroughly pervade the basic vocabulary and grammar, that neither accident nor borrowing will explain them. We need only turn to languages outside the Germanic group to see the contrast, as in 'hand': French [mɛⁿ], Russian [ru'ka], Finnish *käsi;* or 'house': French [mezoⁿ], Russian [dom], Finnish *talo.* Another remarkable feature is the systematic grouping of the differences within the Germanic family. Where Swedish has the compound intonation, there Danish lacks the glottal stop; where the others have initial [f], there Dutch has initial [v]; where the others have [d], there German has [t]. In fact, whole series of forms show the same divergences from one Germanic language to the other. Thus, the divergent syllabic phonemes in the word *house* are paralleled in a whole set of forms:

	ENGLISH	DUTCH	GERMAN	DANISH	SWEDISH
'house'	haws	høys	haws	hu:ʔs	hu:s
'mouse'	maws	møys	maws	mu:ʔs	mu:s
'louse'	laws	løys	laws	lu:ʔs	lu:s
'out'	awt	øyt	aws	u:ʔð	u:t
'brown'	brawn	brøyn	brawn	bru:ʔn	bru:n.

The fact that the differences themselves follow a system, — that the divergence, say, of English and German [aw] and Dutch [øy] appears in a whole series of forms — confirms our surmise that these forms are historically connected. The divergence, we suppose, is due to characteristic changes undergone by some or all of the related languages. If we extend our observation to cover more of the dialects in each area, we find many other varieties, with a similar parallelism. In particular, we find, in our example, that forms with the vowel [uː], such as [huːs, muːs] etc., occur also in local dialects of the English, Dutch, and German areas — as, for instance, in Scotch English.

Further, availing ourselves of the written records of these languages, we find that the oldest records from the English and Dutch-German areas, dating round the eighth and ninth centuries of our era, write the forms in our example uniformly with the letter *u*, as *hus, mus, lus, ut* (southern German *uz*), *brun*. Since the writing of these peoples was based on Latin, where the letter *u* represented vowels of the type [u], we conclude that the divergences in the syllabic of our forms had not yet arisen in the ninth century, and that the syllabic in those days was [u] in all the Germanic languages; other evidence leads us to believe that the vowel was long [uː]. Accordingly, we conclude that the Primitive Germanic parent language spoke these forms with [uː] as the syllabic. It is important to observe, however, that this description of the phoneme is only a supplementary detail; even if we made no surmise as to the acoustic character of the Primitive Germanic phoneme, the regularity of the correspondences, in the way of agreement and in the way of parallel disagreement, could still be explained only on the supposition that some one phoneme of the parent language appeared in the syllabic position of the forms *house, mouse,* and so on.

18. 4.   It is interesting to compare these inferences with the inferences that are made in the more favorable case, where the parent language is known to us from written records. The resemblance between the Romance languages is much like that between the Germanic languages.

	ITALIAN	LADIN	FRENCH	SPANISH	ROUMANIAN
'nose'	'naso	nas	ne	'naso	nas
'head'	'kapo	*k*af	šef	'kabo	kap
'goat'	'kapra	'*k*avra	šeːvr	'kabra	'kaprə
'bean'	'fava	'fave	fɛːv	'aba	'fawə[1]

[1] Macedonian

Here we follow the same procedure as with the Germanic correspondences, observing the local types in each area, and the spellings of the older records. The difference is only this, that written notations of the form of the parent language, Latin, are in most instances available. The Romance words in our example are modern forms of the Latin words which appear in our records as *nasum, caput, capram, fabam.*

After we have learned to draw inferences from the Romance forms, we may find discrepancies between the result of our inferences and the written records of Latin. These discrepancies are especially interesting because of the light they throw on the value of our inferences in cases where no record of the parent language is available. Take, for instance, the syllabic in the following types:

	ITALIAN	LADIN	FRENCH	SPANISH	ROUMANIAN
'flower'	'fjore	flur	flœ:r		'floarə
'knot'	'nodo	nuf	nø		nod
'vow'	'voto	vud	vø	bodas[1]	
'tail'	'koda	'kua	kø	'kola [2]	'koadə

The Latin prototypes appear in the first three of these words, as well as in a number of similar cases, with a syllabic *o*, which we interpret as [o:]: *florem, nodum, uotum.* In our fourth word, accordingly, we infer that the Latin prototype contained this same vowel and had the form *[ko:dam].* An inference of this kind is a *reconstruction;* we mark the reconstructed form, *[ko:dam]* or *cōdam*, with an asterisk. Now, in the written records of Latin, the word for 'tail' appears in a different shape, namely as *caudam* (accusative singular; the nominative is *cauda*). This disagrees with our reconstruction, for ordinarily Latin *au* (presumably [aw]) is reflected in the Romance languages by a different type of vowel-correspondence. Thus, Latin *aurum* 'gold' and *causam* 'thing, affair' appear as:

	ITALIAN	LADIN	FRENCH	SPANISH	ROUMANIAN
'gold'	'ɔro		ɔ:r	'oro	aur
'thing'	'kɔsa	'koze	šo:z	'kosa	

It is true that our Latin manuscripts, written in the Middle Ages, occasionally spell the word for 'tail' as *coda*, but this may be due merely to the errors of copyists; the older manuscripts from which

---

[1] Plural form, meaning 'wedding.'
[2] Re-shaped from Old Spanish *coa*, presumably ['koal].

ours were copied may have had the usual Latin form *cauda*. This error would be natural for copyists whose school pronunciation of ancient Latin did not distinguish between Latin *o* and *au*, and would be almost inevitable for copyists who spoke a form of Latin in which our word already had, as in the present-day languages, the vowel of *florem, nodum, votum* and not that of *aurum, causam*. That some people were in this latter position appears from the gloss, preserved to us in ninth-century manuscripts, which explains the word *cauda* by saying that it means *coda:* apparently, the former seemed antique and difficult, while the latter was intelligible. The conclusive support for our reconstruction appears in this, that inscriptions of early date show occasional spellings of *o* in words that ordinarily have *au*, as POLA for the name *Paulla* in an inscription dating from the year 184 B.C. Further, we learn that this *o*-pronunciation for *au*-forms was a vulgarism. Suetonius (who died about 160 A.D.) tells us that the rhetorician Florus corrected the Emperor Vespasian (died 79 A.D.) for saying *plostra* instead of the more elegant *plaustra* 'wagons'; the next day, the emperor got back at him by calling him *Flaurus* instead of *Florus*. As to our word, a grammarian of the fourth century A.D. speaks of *cauda* and *coda* as variant pronunciations. Moreover, we occasionally find over-elegant forms, like Vespasian's *Flaurus* for *Florus;* an inscription dating from before the beginning of the Christian Era has the spelling AVSTIA for *ostia* [oːstia] 'doors.'   In sum, we conclude that our reconstructed **coda* *[koːda] is by no means illusory, but represents a less elegant pronunciation which really existed in ancient time.

Cases like this give us confidence in the reconstructed forms. Latin writing did not indicate vowel-quantities; a graph like *secale* 'rye' could represent several phonetic types. As this word does not occur in verse, where its position would show us the vowel-quantities (§ 17.10), we should be unable to determine its form, had we not the evidence of the comparative method: forms like Italian *segola* ['segola], French *seigle* [sɛːgl] show us that the Latin graph represents the form ['seːkale]. Students of the Romance languages reconstruct a Primitive Romance ("Vulgar Latin") form before they turn to the written records of Latin, and they interpret these records in the light of the reconstructed form.

18. 5. A reconstructed form, then, is a formula that tells us which identities or systematic correspondences of phonemes appear in a set of related languages; moreover, since these identities and correspondences reflect features that were already present in the parent language, the reconstructed form is also a kind of phonemic diagram of the ancestral form.

In the oldest records of the Germanic languages we find the following forms of the word *father:*

Gothic, text composed in the fourth century A.D., preserved in a sixth-century manuscript: *fadar*, presumably ['fadar]; the phoneme represented by *d* may have been a spirant.

Old Norse, in thirteenth-century manuscripts of texts that were, in part, composed much earlier: *faðer*, *faðir*, presumably ['faðer].

Old English, ninth-century manuscripts: *fæder*, presumably ['fɛder].[1]

Old Frisian, thirteenth-century manuscripts of texts that were composed somewhat earlier: *feder*, presumably ['feder].

Old Saxon (that is, northerly parts of the Dutch-German area), ninth-century manuscripts: *fader*, presumably ['fader].

Old High German (southerly parts of the Dutch-German area), ninth-century manuscripts: *fater*, presumably ['fater].

We sum up these facts by putting down the Primitive Germanic prototype as *['fader]; moreover, we claim that this summarizing formula at the same time shows us the phonemic structure of the prehistoric form.

Our formula embodies the following observations.

(1) All the Germanic languages stress the first syllable of this word, as of most others. We indicate this in our formula by an accent-mark, or, since accent on the first syllable is normal in Germanic, by writing no accent-mark at all. This means, at the same time, that in the Primitive Germanic parent language this word shared with most other words a phonemic feature (call it x) which appears in all the actual Germanic languages as a high stress on the first syllable of the word. Of course, it is almost a certainty that this feature x in the parent speech was the same as appears in all the actual Germanic languages, namely, a high stress on the first syllable, but this additional surmise in no way affects the validity of the main conclusion.

(2) All the old Germanic languages begin the word with [f].

---

[1] The Old English syllable [-der] has in modern English changed to [-ðr̩]: hence we say *father, mother, gather,* etc., where Old English had [-der].

If we had not the older records, we should have to consider the fact that some present-day dialects of the English and of the Dutch-German areas have here a voiced spirant of the type [v], but the geographic distribution would even then show us that [f] was the older type. In any case, the structural value of the symbol [f] in our formula is merely this, that the word *father* in the Germanic languages begins, and in Primitive Germanic began, with the same phoneme as the words *foot, five, fee, free, fare*, and so on, all of which we symbolize by formulas with initial [f].

(3) The [a] in our formula says that we have here the same correspondence as in words like the following:

water: Gothic ['wato:], Old Norse [vatn], Old English ['wɛter], Old Frisian ['weter], Old Saxon ['watar], Old High German ['wassar], Primitive Germanic formulas *['water, 'wato:];

acre: Gothic ['akrs], Old Norse [akr], Old English ['ɛker], Old Frisian ['ekker], Old Saxon ['akkar], Old High German ['akxar], Primitive Germanic formula *['akraz];

day: Gothic [dags], Old Norse [dagr], Old English [dɛj], Old Frisian [dej], Old Saxon [dag], Old High German [tag], Primitive Germanic formula *['dagaz].

In this case the deviations, namely Old English [ɛ] and Old Frisian [e] beside the [a] of the other languages, do not occur in all forms; all the dialects have [a], for instance, in cases like the following:

fare: Gothic, Old English, Old Saxon, Old High German ['faran], Old Norse, Old Frisian ['fara], Primitive Germanic formula *['faranan].

In fact, the English [ɛ] and the Frisian [e] occur under fixed phonetic conditions — namely, in monosyllables, like *day*, and before an [e] of the next syllable, as in *father, water, acre*. This deviation, we infer, is due to a later change, perhaps in a common intermediate Anglo-Frisian parent language. We are safe, in any case, in setting up, for all these words, a single structural phonemic unit [a] in the Primitive Germanic parent language.

(4) The acoustic value of the Gothic letter which we have transliterated as *d* is doubtful; it may have been a stop of the type [d] or a spirant of the type [ð], or it may have fluctuated, in which case [d] and [ð] were variants of one phoneme. The old Scandinavian graph speaks for [ð] in this area. The West Germanic languages have an unmistakable [d], which, in this as in other

cases, appears in South German as [t]. In our Primitive Germanic formula we indicate all this by the symbol [d] or [ð]; the former is preferable because easier to print. Our formula identifies the phoneme with that which appears in cases like the following:

mother: Old Norse ['mo:ðer], Old English ['mo:dor], Old Frisian ['mo:der], Old Saxon ['mo:dar], Old High German ['muotar], Primitive Germanic formula *['mo:der];

mead: Old Norse [mjɔðr], Old English ['meodo], Old Frisian ['mede], Old High German ['metu], Primitive Germanic formula *['meduz];

ride: Old Norse ['ri:ða], Old English ['ri:dan], Old Frisian ['ri:da], Old High German ['ri:tan], Primitive Germanic formula *['ri:danan].

(5) The next phoneme shows us a divergence in Gothic, which is obviously due to later change: Gothic always has *ar* for the unstressed *er* of the other languages, e.g.: Gothic ['hwaθar], Old English ['hweðer] 'which of the two.'

(6) The dialects agree as to the last phoneme, [r].

18. 6. While we have no written records to confirm our reconstructions of Primitive Germanic, we occasionally get almost this from the very ancient Scandinavian runic inscriptions (§ 17.6). Take, for instance, the following reconstructions:

guest: Gothic [gasts], Old Norse [gestr], Old English, Old Frisian [jest], Old Saxon, Old High German [gast], Primitive Germanic formula *['gastiz];

horn: all the old dialects [horn], Primitive Germanic formula *['hornan].

Here our Primitive Germanic reconstructions are longer than the actually attested forms. Space forbids our entering into the reasons that lead us to set up the additional phonemes; suffice it to say that in most cases, as in *guest*, these additional phonemes are made entirely definite by the forms in the actual dialects, while in others, such as *horn*, the presence of additional phonemes in Primitive Germanic is certain from the comparison of the Germanic languages, although the nature of these phonemes is decided only by the considerations which we now approach. I have chosen the words *guest* and *horn* as examples because they occur in a runic inscription on a golden horn, dating probably round 400 A.D., found near Gallehus in Denmark. Transliterated, the inscription reads:

ek hlewagastiz holtiŋaz horna tawido

'I, Fame-Guest, the Holting (man of the family of Holt), made the horn.' The same words in our Primitive Germanic formulas, would appear as *['ek 'hlewa-₁gastiz 'holtingaz 'hornan 'tawido:n], and the inscription confirms the final syllable of our reconstruction of *guest*, and the vowel, at any rate, of the final syllable in our reconstruction of *horn*.

The Finnish, Esthonian, and Lappish languages, belonging to the Finno-Ugrian family (§ 4.7) and therefore unrelated to ours, contain many words which they must have borrowed from a Germanic language at an ancient time — all evidence points to the beginning of the Christian Era. As these languages have since that time gone through entirely different changes than have the Germanic languages, these borrowed forms give us independent evidence as to the ancient form of Germanic words. Our reconstructions of Primitive Germanic forms, like *ring*, Old English [hring], Old Norse [hringr], as *['hringaz], or *king*, Old English ['kyning], as *['kuningaz], or *gold*, Old English [gold] as *['golθan], or *yoke*, Old English [jok], as *['jokan], are confirmed by such Finnish loan-words as *rengas* 'ring,' *kuningas* 'king,' *kulta* 'gold,' *jukko* 'yoke.'

18. 7. The comparative method gives us an even more powerful check upon our Primitive Germanic reconstructions. Since the Germanic languages are a branch of the Indo-European family, our Primitive Germanic forms enter as units into comparison with forms of the other Indo-European languages. The reconstructed forms of Primitive Indo-European give us a scheme of a still earlier structure, out of which the Primitive Germanic structure has grown.

Among our last examples there are two good instances. Our reconstruction of Primitive Germanic *['gastiz] 'guest' matches the Latin form *hostis* 'stranger.' From the comparison of the Slavic forms, Old Bulgarian [gostɪ], Russian [go*st*], and so on, we reconstruct a Primitive Slavic *['gostɪ]; this, however, is under strong suspicion of having been borrowed from a Germanic dialect and must therefore stay out of account. The comparison of the Latin form, however, leads us to set up a Primitive Indo-European formula *[ghostis], which tells us, in shorthand fashion, that the Latin second syllable confirms the final phonemes of our Primitive Germanic formula.

Similarly, on the basis of Gothic [ga'juk] 'pair' and the other old Germanic forms of the word *yoke*, namely, Old Norse [ók], Old English [jok], Old High German [jox], we set up a Primitive Germanic formula *['jokan], confirmed by the Finnish loan-form *jukko*. The phonemes in the second syllable of this reconstructed form would be in some respects indeterminate, were it not that this formula enters in turn into comparison with other forms of the Indo-European group. Sanskrit [ju'gam] leads us to set up a Primitive Indo-Iranian *[ju'gam]. Further, we have Greek [zu'gon] and Latin ['jugum]. The Slavic forms, such as Old Bulgarian [igo], Russian ['igo], lead us to set up a Primitive Slavic formula *['igo]. Cornish *iou*, Welsh *iau*, point to a Primitive Celtic *['ju-gom]. Even languages which have reshaped our word, Lithuanian ['jungas] and Armenian *luc*, give some evidence as to the structure of the word in Primitive Indo-European. All of this evidence we subsume in the formula, Primitive Indo-European *[ju'gom].

The case of the word *father* shows us an inference of a more complex character. Sanskrit [pi'ta:], Greek [pa'te:r], Latin ['pater], Old Irish ['aðir], Primitive Germanic *['fader], are the principal forms which lead us to set up the Primitive Indo-European formula as *[pə'te:r]. The initial phoneme here illustrates the simplest case, a constant and normal set of correspondences: initial [p] of the Indo-European languages in general is matched by [f] in Germanic, and by zero in Celtic; Latin ['porkus] 'pig,' Lithuanian ['paršas], corresponds to Primitive Germanic *['farhaz], Old English [fearh] (modern *farrow*), and Old Irish [ork], and the Primitive Indo-European formula is *['porkos].

The second phoneme in our formula shows a more complex case. In our Primitive Indo-European formulas we distinguish three short-vowel phonemes, [a, o, ə], although no Indo-European language has this threefold distinction. We do this because the correspondences between the languages show three different combinations. We use the symbol [a] in those cases where Indo-Iranian, Greek, Latin, and Germanic agree in having [a], as in

acre: Sanskrit ['ajrah], Greek [a'gros], Latin ['ager], Primitive Germanic *['akraz]: Primitive Indo-European formula *[agros].

We use the symbol [o] for the many cases where Indo-Iranian and Germanic have [a], but Greek, Latin, and Celtic have [o], as in

eight: Sanskrit [aš'ta:w], Greek [ok'to:], Latin ['okto:], Primitive Germanic *['ahtaw], Gothic ['ahtaw], Old German ['ahto]: Primitive Indo-European formula *[ok'to:w].

We use the symbol [ə] for the cases where Indo-Iranian has [i], while the other languages have the same phoneme as in the forms of the first set:

stead: Sanskrit ['sthitih] 'a standing,' Greek ['stasis], Primitive Germanic *['stadiz], Gothic [staθs], Old High German [stat]: Primitive Indo-European formula *[sthətis].

Evidently the forms of the word *father* show this last type of correspondence; hence we use [ə] in our formula. The morphologic structure of Primitive Indo-European, as it appears in the totality of our formulas, confirms our threefold distinction [a, o, ə], in that these three units take part in three different types of morphologic alternation.

The third symbol in our formula, which is the last we shall consider, illustrates a very interesting type of inference. Ordinarily when the other Indo-European languages have a [t], the Germanic languages have a [θ]. Thus,

brother: Sanskrit ['bhra:ta:], Greek ['phra:te:r] ('member of a phratry'), Latin ['fra:ter], Old Bulgarian [bratrʊ], Primitive Germanic *['bro:θer], Gothic ['bro:θar], Old Norse ['bro:ðer], Old English ['bro:ðor], Old High German ['bruoder]: Primitive Indo-European formula *['bhra:te:r];

three: Sanskrit ['trajah], Greek ['trejs], Latin [tre:s], Old Bulgarian [trɪje], Primitive Germanic *[θri:z], Old Norse [θri:r], Old High German [dri:]: Primitive Indo-European formula *['trejes].

The word *father*, together with some others, is anomalous in Primitive Germanic in containing [d] instead of [θ]. One might, of course, assume that two distinct Primitive Indo-European phonemes were here involved, which had coincided as [t] in all the Indo-European languages except Germanic, which alone distinguished them as [θ] versus [d]. In 1876, however, Karl Verner (1846–1896), a Danish linguist, showed that in a number of the cases where Germanic has the troublesome [d], this consonant follows upon a vowel or diphthong which is unstressed in Sanskrit and Greek; this correlation occurs in enough instances, and, in the morphologic structure, systematically enough, to exclude the factor of accident. The contrast of the words *brother* and *father* illustrates this correlation. Since the place of the word-accent is determined by the primary phonemes in Italic, Celtic, and Germanic, we can easily believe that its position in each of these languages is due to later change. Sanskrit and Greek, moreover, agree so often, although the place of the accent in both is highly irregular, that we do not hesitate to attribute this feature to the parent language. We thus face a definite succession of events in the period between Primitive Indo-European and Primitive Germanic — a period to which we give the name *pre-Germanic:*

Primitive Indo-European: [t] a unit phoneme; word-accent on different syllables in different words:

*['bhra:te:r] 'brother' *[pə'te:r] 'father'

Pre-Germanic period:

first change: [t] becomes [θ]:

*['bra:θe:r] *[fa'θe:r]

second change: [θ] after unstressed syllabic becomes [d], presumably a voiced spirant:

*['bra:θe:r] *[fa'de:r]

third change: the accent is shifted to the first syllable of each word; this brings us to

Primitive Germanic *['bro:θer] *['fader].

In a similar way, the correspondences reveal the pre-history of each branch of the Indo-European family. Thus, in the case of Latin *cauda* and *cōda* 'tail,' the Lithuanian word ['kuodas] 'tuft' probably represents the same form of the parent speech; if so, then, in the light of other correspondences, in which Lithuanian [uo] and Latin [o:] appear side by side, we may take *cōda* to be the older of the two Latin forms, and *cauda* to be a hyper-urban (over-elegant) variant (§ 18.4).

Our Primitive Indo-European reconstructions are not subject to any check by means of earlier recorded or reconstructed forms. In the last decades, to be sure, it has been ascertained that the Hittite language, known to us from records in cuneiform writing from 1400 B.C. onward, is distantly related to Indo-European. Accordingly, it has been possible to uncover a few features of a Primitive Indo-Hittite parent language — that is, to trace the earlier history of a few of the features of Primitive Indo-European.

18. 8. The comparative method tells us, in principle, nothing about the acoustic shape of reconstructed forms; it identifies the phonemes in reconstructed forms merely as recurrent units. The Indonesian languages show us a striking example of this. Each language has only a few phonemes of the types [d, g, l, r], but the variety of the correspondences assures us of a larger number of phonemes in the parent language. The acoustic character of these phonemes can only be guessed at; the symbols by which we represent them are merely labels for correspondences. It is worth noticing that we have older written records for none of these languages except Javanese; this in no way affects the application of the comparative method. The eight normal types of correspondence will appear sufficiently if we consider three languages: Tagalog (on the island of Luzon in the Philippines), Javanese, and Batak (on the island of Sumatra). In the following examples the consonant under discussion appears in the middle of the word.

		TAGALOG	JAVANESE	BATAK	PRIMITIVE INDONESIAN
(1)		l	l	l	l
	'choose'	'pi:liʔ	pilik	piʟi	*pilik
(2)		l	r	r	ʟ
	'lack'	'ku:laŋ	kuraŋ	huraŋ	*kuʟaŋ
(3)		l	r	g	ɡ
	'nose'	i'luŋ	iruŋ	iguŋ	*iɡuŋ
(4)		l	ᴅ	d	ᴅ
	'desire'	'hi:lam	iᴅam	idam	*hiᴅam[1]
(5)		r	d	d	d
	'point out'	'tu:ruʔ	tuduk	tudu	*tuduk
(6)		r	ᵈ	ᵈ	ᵈ
	'spur'	'ta:riʔ	taᵈi	taᵈi	*taᵈi
(7)		g	g	g	g
	'sago'	'sa:gu	sagu	sagu	*tagu[2]
(8)		g	zero	r	γ
	'addled'	bu'guk	vuʔ	buruk	*buγuk

18. 9. The comparative method assumes that each branch or language bears independent witness to the forms of the parent language, and that identities or correspondences among the related languages reveal features of the parent speech. This is the same thing as assuming, firstly, that the parent community was completely uniform as to language, and, secondly, that this parent community split suddenly and sharply into two or more daughter communities, which lost all contact with each other.

[1] Javanese [D] is a domal stop, distinct from the dental [d]. The Tagalog word means 'pain, smart.' The Batak form here given is not listed for the Toba dialect, from which our other examples are taken, but it occurs in the Dairi dialect.

[2] The Tagalog form means 'exudation'; in poetic use, also 'sap.'

Often enough, the comparative method assumes successive splittings of this sort in the history of a language. It assumes that Germanic split off neatly from Primitive Indo-European. After this split, any change in Germanic was independent of changes in the sister languages, and any resemblance between Germanic and the sister languages betokens a common inheritance. The differences between Primitive Indo-European and Primitive Germanic are due to changes which occurred during the *pre-Germanic* period. In exactly the same way, the comparative method interprets the special similarities among the West Germanic languages (in contrast with Scandinavian and Gothic) by saying that a West Germanic community split off, neatly and suddenly, from the uniform Primitive Germanic parent community. After this splitting off comes a pre-West-Germanic period, during which there arose the differences that characterize Primitive West Germanic. Again, on the basis of peculiarities common to English and Frisian (such as, especially, the [ɛ, e] for Primitive West Germanic [a], which we noticed above), we may speak of a pre-Anglo-Frisian period, during which there occurred the changes which led to Primitive Anglo-Frisian. Upon this there followed a pre-English period, which leads to the forms that appear in our earliest records of English. Thus, the comparative method reconstructs uniform parent languages existing at points in time, and deduces the changes which took place after each such parent language split, up to the next following parent language or recorded language. The comparative method thus shows us the ancestry of languages in the form of a family-tree, with successive branchings: the points at which branches separate are designated by the word *primitive;* the branches between the points are designated by the prefix *pre-*, and represent periods of linguistic change (Figure 1).

18. 10. The earlier students of Indo-European did not realize that the family-tree diagram was merely a statement of their method; they accepted the uniform parent languages and their sudden and clear-cut splitting, as historical realities.

In actual observation, however, no speech-community is ever quite uniform (§ 3.3). When we describe a language, we may ignore the lack of uniformity by confining ourselves to some arbitrarily chosen type of speech and leaving the other varieties for later discussion, but in studying linguistic change we cannot do this, because all changes are sure to appear at first in the shape of variant features.

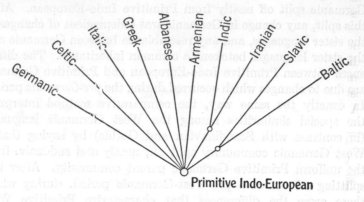

Primitive Indo-European

⋮ English (actual records)
⋮ pre-English period
○ Primitive Anglo-Frisian
⋮ pre-Anglo-Frisian period
○ Primitive West Germanic
⋮ pre-West Germanic period
○ Primitive Germanic

⋮ pre-Germanic period

○ Primitive Indo-European

FIGURE 1. (Above) Family-tree diagram of the relationship of the Indo-European languages. (Below) Part of a family-tree diagram, showing the epochs in the history of English.

At times, to be sure, history shows us a sudden cleavage, such as is assumed by the comparative method. A cleavage of this sort occurs when part of a community emigrates. After the Angles, Saxons, and Jutes settled in Britain, they were fairly well cut off from their fellows who remained on the Continent; from that time on, the English language developed independently, and any resemblance between English and the continental dialects of West Germanic can be taken, in the ordinary case, as evidence for a feature that existed before the emigration of the English. When the Gipsies, in the Middle Ages, started from northwestern India on their endless migration, the changes in their language, from that time on, must have been independent of whatever linguistic changes occurred in their former home.

A less common case of clear-cut division of a speech-community,

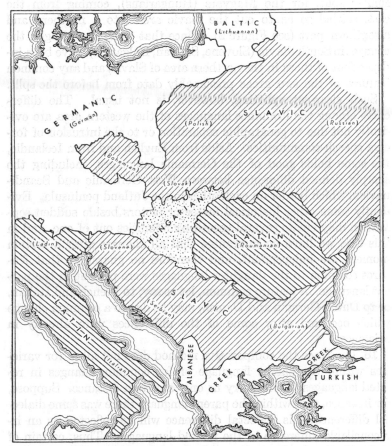

FIGURE 2. Eastern Europe: the splitting of speech-areas by invasion. Latin, once a unit, was split, in the early Middle Ages, by the intrusion of Slavic. In the ninth century this area, in turn, was split by the intrusion of Hungarian.

is splitting by the intrusion of a foreign community. Under the Roman Empire, Latin was spoken over a solid area from Italy to the Black Sea. In the early Middle Ages, Slavs came in from the north and settled so as to cut this area completely in two: since that time, the development of Roumanian, in the east, has gone on independently of the development of the other Romance languages, and a feature common to both Roumanian and the western Romance languages is presumably guaranteed as Latin. In the ninth century, the great Slavic area in turn suffered a similar split, for the Magyars (Hungarians), coming from the east, settled so as to cut the Slavic area into a northern and a southern part (see Figure 2). Since that time, accordingly, the changes in South Slavic (Slovene, Serbian, Bulgarian) have been independent of those in the northern area of Slavic, and any common features of the two areas presumably date from before the split.

Such clear-cut splitting, however, is not usual. The differences among the Romance languages of the western area are evidently not due to geographic separation or to the intrusion of foreign speech-communities. Aside from English and from Icelandic, the same holds good of the Germanic languages, including the sharply defined difference between West Germanic and Scandinavian, which border on each other in the Jutland peninsula. Evidently some other historical factor or factors beside sudden separation may create several speech-communities out of one, and in this case we have no guarantee that all changes after a certain moment are independent, and therefore no guarantee that features common to the daughter languages were present in the parent language. A feature common, let us say, to French and Italian, or to Dutch-German and Danish, may be due to a common change which occurred after some of the differences were already in existence.

18. 11. Since the comparative method does not allow for varieties within the parent language or for common changes in related languages, it will carry us only a certain distance. Suppose, for instance, that within the parent language there was some dialectal difference: this dialectal difference will be reflected as an irreconcilable difference in the related languages. Thus, certain of the inflectional suffixes of nouns contain an [m] in Germanic and Balto-Slavic, but a [bh] in the other Indo-European languages, and there is no parallel for any such phonetic correspondence.

(a) Primitive Indo-European *[-mis], instrumental plural: Gothic ['wulfam] 'to, by wolves,'

Primitive Indo-European *[-miːs], instrumental plural: Lithuanian [nakti'mis] 'by nights,' Old Bulgarian [noštɪmi],

Primitive Indo-European *[-mos], dative-ablative plural: Lithuanian [vil'kams] 'to wolves,' Old Bulgarian [vḷkomʊ],

(b) Primitive Indo-European *[-bhis], instrumental plural: Sanskrit [pad'bhih] 'by feet,' Old Irish ['feraʋ] 'by men,'

Primitive Indo-European *[-bhjos], dative-ablative plural: Sanskrit [pad'bhjah] 'to, from the feet,'

Primitive Indo-European *[-bhos], dative-ablative plural: Latin ['pedibus] 'to, from the feet,' Old Celtic [maːtrebo] 'to the mothers.'

In cases like these, the comparative method does not show us the form of the parent speech (which is defined as a uniform language), but shows us irreconcilably different forms, whose relation, as alternants or as dialectal variants, it does not reveal. Yet these cases are very many.

On the other hand, if, like the older scholars, we insist that the discrepancy is due to a common change in the history of Germanic and Balto-Slavic, then, under the assumptions of the comparative method, we must say that these two branches had a period of common development: we must postulate a Primitive Balto-Slavo-Germanic speech-community, which split off from Primitive Indo-European, and in turn split into Germanic and Balto-Slavic. If we do this, however, we are at once involved in contradictions, because of other, discordant but overlapping, resemblances. Thus, Balto-Slavic agrees with Indo-Iranian, Armenian, and Albanese, in showing sibilants in certain forms where the other languages have velars, as in the word for 'hundred':

Sanskrit [ça'tam], Avestan [satəm], Lithuanian ['šimtas], but Greek [he-ka'ton], Latin ['kentum], Old Irish [keːð], Primitive Indo-European *[km̥'tom]. We suppose that the parent language in such cases had palatalized velar stops.

Likewise, where the four branches just named have velar stops, there the others, in many forms, have combinations of velars with a labial element, or apparent modifications of these; we suppose that the parent language had labialized velar stops, as in the interrogative substitute stem:

Sanskrit [kah] 'who?' Lithuanian [kas], Old Bulgarian [kʊ-to], but Greek ['po-then] 'from where?' Latin [kwo:] 'by whom, by what?' Gothic [hwas] 'who?' Primitive Indo-European *[kʷos] 'who?' and derivatives.

Only in a limited number of cases do the two sets of languages agree in having plain velar stops. Accordingly, many scholars suppose that the earliest traceable division of the Primitive Indo-European unity was into a western group of so-called "*centum*-languages" and an eastern group of "*satem*-languages," although, to be sure, Tocharian, in Central Asia, belonged to the former group. This division, it will be seen, clashes with any explanation that supposes Balto-Slavic and Germanic to have had a common period of special development.

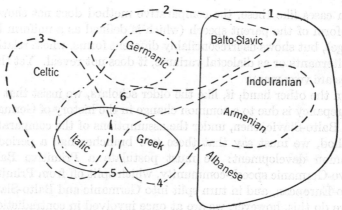

FIGURE 3. Some overlapping features of special resemblance among the Indo-European languages, conflicting with the family-tree diagram. — Adapted from Schrader.
1. Sibilants for velars in certain forms.
2. Case-endings with [m] for [bh].
3. Passive-voice endings with [r].
4. Prefix ['e-] in past tenses.
5. Feminine nouns with masculine suffixes.
6. Perfect tense used as general past tense.

Again, we find special resemblances between Germanic and Italic, as, for instance, in the formation and use of the past-tense verb, or in some features of vocabulary (*goat* : Latin *haedus;* Gothic *gamains* : Latin *commūnis* 'common'). These, too, conflict with the special resemblances between Germanic and Balto-Slavic. In the same way, Italic on the one side shares peculiarities with Celtic and on the other side with Greek (Figure 3).

18. 12. As more and more of these resemblances were revealed, the older scholars, who insisted upon the family-tree diagram, faced an insoluble problem. Whichever special resemblances one took as evidence for closer relationships, there remained others, inconsistent with these, which could be explained only by an entirely different diagram. The decision, moreover, was too important to be evaded, since in each case it profoundly altered the value of resemblances. If Germanic and Balto-Slavic, for instance, have passed through a period of common development, then any agreement between them guarantees nothing about Primitive Indo-European, but if they have not passed through a period of common development, then such an agreement, on the family-tree principle, is practically certain evidence for a trait of Primitive Indo-European.

The reason for these contradictions was pointed out in 1872 by Johannes Schmidt (1843–1901), in a famous essay on the interrelationship of the Indo-European languages. Schmidt showed that special resemblances can be found for any two branches of Indo-European, and that these special resemblances are most numerous in the case of branches which lie geographically nearest each other. Johannes Schmidt accounted for this by the so-called *wave-hypothesis*. Different linguistic changes may spread, like waves, over a speech-area, and each change may be carried out over a part of the area that does not coincide with the part covered by an earlier change. The result of successive waves will be a network of isoglosses (§ 3.6). Adjacent districts will resemble each other most; in whatever direction one travels, differences will increase with distance, as one crosses more and more isogloss-lines. This, indeed, is the picture presented by the local dialects in the areas we can observe. Now, let us suppose that among a series of adjacent dialects, which, to consider only one dimension, we shall designate as A, B, C, D, E, F, G, . . . X, one dialect, say F, gains a political, commercial, or other predominance of some sort, so that its neighbors in either direction, first E and G, then D and H, and then even C and I, J, K, give up their peculiarities and in time come to speak only the central dialect F. When this has happened, F borders on B and L, dialects from which it differs sharply enough to produce clear-cut language boundaries; yet the resemblance between F and B will be greater than that between F and A, and, similarly, among L, M, N, . . . X, the dialects nearest to F will show a greater resemblance to F, in spite of the clearly marked boundary, than will the more distant dialects. The presentation of these factors became known as the *wave-theory*, in contradistinction to the older *family-tree theory* of linguistic relationship. Today we view the wave process and the splitting process merely as two types — perhaps the principal types — of historical processes that lead to linguistic differentiation.

18. 13. The comparative method, then, — our only method for the reconstruction of prehistoric language, — would work accurately for absolutely uniform speech-communities and sudden, sharp cleavages. Since these presuppositions are never fully realized, the comparative method cannot claim to picture the historical process. Where the reconstruction works smoothly, as in the Indo-European word for *father*, or in observations of less ambitious scope (such as, say, reconstructions of Primitive Romance or Primitive Germanic), there we are assured of the structural features of a speech-form in the parent language. Wherever the comparison is at all ambitious as to the reach of time or the breadth of the area, it will reveal incommensurable forms and partial similarities that cannot be reconciled with the family-tree diagram. The comparative method can work only on the assumption of a uniform parent language, but the incommensurable forms (such as *[-mis] and *[-bhis] as instrumental plural case endings in Primitive Indo-European) show us that this assumption is not justified. The comparative method presupposes clear-cut splitting off of successive branches, but the inconsistent partial similarities show us that later changes may spread across the isoglosses left by earlier changes; that resemblance between neighboring languages may be due to the disappearance of intermediate dialects (wave-theory); and that languages already in some respects differentiated may make like changes.

Sometimes additional facts help us to a decision. Thus, the adjective Sanskrit ['pi:va:] 'fat,' Greek ['pi:o:n] occurs only in Indo-Iranian and Greek, but its existence in Primitive Indo-European is guaranteed by the irregular formation of the feminine form, Sanskrit ['pi:vari:], Greek ['pi:ejra]; neither language formed new feminines in this way. On the other hand, the Germanic word *hemp*, Old English ['henep], Middle Dutch ['hannep], and so on, corresponds to Greek ['kannabis]; nevertheless, we learn from Herodotus (fifth century B.C.) that hemp was known to the Greeks only as a foreign plant, in Thrace and Scythia: the word came into Greek (and thence into Latin) and into Germanic (and thence, presumably, into Slavic) from some other language — very likely from a Finno-Ugrian dialect — at some time before the pre-Germanic changes of [k] to [h] and of [b] to [p]. But for this piece of chance information, the correspondence of the Greek and Germanic forms would have led us to attribute this word to Primitive Indo-European.

18. 14. The reconstruction of ancient speech-forms throws some light upon non-linguistic conditions of early times. If we consider, for instance, that the composition of our earliest Indic records can scarcely be placed later than 1200 B.C., or that of the Homeric poems later than 800 B.C., we are bound to place our reconstructed Primitive Indo-European forms at least a thousand years earlier than these dates. We can thus trace the history of language, often in minute detail, much farther back than that of any other of a people's institutions. Unfortunately, we cannot transfer our knowledge to the latter field, especially as the meanings of speech-forms are largely uncertain. We do not know where Primitive Indo-European was spoken, or by what manner of people; we cannot link the Primitive Indo-European speech-forms to any particular type of prehistoric objects.

The noun and the verb *snow* appear so generally in the Indo-European languages that we can exclude India from the range of possible dwellings of the Primitive Indo-European community. The names of plants, even where there is phonetic agreement, differ as to meaning; thus, Latin ['fa:gus], Old English [bo:k] mean 'beech-tree,' but Greek [phe:'gos] means a kind of oak. Similar divergences of meaning appear in other plant-names, such as our words *tree, birch, withe* (German *Weide* 'willow'), *oak, corn,* and the types of Latin *salix* 'willow,' *quercus* 'oak,' *hordeum* 'barley' (cognate with German *Gerste*), Sanskrit ['javah] 'barley.' The type of Latin *glans* 'acorn' occurs with the same meaning in Greek, Armenian, and Balto-Slavic.

Among animal-names, *cow,* Sanskrit [ga:wh], Greek [ˇbows], Latin [bo:s], Old Irish [bo:], is uniformly attested and guaranteed by irregularities of form. Other designations of animals appear in only part of the territory; thus, *goat,* as we have seen, is confined to Germanic and Italic; the type Latin *caper:* Old Norse *hafr* 'goat' occurs also in Celtic; the type Sanskrit [a'jah], Lithuanian [oˇži:s] is confined to these two languages; and the type of Greek ['ajks]

appears also in Armenian and perhaps in Iranian. Other animals
for which we have one or more equations covering part of the
Indo-European territory, are horse, dog, sheep (the word *wool*
is certainly of Primitive Indo-European age), pig, wolf, bear, stag,
otter, beaver, goose, duck, thrush, crane, eagle, fly, bee (with
mead, which originally meant 'honey'), snake, worm, fish. The
types of our *milk* and of Latin *lac* 'milk' are fairly widespread, as
are the word *yoke* and the types of our *wheel* and German *Rad*
'wheel,' and of *axle*. We may conclude that cattle were domesti-
cated and the wagon in use, but the other animal-names do not
guarantee domestication.

Verbs for weaving, sewing, and other processes of work are
widespread, but vague or variable in meaning. The numbers
apparently included 'hundred' but not 'thousand.' Among terms
of relationship, those for a woman's relatives by marriage ('husband's brother,' 'husband's sister,' and so on) show widespread
agreement, but not those for a man's relatives by marriage; one
concludes that the wife became part of the husband's family,
which lived in a large patriarchal group. The various languages
furnish several equations for names of tools and for the metals gold,
silver, and bronze (or copper). Several of these, however, are loan-
words of the type of *hemp;* so certainly Greek ['pelekus] 'axe,'
Sanskrit [para'çuh] is connected with Assyrian [pilakku], and our
axe and *silver* are ancient loan-words. Accordingly, scholars place
the Primitive Indo-European community into the Late Stone Age.

CHAPTER 19

DIALECT GEOGRAPHY

19. 1. The comparative method, with its assumption of uniform parent languages and sudden, definitive cleavage, has the virtue of showing up a residue of forms that cannot be explained on this assumption. The conflicting large-scale isoglosses in the Indo-European area, for instance, show us that the branches of the Indo-European family did not arise by the sudden breaking up of an absolutely uniform parent community (§ 18.11, Figure 3). We may say that the parent community was dialectally differentiated before the break-up, or that after the break-up various sets of the daughter communities remained in communication; both statements amount to saying that areas or parts of areas which already differ in some respects may still make changes in common. The result of successive changes, therefore, is a network of isoglosses over the total area. Accordingly, the study of local differentiations in a speech-area, *dialect geography*, supplements the use of the comparative method.

Local differences of speech within an area have never escaped notice, but their significance has only of late been appreciated. The eighteenth-century grammarians believed that the literary and upper-class standard language was older and more true to a standard of reason than the local speech-forms, which were due to the ignorance and carelessness of common people. Nevertheless, one noticed, in time, that local dialects preserved one or another ancient feature which no longer existed in the standard language. Toward the end of the eighteenth century there began to appear *dialect dictionaries*, which set forth the lexical peculiarities of non-standard speech.

The progress of historical linguistics showed that the standard language was by no means the oldest type, but had arisen, under particular historical conditions, from local dialects. Standard English, for instance, is the modern form not of literary Old English, but of the old local dialect of London which had become first a provincial and then a national standard language, absorbing.

meanwhile, a good many forms from other local and provincial dialects. Opinion now turned to the other extreme. Because a local dialect preserved some forms that were extinct in the standard language, it was viewed as a survival, unchanged, of some ancient type; thus, we still hear it said that the speech of some remote locality is "pure Elizabethan English." Because the admixture of forms from other dialects had been observed only in the standard language, one jumped at the conclusion that local dialects were free from this admixture and, therefore, in a historical sense, more regular. At this stage, accordingly, we find *dialect grammars*, which show the relation of the sounds and inflections of a local dialect to those of some older stage of the language.

Investigation showed that every language had in many of its forms suffered displacements of structure, which were due to the admixture of forms from other dialects. Old English [f], for instance, normally appears as [f] in standard English, as in *father, foot, fill, five*, and so on, but in the words *vat* and *vixen*, from Old English [fɛt] and ['fyksen] 'female fox,' it appears as [v], evidently because these forms are admixtures from a dialect which had changed initial [f] to [v]; and, indeed, this initial [v] appears regularly in some southern English dialects (Wiltshire, Dorset, Somerset, Devon), in forms like ['vaðə, vut, vil, vajv]. Some students hoped, therefore, to find in local dialects the phonemic regularity (that is, adherence to older patterns) that was broken in the standard language. In 1876 a German scholar, Georg Wenker, began, with this end in view, to survey the local dialects in the Rhine country round Düsseldorf; later he extended his survey to cover a wider area, and published, in 1881, six maps as a first instalment of a *dialect atlas* of northern and central Germany. He then gave up this plan in favor of a survey which was to cover the whole German Empire. With government aid, Wenker got forty test-sentences translated, largely by schoolmasters, into more than forty-thousand German local dialects. Thus it was possible to mark the different local varieties of any one feature on a map, which would then show the geographic distribution. Since 1926 these maps, on a reduced scale, have been appearing in print, under the editorship of F. Wrede.

The result, apparent from the very start, of Wenker's study, was a surprise: the local dialects were no more consistent than the standard language in their relation to older speech-forms. *Dialect geography* only confirmed the conclusion of comparative study, namely, that different linguistic changes cover different portions of an area. The new approach yielded, however, a close-range view of the network of isoglosses.

19. 2. At present, then, we have three principal forms of dialect study. The oldest is lexical. At first, the dialect dictionaries included only the forms and meanings which differed from standard usage. This criterion, of course, is irrelevant. Today we expect a dictionary of a local dialect to give all the words that are current in non-standard speech, with phonetic accuracy and with reasonable care in the definition of meanings. A dialect dictionary for a whole province or area is a much bigger undertaking. It should give a phonemic scheme for each local type of speech, and therefore can hardly be separated from a phonologic study. We expect a statement of the geographic area in which every form is current, but this statement can be given far better in the form of a map.

Grammars of local dialects largely confine themselves to stating the correspondence of the phonemes and of the inflectional forms with those of an older stage of the language. The modern demand would be rather for a description such as one might make of any language: phonology, syntax, and morphology, together with copious texts. The history of the forms can be told only in connection with that of the area as a whole, since every feature has been changed or spared only in so far as some wave of change has reached or failed to reach the speakers of the local dialect. The grammar of a whole area represents, again, a large undertaking. The first work of this kind, the single-handed performance of a man of the people, was the Bavarian grammar, published in 1821, of Johann Andreas Schmeller (1785–1852); it is still unsurpassed. For English, we have the phonology of the English dialects in the fifth volume of Ellis's *Early English Pronunciation*, and Joseph Wright's grammar, published in connection with his *English Dialect Dictionary*. Here too, of course, we demand a statement of the topographic extent of each feature, and this, again, can be more clearly given on a map.

Except for the complete and organized description of a single local dialect, then, the map of distribution is the clearest and most compact form of statement. The dialect atlas, a set of such maps, allows us to compare the distributions of different features by comparing the different maps; as a practical help for this comparison, the German atlas provides with each map a loose transparent sheet reproducing the principal isoglosses or other marks of the map. Aside from the self-understood demands of accuracy and consistency, the value of a map depends very largely on the completeness with which the local dialects are registered: the finer the network, the more complete is the tale. In order to record and estimate a local form, however, we need to know its structural pattern in terms of the phonemic system of the local dialect. Furthermore, several variant pronunciations or grammatical or lexical types may be current, with or without a difference of denotation, in a local dialect, and these variants may be decidedly relevant to the history of the change which produced them. Finally, to reproduce the whole grammar and lexicon would require so vast a number of maps that even a very large atlas can only give samples of distribution; we ask for as many maps as possible. In view of all this, a dialect atlas is a tremendous undertaking, and in practice is likely to fall short in one or another respect. The sentences on which the German atlas is based, were written down in ordinary German orthography by schoolmasters and other linguistically untrained persons; the material does not extend to great parts of the Dutch-German area, such as the Netherlands and Belgium, Switzerland, Austria, Baltic German, Yiddish, Transylvanian, and the other speech-islands. The data are largely phonologic, since the informant, except for striking lexical or grammatical differences, would merely transcribe the forms into a spelling that represented the local pronunciation; yet the phonologic aspect is precisely what will be least clear in such a transcription. The data for the French atlas were collected by a trained phonetician, Edmond Edmont; one man, of course, could visit only a limited number of localities and stay but a short time in each. Accordingly, the maps register only something over six-hundred points in the French area (France and adjoining strips in Belgium, Switzerland, and Italy), and the forms were collected in each case from a single informant by means of a questionnaire of some two-thousand words and phrases. However fine his ear, Edmont could not know the phonologic pattern of each local dialect. The results for both phonetics and lexicon are more copious than those of the German atlas, but the looseness of the network and the lack of whole sentences are drawbacks. The atlas itself was planned and worked out by Jules Gilliéron (1854–1926), and has appeared in full (1896–1908), together with a supplement for Corsica. An Italian atlas, by K. Jaberg and J. Jud, has been appearing since 1928; it tries for great accuracy and pays close attention to meanings. Smaller atlases exist for Swabia (by H. Fischer, 28 maps, published, in connection with a careful treatise, in 1895), for Denmark (by V. Bennicke and M. Kristensen, 1898–1912), for Roumania (by G. Weigand, 1909), for Catalonia (by A. Griera, 1923 ff.), and for Brittany (by P. Le Roux, 1924 ff.). Other atlases are in preparation, including a survey of New England under the direction of H. Kurath. A single-handed observer can cover a small part of an area, as did Karl Haag in his study of a district in Southern Swabia (1898); or else, he may restrict himself to one or two features but follow them over a larger district, as did G. G. Kloeke in his study of the vowel phonemes of the words *mouse* and *house* in the Netherlands and Belgium (1927).

Needless to say, the map or atlas may be accompanied by a treatise that interprets the facts or accounts for their origin, as in the publications of Fischer, Haag, and Kloeke. The great atlases have given rise to many studies, such as, notably, Gilliéron's various books and essays, based on the French atlas, and a whole series of studies, under the editorship of F. Wrede, by workers on the German maps.

19. 3. Our knowledge is confined, so far, to the conditions that prevail in long-settled areas. In these, there is no question of uniformity over any sizable district. Every village, or, at most, every cluster of two or three villages, has its local peculiarities of speech. In general, it presents a unique combination of forms, each of which also appears, in other combinations, in some of the neighboring localities. On the map, accordingly, each settlement or small cluster of settlements will be cut off from each of its neighbors by one or more isoglosses. As an example, Figure 4, reproducing a small portion of Haag's map, shows the Swabian village of Bubsheim (about ten miles east by southeast of Rottweil). The nearest neighbors, within a distance of less than five miles, are all separated from Bubsheim by isoglosses; only two of these neighbors agree with each other as to all of the features that were studied by Haag. The appended table (Figure 5) shows under the name of each locality, the forms in which its dialect differs from the forms of Bubsheim, which are given in the first column; where no form is given, the dialect agrees with Bubsheim. The number before each form is the same as the number attached to the corresponding isogloss in Figure 4.

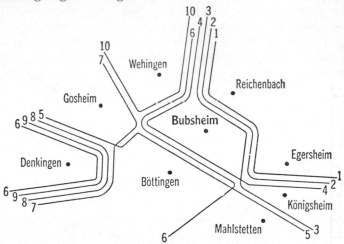

FIGURE 4. Isoglosses around the German village of Bubsheim (Swabia), after Haag. The village of Denkingen has been added, with a few of its isoglosses, in order to show the recurrence of Line 6.

If we followed the further course of these isoglosses, we should find them running in various directions and dividing the territory into portions of differing size. The isoglosses numbered 1, 2, and 3 in our Figures, cut boldly across the German area; Bubsheim agrees, as to these features, with the south and southwest. In contrast with these important lines, others, such as our number 9, surround only a small district: the form ['tru:ⁿke] 'drunk,' which is listed for Denkingen, is spoken only in a small patch of settlements. The isogloss we have numbered as 6 appears on our map as two lines; these are really parts of an irregularly winding line: Denkingen agrees with Bubsheim as to the vowel of the verb *mow*, although the intermediate villages speak differently. We find even isoglosses which divide a town into two parts; thus, along the lower Rhine, just southwest of Duisburg, the town of Kaldenhausen is cut through by a bundle of isoglosses: the eastern and western portions of the town speak different dialects.

The reason for this intense local differentiation is evidently to be sought in the principle of density (§ 3.4). Every speaker is constantly adapting his speech-habits to those of his interlocutors;

BUBSHEIM		REICHENBACH, EGERSHEIM	KÖNIGSHEIM	MAHLSTETTEN	BÖTTINGEN	DENKINGEN	GOSHEIM	WEHINGEN
1. oːfə	'stove'	oːfə						
2. uffi	'up'	nuff						
3. tsiːt	'time'	tsejt	tsejt					
4. baw^n	'bean'		bɔ·^{n}	bo·^{q}	bɔ·^{n}	bɔ·^{n}	bɔ·^{n}	bɔ·^{n}
5. ɛ·t̚	'end'			aj^{n}t	aj^{n}t	aj^{n}t		
6. meːjə	'to mow'				majə		majə	majə
7. farb	'color'					faːrb	faːrb	
8. alt	'old'					aːlt		
9. truŋkə	'drunk'					tru^{n}k^n		
10. gaw^n	'to go'							gɔ·^{n}

FIGURE 5. Ten speech-forms in the local dialect of Bubsheim in Swabia, with the divergent forms of neighboring dialects. Where no form is given, the dialect agrees with Bubsheim. The numbers are those of the isoglosses on the map, Figure 4. — After Haag.

he gives up forms he has been using, adopts new ones, and, perhaps oftenest of all, changes the frequency of speech-forms without entirely abandoning any old ones or accepting any that are really new to him. The inhabitants of a settlement, village, or town, however, talk much more to each other than to persons who live elsewhere. When any innovation in the way of speaking spreads over a district, the limit of this spread is sure to be along some line of weakness in the network of oral communication, and these lines of weakness, in so far as they are topographical lines, are the boundaries between towns, villages, and settlements.

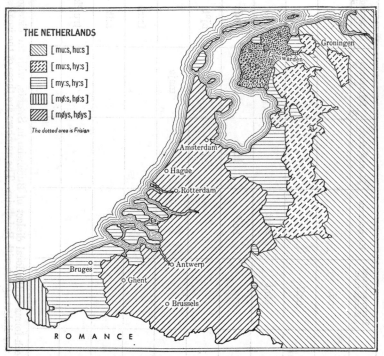

FIGURE 6. Distribution of syllabic sounds in the words *mouse* and *house* in the Netherlands. — After Kloeke.

19. 4. Isoglosses for different forms rarely coincide along their whole extent. Almost every feature of phonetics, lexicon, or grammar has its own area of prevalence — is bounded by its own isogloss. The obvious conclusion has been well stated in the form of a maxim: *Every word has its own history.*

The words *mouse* and *house* had in early Germanic the same vowel phoneme, a long [u:]. Some modern dialects — for instance, some Scotch dialects of English — preserve this sound apparently unchanged. Others have changed it, but keep the ancient structure, in the sense that these two words still have the same syllabic phoneme; this is the case in standard English and in standard German, where both words have [aw], and in standard Dutch, where both have [øʏ]. In the study above referred to, Kloeke traces the syllabics of these two words through the present-day local dialects of Belgium and the Netherlands. Our Figure 6 shows Kloeke's map on a reduced scale.

An eastern area, as the map shows, has preserved the Primitive Germanic vowel [u:] in both words: [mu:s, hu:s].

Several patches, of various size, speak [y:] in both words: [my:s, hy:s].

A district in the extreme west speaks [ø:] in both words: [mø:s, hø:s].

A great central area speaks a diphthong of the type [øʏ] in both words: [møʏs, høʏs]. Since this is the standard Dutch-Flemish pronunciation, it prevails in the usage of standard speakers also in the other districts, but this fact is not indicated on the map.

In these last three districts, then, the sound is no longer that of Primitive Germanic and medieval Dutch, but the structure of our two words is unchanged, in so far as they still agree in their syllabic phoneme.

Our map shows, however, three fair-sized districts which speak [u:] in the word *mouse*, but [y:] in the word *house;* hence, inconsistently, [mu:s, hy:s]. In these districts the structural relation of the two words has undergone a change: they no longer agree as to their syllabic phoneme.

We see, then, that the isogloss which separates [mu:s] from [my:s] does not coincide with the isogloss which separates [hu:s] from [hy:s]. Of the two words, *mouse* has preserved the ancient vowel over a larger territory than *house*. Doubtless a study of other words which contained [u:] in medieval times, would show us still other distributions of [u:] and the other sounds, distributions which would agree only in part with those of *mouse* and *house*.

At some time in the Middle Ages, the habit of pronouncing [y:] instead of the hitherto prevalent [u:] must have originated in some cultural center — perhaps in Flanders — and spread from there over a large part of the area on our map, including the central district which today speaks a diphthong. On the coast at the north of the Frisian area there is a Dutch-speaking district known as *het Bilt*, which was diked in and settled under the leadership of Hollanders at the beginning of the sixteenth century, and, as the map shows, uses the [y:]-pronunciation. It is [y:], moreover, and not the old [u:], that appears in the loan-words which in the early modern period passed from Dutch into the more easterly (Low German) dialects of the Dutch-German area, and into foreign languages, such as Russian and Javanese. The Dutch that was carried to the colonies, such as the Creole Dutch of the Virgin Islands, spoke [y:]. The spellings in written documents and the evidence of poets' rimes confirm this: the [y:]-pronunciation spread abroad with the cultural prestige of the great coastal cities of Holland in the sixteenth and seventeenth centuries.

This wave of cultural expansion was checked in the eastern part of our district, where it conflicted with the expansion of another and similar cultural area, that of the North German Hanseatic cities. Our isoglosses of *mouse* and *house*, and doubtless many others, are results of the varying balance of these two cultural forces. Whoever was impressed by the Hollandish official or merchant, learned to speak [y:]; whoever saw his superiors in the Hanseatic upper class, retained the old [u:]. The part of the population which made no pretensions to elegance, must also have long retained the [u:], but in the course of time the [y:] filtered down even to this class. This process is still going on: in parts of the area where [u:] still prevails — both in the district of [mu:s, hu:s] and in the district of [mu:s, hy:s] — the peasant, when he is on his good behavior, speaks [y:] in words where his everyday speech has [u:]. This flavor of the [y:]-variants appears strikingly in the shape of hyper-urbanisms: in using the elegant [y:], the speaker sometimes substitutes it where it is entirely out of place, saying, for instance, [vy:t] for [vu:t] 'foot,' a word in which neither older nor present-day upper-class Dutch ever spoke an [y:].

The word *house* will occur much oftener than the word *mouse* in official speech and in conversation with persons who represent the cultural center; *mouse* is more confined to homely and familiar situations. Accordingly, we find that the word *house* in the upper-class and central form with [y:] spread into districts where the word *mouse* has persisted in the old-fashioned form with [u:]. This shows us also that the Holland influence, and not the Hanseatic, was the innovator and aggressor; if the reverse had been the case, we should find districts where *house* had [u:] and *mouse* had [y:].

In the sixteenth and seventeenth centuries, even while the [y:]-pronunciation was making its conquests, there arose, it would seem in Antwerp, a still newer pronunciation with [øɥ] instead of the hitherto elegant [y:]. This new style spread to the Holland cities, and with this its fortune was made. The [øɥ]-pronunciation, as in standard Dutch *huis* [høɥs], *muis* [møɥs], is today the only truly urbane form. On our map, the area of this [øɥ] looks as if it had been laid on top of a former solid area of [y:], leaving only disconnected patches uncovered along the edge. This picture of disconnected patches at the periphery is characteristic of older styles, in language or in other activities, that have been superseded by some new central fashion. It is characteristic, too, that the more remote local dialects are taking up a feature, the [y:]-pronunciation, which in more central districts and in the more privileged class of speakers, has long ago been superseded by a still newer fashion.

19. 5. The map in our last example could not show the occurrence of the present-day standard Dutch-Flemish pronunciation with [øɥ] in the districts where it has not conquered the local dialects. To show this would be to cover our whole map with a dense and minute sprinkling of [øɥ]-forms, for the educated or socially better-placed persons in the whole area speak standard Dutch-Flemish.

The persistence of old features is easier to trace than the occurrence of new. The best data of dialect geography are furnished by *relic forms*, which attest some older feature of speech. In 1876, J. Winteler published what was perhaps the first adequate study of a single local dialect, a monograph on his native Swiss-German dialect of the settlement Kerenzen in the Canton of Glarus. In this study, Winteler mentions an archaic imperative form, [lɑx] 'let,' irregularly derived from the stem [lɑs-], and says that he is not certain that anyone still used it at the time of publication; most speakers, at any rate, already used the widespread and more regular form [lɑs] 'let.' A later observer, C. Streiff, writing in 1915, has not heard the old form; it has been totally replaced by [lɑs].

In the same way, Winteler quotes a verse in which the Glarus people are mocked for their use of the present-tense plural verb-

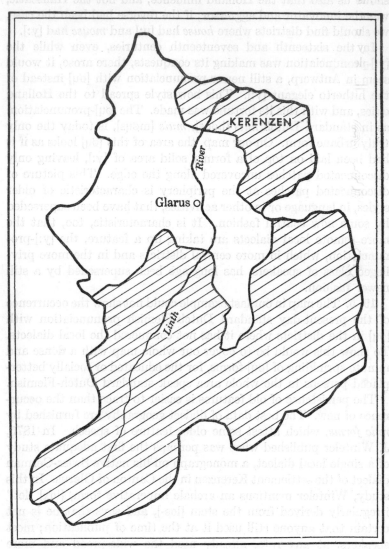

FIGURE 7. The Canton of Glarus, Switzerland. — In 1915 the shaded areas still used the provincial [hajd, wajd] as plurals of "have" and "want to"; the unshaded area used the general Swiss-German forms [hand, wand]. — After Streiff.

forms [hajd] '(we, ye, they) have' and [wajd] '(we, ye, they) want to,' forms which sounded offensively rustic to their neighbors, who used the more generally Swiss provincial forms [hand, wand]. Forty years later, Streiff reports a similar verse, in which the people of the central region of the canton (including the largest

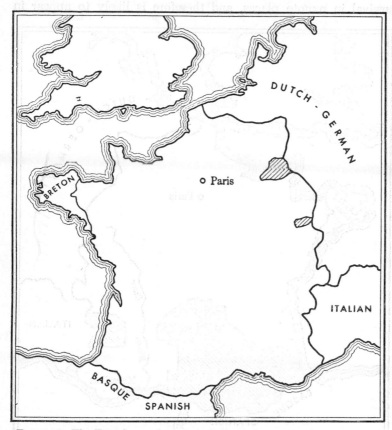

FIGURE 8. The French speech-area. — A discontinuous isogloss encloses the two marginal shaded areas in which reflexes of Latin *multum* "much, very" are still in use. — After Gamillscheg.

community and seat of government, the town of Glarus) mock the inhabitants of the outlying valleys for their use of these same forms, [hajd, wajd]. Our Figure 7, based on Streiff's statements, shows the distribution in 1915: the more urbane and widespread [hand, wand] prevail in the central district along the river Linth,

which includes the capital, Glarus, and communicates freely with
the city of Zurich (toward the northwest); the old rustic forms
are used in the three more remote valleys, including the settlement
of Kerenzen.

The relic form, as this example shows, has the best chance of
survival in remote places, and therefore is likely to appear in

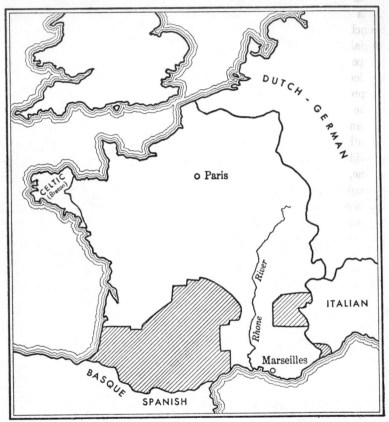

FIGURE 9. The French speech-area. — The unshaded district uses reflexes
of Latin *fallit* in the meaning "it is necessary." The shaded areas use other
forms. — After Jaberg.

small, detached areas. The Latin form *multum* 'much,' surviving, for instance, in Italian *molto* ['molto] and Spanish *mucho*
['mučo] 'much,' *muy* [muj] 'very,' has been replaced in nearly
all of the French area by words like standard French *très* [trɛ]

'very,' a modern form of Latin *trans* 'through, beyond, exceeding,' and *beaucoup* [boku] 'very,' which represents a Latin **bonum colpum* 'a good blow or stroke.' Figure 8 shows the two detached marginal areas in which modern forms of Latin *multum* are still in use.

In Latin, the word *fallit* meant 'he, she, it deceives.' By way of a meaning 'it fails,' this word came to mean, in medieval French, 'it is lacking,' and from this there has developed the modern French use of *il faut* [i fo] 'it is necessary; one must.' This highly specialized development of meaning can hardly have occurred independently in more than one place; the prevalence of the modern locution in the greater part of the French area must be due to spread from a center, presumably Paris. Figure 9 shows us, in the unshaded district, the prevalence of phonetic equivalents of standard French *il faut* in local dialects. The shaded districts use other forms, principally reflexes of Latin *calet* 'it's hot.' It is evident that the modern form spread southward along the Rhône, which is a great highway of commerce. We see here how an isogloss running at right angles to a highway of communication, will not cross it with unchanged direction, but will swerve off, run parallel with the highway for a stretch, and then either cross it or, as in our example, reappear on the other side, and then run back before resuming its former direction. The bend or promontory of the isogloss shows us which of the two speech-forms has been spreading at the cost of the other.

19. 6. If we observe a set of relic forms that exhibit some one ancient feature, we get a striking illustration of the principle that each word has its own history. The Latin initial cluster [sk-] has taken on, in the French area, an initial [e-], a so-called *prothetic vowel*, as, for example, in the following four words with which our Figure 10 is concerned:

	LATIN		MODERN STANDARD FRENCH	
'ladder'	*scala*	['ska:la]	*échelle*	[ešɛl]
'bowl'	*scutella*	[sku'tella]	*écuelle*	[ekɥɛl]
'write'	*scribere*	['skri:bere]	*écrire*	[ekri:r]
'school'	*schola*	['skola]	*école*	[ekɔl]

Our figure shows us six disconnected and, as to commerce, remote districts which still speak forms without the added vowel, such as [kwe:l] 'bowl,' in one or more of these four words. These districts include 55 of the 638 places that were observed by Edmont (§ 19.2). The districts are:

A. A fairly large area in Belgium, overlapping the political border of the French Republic at one point (Haybes, Department of the Ardennes), and covering 23 points of the Atlas.

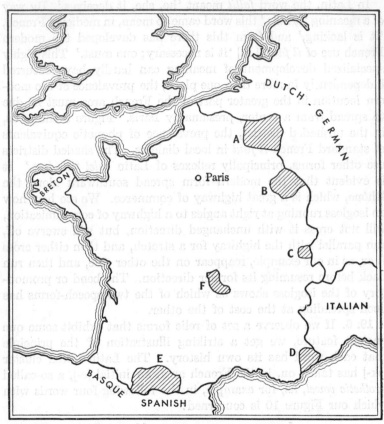

FIGURE 10. The French speech-area. — The shaded districts speak reflexes of Latin [sk-] without an added initial vowel. — After Jaberg.

B. A somewhat smaller area in the Departments of the Vosges and of Meurthe-et-Moselle, overlapping into Lorraine, 14 points.

C. The village of Bobi in Switzerland, 1 point.

D. Mentone and two other villages in the Department of Alpes-Maritimes on the Italian border, 3 points.

E. A fair-sized district along the Spanish border, in the Department of Hautes-Pyrénées, and overlapping into the neighboring Departments, 11 points.

F. A small interior district in the hill-country of the Auvergne, Departments of Haute-Loire and Puy-de-Dôme, 3 points.

Words in which forms without added vowel are still spoken	Number of places where forms without added vowel are still spoken						
	BY DISTRICTS						TOTAL
	A	B	C	D	E	F	
ladder, bowl, write, school	2						2
ladder, bowl, write	11					1	12
ladder, bowl, school				1	3		4
bowl, write, school			1				1
ladder, bowl	5	6		1			12
ladder, write	1						1
ladder, school					5		5
bowl, write	2*					1	3*
ladder	2	8			3		13
bowl				1			1
write						1	1
TOTAL	23	14	1	3	11	3	55*

*One point is doubtful as to 'bowl'

FIGURE 11. Prothetic vowel in French. — Occurrence of the forms in the shaded areas of Figure 10, by communities.

What interests us is the fact that most of the settlements in these backward districts have adopted the prothetic vowel in one, two, or three of our words. Thus, in district B, the village of Sainte-Marguerite (Vosges) says [čo:l] 'ladder' and [kwe:l] 'bowl,' but, in the modern style, [ekrir] 'write' and [eko:l] 'school.' Moreover, the dialects do not agree as to the words in which the innovation is made; thus, in contrast with the preceding case, the village of Gavarnie (Hautes-Pyrénées), in our district E, says ['ska:lo] 'ladder' and ['sko:lo] 'school,' but [esku'de:lo] 'bowl' and [eskri'be] 'write.' Only two points, both in district A, have preserved the old initial type in all four of our words; the others show various combinations of old and new forms. Figure 11 gives, in the first column, the combinations of words in which the old form is still in use, then the number of points (by districts and in total) where each combination has survived. In spite of the great variety

Words in which forms without added vowel are still spoken	Number of places where forms without added vowel are still spoken						
	BY DISTRICTS						TOTAL
	A (23)	B (14)	C (1)	D (3)	E (11)	F (3)	
'ladder'	21	14		2	11	1	49
'bowl'	20*	6	1	3	3	2	35*
'write'	16		1			3	20
'school'	2		1	1	8		12

One point is doubtful

FIGURE 12. Prothetic vowel in French. — Occurrence of the forms in the shaded areas of Figure 10, by words.

that appears in this table, the survey by individual words, in Figure 12, shows that the homely terms 'ladder' and 'bowl' appear more often in the old form than do 'write' and 'school,' which are associated with official institutions and with a wider cultural outlook. To be sure, at Bobi (district C) it is precisely 'ladder' which has the new form, but wherever the field of observation is larger, as in districts A, B, and E, or in the total, the terms for 'ladder' and 'bowl' tend to lead in the number of conservative forms.

19. 7. The final result of the process of spread is the complete submergence of the old forms. Where we find a great area in which some linguistic change has been uniformly carried out, we may be sure that the greater part of the uniformity is due to geographic leveling. Sometimes place-names show us the only trace of the struggle. In the German area generally, two ancient diphthongs, which we represent as [ew] and [iw] are still distinct, as in standard New High German, with [i:] for ancient [ew], *Fliege* 'fly' (noun), *Knie* 'knee,' *Stiefvater* 'step-father,' *tief* 'deep,' but, with [oj] for ancient [iw], *scheu* 'shy,' *teuer* 'dear,' *neun* 'nine.' The dialect of Glarus has apparently lost the distinction, as have adjoining dialects, wherever a labial or velar consonant followed the diphthong:

old [ew] before labial or velar:

	PRIMITIVE GERMANIC TYPE	GLARUS
fly	*['flewgo:n]	['fly:gə]
knee	*['knewan]	[xny:]
step-	*['stewpa-]	['šty:f-fɑtər]

old [iw]:

shy	*['skiwhjaz]	[šy:x]
dear	*['diwrjaz]	[ty:r]
nine	*['niwni]	[ny:n]

Apparently, then, these two old types are both represented in Glarus by modern [y:], in accordance with the general South-German development. A single form suggests that the [y:] for old [ew] is really an importation, namely, the word *deep*, Primitive Germanic type *['dewpaz], which appears in Glarus as [tœjf]. Our suspicion that the diphthong [œj] is the older representative of [ew] before labials and velars in this region, is confirmed by a place-name: ['xnœj-grɑ:t], literally 'Knee-Ridge.'

The southwestern corner of German-speaking Switzerland has changed the old Germanic [k] of words like *drink* to a spirant [x] and has lost the preceding nasal, as in ['tri:xə] 'to drink.' This is today a crass localism, for most of Switzerland, along with the rest of the Dutch-German area, speaks [k]. Thus, Glarus says ['trɪŋkə] 'to drink,' in accord with standard German *trinken*. Place-names, however, show us that the deviant pronunciation once extended over a much larger part of Switzerland. Glarus, well to the east, alongside the common noun ['wɪŋkəl] 'angle, corner,' has the place-name of a mountain pasture ['wɪxlə] 'Corners,' and alongside [xrɑŋk] 'sick' (formerly, 'crooked') the name of another pasture ['xrawx-tɑːl] 'Crank-Dale,' that is, 'Crooked-Valley.'

19. 8. Dialect geography thus gives evidence as to the former extension of linguistic features that now persist only as relic forms. Especially when a feature appears in detached districts that are separated by a compact area in which a competing feature is spoken, the map can usually be interpreted to mean that the detached districts were once part of a solid area. In this way, dialect geography may show us the stratification of linguistic features; thus, our Figure 6, without any direct historical supplementation, would tell us that the [uː]-forms were the oldest, that they were superseded by the [yː]-forms, and these, in turn, by the diphthongal forms.

Since an isogloss presumably marks a line of weakness in the density of communication, we may expect the dialect map to show us the communicative conditions of successive times. The inhabitants of countries like England, Germany, or France, have always applied provincial names to rough dialectal divisions, and spoken of such things as "the Yorkshire dialect," "the Swabian dialect," or "the Norman dialect." Earlier scholars accepted these classifications without attempting to define them exactly; it was hoped, later, that dialect geography would lead to exact definitions. The question gained interest from the wave-theory (§ 18.12), since the provincial types were examples of the differentiation of a speech-area without sudden cleavage. Moreover, the question took on a sentimental interest, since the provincial divisions largely represent old tribal groupings: if the extension of a dialect, such as, say, the "Swabian dialect" in Germany, could be shown to coincide with the area of habitation of an ancient tribe, then language would again be throwing light on the conditions of a bygone time.

In this respect, however, dialect geography proved to be disappointing. It showed that almost every village had its own dialectal features, so that the whole area was covered by a network of isoglosses. If one began by setting up a list of characteristic provincial peculiarities, one found them prevailing in a solid core, but shading off at the edges, in the sense that each characteristic was bordered by a whole set of isoglosses representing its presence in different words — just as the *house* and *mouse* isoglosses for [y:] and [u:] do not coincide in the eastern Netherlands (Figure 6). A local dialect from the center of Yorkshire or Swabia or Normandy could be systematically classed in terms of its province, but at the outskirts of such a division there lie whole bands of dialects which share only part of the provincial characteristics. In this situation, moreover, there is no warrant for the initial list of characteristics. If these were differently selected — say, without regard to the popularly current provincial classification — we should obtain entirely different cores and entirely different zones of transition.

Accordingly, some students now despaired of all classification and announced that within a dialect area there are no real boundaries. Even in a domain such as that of the western Romance languages (Italian, Ladin, French, Spanish, Portuguese) it was urged that there were no real boundaries, but only gradual transitions: the difference between any two neighboring points was no more and no less important than the difference between any two other neighboring points. Opposing this view, some scholars held fast to the national and provincial classifications, insisting, perhaps with some mystical fervor, on a terminology of cores and zones.

It is true that the isoglosses in a long-settled area are so many as to make possible almost any desired classification of dialects and to justify almost any claim concerning former densities of communication. It is easy to see, however, that, without prejudice of any kind, we must attribute more significance to some isoglosses than to others. An isogloss which cuts boldly across a whole area, dividing it into two nearly equal parts, or even an isogloss which neatly marks off some block of the total area, is more significant than a petty line enclosing a localism of a few villages. In our Figures 4 and 5, isoglosses 1, 2, 3, which mark off southwestern German from the rest of the German area, are evidently more significant than, say, isogloss 9, which encloses only a few villages. The great isogloss shows a feature which has spread over a large domain; this spreading is a large event, simply as a fact in the history of language, and, may reflect, moreover, some non-linguistic cultural movement of comparable strength. As a criterion of description, too, the large division is, of course, more significant than small ones; in fact, the popular classification of dialects is evidently based upon the prevalence of certain peculiarities over large parts of an area.

Furthermore, a set of isoglosses running close together in much the same direction — a so-called *bundle* of isoglosses — evidences a larger historical process and offers a more suitable basis of classification than does a single isogloss that represents, perhaps, some unimportant feature. It appears, moreover, that these two characteristics, topographic importance and bundling, often go hand in hand. Thus, France is divided by a great bundle of isoglosses running east and west across the area. This division reflects the medieval division of France into the two cultural and linguistic domains of French and Provençal.

The most famous bundle of this kind, perhaps, is the east-and-west bundle which runs across the Dutch-German area, separating Low German from High German. The difference is in the treatment of the Primitive Germanic unvoiced stops [p, t, k], which in the south have been shifted to spirants and affricates. If we take standard Dutch and standard German as representatives of the two types, our isoglosses separate forms like these:

	Northern	Southern
make	['ma:ke]	['maxen]
I	[ik]	[ix]
sleep	['sla:pe]	['šla:fen]
thorp 'village'	[dorp]	[dorf]
pound	[punt]	[pfunt]
bite	['bejte]	['bajsen]
that	[dat]	[das]
to	[tu:]	[tsu:]

The isoglosses of these and other forms that contain Primitive Germanic [p, t, k] run in a great bundle, sometimes coinciding, but at other times diverging, and even crossing each other. Thus, round Berlin, the isogloss of *make*, together with a good many others, makes a northward bend, so that there one says [ik] 'I' with unshifted [k], but ['maxen] 'make' with [k] shifted to [x]; on the other hand, in the west the isogloss of *I* swerves off in a northwesterly direction, so that round Düsseldorf one says [ix] 'I' with the shifted sound, but ['ma:ken] 'make' with the old [k] preserved.

In this way we find that the topographic distribution of linguistic features within a dialect area is not indifferent, and exhibits decided cleavages. We must make only two obvious reservations: we cannot guarantee to preserve the popular terminology by provinces, but, if we retain provincial names, must redefine them; and we can bound our divisions either imperfectly, by zones, or arbitrarily, by selecting some one isogloss as the representative of a whole bundle.

19. 9. Having found the linguistic divisions of an area, we may compare them with other lines of cleavage. The comparison shows that the important lines of dialectal division run close to political lines. Apparently, common government and religion, and especially the custom of intermarriage within the political unit, lead to relative uniformity of speech. It is estimated that, under older conditions, a new political boundary led in less than fifty years to some linguistic difference, and that the isoglosses along a political boundary of long standing would persist, with little shifting, for some two-hundred years after the boundary had been abolished. This seems to be the primary correlation. If the important isoglosses agree with other lines of cultural division — as, in northern Germany, with a difference in the construction of farm-houses — or if they agree with geographic barriers, such as rivers or mountain-ranges, then the agreement is due merely to the fact that these features also happen to concord with political divisions.

This has been shown most plainly in the distribution of the important German isoglosses along the Rhine. Some forty kilometers east of the Rhine the isoglosses of the great bundle that separates Low German and High German begin to separate and spread out northwestward and southwestward, so as to form what has been called the "Rhenish fan" (Figure 13). The isogloss of northern [k] versus southern [x] in the word *make*, which has been taken, arbitrarily, as the critical line of division, crosses the Rhine just north of the town of Benrath and, accordingly, is called the "Benrath line."   It is found, now, that this line corresponds roughly to an ancient northern boundary of the territorial domains of Berg (east of the Rhine) and Jülich (west of the Rhine). The isogloss of northern [k] versus southern [x] in the word *I* swerves off northwestward, crossing the Rhine just north of the village of Ürdingen, and is known accordingly, as the "Ürdingen line;" some students take this, rather than the line of *make*, as the arbitrary boundary between Low and High German. The Ürdingen line corresponds closely to the northern boundaries of the pre-Napoleonic Duchies, abolished in 1789, of Jülich and Berg — the states whose earlier limit is reflected in the Benrath line — and of the Electorate of Cologne. Just north of Ürdingen, the town of Kaldenhausen is split by the Ürdingen line into a western section which says [ex] and an eastern which says [ek];

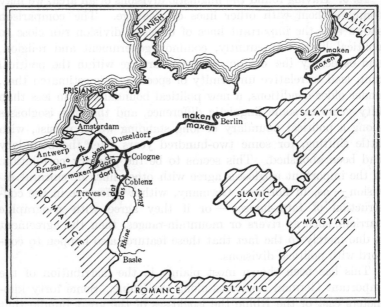

FIGURE 13. The Dutch-German speech-area, showing the isogloss of [k] versus [x] in the word *make*, and, in the western part, the divergence of three other isoglosses which in the east run fairly close to that of *make*. — After Behaghel.

we learn that up to 1789 the western part of the town belonged to the (Catholic) Electorate of Cologne, and the eastern part to the (Protestant) County of Mörs. Our map shows also two isoglosses branching southwestward. One is the line between northern [p] and southern [f] in the word [dorp — dorf] 'village'; this line agrees roughly with the southern boundaries in 1789 of Jülich, Cologne, and Berg, as against the Electorate of Treves. In a still more southerly direction there branches off the isogloss between northern [t] and southern [s] in the word [dat — das] 'that,' and this line, again, coincides approximately with the old southern boundary of the Electorate and Archbishopric of Treves.

All this shows that the spread of linguistic features depends upon social conditions. The factors in this respect are doubtless the density of communication and the relative prestige of different social groups. Important social boundaries will in time attract isogloss-lines. Yet it is evident that the peculiarities of the several linguistic forms themselves play a part, since each is likely to show an isogloss of its own. In the Netherlands we saw a new form of the word *house* spreading farther than a new form of the homely word *mouse* (§ 19.4). We can hope for no scientifically usable analysis, such as would enable us to predict the course of every isogloss: the factors of prestige in the speakers and of meaning (including connotation) in the forms cut off our hope of this. Nevertheless, dialect geography not only contributes to our understanding of the extra-linguistic factors that affect the prevalence of linguistic forms, but also, through the evidence of relic forms and stratifications, supplies a great many details concerning the history of individual forms.

CHAPTER 20

PHONETIC CHANGE

20. 1. Written records of earlier speech, resemblance between languages, and the varieties of local dialects, all show that languages change in the course of time. In our Old English records we find a word *stan* 'stone,' which we interpret phonetically as [staːn]; if we believe that the present-day English word *stone* [stown] is the modern form, by unbroken tradition, of this Old English word, then we must suppose that Old English [aː] has here changed to modern [ow]. If we believe that the resemblances are due not to accident, but to the tradition of speech-habits, then we must infer that the differences between the resemblant forms are due to changes in these speech-habits. Earlier students recognized this; they collected sets of resemblant forms (etymologies) and inferred that the differences between the forms of a set were due to linguistic change, but, until the beginning of the nineteenth century, no one succeeded in classifying these differences. The resemblances and differences varied from set to set. An Old English *bat*, which we interpret phonetically as [baːt], is in one meaning paralleled by modern English *boat* [bowt], but in another meaning by modern English *bait* [bejt]. The initial consonants are the same in Latin *dies* and English *day*, but different in Latin *duo* and English *two*. The results of linguistic change presented themselves as a hodge-podge of resemblances and differences. One could suspect that some of the resemblances were merely accidental ("false etymologies"), but there was no test. One could reach no clear formulation of linguistic relationship — the less so, since the persistence of Latin documents through the Middle Ages alongside of documents in the Romance languages distorted one's whole view of linguistic chronology.

It is not useless to look back at those times. Now that we have a method which brings order into the confusion of linguistic resemblances and throws some light on the nature of linguistic relationship, we are likely to forget how chaotic are the results of linguistic change when one has no key to their classification.

Since the beginning of the nineteenth century we have learned to classify the differences between related forms, attributing them to several kinds of linguistic change. The data, whose variety bewildered earlier students, lend themselves with facility to this classification. Resemblances which do not fit into our classes of change, are relatively few and can often be safely ruled out as accidental; this is the case, for instance, with Latin *dies* : English *day*, which we now know to be a false etymology.

The process of linguistic change has never been directly observed; we shall see that such observation, with our present facilities, is inconceivable. We are assuming that our method of classification, which works well (though not by any means perfectly), reflects the actual factors of change that produced our data. The assumption that the simplest classification of observed facts is the true one, is common to all science; in our case, it is well to remember that the observed facts (namely, the results of linguistic change as they show themselves in etymologies) resisted all comprehension until our method came upon the scene. The first step in the development of method in historical linguistics was the seeking out of uniform *phonetic correspondences;* we take these correspondences to be the results of a factor of change which we call *phonetic change.*

20. 2. At the beginning of the nineteenth century we find a few scholars systematically picking out certain types of resemblance, chiefly cases of *phonetic* agreement or correspondence. The first notable step was Rask's and Grimm's observation (§ 1.7) of correspondences between Germanic and other Indo-European languages. From among the chaotic mass of resemblant forms, they selected certain ones which exhibited uniform phonetic correlations. Stated in present-day terms, these correlations appear as follows:

(1) Unvoiced stops of the other languages are paralleled in Germanic by unvoiced spirants:

[p − f] Latin *pēs* : English *foot;* Latin *piscis* : English *fish;* Latin *pater* : English *father;*

[t − θ] Latin *trēs* : English *three;* Latin *tenuis* : English *thin;* Latin *tacēre* 'to be silent' : Gothic ['θahan];

[k − h] Latin *centum* : English *hundred;* Latin *caput* : English *head;* Latin *cornū* : English *horn.*

(2) Voiced stops of the other languages are paralleled in Germanic by unvoiced stops:

[b – p] Greek ['kannabis] : English *hemp;*
[d – t] Latin *duo* : English *two;* Latin *dens* : English *tooth;* Latin *edere* : English *eat;*
[g – k] Latin *grānum* : English *corn;* Latin *genus* : English *kin;* Latin *ager* : English *acre.*

(3) Certain aspirates and spirants of the other languages (which we denote today as "reflexes of Primitive Indo-European voiced aspirates") are paralleled in Germanic by voiced stops and spirants:

Sanskrit [bh], Greek [ph], Latin [f], Germanic [b, v]: Sanskrit ['bhara:mi] 'I bear,' Greek ['phero:], Latin *ferō* : English *bear;* Sanskrit ['bhra:ta:], Greek ['phra:te:r], Latin *frāter* : English *brother;* Latin *frangere* : English *break;*

Sanskrit [dh], Greek [th], Latin [f], Germanic [d, ð]: Sanskrit ['a-dha:t] 'he put,' Greek ['the:so:] 'I shall put,' Latin *fēcī* 'I made, did' : English *do;* Sanskrit ['madhu] 'honey, mead,' Greek ['methu] 'wine' : English *mead;* Sanskrit ['madhjah], Latin *medius* : English *mid;*

Sanskrit [h], Greek [kh], Latin [h], Germanic [g, γ]: Sanskrit [ha^n'sah] : English *goose;* Sanskrit ['vahati] 'he carries on a vehicle,' Latin *vehit* : Old English *wegan* 'to carry, move, transport'; Latin *hostis* 'stranger, enemy' : Old English *giest* 'guest.'

The only reason for assembling cases like these is the belief that the correlations are too frequent or in some other way too peculiar to be due to chance.

20. 3. Students of language have accepted these correlations (calling them, by a dangerous metaphor, Grimm's "law"), because the classification they introduce is confirmed by further study: new data show the same correspondences, and cases which do not show these correspondences lend themselves to other classifications.

For instance, from among the cases which do not show Grimm's correspondences, it is possible to sort out a fair-sized group in which unvoiced stops [p, t, k] of the other languages appear also in Germanic; thus, the [t] of the other languages is paralleled by Germanic [t] in cases like the following:

Sanskrit ['asti] 'he is,' Greek ['esti], Latin *est* : Gothic [ist] 'is'; Latin *captus* 'taken, caught' : Gothic [hafts] 'restrained'; Sanskrit [aš'ta:w] 'eight,' Greek [ok'to:] Latin *octō* : Gothic ['ahtaw].

Now, in all these cases the [p, t, k] in Germanic is immediately preceded by an unvoiced spirant [s, f, h], and a survey of the cases which conform to Grimm's correspondences shows that in them the Germanic consonant is never preceded by these sounds. Grimm's correlations have thus, by leaving a residue, led us to find another correlation: after [s, f, h] Germanic [p, t, k] parallel the [p, t, k] of the other Indo-European languages.

Among the residual forms, again, we find a number in which initial voiced stops [b, d, g] of Germanic are paralleled in Sanskrit not by [bh, dh, gh], as Grimm would have it, but by [b, d, g], and in Greek not by the expected [ph, th, kh], but by [p, t, k]. An example is Sanskrit ['bo:dha:mi] 'I observe,' Greek ['pewthomaj] 'I experience' : Gothic [ana-'biwdan] 'to command,' Old English ['be:odan] 'to order, announce, offer,' English *bid*. In 1862, Hermann Grassmann (1809–1877) showed that this type of correlation appears wherever the next consonant (the consonant after the intervening vowel or diphthong) belongs to Grimm's third type of correspondences. That is, Sanskrit and Greek do not have aspirate stops at the beginning of two successive syllables, but, wherever the related languages show this pattern, have the first of the two stops unaspirated: corresponding to Germanic *[bewda-], we find in Sanskrit not *[bho:dha-] but [bo:dha-], and in Greek not *[phewtho-] but [pewtho-]. Here too, then, the residual data which are marked off by Grimm's correspondences, reveal a correlation.

In this case, moreover, we get a confirmation in the structure of the languages. In Greek, certain forms have a reduplication (§ 13.8) in which the first consonant of the underlying stem, followed by a vowel, is prefixed: ['do:so:] 'I shall give,' ['di-do:mi] 'I give.' We find, now, that for stems with an initial aspirate stop the reduplication is made with a plain stop: ['the:so:] 'I shall put,' ['ti-the:mi] 'I put.' The same habit appears elsewhere in Greek morphology; thus, there is a noun-paradigm with nominative singular ['thriks] 'hair,' but other case-forms like the accusative ['trikha]: when the consonant after the vowel is aspirated, the initial consonant is [t] instead of [th]. Similarly, in Sanskrit, the normal reduplication repeats the first consonant: ['a-da:t] 'he gave,' ['da-da:mi] 'I give,' but for an initial aspirate the reduplication has a plain stop: ['a-dha:t] 'he put,' ['da-dha:mi] 'I put,' and similar alternations appear elsewhere in Sanskrit morphology.

These alternations are obviously results of the sound-change discovered by Grassmann.

20. 4. If our correspondences are not due to chance, they must result from some historical connection, and this connection the comparative method reconstructs, as we have seen, by the assumption of common descent from a parent language. Where the related languages agree, they are preserving features of the parent language, such as, say, the [r] in the word *brother*, the [m] in the words *mead* and *mid* (§ 20.2), or the [s] in the verb-forms for 'he is' (§ 20.3). Where the correspondence connects markedly different phonemes, we suppose that one or more of the languages have changed. Thus we state Grimm's correspondences by saying:

(1) Primitive Indo-European unvoiced stops [p, t, k] changed in pre-Germanic to unvoiced spirants [f, θ, h];

(2) Primitive Indo-European voiced stops [b, d, g] changed in pre-Germanic to unvoiced stops [p, t, k];

(3) Primitive Indo-European voiced aspirate stops [bh, dh, gh] changed in pre-Germanic to voiced stops or spirants [b, d, g], in pre-Greek to unvoiced aspirate stops [ph, th, kh], in pre-Italic and pre-Latin to [f, θ, h]. In this case the acoustic shape of the Primitive Indo-European phonemes is by no means certain, and some scholars prefer to speak of unvoiced spirants [f, θ, x]; similarly, we do not know whether the Primitive Germanic reflexes were stops or spirants, but these doubts do not affect our conclusions as to the phonetic pattern.

The correspondences where [p, t, k] appear also in Germanic demand a restriction for case (1): immediately after a consonant (those which actually occur are [s, p, k]), the Primitive Indo-European unvoiced stops [p, t, k] were not changed in pre-Germanic.

Grassmann's correspondences we state historically by saying that at a certain stage in the history of pre-Greek, forms which contained two successive syllables with aspirate stops, lost the aspiration of the first stop. Thus, we reconstruct:

PRIMITIVE INDO-EUROPEAN	>	PRE-GREEK	>	GREEK
*['bhewdhomaj]		*['phewthomaj]		['pewthomaj]
*['dhidhe:mi]		*['thithe:mi]		['tithe:mi]
*['dhrighm̥]		*['thrikha]		['trikha].

On the other hand, in the nominative singular of the word for 'hair,' we suppose that there never was an aspirate after the vowel·

Primitive Indo-European *[dhriks] appears as Greek [thriks]. We infer a similar change for pre-Indo-Iranian: a Primitive Indo-European *[bhewdho-] appearing in Sanskrit as [bo:dha-], a Primitive Indo-European *[dhedhe:-] as [dadha:-], and so on.

A further step in the reconstruction of the historical events proceeds from the fact that the loss of aspiration results in Sanskrit in [b, d, g], but in Greek in [p, t, k]. This implies that the Primitive Indo-European [bh, dh, gh] had already become unvoiced [ph, th, kh] in pre-Greek when the loss of aspiration took place. Since this unvoicing does not occur in Indo-Iranian, we conclude that the de-aspiration in pre-Greek and the de-aspiration in pre-Indo-Iranian took place independently.

The interpretation, then, of the phonetic correspondences that appear in our resemblant forms, assumes that *the phonemes of a language are subject to historical change.* This change may be limited to certain phonetic conditions; thus, in pre-Germanic, [p, t, k] did not change to [f, θ, h] when another unvoiced consonant immediately preceded, as in *[kəptos] > Gothic [hafts]; in pre-Greek, [ph, th, kh] became [p, t, k] only when the next syllable began with an aspirate. This type of linguistic change is known as *phonetic change* (or *sound change*). In modern terminology, the assumption of sound-change can be stated in the sentence: *Phonemes change.*

20. 5. When we have gathered the resemblant forms which show the recognized correlations, the remainders will offer two self-evident possibilities. We may have stated a correlation too narrowly or too widely: a more careful survey or the arrival of new data may show the correction. A notable instance of this was Grassmann's discovery. The fact that residues have again and again revealed new correlations, is a strong confirmation of our method. Secondly, the resemblant forms may not be divergent pronunciations of the same earlier form. Grimm, for instance, mentioned Latin *dies* : English *day* as an etymology which did not fall within his correlations, and since his time no amount of research has revealed any possibility of modifying the otherwise valid correlation-classes so that they may include this set. Similarly, Latin *habēre* 'to have' : Gothic *haban*, Old High German *habēn*, in spite of the striking resemblance, conflicts with types of correlation that otherwise hold good. In such cases, we may attribute the resemblance to accident, meaning by this that it is not due to any historical connection; thus, Latin *dies* : English *day* is now regarded by everyone as a "false etymology." Or else, the resemblance may be due to grammatical resemblance of forms in the parent language; thus, Latin *habēre* 'to have' and Old High German *habēn* 'to have' may be descendants, respectively, of two stems, *[gha'bhe:-] and *[ka'bhe:-] which were morphologically parallel in Primitive Indo-European. Finally, our resemblant forms may owe their likeness to a historical connection other than descent from a common prototype. Thus, Latin *dentālis* 'pertaining to a tooth' and English *dental* resemble each other, but do not show the correlations (e.g. Latin *d* : English *t*) which appear in Latin and English reflexes of a common Primitive Indo-European prototype. The reason is that *dental* is merely the English-speaker's reproduction of the Latin word.

To sum up, then, the residual forms which do not fit into recognized types of phonetic correlation may be:

(1) descendants of a common ancestral form, deviant only because we have not correctly ascertained the phonetic correlation, e.g. Sanskrit ['bo:dha:mi] and English *bid*, before Grassmann's discovery;

(2) not descendants of a common ancestral form, in which case the resemblance may be due to

(a) accident, e.g. Latin *dies* : English *day;*

(b) morphologic partial resemblance in the parent language, e.g. Latin *habēre* : English *have;*

(c) other historical relations, e.g. Latin *dentālis* : English *dental.*

If this is correct, then the study of residual resemblant forms will lead us to discover new types of phonetic correlation (1), to weed out false etymologies (2a), to uncover the morphologic structure of the parent speech (2b), or to recognize types of linguistic change other than sound-change (2c). If the study of residual forms does not lead to these results, then our scheme is incorrect.

20. 6. During the first three quarters of the nineteenth century no one, so far as we know, ventured to limit the possibilities in the sense of our scheme. If a set of resemblant forms did not fit into the recognized correlations, scholars felt free to assume that these forms were nevertheless related in exactly the same way as the normal forms — namely, by way of descent from a common ancestral form. They phrased this historically by saying that a speech-sound might change in one way in some forms, but might change in another way (or fail to change) in other forms. A Primitive Indo-European [d] might change to [t] in pre-Germanic in most forms, such as *two* (: Latin *duo*), *ten* (: Latin *decem*), *tooth* (: Latin *dens*), *eat* (: Latin *edere*), but remain unchanged in some other forms, such as *day* (: Latin *dies*).

On the whole, there was nothing to be said against this view — in fact, it embodied a commendable caution — unless and until an extended study of residual forms showed that possibilities (1) and (2a, b, c) were realized in so great a number of cases as to rule out the probability of sporadic sound-change. In the seventies of the nineteenth century, several scholars, most notably, in the year 1876, August Leskien (§ 1.9), concluded that exactly this had taken place: that the sifting of residual forms had resulted so often in the discovery of non-contradictory facts (1, 2b, 2c) or in the weeding out of false etymologies (2a), as to warrant linguists in supposing that the change of phonemes is absolutely regular. This meant, in terms of our method, that all resemblances between forms which do not fall into the recognized correspondence-classes are due to features of sound-change which we have failed to recognize (1), or else are not divergent forms of a single prototype, either because the etymology is false (2a), or because some factor other than sound-change has led to the existence of resemblant forms (2b, c). Historically interpreted, the statement means that sound-change is merely a change in the speakers' manner of producing phonemes and accordingly affects a phoneme at every occurrence, regardless of the nature of any particular linguistic form in which the phoneme happens to occur. The change may concern some habit of articulation which is common to several phonemes, as in the unvoicing of voiced stops [b, d, g] in pre-Germanic. On the other hand, the change may concern some habit of articulating successions of phonemes, and therefore take place only under particular phonetic conditions, as when [p, t, k] in pre-Germanic became [f, θ, h] when not preceded by another sound of the same group or by [s]; similarly, [ph, th, kh] in pre-Greek became [p, t, k] only when the next syllable began with an aspirate. The limitations of these *conditioned sound-changes* are, of course, purely phonetic, since the change concerns only a habit of articulatory movement; phonetic change is independent of non-phonetic factors, such as the meaning, frequency, homonymy, or what not, of any particular linguistic form. In present-day terminology the whole assumption can be briefly put into the words: *phonemes change,* since the term *phoneme* designates a meaningless minimum unit of signaling.

The new principle was adopted by a number of linguists, who received the nickname of "neo-grammarians." On the other hand, not only scholars of the older generation, such as Georg Curtius (1820–1885), but also some younger men, most notably Hugo Schuchardt (1842–1927), rejected the new hypothesis. The discussion of the pro's and con's has never ceased; linguists are as much divided on this point today as in the 1870's.

A great part of this dispute was due merely to bad terminology. In the 1870's, when technical terms were less precise than today, the assumption of uniform sound-change received the obscure and metaphorical wording, "Phonetic laws have no exceptions." It is evident that the term "law" has here no precise meaning, for a sound-change is not in any sense a law, but only a historical occurrence. The phrase "have no exceptions" is a very inexact way of saying that non-phonetic factors, such as the frequency or meaning of particular linguistic forms, do not interfere with the change of phonemes.

The real point at issue is the scope of the phonetic correspond‧ence-classes and the significance of the residues. The neo-gram‧marians claimed that the results of study justified us in making the correspondence-classes non-contradictory and in seeking a complete analysis of the residues. If we say that Primitive Indo-European [d] appears in Germanic as [t], then, according to the neo-grammarians, the resemblance of Latin *dies* and English *day* or of Latin *dentālis* and English *dental,* cannot be classed simply as "an exception" — that is, historically, as due to the pre-Germanic speakers' failure to make the usual change of habit — but presents a problem. The solution of this problem is either the abandonment of the etymology as due to accidental resemblance (Latin *dies* : English *day*), or a more exact formulation of the phonetic correspondence (Grassmann's discovery), or the recognition of some other factors that produce resemblant forms (Latin *dentālis* borrowed in English *dental*). The neo-grammarian insists, particularly, that his hypothesis is fruitful in this last direction: it sorts out the resemblances that are due to factors other than phonetic change, and accordingly leads us to an understanding of these factors.

The actual dispute, then, concerns the weeding-out of false etymologies, the revision of our statements of phonetic correspondence, and the recognition of linguistic changes other than sound-change.

20. 7. The opponents of the neo-grammarian hypothesis claim that resemblances which do not fit into recognized types of phonetic correspondence may be due merely to sporadic occurrence or deviation or non-occurrence of sound-change. Now, the very foundation of modern historical linguistics consisted in the setting up of phonetic correspondence-classes: in this way alone did Rask and Grimm bring order into the chaos of resemblances which had bewildered all earlier students. The advocates of sporadic sound-change, accordingly, agree with the neo-grammarians in discarding such etymologies as Latin *dies* : English *day*, and retain only a few, where the resemblance is striking, such as Latin *habēre* : Old High German *habēn*, or Sanskrit [ko:kilah], Greek ['kokkuks], Latin *cuculus* : English *cuckoo*. They admit that this leaves us no criterion of decision, but insist that our inability to draw a line does not prove anything: exceptional sound-changes occurred, even though we have no certain way of recognizing them.

The neo-grammarian sees in this a serious violation of scientific method. The beginning of our science was made by a procedure which implied regularity of phonetic change, and further advances, like Grassmann's discovery, were based on the same implicit assumption. It may be, of course, that some other assumption would lead to an even better correlation of facts, but the advocates of sporadic sound-change offer nothing of the kind; they accept the results of the actual method and yet claim to explain some facts by a contradictory method (or lack of method) which was tried and found wanting through all the centuries that preceded Rask and Grimm.

In the historical interpretation, the theory of sporadic sound-change faces a very serious difficulty. If we suppose that a form like *cuckoo* resisted the pre-Germanic shift of [k] to [h] and still preserves a Primitive Indo-European [k], then we must also suppose that during many generations, when the pre-Germanic people had changed their way of pronouncing Primitive Indo-

European [k] in most words, and were working on through successive acoustic types such as, say, [kh — kx — x — h], they were still in the word *cuckoo* pronouncing an unchanged Primitive Indo-European [k]. If such things happened, then every language would be spotted over with all sorts of queer, deviant sounds, in forms which had resisted sound-change or deviated from ordinary changes. Actually, however, a language moves within a limited set of phonemes. The modern English [k] in *cuckoo* is no different from the [k] in words like *cow, calf, kin,* which has developed normally from the Primitive Indo-European [g]-type. We should have to suppose, therefore, that some later change brought the preserved Primitive Indo-European [k] in *cuckoo* into complete equality with the Germanic [k] that reflects a Primitive Indo-European [g], and, since every language moves within a limited phonetic system, we should have to suppose that in every case of sporadic sound-change or resistance to sound-change, the discrepant sound has been reduced to some ordinary phonemic type in time to escape the ear of the observer. Otherwise we should find, say, in present-day standard English, a sprinkling of forms which preserved sounds from eighteenth-century English, early modern English, Middle English, Old English, Primitive Germanic, and so on — not to speak of deviant sounds resulting from sporadic changes in some positive direction.

Actually, the forms which do not exhibit ordinary phonetic correlations, conform to the phonemic system of their language and are peculiar only in their correlation with other forms. For instance, the modern standard English correspondents of Old English [o:] show some decided irregularities, but these consist simply in the presence of unexpected phonemes, and never in deviation from the phonetic system. The normal representation seems to be:

[ɑ] before [s, z] plus consonant other than [t]: *goshawk, gosling, blossom;*

[ɔ] before Old English consonant plus [t]: *foster, soft, sought* (Old English *sōhte*), *brought, thought;*

[u] before [k] *book, brook* (noun), *cook, crook, hook, look, rook, shook, took;*

[o] before [n] plus consonant other than [t] and before consonant plus [ɽ]: *Monday, month; brother, mother, other, rudder;*

[ow] before [nt] and [r] and from the combination of Old English

[o:w]: *don't; floor, ore, swore, toward, whore; blow* ('bloom'), *flow, glow, grow, low* (verb), *row, stow;*

[uw] otherwise: *do, drew, shoe, slew, too, to, woo, brood, food, mood, hoof, roof, woof, cool, pool, school, stool, tool, bloom, broom, doom, gloom, loom, boon, moon, noon, soon, spoon, swoon, whoop, goose, loose, boot, moot, root, soot, booth, sooth, tooth, smooth, soothe, behoove, prove, ooze.*

If we take the correlation of Old English [o:] with these sounds as normal under the phonetic conditions of each case, then we have the following residue of contradictory forms:

[a] *shod, fodder;*

[aw] *bough, slough;*

[e] *Wednesday;*

[o] *blood, flood, enough, tough, gum, done, must, doth, glove;*

[ow] *woke;*

[u] *good, hood, stood, bosom, foot,* and optionally *hoof, roof, broom, soot;*

[uw] *moor, roost.*

All of these seven deviant types contain some ordinary English phoneme; the [o], for instance, in *blood,* etc., is the ordinary [o]-phoneme, which represents Old English [u] in words like *love, tongue, son, sun, come.* In every case, the discrepant forms show not queer sounds, but merely normal phonemes in a distribution that runs counter to the expectations of the historian.

20. 8. As to the correction of our correspondence-groups by a careful survey of the residual cases, the neo-grammarians soon got a remarkable confirmation of their hypothesis in Verner's treatment of Germanic forms with discrepant [b, d, g] in place of [f, θ, h] (§ 18.7). Verner collected the cases like Latin *pater :* Gothic ['fadar], Old English ['fɛder], where Primitive Indo-European [t] appears in Germanic as [d, ð], instead of [θ]. Now, the voicing of spirants between vowels is a very common form of sound-change, and has actually occurred at various times in the history of several Germanic languages. Primitive Germanic [θ] appears as a voiced spirant, coinciding with the reflex of Primitive Germanic [d], in Old Norse, which says, for instance, ['bro:ðer], with the same consonant as ['faðer]. In Old English, too, the Primitive Germanic [θ] had doubtless become voiced between vowels, as in ['bro:ðor], although it did not coincide with [d], the reflex of Primitive Germanic [d], as in ['fɛder]. In both Old

Norse and Old English, Primitive Germanic [f] had become voiced [v] between vowels, as in Old English *ofen* ['oven] 'oven' (Old High German *ofan* ['ofan]), coinciding with the [v] that represented Primitive Germanic [b], as in Old English *yfel* ['yvel] 'evil' (Old High German *ubil* ['ybil]). Nothing could be more natural, therefore, if one admitted the possibility of irregular sound-change, than to suppose that the voicing of intervocalic spirants had begun sporadically in some words already in pre-Germanic time, and that a Primitive Germanic *['fader] alongside *['bro:θer] represented merely the beginning of a process that was to find its completion in the Old Norse, Old English, and Old Saxon of our actual records. Yet in 1876 Verner's study of the deviant forms showed an unmistakable correlation: in a fair number of cases and in convincing systematic positions, the deviant [b, d, g] of Germanic appeared where Sanskrit and Greek (and therefore, presumably, Primitive Indo-European) had an unaccented vowel or diphthong before the [p, t, k], as in Sanskrit [pi'ta:], Greek [pa-'te:r] : Primitive Germanic *['fader], contrasting with Sanskrit ['bhra:ta:], Greek ['phra:te:r] : Primitive Germanic *['bro:θer]. Similarly, Sanskrit ['çvaçurah] 'father-in-law,' reflecting, presumably a Primitive Indo-European *['swekuros], shows in Germanic the normal reflex of [h] for [k], as in Old High German ['swehar], but Sanskrit [çva'çru:h] 'mother-in-law,' reflecting a Primitive Indo-European *[swe'kru:s] appears in Germanic with [g], as in Old High German ['swigar], representing the Primitive Indo-European [k] after the unstressed vowel.

A confirmation of this result was the fact that the unvoiced spirant [s] of Primitive Indo-European suffered the same change under the same conditions: it appears in Germanic as [s], except when the preceding syllabic was unaccented in Primitive Indo-European; in this case, it was voiced in pre-Germanic, and appears as Primitive Germanic [z], which later became [r] in Norse and in West Germanic. In a number of irregular verb-paradigms the Germanic languages have medial [f, θ, h, s] in the present tense and in the singular indicative-mode forms of the past tense, but [b, d, g, z] in the plural and subjunctive forms of the past tense and in the past participle, as, for instance, in Old English:

['weorθan] 'to become,' [he: 'wearθ] 'he became,' but [we: 'wurdon] 'we became';

['ke:osan] 'to choose,' [he: 'ke:as] 'he chose,' but [we: 'kuron] 'we chose';

['wesan] 'to be,' [he: 'wɛs] 'he was,' but [we: 'wɛːron] 'we were.'

This alternation, Verner showed, corresponds to the alternation in the position of the word-accent in similar Sanskrit paradigms, as, in the verb-forms cognate with the above:

['vartate:] 'he turns, becomes,' [va-'varta] 'he turned,' but [va-vr̥ti'ma] 'we turned';

*['jo:šati] 'he enjoys,' [ju-'jo:ša] 'he enjoyed,' but [ju-juši'ma] 'we enjoyed';

['vasati] 'he dwells,' [u-'va:sa] 'he dwelt,' but [u:ši'ma] 'we dwelt.'

This was so striking a confirmation of the hypothesis of regular sound-change, that the burden of proof now fell upon the opponents of the hypothesis: if the residual forms can show such a correlation as this, we may well ask for very good reasons before we give up our separation of forms into recognized correspondences and remainders, and our principle of scanning residual forms for new correspondences. We may doubt whether an observer who was satisfied with a verdict of "sporadic sound-change" could ever have discovered these correlations.

In a small way, the accidents of observation sometimes furnish similar confirmations of our method. In the Central Algonquian languages — for which we have no older records — we find the following normal correspondences, which we may symbolize by "Primitive Central Algonquian" reconstructed forms:

	Fox	Ojibwa	Menomini	Plains Cree	Primitive Central Algonquian
(1)	hk	šk	čk	sk	čk
(2)	šk	šk	sk	sk	šk
(3)	hk	hk	hk	sk	xk
(4)	hk	hk	hk	hk	hk
(5)	k	ng	hk	hk	nk

Examples:

(1) Fox [kehkjɛ:wa] 'he is old,' Menomini [kɛčki:w], PCA *[kečkjɛ:wa].

(2) Fox [aškutɛ:wi] 'fire,' Ojibwa [iškudɛ:], Menomini [esko:tɛ:w], Cree [iskute:w], PCA *[iškutɛ:wi].

(3) Fox [mahkese:hi] 'moccasin,' Ojibwa [mahkizin], Menomini [mahkɛ:sen], Cree [maskisin], PCA *[maxkesini].

(4) Fox [no:hkumesa] 'my grandmother,' Ojibwa [no:hkumis], Menomini [no:hkumɛh], Cree [no:hkum], PCA *[no:hkuma].

(5) Fox [takeškawɛ:wa] 'he kicks him,' Ojibwa [tangiškawa:d], Menomini [tahkɛ:skawɛ:w], Cree [tahkiskawe:w], PCA *[tankeškawɛ:wa].

Now, there is a residual morpheme in which none of these correspondences holds good, namely the element which means 'red':

(6) Fox [meškusiwa] 'he is red,' Ojibwa [miškuzi], Menomini [mɛhko:n], Cree [mihkusiw], PCA *[meçkusiwa].

Under an assumption of sporadic sound-change, this would have no significance. After the sixth correspondence had been set up, however, it was found that in a remote dialect of Cree, which agrees in groups (1) to (5) with the Plains Cree scheme, the morpheme for 'red' has the peculiar cluster [htk], as in [mihtkusiw] 'he is red.' In this case, then, the residual form showed a special phonetic unit of the parent speech.

The assumption of regular (that is, purely phonemic) sound-change is justified by the correlations which it uncovers; it is inconsistent to accept the results which it yields and to reject it whenever one wants a contradictory assumption ("sporadic sound-change") to "explain" difficult cases.

20. 9. The relation of our residual forms to factors of linguistic history other than sound-change, is the crucial point in the dispute about the regularity of sound-change. The neo-grammarians could not claim, of course, that linguistic resemblances ever run in regular sets. The actual data with which we work are extremely irregular, — so irregular that centuries of study before the days of Rask and Grimm had found no useful correlations. The neo-grammarians did claim, however, that factors of linguistic change other than sound-change will appear in the residual forms after we have ruled out the correlations that result from sound-change. Thus, Old English [a:] in stressed syllables appears in modern English normally as [ow], as in *boat* (from Old English [ba:t]), *sore, whole, oath, snow, stone, bone, home, dough, goat,* and many other forms. In the residue, we find forms like Old English [ba:t] : *bait,* Old English [ha:l] : *hale,* Old English [swa:n] 'herdsman' : *swain.* Having found that Old English [a:] appears in modern standard English as [ow], we assign the forms with the discrepant modern English [ej] to a residue. The forms in this residue are not the results of a deviant, sporadic sound-change of Old English [aː] to modern English [ej]; their deviation is due not to sound-change, but to another factor of linguistic change. The forms like *bait, hale, swain* are not the modern continuants of Old English forms with [aː], but borrowings from Scandinavian. Old Scandinavian had [ej] in forms where Old English had [aː]; Old Scandinavian (Old Norse) said [stejnn, bejta, hejll, swejnn] where Old English said [staːn, baːt, haːl, swaːn]. The regularity of correspondence is due, of course, to the common tradition from Primitive Germanic. After the Norse invasion of England, the English language took over these Scandinavian words, and it is the Old Norse diphthong [ej] which appears in the deviant forms with modern English [ej].

In cases like these, or in cases like Latin *dentālis* : English *dental*, the opponents of the neo-grammarian hypothesis raise no objection, and agree that *linguistic borrowing* accounts for the resemblance. In many other cases, however, they prefer to say that irregular sound-change was at work, and, strangely enough, they do this in cases where only the neo-grammarian hypothesis yields a significant result.

Students of dialect geography are especially given to this confusion. In any one dialect we usually find an ancient unit phoneme represented by several phonemes — as in the case of Old English [oː] in modern English *food, good, blood,* and so on (§ 20.7). Often one of these is like the old phoneme and the others appear to embody one or more phonetic changes. Thus, in Central-Western American English, we say *gather* with [ɛ], *rather* with [ɛ] or with [a], and *father* always with [a]. Some speakers have [juw] in words like *tune, dew, stew, new;* some have [uw] in the first three types, but keep [juw] ordinarily after [n-]; others speak [uw] in all of them. Or, again, if we examine adjacent dialects in an area, we find a gradation: some have apparently carried out a sound-change, as when, say, in Dutch, some districts in our Figure 6 have [yː] for ancient [uː] in the words *mouse* and *house;* next to these we may find dialects which have apparently carried out the change in some of the forms, but not in others, as when some districts in our Figure 6 say [hyːs] with the changed vowel, but [muːs] with the unchanged; finally, we reach a district where the changed forms are lacking, such as, in Figure 6, the area where the old forms [muːs, huːs] are still being spoken. Under a hypothesis of sporadic sound-change, no definite conclusions could be drawn, but under the assumption of regular sound-change, distributions of this sort can at once be interpreted: an irregular distribution shows that the new forms, in a part or in all of the area, are due not to sound-change, but to borrowing. The sound-change took place in some one center and, after this, forms which had undergone the change spread from this center by linguistic borrowing. In other cases, a community may have made a sound-change, but the changed forms may in part be superseded by unchanged forms which spread from a center which has not made the change. Students of dialect geography make this inference and base on it their reconstruction of linguistic and cultural movements, but many of these students at the same time profess to reject the assumption of regular phonetic change. If they stopped to examine the implications of this, they would soon see that their work is based on the supposition that sound-change is regular, for, if we admit the possibility of irregular sound-change, then the use of [hy:s] beside [mu:s] in a Dutch dialect, or of ['raðr̩] *rather* beside ['gɛðr̩] *gather* in standard English, would justify no deductions about linguistic borrowing.

20. 10. Another phase of the dispute about the regularity of sound-change concerns residual forms whose deviation is connected with features of meaning. Often enough, the forms that deviate from ordinary phonetic correlation belong to some clearly marked semantic group.

In ancient Greek, Primitive Indo-European [s] between vowels had been lost by sound-change. Thus, Primitive Indo-European *['ɡewso:] 'I taste' (Gothic ['kiwsa] 'I choose') appears in Greek as ['gewo:] 'I give a taste'; Primitive Indo-European *['ɡenesos] 'of the kin' (Sanskrit ['janasah]) appears as Greek ['geneos], later ['genows]; Primitive Indo-European *['e:sm̩] 'I was' (Sanskrit ['a:sam]) appears in Greek as [ˇe:a], later [ˇe:].

Over against cases like these, there is a considerable residue of forms in which an old intervocalic [s] seems to be preserved in ancient Greek. The principal type of this residue consists of aorist-tense (that is, past punctual) verb-forms, in which the suffix [-s-] of this tense occurs after the final vowel of a root or verb-stem. Thus, the Greek root [plew-] 'sail' (present tense ['plewo:] 'I sail,' paralleled by Sanskrit ['plavate:] 'he sails') has the aorist form ['eplewsa] 'I sailed'; the Greek aorist ['etejsa] 'I paid a penalty' parallels

Sanskrit ['ača:jšam] 'I collected'; the Greek root [ste:-] 'stand' (present tense ['histe:mi] 'I cause to stand') has the aorist form ['este:sa] 'I caused to stand,' parallel with Old Bulgarian [staxʊ] 'I stood up,' Primitive Indo-European type *['esta:sm̥]; a Primitive Indo-European aorist type *['ebhu:sm̥] (Old Bulgarian [byxʊ] 'I became') is apparently represented by Greek ['ephu:sa] 'I caused to grow.' Opponents of the neo-grammarian method suppose that when intervocalic [s] was weakened and finally lost during the pre-Greek period, the [s] of these forms resisted the change, because it expressed an important meaning, namely that of the aorist tense. A sound-change, they claim, can be checked in forms where it threatens to remove some semantically important feature.

The neo-grammarian hypothesis implies that sound-change is unaffected by semantic features and concerns merely the habits of articulating speech-sounds. If residual forms are characterized by some semantic feature, then their deviation must be due not to sound-change, but to some other factor of linguistic change — to some factor which is connected with meanings. In our example, the sound-change which led to the loss of intervocalic [s] destroyed every intervocalic [s]; forms like Greek ['este:sa] cannot be continuants of forms that existed before that sound-change. They were created after the sound-change was past, as new combinations of morphemes in a complex form, by a process which we call *analogic new combination* or *analogic change*. In many forms where the aorist-suffix was not between vowels, it had come unscathed through the sound-change. Thus, a Primitive Indo-European aorist *['ele:jkʷsm̥] 'I left' (Sanskrit ['ara:jkšam]) appears in Greek, by normal phonetic development, as ['elejpsa]; Primitive Indo-European *[eje:wksm̥] 'I joined' (Sanskrit ['aja:wkšam]) appears as Greek ['ezewksa]; the Primitive Indo-European root *[ɡews-] 'taste' (Greek present ['gewo:], cited above), combining with the aorist-suffix, would give a stem *[ɡe:ws-s-]: as double [ss] was not lost in pre-Greek, but merely at a later date simplified to [s], the Greek aorist ['egewsa] 'I gave a taste' is the normal phonetic type. Accordingly, the Greek language possessed the aorist suffix [-s-]; at all times this suffix was doubtless combined with all manner of verbal stems, and our aorists with the [-s-] between vowels are merely combinations which were made after the sound-change which affected [-s-] had ceased to work. On models like the inherited present-tense ['gewo:] with aorist ['egewsa], one formed, for the present-tense ['plewo:], a new aorist ['eplewsa]. In sum, the residual forms are not due to deflections of the process of sound-change, but reveal to us, rather, a different factor of linguistic change — namely, analogic change.

In much the same way, some students believe that sounds which bear no important meaning are subject to excess weakening and to loss by irregular sound-change. In this way they explain, for instance, the weakening of *will* to [l] in forms like *I'll go.* The neo-grammarian would attribute the weakening rather to the fact that the verb-form in phrases like these is atonic: in English, unstressed phonemes have been subjected to a series of weakenings and losses.

20. 11. The neo-grammarians define sound-change as a purely phonetic process; it affects a phoneme or a type of phonemes either universally or under certain strictly phonetic conditions, and is neither favored nor impeded by the semantic character of the forms which happen to contain the phoneme. The effect of sound-change, then, as it presents itself to the comparatist, will be a set of regular phonemic correspondences, such as Old English [sta:n, ba:n, ba:t, ga:t, ra:d, ha:l]: modern English [stown, bown, bowt, gowt, rowd, howl] *stone, bone, boat, goat, road (rode), whole.* However, these correspondences will almost always be opposed by sets or scatterings of deviant forms, such as Old English [ba:t, swa:n, ha:l] versus modern English [bejt, swejn, hejl] *bait, swain, hale,* because phonetic change is only one of several factors of linguistic change. We must suppose that, no matter how minute and accurate our observation, we should always find deviant forms, because, from the very outset of a sound-change, and during its entire course, and after it is over, the forms of the language are subject to the incessant working of other factors of change, such as, especially, borrowing and analogic combination of new complex forms. The occurrence of sound-change, as defined by the neo-grammarians, is not a fact of direct observation, but an assumption. The neo-grammarians believe that this assumption is correct, because it alone has enabled linguists to find order in the factual data, and because it alone has led to a plausible formulation of other factors of linguistic change.

Theoretically, we can understand the regular change of phonemes, if we suppose that language consists of two layers of habit. One layer is phonemic: the speakers have certain habits of voic-

ing, tongue-movement, and so on. These habits make up the phonetic system of the language. The other layer consists of formal-
semantic habits: the speakers habitually utter certain combinations
of phonemes in response to certain types of stimuli, and respond
appropriately when they hear these same combinations. These
habits make up the grammar and lexicon of the language.

One may conceivably acquire the phonetic habits of a language
without using any of its significant forms; this may be the case of
a singer who has been taught to render a French song in correct
pronunciation, or of a mimic who, knowing no French, can yet
imitate a Frenchman's English. On the other hand, if the phonemes of a foreign language are not completely incommensurable
with ours, we may utter significant forms in this language without
acquiring its phonetic habits; this is the case of some speakers of
French and English, who converse freely in each others' languages,
but, as we say, with an abominable pronunciation.

Historically, we picture phonetic change as a gradual favoring
of some non-distinctive variants and a disfavoring of others. It
could be observed only by means of an enormous mass of mechan-
ical records, reaching through several generations of speakers. The
hypothesis supposes that such a collection — provided that we
could rule out the effects of borrowing and analogic change —
would show a progressive favoring of variants in some one direction, coupled with the obsolescence of variants at the other extreme. Thus, Old English and Middle English spoke a long mid
vowel in forms like *gos* 'goose' and *ges* 'geese.' We suppose that
during a long period of time, higher variants were favored and
lower variants went out of use, until, in the eighteenth century, the
range of surviving variants could be described as a high-vowel
type [u:, i:]; since then, the more diphthongal variants have been
favored, and the simple-vowel types have gone out of use.

The non-distinctive acoustic features of a language are at all
times highly variable. Even the most accurate phonetic record
of a language at any one time could not tell us which phonemes
were changing. Moreover, it is certain that these non-distinctive,
sub-phonemic variants are subject to linguistic borrowing (imitation) and to analogic change (systematization). This appears
from the fact that whenever the linguist deals with a sound-change
— and certainly in some cases his documents or his observations
must date from a time very shortly after the occurrence of the

change — he finds the results of the sound-change disturbed by these other factors. Indeed, when we observe sub-phonemic variants, we sometimes find them distributed among speakers or systematized among forms, quite in the manner of linguistic borrowing and of analogic change. In the Central-Western type of American English, vowel-quantities are not distinctive, but some speakers habitually (though perhaps not invariably) use a shorter variant of the phoneme [a] before the clusters [rk, rp], as in *dark, sharp*, and before the clusters [rd, rt] followed by a primary suffix [-ɽ, -ṇ], as in *barter, Carter, garden, marten (Martin)*. Before a secondary suffix, [-ɽ, -ṇ], however, the longer variant is used, as in *starter, carter* ('one who carts'), *harden;* here the existence of the simple words (*start, cart, hard*), whose [a] is not subject to shortening, has led to the favoring of the normal, longer variant. The word *larder* (not part of the colloquial vocabulary) could be read with the shorter variant, but the agent-noun *larder* ('one who lards') could be formed only with the longer type of the [a]-phoneme. This distribution of the sub-phonemic variants is quite like the results of analogic change, and, whatever its origin, the distribution of this habit among speakers is doubtless effected by a process of imitation which we could identify with linguistic borrowing. If the difference between the two variants should become distinctive, then the comparatist would say that a sound-change had occurred, but he would find the results of this sound-change overlaid, from the very start, by the effects of borrowing and of analogic change.

We can often observe that a non-distinctive variant has become entirely obsolete. In eighteenth-century English, forms like *geese, eight, goose, goat* had long vowels of the types [iː, eː, uː, oː], which since then have changed to the diphthongal types [ij, ej, uw, ow]. This displacement has had no bearing on the structure of the language; a transcription of present-day standard English which used the symbols [iː, eː, uː, oː] would be perfectly adequate. It is only the phonetician or acoustician who tells us that there has been a displacement in the absolute physiologic and acoustic configuration of these phonemes. Nevertheless, we can see that the non-diphthongal variants, which at first were the predominant ones, are today obsolete. The speaker of present-day standard English who tries to speak a language like German or French which has undiphthongized long vowels, has a hard time learning to produce these types. It is as hard for him to artic-ulate these acoustic types (which existed in English not so many generations ago) as it is for the Frenchman or the German to produce the English diphthongal types. The speaker learns only with difficulty to produce speech-sounds that do not occur in his native language, even though the historian, irrelevantly, may assure him that an earlier stage of his language possessed these very sounds.

We can speak of sound-change only when the displacement of habit has led to some alteration in the structure of the language. Most types of American English speak a low vowel [ɑ] in forms like *got, rod, not,* where British English has kept an older mid-vowel type [ɔ]. In some types of American standard English, this [ɑ] is distinct from the [a] of forms like *calm, far, pa* — so that *bother* does not rime with *father,* and *bomb,* is not homonymous with *balm:* there has been no displacement of the phonemic system. In other types of American standard English, however, the two phonemes have coincided: *got, rod, bother, bomb, calm, far, pa, father, balm* all have one and the same low vowel [a], and we say, accordingly, that a sound-change has taken place. Some speakers of this (as well as some of the other) type pronounce *bomb* as [bom]: this form is due to some sort of linguistic borrowing and accordingly cannot exhibit the normal correlation.

The initial clusters [kn-, gn-], as in *knee, gnat,* lost their stop sound early in the eighteenth century: hereby *knot* and *not, knight* and *night, gnash* and *Nash* became homonymous. English-speakers of today learn only with difficulty to produce initial clusters like these, as, say, in German *Knie* [kni:] 'knee.'

In Dutch-German area, the Primitive Germanic phoneme [θ] changed toward [ð] and then toward [d]; by the end of the Middle Ages this [d] coincided, in the northern part of the area, with Primitive Germanic [d]. Hence modern standard Dutch has ini-tial [d] uniformly, both in words like *dag* [dax] 'day,' *doen* [du:n] 'do,' *droom* [dro:m] 'dream,' where English has [d], and in words like *dik* [dik] 'thick,' *doorn* [do:rn] 'thorn,' *drie* [dri:] 'three,' where English has [θ]. The distinction has been entirely obliterated, and could be re-introduced only by borrowing from a language in which it has been preserved. Needless to say, the Dutchman or North German has as hard a time learning to utter an Eng-lish [θ] as though this sound had never existed in his language.

The favoring of variants which leads to sound-change is a historical occurrence; once it is past, we have no guarantee of its happening again. A later process may end by favoring the very same acoustic types as were eliminated by an earlier change. The Old and Middle English long vowels [i:, u:], as in [wi:n, hu:s], were eliminated, in the early modern period, by change toward the diphthongal types of the present-day *wine, house.* At about the same time, however, the Old and Middle English long mid vowels, as in [ge:s, go:s], were being raised, so that eighteenth-century English again had the types [i:, u:] in words like *geese, goose.* The new [i:, u:] arrived too late to suffer the change to [aj, aw] which had overtaken the Middle English high vowels. Similarly, we must suppose that the pre-Greek speakers of the generations that were weakening the phoneme [s] between vowels, could learn only with difficulty to utter such a thing as a distinct simple [s] in intervocalic position, but, after the change was over, the simplification of long [ss] re-introduced this phonetic type, and (doubtless independently of this) new combinations of the type ['este:sa] (§ 20.10) were again fully pronounceable. In this way, we can often determine the succession (*relative chronology*) of changes. Thus, it is clear that in pre-Germanic time, the Primitive Indo-European [b, d, g] can have reached the types of Primitive Germanic [p, t, k] only *after* Primitive Indo-European [p, t, k] had already been changed somewhat in the direction of the types of Primitive Germanic [f, θ, h] — for the actual Germanic forms show that these two series of phonemes did not coincide (§ 20.2).

CHAPTER 21

TYPES OF PHONETIC CHANGE

21. 1. Phonetic change, as defined in the last chapter, is a change in the habits of performing sound-producing movements. Strictly speaking, a change of this kind has no importance so long as it does not affect the phonemic system of the language; in fact, even with perfect records at our command, we should probably be unable to determine the exact point where a favoring of certain variants began to deserve the name of a historical change. At the time when speakers of English began to favor the variants with higher tongue-position of the vowels in words like *gōs* 'goose' and *gēs* 'geese,' the dislocation was entirely without significance. The speakers had no way of comparing the acoustic qualities of their vowels with the acoustic qualities of the vowels which their predecessors, a few generations back, had spoken in the same linguistic forms. When they heard a dialect which had not made the change, they may have noticed a difference, but they could have had no assurance as to how this difference had arisen. Phonetic change acquires significance only if it results in a change of the phonemic pattern. For instance, in the early modern period, the Middle English vowel [ɛ:], as in *sed* [sɛ:d] 'seed,' was raised until it coincided with the [e:] in *ges* [ge:s] 'geese,' and this coincidence for all time changed the distribution of phonemes in the forms of the language. Again, the Middle English short [e] in a so-called "open" syllable — that is, before a single consonant followed by another vowel, as in *ete* ['ete] 'eat' — was lengthened and ultimately coincided with the long vowels just mentioned. Accordingly, the phonemic structure of modern English is different from that of medieval English. Our phoneme [ij] continues, among others, these three older phonemes; we may note, especially, that this coincidence has given rise to a number of homonyms.

Old and Middle English [e:] has changed to modern [ij] in *heel, steel, geese, queen, green, meet* (verb), *need, keep.*

Old and Middle English [ɛ:] has changed to modern [ij] in *heal, meal* ('taking of food'), *cheese, leave, clean, lean* (adjective), *street, mead* ('meadow'), *meet* (adjective).

Old and Middle English [e] has changed to modern [ij] in *steal, meal* ('flour'), *weave, lean* (verb), *quean, speak, meat, mete, eat, mead* ('fermented drink').

On the other hand, the restriction of this last change to a limited phonetic position, has produced different phonemes in forms that used to have the same phoneme: the old [e] was lengthened in Middle English *weve* < *weave,* but not in Middle English *weft* < *weft.* In the same way, a phonetic change which consisted of shortening long vowels before certain consonant-clusters has produced the difference of vowel between *meadow* (< Old English ['mɛ:dwe]) and *mead,* or between *kept* (< Old English ['ke:pte]) and *keep.*

A few hundred years ago, initial [k] was lost before [n]: the result was a change in the phonemic system, which included such features as the homonymy of *knot* and *not,* or of *knight* and *night,* and the alternation of [n-] and [-kn-] in *know, knowledge : acknowledge.*

21. 2. The general direction of a great deal of sound-change is toward a simplification of the movements which make up the utterance of any given linguistic form. Thus, consonant-groups are often simplified. The Old English initial clusters [hr, hl, hn, kn, gn, wr] have lost their initial consonants, as in Old English *hring* > *ring, hlēapan* > *leap, hnecca* > *neck, cnēow* > *knee, gnagan* > *gnaw, wringan* > *wring.* The loss of the [h] in these groups occurred in the later Middle Ages, that of the other consonants in early modern time; we do not know what new factor intervened at these times to destroy the clusters which for many centuries had been spoken without change. The [h]-clusters are still spoken in Icelandic; initial [kn] remains not only in the other Germanic languages (as, Dutch *knie* [kni:], German *Knie* [kni:], Danish [knɛ:ʔ], Swedish [kne:]), but also in the English dialects of the Shetland and Orkney Islands and northeastern Scotland. The [gn] persists almost as widely — in English, more widely; [wr-], in the shape of [vr-], remains in Scandinavian, the northern part of the Dutch-German area, including standard Dutch, and in several scattered dialects of English. As long as we do not know what factors led to these changes at one time and place but not at another, we cannot claim to know the causes of the change —

that is, to predict its occurrence. The greater simplicity of the favored variants is a permanent factor; it can offer no possibilities of correlation.

Simplification of final consonant-clusters is even more common. A Primitive Indo-European *[pe:ts] 'foot' (nominative singular) appears in Sanskrit as [pa:t] and in Latin as *pes* [pe:s]; a Primitive Indo-European *['bheronts] 'bearing' (nominative singular masculine) appears in Sanskrit as ['bharan], and in Latin as *ferens* ['ferens], later ['fere:s]. It is this type of change which leads to habits of permitted final (§ 8.4) and to morphologic alternations of the type described in § 13.9. Thus, a Primitive Central Algonquian *[axkehkwa] 'kettle,' plural *[axkehkwaki], reflected in Fox [ahko:hkwa, ahko:hko:ki], loses its final vowel and part of the consonant-cluster in Cree [askihk, askihkwak] and in Menomini [ahkɛ:h, ahkɛ:hkuk], so that the plural-form in these languages contains a consonant-cluster that cannot be determined by inspection of the singular form. In English, final [ŋg] and [mb] have lost their stop; hence the contrast of *long : longer* [lɔŋ — 'lɔŋgr̩], *climb : clamber* [klajm — 'klɛmbr̩].

Sometimes even single final consonants are weakened or disappear. In pre-Greek, final [t, d] were lost, as in Primitive Indo-European *[tod] 'that,' Sanskrit [tat]: Greek [to]; final [m] became [n], as in Primitive Indo-European *[ju'gom] 'yoke,' Sanskrit [ju'gam]: Greek [zu'gon]. The same changes seem to have occurred in pre-Germanic. Sometimes all final consonants are lost and there results a phonetic pattern in which every word ends in a vowel. This happened in pre-Slavic, witness forms like Old Bulgarian [to] 'that,' [igo] 'yoke.' It is a change of this sort that accounts for morphologic situations like that of Samoan (§ 13.9); a Samoan form like [inu] 'drink' is the descendant of an older *[inum], whose final consonant has been kept in Tagalog [i'num].

When changes of this sort appear at the beginning or, more often, at the end of words, we have to suppose that the languages in which they took place had, at the time, some phonetic marking of the word-unit. If there were any forms in which the beginning or the end of a word had not the characteristic initial or final pronunciation, these forms would not suffer the change, and would survive as sandhi-forms. Thus, in Middle English, final [n] was lost, as in *eten > ete* 'eat,' but the article *an* before vowels must have been pronounced as if it were part of the following word — that is, without the phonetic peculiarities of final position — so that the [n] in this case was not lost (like a final [n]), but preserved (like a medial [n]): *a house* but *an arm*. Latin *vōs* 'ye' gives French *vous* [vu], but Latin phrase-types like *vōs amātis* 'ye love' are reflected in the French sandhi-habit of saying *vous aimez* [vuz eme]. Latin *est* 'he is' gave French *est* [ɛ] 'is,' but the phrase-type of Latin *est ille?* 'is that one?' appears in the French sandhi-form in *est-il?* [ɛt i?] 'is he?' In the same way, a Primitive Indo-European *['bheronts] is reflected not only in Sanskrit ['bharan], above cited, but also in the Sanskrit habit of adding a sandhi [s] when the next word began with [t], as in ['bharaⁿs 'tatra] 'carrying there.'

21. 3. Simplification of consonant-clusters is a frequent result of sound-change. Thus, a pre-Latin *['fulgmen] 'flash (of lightning)' gives a Latin *fulmen*. Here the group [lgm] was simplified by the change to [lm], but the group [lg], as in *fulgur* 'flash,' was not changed, and neither was the group [gm], as in *agmen* 'army.' In describing such changes, we speak of the conditions as *conditioning factors* (or *causing factors*) and say, for instance, that one of these was absent in cases like *fulgur* and *agmen*, where the [g], accordingly, was preserved. This form of speech is inaccurate, since the change was really one of [lgm] to [lm], and cases like *fulgur*, *agmen* are irrelevant, but it is often convenient to use these terms. The result of a conditioned change is often a morphologic alternation. Thus, in Latin, we have the suffix *-men* in *agere* 'to lead': *agmen* 'army' but *fulgere* 'to flash': *fulmen* 'flash (of lightning).' Similarly, pre-Latin [rkn] became [rn]; beside *pater* 'father': *paternus* 'paternal,' we have *quercus* 'oak' : *quernus* 'oaken.'

Quite commonly, clusters change by way of *assimilation:* the position of the vocal organs for the production of one phoneme is altered to a position more like that of the other phoneme. The commoner case is *regressive* assimilation, change of the prior phoneme.

Thus, the voicing or unvoicing of a consonant is often altered into agreement with that of a following consonant; the [s] of *goose* and *house* has been voiced to [z] in the combinations *gosling*, *husband*. This, again, may give rise to morphologic alternations. In the history of Russian the loss of two short vowels (I shall transcribe them as [ɪ] and [ʊ]) produced consonant-clusters; in these clusters a stop or spirant was then assimilated, as to voicing, to a following stop or spirant. The old forms can be seen in Old

Bulgarian, which did not make the changes in question. Thus *['svatɪba] 'marriage' gives Russian ['svadba]; compare Russian [svat] 'arranger of a marriage.' Old Bulgarian [otʊbe:žati] 'to run away' appears in Russian as [odbe'žat]; compare the simple Old Bulgarian [otʊ] 'from, away from' : Russian [ot]. On the other hand, Old Bulgarian [podʊkopati] 'to undermine' appears in Russian as [potko'pat]; contrast Old Bulgarian [podʊ igo] 'under the yoke' : Russian ['pod igo].

The assimilation may affect the action of the velum, tongue, or lips. If some difference between the consonants is kept, the assimilation is *partial;* thus in pre-Latin [pn] was assimilated to [mn], as in Primitive Indo-European *['swepnos] 'sleep,' Sanskrit ['svapnah] : Latin *somnus.* If the difference entirely disappears, the assimilation is *total,* and the result is a long consonant, as in Italian *sonno* ['sɔnno]. Similarly, Latin *octō* 'eight' > Italian *otto* ['ɔtto]; Latin *ruptum* 'broken' > Italian *rotto* ['rɔtto].

In *progressive* assimilation the latter consonant is altered. Thus, pre-Latin *[kolnis] 'hill' gives Latin *collis;* compare Lithuanian ['ka:lnas] 'mountain.' Our word *hill* underwent the same change [ln] > [ll] in pre-Germanic; witness Primitive Indo-European *[pl̥:'nos] 'full,' Sanskrit [pu:r'ɴah], Lithuanian ['pilnas] : Primitive Germanic *['follaz], Gothic *fulls,* Old English *full,* or Primitive Indo-European *['wl̥:na:] 'wool,' Sanskrit ['u:rɴa:], Lithuanian ['vilna] : Primitive Germanic *['wollo:], Gothic *wulla,* Old English *wull.*

21. 4. A great many other changes of consonants can be viewed as assimilative in character. Thus, the unvoicing of final consonants, which has occurred in the history of various languages, can be viewed as a sort of regressive assimilation: the open position of the vocal chords which follows upon the end of speech, is anticipated during the utterance of the final consonant. Thus, many dialects of the Dutch-German area, including the standard languages, have unvoiced all final stops and spirants; the result is an alternation of unvoiced finals with voiced medials (§ 13.9):

Old High German *tag* 'day' > New High German *Tag* [ta:k], but, plural, *taga* 'days' > *Tage* ['ta:ge], with unchanged [g];

Old High German *bad* 'bath' > New High German *Bad* [ba:t], but, genitive case, *bades* > *Bades* ['ba:des];

Old High German *gab* '(he) gave' > New High German *gab* [ga:p], but, plural, *gābun* '(they) gave' > *gaben* ['ga:ben].

The voiced consonant may be preserved in sandhi — that is, in traditional phrase-types where it did not come at the end of speech. This does not happen in standard German; here the final-form has been carried out for every word-unit. In Russian, however, we have not only the final-form, by which an old [podʊ], after loss of the vowel, became [pot], but also phrasal types like ['pod igo] 'under the yoke.' There is a type of Dutch pronunciation where an old *hebbe* '(I) have' appears, after loss of the final vowel, not only in the final-form with [-p], as in *ik heb* [ek 'hep], but also in the phrasal sandhi-type, *heb ek?* ['heb ek?] 'have I?' This is the origin of reminiscent sandhi (§ 12.5).

A very common type of change is the weakening of consonants between vowels or other open sounds. This, too, is akin to assimilation, since, when the preceding and following sounds are open and voiced, the less marked closure or the voicing of a stop or spirant represents an economy of movement. The change which gave rise to the American English voiced tongue-flip variety of [t], as in *water, butter, at all* (§ 6.7), was surely of this sort. Latin [p, t, k] between vowels are largely weakened in the Romance languages: Latin *rīpam* 'bank, shore,' *sētam* 'silk,' *focum* 'hearth' appear in Spanish as *riba, seda, fuego* 'fire,' where the [b, d, g] are largely spirant in character, and in French as *rive, soie, feu* [riːv, swa, fø]. Some languages, such as pre-Greek, lose sounds like [s, j, w] between vowels. The Polynesian languages and, to some extent, the medieval Indo-Aryan languages, show a loss of the old structure of medial consonants, much like that in the French forms just cited. In the history of English, loss of [v] is notable, as in Old English ['hɛvde, 'havok, 'hlaːvord, 'hlaːvdije, 'heːavod, 'navogaːr] > modern *had, hawk, lord, lady, head, auger;* this change seems to have occurred in the thirteenth century.

If the conditioning factors are removed by subsequent change, the result is an irregular alternation. In this way, arose, for example, the sandhi-alternation of initial consonants in Irish (§ 12.4). In the history of this language, stops between vowels were weakened to spirants, as in Primitive Indo-European *['piboːmi] 'I drink,' Sanskrit ['pibaːmi]: Old Irish *ebaim* ['evim]. Apparently the language at this stage gave little phonetic recognition to the word-unit, and carried out this change in close-knit phrases, changing, for instance, an *[eso bowes] 'his cows' (compare Sanskrit [a'sja 'gaːvah]) to what is now [a vaː], in contrast with the absolute form [ba:] 'cows.' This type of sandhi is preserved in a limited number of cases, as, in our instance, after the pronoun [a] 'his.' In the same way, [s] between vowels was weakened to [h] and then lost: a Primitive Indo-European *['sweso:r] 'sister,' Sanskrit ['svasa:], giving first, presumably, *['sweho:r], and then Old Irish *siur*. Final [s] similarly was lost: a Gallic *tarbos* 'bull' appears in Old Irish as *tarb*. We have to suppose, now, that the change [s > h] between vowels took place also in close-knit phrases, so that an *[esa:s o:wjo] 'her egg' (compare Sanskrit [a'sja:h] 'her,' with [-h] from [-s]) resulted in a modern [a huv] 'her egg,' in contrast with the independent [uv] 'egg' — again, a habit preserved only in certain combinations, as after the word for 'her.' Similarly, [m] was first changed to [n] and then lost at the end of words, but between vowels was preserved; both treatments appear in *[nemo:tom] 'holy place,' Old Gallic [neme:ton], Old Irish *nemed*. At the stage where [-m] had become [-n], an old *[sen-to:m o:wjo:m] 'of these eggs' (compare the Greek genitive plural ['to:n]) gave what is now [na nuv], in contrast with the absolute [uv] 'egg.' To a similar, but more complicated development we owe the sandhi-alternant with initial [t], as in [an tuv] 'the egg'; ultimately this is due to the fact that the Primitive Indo-European nominative-accusative singular neuter pronoun-forms ended in [d], as Sanskrit [tat] 'that,' Latin *id* 'it.'

We may interpret the pre-Germanic change discovered by Verner (§§ 18.7; 20.8) as a weakening of unvoiced spirants [f, θ, h, s] between musical sounds to voiced [v, ð, γ, z]; then the restriction of the change to cases where the preceding vowel or diphthong was unstressed is subject to a further interpretation of the same sort: after a loudly stressed vowel there is a great amount of breath stored up behind the vocal chords, so that their opening for an unvoiced spirant is easier than their closure for a voiced. We cannot view these interpretations as correlating ("causal") explanations, however, for enough languages keep unvoiced spirants intact between vowels, while others change them to voiced regardless of high stress on a preceding vowel. Here, too, the conditioning factor was afterwards removed by other changes: in an early pre-Germanic *['werθonon] 'to become' versus *[wurðu'me] 'we became,' the alternation [θ:ð] depended on the place of the stress; later, when the stress had changed to the first syllable of all words, the alternation in Primitive Germanic

*['werθanan — 'wurdumɔ], Old English ['weorθan — 'wurdon], was
an arbitrary irregularity, just as is the parallel *was : were*, from
Primitive Germanic *['wase — 'we:zume], in modern English.
A similar change occurred much later in the history of English; it accounts for such differences as *luxury : luxurious* ['lokš-
ṛij — log'žuwrjos] in a common type of pronunciation, and for the
two treatments of French [s] in forms like *possessor* [po'zesṛ].
This change involved the voicing of old [s] after an unstressed
vowel in suffixes, as in *glasses, misses, Bess's;* a few forms like
dice (plural of *die*) and *pence* show the preservation of [s] after
a stressed vowel.   Immediately after this change the stressed
forms must have been *off* [of], *with* [wiθ], *is* [is], *his* [his], and the
atonic forms *of* [ov] and [wiδ, iz, hiz,] but this alternation has
been destroyed: *off* and *of* have been redistributed by analogic
change, [wiθ] survives as a variant of [wiδ], and the [s]-forms of
is and *his* have fallen into disuse.

21. 5. Consonants are often assimilated to the tongue-position
of preceding or following vowels. The commonest case is the assimilation especially of dentals and velars to a following front
vowel; this is known as *palatalization*. A change of this kind which
did not cause phonemic alterations, must have occurred not too
long ago in English, for phoneticians assure us that we make the
tongue-contact of [k, g] farther forward before a front vowel, as
in *kin, keep, kept, give, geese, get*, than before a back vowel, as in
cook, good. In pre-English there occurred a change of the same
sort which led to alteration of the phonemic structure. To begin
with, the palatalized form of [g] — presumably this phoneme had
a spirant character — coincided with another phoneme, [j]. The
change in phonemic distribution appears plainly when we compare
the cognate forms from North German (Old Saxon), where the
old phonemic distribution remained intact:

NORTH GERMAN	PRE-ENGLISH	>	OLD ENGLISH	>	MODERN ENGLISH
gold	*[gold]		*gold*	[gold]	*gold*
gōd	*[go:d]		*god*	[go:d]	*good*
geldan	*['geldan]		*gieldan*	['jeldan]	*yield*
garn	*[gɛrn]		*gearn*	[jarn]	*yarn*
jok	*[jok]		*geoc*	[jok]	*yoke*
jār	*[je:r]		*gear*	[je:ar]	*year*

Another way in which the pre-English palatalization in time affected the structure of the language, was by the obscuration of the conditioning factor. The back vowels [o, u], which did not affect a preceding velar, were changed, under certain conditions, to front vowels [ø, y] and later to [e, i], which coincided with old front vowels that had effected palatalization. Hence, in the later stages of English, both palatalized and unpalatalized velars occurred before front vowels.

Palatalized velars, before old front vowels:

PRE-ENGLISH	>	OLD ENGLISH	>	MODERN ENGLISH
*['kɛ:si]		ciese	['ki:ese]	cheese
*[kinn]		cinn	[kin]	chin
*['geldan]		gieldan	['jeldan]	yield
*[gɛrn]		gearn	[jarn]	yarn

Unpalatalized velars, before new front vowels:

PRE-ENGLISH	>	OLD ENGLISH	>	MODERN ENGLISH
*['ko:ni > 'kø:ni]		cene	['ke:ne]	keen
*['kunni > 'kynni]		cynn	[kyn]	kin
*['go:si > 'gø:si]		ges	[ge:s]	geese
*['guldjan > 'gyldjan]		gyldan	['gyldan]	gild

A third factor of the same kind was the loss, by later sound-change, of the conditioning feature, — that is, of the front vowel [e, i, j] which had caused the palatalization:

Palatalized velars, followed, at the critical time, by a front vowel:

PRE-ENGLISH	>	OLD ENGLISH	>	MODERN ENGLISH
*['drenkjan]		drencean	['drenkan]	drench
*['stiki]		stice	['stike]	stitch
*['sengjan]		sengan	['sengan]	singe
*['bryggju]		brycg	[brygg]	bridge

Unpalatalized velars, not followed by front vowel:

PRE-ENGLISH	>	OLD ENGLISH	>	MODERN ENGLISH
*['drinkan]		drincan	['drinkan]	drink
*['stikka]		sticca	['stikka]	stick
*['singan]		singan	['singan]	sing
*['frogga]		frogga	['frogga]	frog

The sound-change which we call palatalization changes consonants at first to varieties which the phonetician calls palatalized;
the modern English forms in our preceding examples, with their
[č, ǰ, j], show us that these palatalized types may undergo further
changes. These, in fact, are extremely common, although their
direction varies. In the case of both velars and dentals, affricate
types [č, ǰ] and sibilant types, both abnormal [š, ž] and normal [s, z],
are fairly frequent. In modern English we have a development
of [tj > č, dj > ǰ, sj > š, zj > ž], as in *virtue, Indian, session,
vision* ['vṛčuw, 'inǰṇ, 'sešṇ, 'vižṇ]; more formal variants, such as
['vṛtjuw, 'indjṇ], have arisen by later changes. The Romance
languages exhibit a great variety of development of palatalized
velars:

	LATIN >	ITALIAN	FRENCH	SPANISH
'hundred'	*centum*	*cento*	*cent*	*ciento*
	['kentum]	['čɛnto]	[sɑⁿ]	['θjento]
'nation'	*gentem*	*gente*	*gens*	*gente*
	['gentem]	['ǰɛnte]	[žɑⁿ]	['xente]

Part of the French area has a palatalization of [k] before [a];
in the Middle Ages, when English borrowed many French words,
this had reached the stage of [č], so that a Latin type like *cantare*
[kan'taːre] 'to sing' > Old French *chanter* [čan'teːr] appears in
English as *chant;* similarly, Latin *cathedram* ['katedram] appears
as *chair;* Latin *catenam* [ka'teːnam] as *chain;* Latin *cameram* ['kam-
eram] as *chamber.* In modern standard French, further change
of this [č] has led to [š]: *chanter, chaire, chaîne, chambre* [šɑⁿte,
šeːr, šeːn, šɑⁿbr].

Palatalization has played a great part in the history of the
Slavic languages: it has occurred at different times with different
results, and has affected every type of consonant, including even
labials.

A case of palatalization whose causing factor was obscured by
later change, played an important part in the development of
Indo-European studies. In the Indo-Iranian languages a single
vowel-type [a] corresponds to the three types [a, e, o] of the other
Indo-European languages. Thus, Latin *ager* 'field,' *equos* 'horse,'
octō 'eight' are cognate with Sanskrit ['aǰrah, 'açvah, aš'ʈaːw].
For a long time students believed that the Indo-Iranian languages
had here preserved the Primitive Indo-European state of affairs.

and that the diverse vowels of the European languages were due to later change, made during a common pre-European period. Before the [a] of the Indo-Iranian languages, Primitive Indo-European, velars [k, g] appeared sometimes unchanged and sometimes as [č, ǰ]. In the 1870's several students independently saw that these latter reflexes are probably due to palatalization, and, in fact, correlate fairly well with the cases where the European languages have [e]. Thus we find, with back vowels in the languages of Europe and velar stops in Indo-Iranian, correspondences like

Primitive Indo-European *[kʷod], Latin *quod* [kwod] 'what': Sanskrit kat- (as first member in compounds);

Primitive Indo-European *[gʷo:ws], Old English *cu* [ku:] 'cow': Sanskrit [ga:wh].

On the other hand, with the front vowel [e] in the languages of Europe and affricates instead of velar stops in Indo-Iranian, we find correspondences like

Primitive Indo-European *[kʷe], Latin *que* [kwe] 'and' : Sanskrit [ča];

Primitive Indo-European *[gʷe:nis], Gothic *qens* [kwe:ns] 'wife': Sanskrit [-ja:nih] (final member in compounds).

From cases like these we conclude that the uniform [a] of Indo-Iranian is due to a later development: in pre-Indo-Iranian there must have been an [e] distinct from the other vowels, and this [e] must have caused palatalization of preceding velar stops. Since this [e], moreover, agrees with the [e] of the European languages, the distinction must have existed in Primitive Indo-European, and cannot be due to a joint innovation by the languages of Europe. This discovery put an end to the notion of a common parent speech intermediate between Primitive Indo-European and the European (as opposed to the Indo-Iranian) languages.

21. 6. The weakening or loss of consonants is sometimes accompanied by *compensatory lengthening* of a preceding vowel. The Old English combination [ht], preserved to this day in northern dialects, has lost the [h] and lengthened the preceding vowel in most of the area. Thus, Old English *niht* [niht, nixt] 'night,' modern Scotch [nixt, next], became [ni:t], whence modern *night* [najt]. Loss of a sibilant before voiced non-syllabics with compensatory lengthening of a vowel is quite common, as in pre-Latin *['dis-lego:] 'I pick out, I like' > Latin *dīligō* (compare *dis-* in *dispendō* 'I

weigh out,' and *legō* 'I pick, gather'); early Latin *cosmis* 'kind'
> Latin *cōmis;* pre-Latin *['kaznos] 'gray-haired' > Latin *cānus*
(compare, in Paelignian, a neighboring Italic dialect, *casnar* 'old
man'); Primitive Indo-European *[nisdos] 'nest' (compare English
nest) > Latin *nīdus.*

If the lost consonant is a nasal, the preceding vowel is often
nasalized, with or without compensatory lengthening and other
changes. This is the origin of the nasalized vowels of many languages, as of French: Latin *cantāre* > French *chanter* [šaⁿte],
Latin *centum* > French *cent* [saⁿ], and so on. The morphology of
Old Germanic shows parallel forms with and without nasal, such
as Gothic ['bringan — 'braːhta] 'bring, brought,' ['θankjan —
'θaːhta] 'think, thought.' The forms without [n] all have an [h]
immediately following a long vowel. The suspicion that in these
forms an [n] has been lost with compensatory lengthening, is
confirmed by a few comparisons with other Indo-European languages, such as Latin *vincere* 'to conquer' : Gothic ['wiːhan] 'to
fight.' Further, we have a twelfth-century Icelandic grammarian's
statement that in his language forms like [θeːl] 'file' (from *['θin-
hloː]) had a nasalized vowel. In Old English, the [aː] of the other
Germanic languages, in forms like these, is represented by [oː],
as in ['broːhte] 'brought,' ['θoːhte] 'thought.' We have reason to
believe that this divergent vowel quality is a reflex of older na-
salization, because in other cases also, Old English shows us an
[oː] as a reflex of an earlier nasalized [a]. The loss of [n] before [h]
occurred in pre-Germanic; before the other unvoiced spirants
[f, s, θ] an [n] remained in most Germanic dialects, but was lost,
with compensatory lengthening, in English, Frisian, and some of
the adjacent dialects. In these cases, too, we find an [oː] in Old
English as the reflex of a lengthened and nasalized [a]. Thus, the
words *five, us, mouth, soft, goose, other* appear in the oldest German
documents as [finf, uns, mund, sanfto, gans, 'ander] (with [d] as
reflex of an old [θ]), but in Old English as [fiːf, uːs, muːθ, 'soːfte,
goːs, 'oːðer].

When a consonant has been lost between vowels, the resulting
succession of vowels often suffers *contraction* into a single vowel or
diphthongal combination. Our earliest English records still show
us an [h] between vowels, but very soon afterward this *h* disappears
from the texts, and single vowels are written. Thus, the word *toe*
appears first as *tahæ*, presumably ['taːhɛ], but soon as *ta* [taː];

a pre-English type *['θanho:n] 'clay' appears first as *thohæ*
['θo:hɛ], then as [θo:]; Gothic ['ahwa] 'river' (cognate with Latin
aqua 'water') is paralleled by Old English *ea* [e:a], from pre-
English *['ahwu]; Gothic ['sehwan] 'to see' is matched by Old
English *seon* [se:on].

21. 7. Vowels are often assimilated to vowels that precede or
follow in the next syllable. During the early Middle Ages, changes
of this kind occurred in several Germanic dialects. These changes
in the Germanic languages are known by the name of *umlaut;* somewhat confusingly, this term is applied also to the resultant grammatical alternations. The commonest type of umlaut is the partial
assimilation of a stressed back vowel to a following [i, j]. The
resulting alternations, after the loss of the conditioning [i, j], became purely grammatical:

Pre-English	>	Old English	>	Modern English
*[gold]		gold		gold
*['guldjan] ¹		gyldan		gild
*[mu:s]		mus	[mu:s]	mouse
*['mu:si]		mys	[my:s]	mice
*[fo:t]		fot	[fo:t]	foot
*['fo:ti]		fet	[fe:t]	feet
*[gans]		gos	[go:s]	goose
*['gansi]		ges	[ge:s]	geese
*[drank]		dranc	[drank]	drank
*['drankjan]		drencean	['drenkan]	drench

Old Norse had also other types of umlaut, such as assimilation
of [a] toward the back-vowel quality of a following [u], as in
*['saku] 'accusation' (compare Old English *sacu* 'dispute') > Old
Norse [sɔk]. Similar changes, supplemented, no doubt by regularizing new-formations, must have led to the vowel-harmony that
prevails in Turco-Tartar and some other languages (§ 11.7).

The effect of simplification appears most plainly in shortening
and loss of vowels. In the final syllables of words, and especially
in final position, this occurs in all manner of languages. Among the
Central Algonquian languages, Fox alone has kept the final vowels:
Primitive Central Algonquian *[eleniwa] 'man' > Fox [neniwa],
Ojibwa [inini], Menomini [enɛ:niw], Plains Cree [ijiniw]. Certain

¹ The [u] in this form is due to an earlier assimilation of [o] to the high-vowel
position of the following [j].

types of two-syllable words are exempt from this shortening: *[ehkwa] 'louse' > Fox [ehkwa], Ojibwa [ihkwa], Menomini [ehkuah], Cree [ihkwa].

Languages with strong word-stress often weaken or lose their unstressed vowels. The loss of final vowels, as in Old English (*ic*) *singe* > (*I*) *sing*, is known as *apocope;* that of medial vowels, as in Old English *stānas* > *stones* [stownz], as *syncope*. The contrast between the long forms of Primitive Germanic, the shorter forms of Old English, and the greatly reduced words of modern English, is due to a succession of such changes. Thus, a Primitive Indo-European *['bheronom] 'act of bearing,' Sanskrit ['bhara-ɴam], Primitive Germanic *['beranan], gives Old English *beran*, Middle English *bere*, and then modern (*to*) *bear*. The habit of treating certain words in the phrase as if they were part of the preceding or following word, was inherited from Primitive Indo-European; when, in pre-Germanic time, a single high stress was placed on each word, these atonic forms received none; later, the weakening of unstressed vowels led to sandhi-variants, stressed and unstressed, of such words. Weakenings of this kind have occurred over and over again in the history of English, but the resultant alternations have been largely removed by re-formations which consisted either of using the full forms in unstressed positions, or of using the weakened forms in stressed positions. Our *on*, for instance, was in the medieval period the unweakened form; the weakened form of this word was *a*, as in *away*, from Old English *on weg* [on 'wej]; this weakened form survives only in a limited number of combinations, such as *away, ashore, aground, aloft*, and the unweakened *on* is now used in atonic position, as in *on the table*, but has here been subjected to a new weakening, which has resulted in unstressed [on] beside stressed [ɑn], as in *go on* [gow 'ɑn]. In contrast with this, our pronoun *I*, which we use in both stressed and unstressed positions, reflects an old unstressed form, in which the final consonant of Old English *ic* has been lost; the old stressed form survives in the [ič] 'I' of a few local dialects. These changes have left their mark in the unstressed sandhi-variants of many words, such as *is*, but [z] in *he's here; will*, but [l] in *I'll go; not*, but [ṇt] in *isn't;* and in the weakened forms of some unstressed compound members: *man*, but [-mṇ] in *gentleman; swain* but [-sṇ] in *boatswain*. The same factor accounts for the shortness of French words compared to Latin; as in *centum* > *cent* [sɑⁿ]; since the time of these shortenings, however, French has lost the strong word-stress and ceased shortening its forms.

If a language goes through this kind of change at a time when morphologically related forms stress different syllables, the result may be an extremely irregular morphology. We can see the beginnings of this in our foreign-learned vocabulary, which stresses different syllables in different derivatives: *angel* ['ejnǰl̩], but *angelic* [ɛn'ǰelik]. In Primitive Germanic the prefixes were unstressed in verb-forms but stressed in most other words; the weakenings that ensued broke up some morphologic sets, such as

pre-English *[bi-'haːtan] 'to threaten' > Old English *behatan* [be'haːtan], but

pre-English *['bi-haːt] 'a threat' > Old English *beot* [beːot].

A similar process rendered the morphology and, as to sandhi, the syntax of Old Irish extremely irregular:

pre-Irish *['bereti] 'he bears' > Old Irish *berid* ['beriδ];

pre-Irish *[eks 'beret] 'he bears out, brings forth' > Old Irish *asbeir* [as'ber] 'he says';

pre-Irish *[ne esti 'eks beret] 'not it-is that-he-forth-brings' (that is, 'he does not bring forth') > Old Irish *nī epir* [ni: 'epir] 'he does not say.'

21. 8. Some changes which superficially do not seem like weakenings or abbreviations of movement, may yet involve a simplification. In a good many languages we find an intermediate consonant arising in a cluster. A Primitive Indo-European [sr] appears as [str] in Germanic and in Slavic; thus, Primitive Indo-European *[srow-] (compare Sanskrit ['sravati] 'it flows') is reflected in Primitive Germanic *['strawmaz] 'stream,' Old Norse [strawmr], Old English [streːam], and in Old Bulgarian [struja] 'stream.' English, at more than one time, has inserted a [d] in the groups [nr, nl] and a [b] in the groups [mr, ml]: Old English ['θunrian] > (*to*) *thunder;* Old English ['alre] (accusative case) > *alder;* Gothic has ['timrjan] 'to construct' as well as ['timbrjan], but Old English has only ['timbrian] and [je'timbre] 'carpentry-work,' whence modern *timber;* Old English ['θymle] > *thimble.* These changes involve no additional movement, but merely replace simultaneous movements by successive. To pass from [n] to [r], for instance, the speaker must simultaneously raise his velum and move his tongue from the closure position to the trill position:

[n]   [r]

velum lowered ⟫⟶ velum raised

dental closure ⟫⟶ trill position

If, with a less delicate co-ordination, the velum is raised before the change of tongue-position, there results a moment of unnasalized closure, equivalent to the phoneme [d]:

[n]   [d]   [r]

velum lowered ⟫⟶ velum raised

dental closure   ⟫⟶ trill position

The second of these performances is evidently easier than the first.

In other cases, too, an apparent lengthening of a form may be viewed as lessening the difficulty of utterance. When a relatively sonorous phoneme is non-syllabic, it often acquires syllabic function; this change is known by the Sanskrit name of *samprasarana*. Thus, in sub-standard English, *elm* [elm] has changed to ['elm̥]. This is often followed by another change, known as *anaptyxis*, the rise of a vowel beside the sonant, which becomes non-syllabic. Primitive Indo-European *[aɡros] 'field' gives pre-Latin *[agr]; in this the [r] must have become syllabic, and then an anaptyctic vowel must have arisen, for in the historical Latin form *ager* ['ager] the *e* represents a fully formed vowel. Similarly, Primitive Germanic forms like *['akraz] 'field,' *['foglaz] 'bird,' *['tajknan] 'sign,' *['majθmaz] 'precious object' lost their unstressed vowels in all the old Germanic dialects. The Gothic forms [akrs, fugls, tajkn, majθms] may have been monosyllabic or may have had syllabic sonants; anaptyxis has taken place in the Old English forms ['ɛker, 'fugol, 'ta:ken, 'ma:ðom], though even here spellings like *fugl* are not uncommon.

Another change which may be regarded as a simplification occurs in the history of some stress-using languages: the quantities of stressed vowels are regulated according to the character of the following phonemes. Generally, long vowels remain long and short vowels are lengthened in "open" syllables, that is, before a single consonant that is followed by another vowel; in other positions, long vowels are shortened and short ones kept short. Thus, Middle English long vowels remained long in forms like *clene* ['klɛ:ne] > *clean*, *kepe* ['ke:pe] > *keep*, *mone* ['mo:ne] > *moon*, but were shortened in forms like *clense* > *cleanse*, *kepte* > *kept*, *mon(en)dai* > *Monday;* and short vowels were lengthened in forms like *weve* ['weve] > *weave*, *stele* ['stele] > *steal*, *nose* ['nose] > *nose*, but stayed short in forms like *weft*, *stelth* > *stealth*, *nos(e)thirl* > *nostril*. In some languages, such as Menomini, we find a very complicated regulation of long and short vowels according to the preceding and following consonants and according to the number of syllables intervening after the last preceding long vowel.

The complete loss of quantitative differences, which occurred, for instance, in medieval Greek and in some of the modern Slavic languages, makes articulation more uniform. The same can be said of the abandonment of distinctions of syllable-pitch, which has occurred in these same languages; similarly, the removal of word-accent uniformly to some one position such as the first syllable, in pre-Germanic and in Bohemian, or the next-to-last, in Polish, probably involves a facilitation.

In the same sense, the loss of a phonemic unit may be viewed as a simplification. Except for English and Icelandic, the Germanic languages have lost the phoneme [θ] and its voiced development [ð]; the reflexes coincide in Frisian and in Scandinavian largely with [t], as in Swedish *torn* [to:rn] : *thorn*, with the same initial as *tio* ['ti:e] : *ten*, and in the northern part of the Dutch-German area with [d], as in Dutch *doorn* [do:rn] : *thorn*, with the same initial as *doen* [du:n] : *do*. Old English [h] before a consonant, as in *niht* 'night,' or in final position, as in *seah* '(I) saw,' was acoustically doubtless an unvoiced velar or palatal spirant; in most of the English area this sound has been lost or has coincided with other phonemes.

21. 9. Although many sound-changes shorten linguistic forms, simplify the phonetic system, or in some other way lessen the labor of utterance, yet no student has succeeded in establishing a correlation between sound-change and any antecedent phenomenon: the causes of sound-change are unknown. When we find a large-scale shortening and loss of vowels, we feel safe in assuming that the language had a strong word-stress, but many languages with strong word-stress do not weaken the unstressed vowels; examples are Italian, Spanish, Bohemian, Polish. The English change of [kn-, gn-] to [n-] seems natural, after it has occurred, but why did it not occur before the eighteenth century, and why has it not occurred in the other Germanic languages?

Every conceivable cause has been alleged: "race," climate, topographic conditions, diet, occupation and general mode of life, and so on. Wundt attributed sound-change to increase in the rapidity of speech, and this, in turn, to the community's advance in culture and general intelligence. It is safe to say that we speak as rapidly and with as little effort as possible, approaching always the limit where our interlocutors ask us to repeat our utterance, and that a great deal of sound-change is in some way connected with this factor. No permanent factor, however, can account for specific changes which occur at one time and place and not at another. The same consideration holds good against the theory that sound-change arises from imperfections in children's learning of language. On the other hand, temporary operation of factors like the above, such as change of habitat, occupation, or diet, is ruled out by the fact that sound-changes occur too often and exhibit too great a variety.

The *substratum theory* attributes sound-change to transference of language: a community which adopts a new language will speak it imperfectly and with the phonetics of its mother-tongue. The transference of language will concern us later; in the present connection it is important to see that the substratum theory can account for changes only during the time when the language is spoken by persons who have acquired it as a second language. There is no sense in the mystical version of the substratum theory, which attributes changes, say, in modern Germanic languages, to a "Celtic substratum" — that is, to the fact that many centuries ago, some adult Celtic-speakers acquired Germanic speech. Moreover, the Celtic speech which preceded Germanic in southern Germany, the Netherlands, and England, was itself an invading language: the theory directs us back into time, from "race" to "race," to account for vague "tendencies" that manifest themselves in the actual historical occurrence of sound-change.

Aside from their failure to establish correlations, theories of this kind are confuted by the fact that when sound-change has removed some phonetic feature, later sound-change may result in the renewal of just this feature. If we attribute some particular character to the Primitive Indo-European unvoiced stops [p, t, k] — supposing, for the sake of illustration, that they were unaspirated fortes — then the pre-Germanic speakers who had begun to change these sounds in the direction of spirants [f, θ, h], were doubtless incapable of pronouncing the original sounds, just as the English-speaker of today is incapable of pronouncing the French unaspirated [p, t, k]. At a later time, however, Primitive Indo-European [b, d, g] were changed in pre-Germanic to unvoiced stops [p, t, k]. These sounds did not coincide with those of the first group: the sounds of the first group had no longer the [p, t, k] character, having changed to aspirates or affricates or perhaps already to spirants; the sounds of the second group, on the other hand, were not subjected to the same change as those of the first group, because, as we say, the sound-change of [p, t, k] to [f, θ, h] was *past*. More accurately, we should say that the sound-change of [p, t, k] was *already under way:* the new [p, t, k] constituted a different habit, which did not take part in the displacement of the old habit. In time, the new [p, t, k] became aspirated, as they are in present-day English; so that, once more, we are incapable of pronouncing unaspirated unvoiced stops.

The English sound-changes that are known under the name of "the great vowel-shift," are of a type that has little effect beyond altering the acoustic shape of each phoneme; the long vowels were progressively shifted upward and into diphthongal types:

MIDDLE ENGLISH	>	EARLY MODERN	>	PRESENT-DAY	
['na:me]		[ne:m]		[nejm]	*name*
[de:d]		[di:d]		[dijd]	*deed*
[ge:s]		[gi:s]		[gijs]	*geese*
[wi:n]		[wejn]		[wajn]	*wine*
[stɔ:n]		[sto:n]		[stown]	*stone*
[go:s]		[gu:s]		[guws]	*goose*
[hu:s]		[hows]		[haws]	*house*

Another theory seeks the cause of some sound-changes in formal conditions of a language, supposing that forms of weak meaning are slurred in pronunciation and thereby permanently weakened or lost. We have met this doctrine as one of those which deny the occurrence of purely phonemic changes (§ 20.10). We have no gauge by which we could mark some formal features of a language as semantically weak or superfluous. If we condemn all features of meaning except business-like denotations of the kind that could figure in scientific discourse, we should have to expect, on this theory, the disappearance of a great many forms in almost every language. For instance, the inflectional endings of adjec-

tives in modern German are logically superfluous; the use of adjectives is quite like the English, and a text in which these endings are covered up is intelligible.

In fact, sound-changes often obliterate features whose meaning
is highly important. No grammatical difference could be more
essential than is that of actor and verbal goal in an Indo-European
language. Yet the difference between the Primitive Indo-European
nominative in *[-os], as in Sanskrit ['vr̥kah], Greek ['lukos], Latin
lupus, Primitive Germanic *['wolfaz], Gothic *wulfs*, and the accusative in *[-om], as in Sanskrit ['vr̥kam], Greek ['lukon], Latin
lupum, Primitive Germanic *['wolfan], Gothic *wulf*, had been
obliterated by the weakening of the word-final in pre-English,
so that the two cases were merged, even in our earliest records,
in the form *wulf* 'wolf'. In Old English a few noun-types, such
as nominative *caru* : accusative *care* 'care,' still had the distinction;
by the year 1000 these were probably merged in the form ['kare],
thanks to the weakening of unstressed vowels. In the same way,
sound-change leads to all manner of homonymies, such as *meet :
meat; meed : mead* ('meadow'): *mead* ('drink'), *knight : night*.
The classical instance of this is Chinese, for it can be shown that
the vast homonymy of the present-day languages, especially of
North Chinese, is due to phonetic changes. Homonymy and
syncretism, the merging of inflectional categories, are normal results of sound-change.

The theory of semantic weakness does seem to apply, however,
to fixed formulas with excess slurring (§ 9.7). Historically, these
formulas can be explained only as weakenings far in excess of
normal sound-change. Thus, *good-bye* represents an older *God be
with ye*, *ma'm* an older *madam*, Spanish *usted* [u'sted] an older
vuestra merced ['vwestra mer'θed], and Russian [s], as in [da s]
'yes, sir,' an older ['sudar] 'lord.' In these cases, however, the
normal speech-form exists by the side of the slurred form. The
excess weakening in these forms has not been explained and doubtless is connected in some way with what we may call the sub-
linguistic status of these conventional formulae. In any event, their
excess weakening differs very much from ordinary phonetic change.

Since a sound-change is a historical happening, with a beginning
and an end, limited to a definite time and to a definite body of
speakers, its cause cannot be found in universal considerations
or by observing speakers at other times and places. A phoneti-

cian tried to establish the cause of a change of the type [azna >
asna], which occurred in the pre-history of the Avesta language,
by observing in the laboratory a number of persons who were
directed to pronounce the sequence [azna] many times in succession.   Most of the persons — they were Frenchmen — yielded
no result, but at last came one who ended by saying [asna].   The
phonetician's joy was not clouded by the fact that this last person
was a German, in whose native language [z] occurs only before
syllabics.

It has been suggested that if a phoneme occurs in a language
with more than a certain relative frequency (§ 8.7), this phoneme
will be slurred in articulation and subjected to change. The upper
limit of tolerable frequency, it is supposed, varies for different
types of phonemes; thus, [t] represents in English more than 7
per cent of the total of uttered phonemes, and in several other
languages (Russian, Hungarian, Swedish, Italian) the unvoiced
dental stop runs to a similar percentage, while the type [d], on the
other hand, with a lower relative frequency (in English it is less
than 5 per cent) would in any language suffer sound-change,
according to this theory, before it reached a relative frequency
like that of English [t]. The relative frequency of a phoneme is
governed by the frequency of the significant forms that contain
it; thus, [ð] in English is evidently favored by the high frequency
of the word *the*. The frequency of significant forms is subject, as
we shall see, to unceasing fluctuation, in accordance with changes
in practical life. This theory, therefore, has the merit of correlating sound-change with an ever present and yet highly variable
factor. It could be tested if we could determine the absolute upper
limit for types of phonemes, and the actual frequency of a phoneme
at a stage of a language just before this phoneme was changed —
as, say, of [v] in English just before the change *havok* > *hawk*.
We should then still have to account for the specific nature of the
change, since phonemes of any one general type have changed in
different ways in the history of various languages. Against the
theory we must weigh the great phonetic difference between languages and the high frequency, in some languages, of what we may
call unusual phonetic types; [ð], which plays such a great part
in English, was at one time eliminated (by a pre-West-Germanic
change to [d]) and has remained so in Dutch-German; later it was
re-introduced into English by a change from [θ] to [ð].

21. 10. Certain linguistic changes which are usually described as sound-change, do not come under the definition of phonetic change as a gradual alteration of phonemic units. In various parts of Europe, for instance, the old tongue-tip trill [r] has been replaced, in modern times, by a uvular trill. This has happened in Northumbrian English, in Danish and southern Norwegian and Swedish, and in the more citified types of French (especially in Paris) and Dutch-German. Aside from its spread by borrowing, the new habit, in whatever times and places it may first have arisen, could have originated only as a sudden replacement of one trill by another. A replacement of this sort is surely different from the gradual and imperceptible alterations of phonetic change.

Some changes consist in a redistribution of phonemes. The commonest of these seems to be *dissimilation:* when a phoneme or type of phoneme recurs within a form, one of the occurrences is sometimes replaced by a different sound. Thus, Latin *peregrīnus* 'foreigner, stranger' is replaced in the Romance languages by a type **pelegrīnus*, as in Italian *pellegrino*, and in English *pilgrim*, borrowed from Romance; the first of the two [r]'s has been replaced by [l]. In the languages of Europe, the sounds [r, l, n] are especially subject to this replacement; the replacing sound is usually one of the same group. Where the replacement occurs, it follows quite definite rules, but we cannot predict its occurrence. The change, if carried out, would produce a state of affairs where recurrence of certain sounds, such as [r] and [l], was not allowed within a word — the state of affairs which actually prevails in the modern English derivation of symbolic words, where we have *clatter, blubber,* but *rattle, crackle* (§ 14.9). Probably this type of change is entirely different from ordinary phonetic change.

There is also a type of dissimilation in which one of the like phonemes is dropped, as when Latin *quinque* ['kwi:nkwe] 'five' is replaced, in Romance, by a type **['ki:nkwe]*, Italian *cinque* ['činkwe], French *cinq* [sɛ^{n}k].

There are several other kinds of phonetic replacement which cannot properly be put on a level with ordinary sound-change. In *distant assimilation* a phoneme is replaced by another of related acoustic type which occurs elsewhere in the same word. Thus, Primitive Indo-European **['penk^{w}e]* 'five,' Sanskrit ['panča], Greek ['pente] appears in Latin not as **[pinkwe]*, but as *quīnque*. In pre-Germanic this word seems to have suffered the reverse assimilation, to *['pempe], for we have Primitive Germanic *['fimfe] in Gothic and Old High German *fimf*, Old English *fīf*, and so on. Sanskrit has [ç — ç] in words where we expect [s — ç].

Metathesis is the interchange of two phonemes within a word. Beside the expected *āscian* 'ask,' Old English has also *ācsian*. In Tagalog some morphologic alternations seem to be due to changes of this kind; thus, the suffix [-an], as in [a'sin] 'salt' : [as'nan] 'what is to be salted,' is sometimes accompanied by interchange of two consonants that come together: [a'tip] 'roofing' : [ap'tan] 'what is to be roofed'; [ta'nim] 'that planted' : [tam'nan] 'what is to have plants put into it.' In the languages of Europe distant metathesis of [r-l] is fairly common. To Old English *alor* 'alder' there corresponds in Old High German not only *elira* but also *erila* (> modern *Erle*). For Gothic ['werilo:s] 'lips,' Old English has *weleras*. Latin *parabola* 'word' (a borrowing from Greek) appears in Spanish as *palabra*.

When a phoneme or group of phonemes recurs within a word, one occurrence, together with the intervening sounds, may be dropped: this change is known as *haplology*. Thus, from Latin *nūtriō* 'I nourish' the regular feminine agent-noun would be **nūtrī-trīx* 'nurse,' but the form is actually *nūtrīx*. Similarly, the compound which would normally have the form **stīpi-pendium* 'wage-payment' appears actually as *stīpendium*. Ancient Greek [amphi-pho'rews] 'both-side-carrier' appears also as [ampho'rews] 'amphora.' Changes like these are very different from those which are covered by the assumption of sound-change; it is possible that they are akin rather to the types of linguistic change which we have still to consider — analogic change and borrowing.

CHAPTER 22

FLUCTUATION IN THE FREQUENCY OF FORMS

22. 1. The assumption of phonetic change divides linguistic changes into two principal types. Phonetic change affects only the phonemes, and alters linguistic forms only by altering their phonetic shape. The English form *wolf* is the modern pronunciation of Primitive Germanic nominative *['wolfaz], accusative *['wolfan], and several other case-forms, and the merging of these (syncretism) is merely the result of the phonetic change. English [mijd] *meed, mead* is the modern pronunciation of Old English [mɛ:d] 'meadow,' [me:d] 'reward,' and ['medu] 'honey-drink'; the homonymy results simply from the change in habits of articulation. When we have listed the phonetic correlations, there remain a great many discrepancies. Thus, having found that Old English [a:] appears in modern standard English as [ow], as in [ba:t] > *boat*, and so on, we see a discrepancy in the parallelism of Old English [ba:t] 'bait' with the modern *bait*. Seeing Old English initial [f] preserved in *father, five, foot*, and so on, we find a discrepancy in the sets Old English [fɛt] : modern *vat* and Old English ['fyksen] : modern *vixen*. While the modern form *cow* stands in a normal phonetic correlation with Old English [ku:], just as *house, mouse, out* correspond to Old English [hu:s, mu:s, u:t], the plural *cows* cannot be the modern form of the Old English plural [ky:] 'cows,' in view of cases like Old English [hwy:] > *why*, [fy:r] > *fire*, [my:s] > *mice*. If we adhere to the assumption of regular phonetic change, we cannot class forms like *bait, vat, vixen, cows* as modern pronunciations of Old English forms, but must view them as the products of factors other than simple tradition. Our problem, therefore, is to find among these residual forms some uniformity or correlation; to the extent that we succeed in this, we shall have confirmed the value of the assumption of phonetic change and of the particular phonetic correspondences we have set up. The neo-grammarians claim that the assumption of phonetic change leaves residues which show striking correlations and allow us to understand the factors of linguistic change other than sound-change. The opponents of the neo-grammarian hypothesis imply that a different assumption concerning sound-change will leave a more intelligible residue, but they have never tested this by re-classifying the data.

If the residual forms are not continuants of ancient forms with only the alterations of sound-change, then they must have come into the language as innovations. We shall see that two kinds of innovation account for the residual forms — namely, the adoption of forms from other languages (*bait* from Old Norse) or other dialects (*vat, vixen* from southern-English local dialects) and the combining of new complex forms (*cow-s* on the pattern "singular noun plus plural-suffix gives plural noun"). These two kinds of innovation, *borrowing* and *analogic change*, will occupy us in the following chapters; now we are concerned merely with the claim that the forms which are not accounted for by phonetic correlation, got into the language at various points in time.

22. 2. If a form which has been introduced into a language prevails in general usage — as, for instance, *cows* prevails as the ordinary plural of *cow* — we have to suppose that it has gained in popularity since its first introduction. Conversely, if an old form — such as the Old English plural [ky:], which, by phonetic development, would today be pronounced *[kaj] — has disappeared, we must suppose that it went through a period of decline, during which it was used less and less as the years went by. *Fluctuation in the frequency of speech-forms* is a factor in all non-phonetic changes. This fluctuation can be observed, to some extent, both at first hand and in our written records. For instance, since the introduction of the automobile, the word *garage*, borrowed from French, has become very common. We can actually name the speakers who first used the words *chortle, kodak,* and *blurb;* since the moment of that first use, each of these words has become common. The disappearance of a form cannot be observed at first hand, since we can have no assurance that it will not be used again, but in older written records we find many speech-forms that are no longer in use. In Old English, ['weorθan] 'to become' was one of the commonest words: [he: 'wearθ 'torn] 'he got angry,' [he: je'wearθ 'mɛ:re] 'he became famous,' [he: 'wearθ of'slɛjen] 'he got killed,' [heo 'wearθ 'widuwe] 'she became a widow.' In the Dutch-German area this verb, Dutch *worden* ['wurde], German *werden* ['verden], is still so used. The ordinary Old English word for 'large,' *mycel,* survives in Scotch *mickle,* but has disappeared from standard English. In our fragments of the Gothic Bible-translation, the word *mother* is entirely replaced by a term ['ajθi:], and the word *father* occurs only once (*Galatians* 4, 6) and is in all other passages replaced by ['atta], a word familiar to us from the Gothic nickname of the king of the Huns, *Attila* 'little father.' This, apparently in its original connotation a nursery-word, is perhaps somehow connected with the Slavic term for 'father,' Primitive Slavic *[otɪ'tsɪ], Russian [o'tets], which in pre-Slavic must have crowded out the reflex of Primitive Indo-European *[pə'te:r].

Most frequently we observe the complementary fluctuation of two forms; thus, *it's I* and *it's me* or *rather* with [ɛ] and with [a], are evidently *rival forms* in present-day American English. The plural-form *kine* beside *cows* is still very rarely used as a poetic archaism. In Elizabethan writings we still find the spelling *fat* for *vat,* evidencing a survival of Old English [fɛt], which has since been crowded out by *vat.* Where a speaker knows two rival forms, they differ in connotation, since he has heard them from different persons and under different circumstances.

Fluctuations in the frequency of forms could be accurately observed if we had a record of every utterance that was made in a speech-community during whatever period of time we wanted to study. We could then keep a tally-sheet for every form (including grammatical forms, such as the type *he ran away; he fell down* in contrast with *away he ran; down he fell*); whenever an utterance was made, we could score a point on the tally-sheet of every form in this utterance. In this way we should obtain tables or graphs which showed the ups and downs in frequency of every form during the time covered by our records. Such a system of scoring will doubtless remain beyond our powers, but this imaginary system gives us a picture of what is actually going on at all times in every speech-community. We can observe the fluctuation with the naked eye when it is especially rapid, as in the sudden rise and equally sudden disuse of popular slangy witticisms. On a smaller scale, but contributing to the total fluctuations in the community, small groups and individuals indulge in similar whims; everyone can recall old favorite words and phrases which he and perhaps his associates once used at every turn. Most fluctuation is less rapid and escapes direct observation, but reveals itself in its results — in the differences of vocabulary and grammar which appear when we compare different historical stages of a language, or dialects of an area, or related languages.

Leaving aside the origination of new forms, which will concern us in the following chapters, we must now consider the factors which lead to the rise or to the decline in frequency of speech-forms. Until recently this topic was neglected, and our knowledge is still far from satisfactory.

22. 3. We naturally ask at once whether any linguistically definable characteristics of a form may favor or disfavor its use. The stylist and the rhetorician tell us that some speech-forms sound better than others. The only criterion of a phonetic sort seems to be this, that repetition of phonemes or sequences is often avoided: a phrase like *the observation of the systematization of education* is disfavored. In ordinary speech, however, euphony seems to play no part; the stock examples of troublesome phonetics are far-fetched combinations like *Peter Piper picked a peck of pickled peppers* or *she sells sea-shells*. On the other hand, various patternings of recurrent phonemes, such as alliteration (*hearth and home, cabbages and kings*), assonance (*a stitch in time saves nine*), and rime, and rhythmic repetitions (*first come, first served*), seem to favor many a speech-form.

In all ordinary cases, semantic rather than formal factors contribute to the favor or disfavor of a form. It is natural to suppose, however, that a form which differs strikingly from the other forms of comparable meaning, will be disfavored. Several students have conjectured that certain speech-forms fell into disuse because they were shorter than ordinary speech-forms of similar meaning. Gilliéron believed that Latin *apis* 'bee' has died out in nearly all dialects of the French area because its modern pronunciation would consist of only a single phoneme [e]. It would be no counter-argument to say that French has grammatical and relational words of this pattern, such as *et* [e] 'and,' but a case like *eau* [o] 'water' (< *aquam*) does militate against the theory. It seems that some verb-forms in the older stages of the Indo-European languages fell into disuse because they were shorter than ordinary forms of the same kind. The Menomini language, like French and English, seems to tolerate words of all sizes. Menomini [o:s] 'canoe' is shorter than ordinary nouns, and [uah] 'he uses it' shorter than ordinary verb-forms. These forms, which are ancient inheritances, have been largely replaced in the sister languages: Primitive Central Algonquian *[o:ši] 'canoe' by longer derivative nouns, such as Fox [anakɛ:weni], Cree and Ojibwa [či:ma:n], — though Cree has also [o:si] — and Primitive Central Algonquian *[o:wa] 'he uses it' by a reduplicated form, Fox [ajo:-wa] or by other words, such as Cree [a:pačihta:w]. All this, however, is doubtful.

The semantic factor is more apparent in the disfavoring of speech-forms that are homonymous with tabu-forms. The reader will have no difficulty in finding speech-forms that he avoids for this reason. In America, *knocked up* is a tabu-form for 'rendered pregnant'; for this reason, the phrase is not used in the British sense 'tired, exhausted.' In older French and English there was a word, French *connil, connin*, English *coney*, for 'rabbit'; in both languages this word died out because it resembled a word that was under a tabu of indecency. For the same reason, *rooster* and *donkey* are replacing *cock* and *ass* in American English. In such cases there is little real ambiguity, but some hearers react nevertheless to the powerful stimulus of the tabu-word; having called forth ridicule or embarrassment, the speaker avoids the innocent homonym. It is a remarkable fact that the tabu-word itself has a much tougher life than the harmless homonym.

22. 4. These cases suggest that homonymy in general may injure the frequency of a form. Many homonyms are distinguished by differences of grammatical function, as are *leader* (noun) and *lead'er* (infinitive phrase) or *bear* (noun), *bear* (verb), and *bare* (adjective); in French, [sɑⁿ] is *sang* 'blood,' *cent* 'hundred,' *sans* 'without,' *sent* 'feels, smells,' and *s'en* 'oneself of it,' as in *s'en aller* 'to go away.' Even with largely similar grammatical functions, homonymies like *pear, pair* or *piece, peace* or *mead, meed* do not seem to lessen the frequency of forms.

Nevertheless, there is some evidence that homonymy may lead to troubles of communication which result in disuse of a form. The classical instance is Gilliéron's explanation of the disappearance of Latin *gallus* 'cock' in southwestern France (Figure 14). In southern France generally this word is still in use in its modern forms, such as [gal] or [žal]. A fair-sized area in the extreme south, however, uses for 'cock' another Latin word, *pullus*, modern [pul], which originally meant 'chick.' Now, the southwestern corner of the French area has made a sound-change by which

Latin [ll] at the end of a word has become [t]; thus, Latin *bellus* 'pretty,' modern [bɛl],[1] appears in the southwestern corner as [bɛt]. The isogloss of this sound-change cuts the *pullus*-district into an eastern part, where one says [pul] and a western part where one says [put]. Outside the *pullus*-district we should accordingly expect to find a form *[gat] 'cock,' corresponding to the

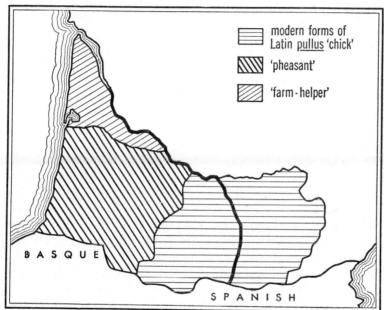

modern forms of Latin *pullus* 'chick'

'pheasant'

'farm-helper'

FIGURE 14. The southwestern part of the French dialect-area. — Southwest of the heavy line ■■■■ Latin [ll] appears in final position as [t]. The unshaded part of the area uses modern forms of Latin *gallus* "cock." The shaded areas use other words for "cock." — After Dauzat.

[gal] of ordinary southern French, but actually this form nowhere appears: the entire [-t]-area, in so far as it does not say [put], calls the cock by queer and apparently slangy names, either by local forms of the word *pheasant*, such as [azaⁿ], from Latin *phāsiānus*, or by a word [begej] which means 'farm-helper, handyman' and is thought to represent Latin *vicārius* 'deputy, proxy, vicar.'

Now, Gilliéron points out, the form *[gat] 'cock' in this district would be homonymous with the word 'cat,' namely [gat],

[1] Standard French *bel* [bɛl] before vowels, *beau* [bo] before consonants.

from Latin *gattus*. This homonymy must have caused trouble in practical life; therefore *[gat] 'cock' was avoided and replaced by makeshift words.

What lends weight to this theory is the remarkable fact that the isogloss which separates the queer words [aza^n] and [be-gej] from the ordinary [gal], coincides exactly with the isogloss between [-t] and [-l]; this is highly significant, because isoglosses — even isoglosses representing closely related features — very rarely coincide for any considerable distance.

Adjoining this stretch, the isogloss between [-t] and [-l] coincides for a ways with the isogloss between [put] and [gal]. This too is striking and seems to be explicable only if we suppose that this part of the [-t]-region formerly used *gallus* and, when the change of [-ll] to [-t] had occurred, replaced the troublesome *[gat] by borrowing [put] from the neighboring *pullus*-district.

On the rest of its course, the isogloss between [-t] and [-l] cuts through the *pullus*-district, and merely separates western [put] from eastern [pul]; in the *pullus*-district the sound-change caused no homonymy and left the lexicon undisturbed.

One may ask why *[gat] 'cock' rather than [gat] 'cat' was affected by the homonymy. Dauzat points out that the morpheme *[gat] 'cock' occurred only in this one word, since the derived form, Latin *gallīna* 'hen' was subject to a different change, giving [garina], while [gat] 'cat,' on the other hand, was backed by a number of unambiguous derivatives, such as the equivalents of standard French *chatte* 'she-cat,' *chaton* 'kitten,' *chatière* 'cat-hole.'

While few instances are as cogent as this, it is likely that homonymy plays more than an occasional part in the obsolescence of forms. A few centuries ago, English had not only our present-day verb *let* (which represents the paradigm of Old English ['lɛ:tan]), but also a homonymous verb which meant 'to hinder' (representing Old English ['lettan]); we still have the phrases *without let or hindrance* and *a let ball*, at tennis. When Shakspere has Hamlet say *I'll make a ghost of him that lets me*, he means 'of him that hinders me.' After it had become homonymous with *let* 'permit,' this word must have been singularly ineffective. A speaker who wanted his hearers to stop someone — say, a child that was running into danger, or a thief — and cried *Let him!* might find his hearers standing aside to make way. Then he would have to add

Stop him! or *Hold him!* After a few such experiences he would use one of the effective forms at the first trial.

22. 5. We frequently find regular, or at least more regular, combinations by the side of irregular complex forms, as, *roofs, hoofs, dwarfs* by the side of *rooves, hooves, dwarves,* or *dreamed, learned* by the side of *dreamt, learnt,* or *you ought to* by the side of *you had better.* In some cases the irregular form is decidedly infrequent, as in *cows, eyes, shoes, brothers* versus *kine, eyne, shoon, brethren.* Other examples are, regular *forehead* ['fowr-ˌhed], *gooseberry* ['guws-ˌberij], *seamstress* ['sijmstres] against irregular ['fɑred, 'guwzbr̥ij, 'semstres]. History shows us that in such cases the irregular form frequently dies out, or survives only in special senses, as when *sodden,* the old participle of *seethe,* survives only in a transferred meaning. The plurals of *goat, book, cow,* if we continued using the Old English forms [gɛ:t, be:k, ky:] would be today *[gijt, bijč, kaj]. Whenever we know the history of a language through any considerable period, we find many cases of this kind, but the operation of this factor is obscure, because in many cases the regular form makes no headway at all. The utterance of a regular *foots* instead of *feet,* or *bringed* instead of *brought* is so rare as to be classed as a childish "mistake" or, in older people, as a "slip of the tongue." Languages seem to differ in toleration of irregular forms, but in general it would seem that a regular rival, given a good start, has much the better chance. Very common forms, such as in English the paradigm of the verb *be* and the pronouns *I, we, he, she, they,* with their over-differentiation, persist in spite of great irregularity.

22. 6. For the most part, fluctuation does not depend upon formal features, but upon meaning, and accordingly escapes a purely linguistic investigation. The changes which are always going on in the practical life of a community, are bound to affect the relative frequencies of speech-forms. The introduction of railways, street-cars, and motor-cars has lessened the frequency of many terms relating to horses, wagons, and harness, and increased that of terms relating to machinery. Even in the most remote and conservative community there is a constant displacement of things talked about; if nothing else should alter, there is at least the change of birth and death.

A new object or practice which gains in vogue, carries a speech-form, old or new, into increased frequency; examples are many in modern life, such as the terms of motoring, flying, and wireless. If the practical situation ceases to exist, the forms which are used in this situation are bound to become less common and may die out. The terms of falconry, for instance, have suffered this fate. Though we still hear beauty in Othello's words, we do not understand them:

If I do prove her haggard,
Though that her jesses were my dear heart-strings,
I'd whistle her off, and let her down the wind,
To prey at fortune.

The word *haggard* was used of a wild-caught, unreclaimed mature hawk; *jesses* were leather straps fastened to the legs of a hawk, and were not removed when the hawk was unleashed; if a hawk flew with the wind behind her, she seldom returned.

In the early centuries of our era, some of the Germanic tribes contained a class of people called [la:t], South-German [la:ts], who were intermediate in rank between freemen and serfs. The English form of this word, [le:t], occurs only once in our records, in the oldest English law-code, and even here the word is explained — incorrectly, at that — by the word [θe:ow] 'serf' written above the line. The new social organization of the English-speaking tribes in Britain contained no such class of people, and the word went out of use along with the institution.

22. 7. Words that are under a ritual or ill-omened tabu, are likely to disappear. The Indo-European languages use the most varied words for 'moon'; it is notable that Russian has borrowed Latin ['lu:na] as [lu'na], though otherwise it makes scarcely any but highly learned borrowings from Latin. It may be due to a ritual or hunters' tabu that the Primitive Indo-European word for 'bear,' surviving in Sanskrit ['r̥kšah], Greek ['arktos], Latin *ursus*, has disappeared in Germanic and in Balto-Slavic. In Slavic it has been replaced by the type of Russian [*med'vet*], originally a transparent compound meaning 'honey-eater.' The like of this seems to have happened in Menomini, where the old word for 'bear,' preserved in Fox [mahkwa], Cree [maskwa], has been replaced by [awɛ:hsɛn̓], a diminutive formation that seems to have meant originally 'little what-you-may-call-him.' Cree ['ma:či:w] 'he goes hunting' originally meant simply 'he goes away' — presumably there was danger of being overheard by the game or by

its spiritual representatives. The term for the 'left' side appears
to have been replaced in various languages; the Indo-European
languages use many words, among which Ancient Greek [ew-'o:-
numos], literally 'of good name,' is evidently euphemistic. One
can often observe people avoiding unpleasant words, such as *die,
death* — these words in pre-Germanic replaced the Primitive Indo-
European term represented by Latin *morī* 'to die' — or names of
serious diseases. The term *undertaker* was, to begin with, vaguely
evasive, but the undertakers are now trying to replace it by *morti-
cian.* In cases like these, where the unpleasantness inheres in
the practical situation, the speech-form becomes undesirable as
soon as it is too specifically tied up with the painful meaning.

Tabus of indecency do not seem to lead to obsolescence; the
tabu-forms are excluded in many or most social situations, but
by no means avoided in others. The substitutes may in time become too closely associated with the meaning and in turn become
tabu. Our word *whore,* cognate with Latin *cārus* 'dear,' must have
been at one time a polite substitute for some word now lost to us.
On the whole, however, words of this type do not seem especially
given to obsolescence.

The practical situation works in favor of words that call forth
a good response. In commerce, the seller finds advantage in label-
ing his goods attractively. This is probably why terms for the
young of animals sometimes replace the more general name of
the species, as when we say *chicken* for 'hen.' French *poule* [pul]
'hen' and dialectal [pul] 'cock' continue a Latin word for 'chick.'
The word *home* for 'house' has doubtless been favored by speculative builders. In Germany, an *express* train has come to mean
a slow train, as has *Schnellzug* ['šnel-ˌtsu:k], literally 'fast-train';
a really fast train is *Blitzzug* ['blits-ˌtsu:k], literally 'lightning-
train' — just as in the United States *first class* on a railroad means
the ordinary day-coach accommodation.

There is an advantage, often, in applying well-favored terms to
one's hearer. The habit of using the plural pronoun 'ye' instead
of the singular 'thou,' spread over Europe during the Middle
Ages. In English, *you* (the old dative-accusative case-form of *ye*)
has crowded *thou* into archaic use; in Dutch, *jij* [jej] has led to
the entire obsolescence of *thou,* and has in turn become the intimate form, under the encroachment of an originally still more
honorific *u* [y:], representing *Uwe Edelheid* ['y:we 'e:delhejt] 'Your

Nobility.' Honorifics of this sort often replace the ordinary second-person substitutes (§ 15.7). Similarly, one speaks in honorific terms of what pertains to the hearer. In Italian, 'my wife' is *mia moglie* [mia 'moʎe], but for 'your wife' one says rather *la sua signora* [la sua si'ɲora] 'your lady.' In French and in German one prefixes 'Mr., Mrs., Miss' to the mention of the hearer's relatives, as, *madame votre mère* [madam vɔtr mɛːr] 'your mother'; in German, moreover, one likes to use for the hearer's husband or wife archaic terms of distinguished flavor: *meine Frau* [majne 'fraw] 'my wife,' but *Ihre Frau Gemahlin* ['iːre fraw ge'maːlin] 'your Mrs. consort,' and *mein Mann* [majn 'man] 'my husband', but *Ihr Herr Gemahl* [iːr her ge'maːl] 'your Mr. consort.' In the Central Algonquian languages the literal terms for both 'my wife' and 'thy wife' are tabu — ogres use them in fairy-tales — and one says rather 'the old woman' or 'the one I live with' or even 'my cook.'

In general, honorific terms for persons spread at the cost of plain ones; *gentleman* and *lady* are more genteel than *man* and *woman*.

22. 8. General effectiveness, in the shape of violence or wit, is a powerful factor in fluctuation, which unfortunately quite escapes the linguist's control. It leads, for instance, to the sudden rise and fall of slang expressions. Round 1896 or so, a transferred use of the word *rubber* in the sense of 'stare, pry' played a great part in slang; ten years later it was obsolescent, and only *rubberneck-wagon* 'sight-seeing omnibus' has now any great frequency. Then, round 1905, an interjection *skidoo* 'be off' and, in the same meaning, an interjectional use of *twenty-three*, came into fashion and as suddenly died out. The rise of such forms is due, apparently, to their effectiveness in producing a response from the hearer. At first they owe this to their novelty and apt yet violent transference of meaning; later, the hearer responds well because he has heard them in favorable situations and from attractive people. All these favorable factors disappear from sheer repetition; the novelty wears off, the violent metaphor lapses when the transferred meaning becomes more familiar than the central meaning; the average of situations and speakers associated with the form becomes indifferent. Thereupon the slang form dies out. In some cases, however, the older form has meanwhile gone out of use or become archaic or specialized; the witticism, having lost its point, remains in use as a normal form. Thus, Latin *caput* 'head' survives in Italian and French in specialized and transferred senses, but in the central meaning has been displaced by reflexes of Latin *testa* 'potsherd, pot,' Italian *testa* ['testa], French *tête* [tɛːt]. Similarly, in German, the cognate of our *head*, namely *Haupt* [hawpt], survives in transferred uses and as a poetic archaism, but has been replaced, in the sense of 'head' by *Kopf*, cognate with English *cup*. The forceful or witty term, weakened through frequency, may suffer encroachment by new rivals, as in the countless slang words for 'head' or 'man' or 'girl' or 'kill,' or in a set like *awfully, terribly, frightfully* (*glad to see you*).

This factor is easily recognized in extreme cases, but figures doubtless in many more which elude our grasp, especially when the fluctuation is observable only from far-off time.

22. 9. The most powerful force of all in fluctuation works quite outside the linguist's reach: the speaker favors the forms which he has heard from certain other speakers who, for some reason of prestige, influence his habits of speech. This is what decides, in countless instances, whether one says *it's me* or *it's I*, *rather* with [ɛ] or with [a], *either* and *neither* with [ij] or with [aj], *roofs* or *rooves*, *you ought to* or *you'd better*, and so on, through an endless list of variants and nearly synonymous forms. Dialect geography and the history of standard languages show us how the speech of important communities is constantly imitated, now in one feature and now in another, by groups and persons of less prestige. The more striking phases of this leveling process will concern us in connection with linguistic borrowing. We may suppose that many features of lexicon and grammar, and some features of phonetics, have a social connotation, different for different groups and even for individual speakers. In the ideal diagram of density of communication (§ 3.4) we should have to distinguish the arrows that lead from each speaker to his hearers by gradations representing the prestige of the speaker with reference to each hearer. If we had a diagram with the arrows thus weighted, we could doubtless predict, to a large extent, the future frequencies of linguistic forms. It is in childhood, of course, that the speaker is most affected by the authority of older speakers, but all through life he goes on adapting his speech to the speech of the persons whom he strives to resemble or to please.

CHAPTER 23

ANALOGIC CHANGE

23. 1. Many speech-forms are not continuants of forms that existed in an older stage of the same language. This is obvious in the case of borrowings: a word like *toboggan*, taken over from an American Indian language, cannot have been used in English before the colonization of America, and, of course, we do not find it in documents of the English language which date from before that time. In very many instances, however, the new form is not borrowed from a foreign language. Thus, the plural-form *cows* does not appear in Old and Middle English. The Old English plural of *cu* [ku:] (whence modern *cow*) is *cy* [ky:], which survives, as [kaj], in a number of modern English dialects. Round the year 1300 there appears in our records a form *kyn*, which survives in the modern archaic-poetic form *kine*. Only some centuries later do we meet the form *cows;* the *New English Dictionary's* first reference, from the year 1607, has it as an alternative of the older form: *Kine or Cows.* Evidently *cows* is not the continuant, with only phonetic change, of *kine*, any more than *kine* bears this relation to *kye:* in both cases a new speech-form has come into the language.

The fact that the form *cows* is not the continuant, with only alterations of sound-change, of the older forms, is self-evident. Strictly speaking, however, this is only an inference which we make from the primary fact of phonetic discrepancy. We know that Old English [y:] appears in modern standard English as [aj], e.g. in *why, mice, bride* from Old English [hwy:, my:s, bry:d], and that modern [aw], as in *cows*, represents an Old English [u:], as in *cow, how, mouse, out* from Old English [ku:, hu:, mu:s, u:t]. Further, we know that modern [z], as in *cows*, is not added by any sound-change, but represents Old English [s], as in *stones* from Old English ['sta:nas]. In many cases, however, the novelty of a speech-form is not so apparent and is revealed only by a systematic comparison of sounds. The form *days* superficially resembles the Old English plural-form *dagas*, which we interpret as ['dagas], presumably with a spirant [g], but the phonetic development of the

Old English sound-group [ag] appears rather in forms like ['sage] > *saw* (implement), ['sagu] > *saw* 'saying,' ['hagu-'θorn] > *hawthorn*, ['dragan] > *draw*. This is confirmed by the fact that in earlier Middle English we find spellings like *daues, dawes* for the plural of *dei* 'day,' and that spellings which agree with the modern form *days* appear only round the year 1200. If our statements of phonetic correspondence are correct, the residues will contain the new forms. One of the strongest reasons for adopting the assumption of regular phonetic change is the fact that the constitution of the residues (aside from linguistic borrowings, which we shall consider in later chapters) throws a great deal of light upon the origin of new forms. Most of the word-forms which arise in the course of time and reveal themselves by their deviation from normal phonetic correspondence, belong to a single well-defined type. This cannot be due to accident: it confirms the assumption of phonetic change, and, on the other hand allows us to study the process of new-formation.

The great mass of word-forms that arise in the course of history consists in new combinations of complex forms. The form *cows*, arising by the side of *kye, kine*, consists of the singular *cow* (< Old English [ku:]) plus the plural-suffix [-z] (< Old English [-as]); similarly, *days*, arising by the side of older *daws*, consists of the singular *day* (< Old English [dɛj]) plus the same suffix. A vast number of such instances, from the history of the most diverse languages, leads us to believe that the analogic habits (§ 16.6) are subject to displacement — that at a time when the plural of *cow* was the irregular form *kine*, the speakers might create a regular form *cows*, which then entered into rivalry with the old form. Accordingly, this type of innovation is called *analogic change*. Ordinarily, linguists use this term to include both the original creation of the new form and its subsequent rivalry with the old form. Strictly speaking, we should distinguish between these two events. After a speaker has heard or uttered the new form (say, *cows*), his subsequent utterance of this form or of the older form (*kine*) is a matter of fluctuation, such as we considered in the last chapter; what we did not there consider and what concerns us now, is the utterance, by someone who has never heard it, of a new combination, such as *cow-s* instead of *kine*.

23. 2. In most cases — and these are the ones we come nearest to understanding — the process of uttering a new form is quite like that of ordinary grammatical analogy. The speaker who, without having heard it, produced the form *cows*, uttered this form just as he uttered any other regular plural noun, on the scheme

$$sow : sows = cow : x.$$

The model set (*sow : sows*) in this diagram represents a series of models (e.g. *bough : boughs, heifer : heifers, stone : stones,* etc., etc.), which, in our instance, includes all the regular noun-paradigms in the language. Moreover, the sets at either side of the sign of equality are not limited to two members. The independent utterance of a form like *dreamed* instead of *dreamt* [dremt], could be depicted by the diagram:

$$scream : screams : screaming : screamer : screamed$$
$$= dream : dreams : dreaming : dreamer : x$$

Psychologists sometimes object to this formula, on the ground that the speaker is not capable of the reasoning which the proportional pattern implies. If this objection held good, linguists would be debarred from making almost any grammatical statement, since the normal speaker, who is not a linguist, does not describe his speech-habits, and, if we are foolish enough to ask him, fails utterly to make a correct formulation. Educated persons, who have had training in school grammar, overestimate their own ability in the way of formulating speech-habits, and, what is worse, forget that they owe this ability to a sophisticated philosophical tradition. They view it, instead, as a natural gift which they expect to find in all people, and feel free to deny the truth of any linguistic statement which the normal speaker is incapable of making. We have to remember at all times that the speaker, short of a highly specialized training, is incapable of describing his speech-habits. Our proportional formula of analogy and analogic change, like all other statements in linguistics, describes the action of the speaker and does not imply that the speaker himself could give a similar description.

In studying the records of past speech or in comparing related languages and dialects, the linguist will recognize many differences of word-form, such as the emergence of *cows* beside older *kine*. The habits of morphology are fairly rigid; word-lists and tables of inflection are relatively easy to prepare and help us to detect innovations. It is otherwise with phrasal forms. Aside from the imperfection of our descriptive technique in syntax, retarded, as it has been, by philosophic habits of approach, the syntactic positions of a language can be filled by so many different forms that a survey is hard to make. The linguist who suspects that a certain phrase departs from the older syntactic habits of its language, may yet find it difficult or impossible to make sure that this older usage really excluded the phrase, or to determine the exact boundary between the older and the newer usage. Nevertheless, we can sometimes recognize syntactic innovations on the proportional pattern. From the sixteenth century on, we find English subordinate clauses introduced by the word *like*. We can picture the innovation in this way:

to do better than Judith : to do better than Judith dia
= *to do like Judith   : x,*

where the outcome is the construction *to do like Judith did*.

A phrasal innovation which does not disturb the syntactic habit may involve a new lexical use. In this case, our lack of control over meanings, especially, of course, where the speech of past times is concerned, acts as an almost insuperable hindrance. The practical situations which make up the meaning of a speech-form are not strictly definable: one could say that every utterance of a speech-form involves a minute semantic innovation. In older English, as in some modern dialects, the word *meat* had a meaning close to that of *food*, and the word *flesh* was used freely in connection with eating, as in this passage (from the year 1693): *who flesh of animals refused to eat, nor held all sorts of pulse for lawful meat.* A compound *flesh-meat* served, for a while, as a compromise. The prevalence of *food* and *fodder* where at an earlier time the word *meat* was common, and the prevalence of *flesh-meat* and *meat* where at an earlier time *flesh* would have been the normal term, must be attributed to a gradual shifting of usage. The difficulty of tracing this has led linguists to view the process as a kind of whimsical misapplication of speech-forms. If we remember that the meaning of a speech-form for any speaker is a product of the situations and contexts in which he has heard this form, we can see that here too a displacement must be merely an extension of some pattern:

leave the bones and bring the flesh : leave the bones and bring the meat
= *give us bread and flesh   : x,*

resulting in *give us bread and meat.* Doubtless we have to do, in both grammatical and lexical displacements, with one general type of innovation; we may call it *analogic-semantic change.* We shall leave the lexical phase of this, *semantic change,* for the next chapter, and consider first the more manageable phase which involves grammatical habits.

23. 3. We can distinguish only in theory between the actual innovation, in which a speaker uses a form he has not heard, and the subsequent rivalry between this new form and some older form. An observer who, a few years ago, heard the form *radios,* might suspect that the speaker had never heard it and was creating it on the analogy of ordinary noun-plurals; the observer could have no assurance of this, however, since the form could be equally well uttered by speakers who had and by those who had not heard it before. Both kinds of speakers, knowing the singular *radio,* would be capable of uttering the plural in the appropriate situation.

It may be worth noticing that in a case like this, which involves clear-cut grammatical categories, our inability to define meanings need give us no pause. A formula like

SINGULAR PLURAL

$$piano : pianos$$
$$= radio : x$$

will hold good even if our definitions of the meanings of these categories (e.g. 'one' and 'more than one') should turn out to be inexact.

The form *radios* did not conflict with any older form. The difficulty about most cases of analogic change is the existence of an older form. An observer round the year 1600 who heard, let us suppose, the earliest utterances of the form *cows,* could probably have made the same observations as we, a few years ago, could make about the form *radios:* doubtless many speakers uttered it independently, and could not be distinguished from speakers who had already heard it. However, the utterances of the form *cows* must have been more thinly sown, since there was also the traditional form *kine.* In the ensuing rivalry, the new form had the advantage of regular formation. It is safe to say that the factors which lead to the origination of a form are the same as those which favor the frequency of an existing form.

We do not know why speakers sometimes utter new combinations instead of traditional forms, and why the new combinations sometimes rise in frequency. A form like *foots*, instead of *feet*, is occasionally uttered by children; we call it a "childish error" and expect the child soon to acquire the traditional habit. A grown person may say *foots* when he is tired or flustered, but he does not repeat the form and no one adopts it; we call it a "slip of the tongue."

It seems that at any one stage of a language, certain features are relatively stable and others relatively unstable. We must suppose that in the sixteenth century, owing to antecedent developments, there were enough alternative plural-forms (say, *eyen : eyes, shoon : shoes, brethren : brothers*) to make an innovation like *cows* relatively inconspicuous and acceptable. At present, an innovation like *foots* seems to have no chance of survival when it is produced from time to time; we may suppose that innovation and fluctuation are at work rather in the sphere of plurals with spirant-voicing: *hooves : hoofs, laths* [leðz : leθs], and so on.

The creation of a form like *cow-s* is only an episode in the rise in frequency of the regular plural-suffix [-ez, -z, -s]. Analogic-semantic change is merely fluctuation in frequency, in so far as it displaces grammatical and lexical types. The extension of a form into a new combination with a new accompanying form is probably favored by its earlier occurrence with phonetically or semantically related forms. Thus, the use of [-z] with *cow* was probably favored by the existence of other plurals in [-aw-z], such as *sows, brows*. Similarity of meaning plays a part: *sows, heifers, ewes* will attract *cows*. Frequent occurrence in context probably increases the attraction of a model. The Latin noun *senatus* [se'na:tus] 'senate' had an irregular inflection, including a genitive *senatus* [se'na:tu:s]; by the side of this there arose a new genitive on the regular model, *senati* [se'na:ti:]. It has been suggested that the chief model for this innovation was the regular noun *populus* ['populus] 'people,' genitive *populi* ['populi:], for the two words were habitually used together in the phrase *senatus populusque* [se'na:tus popu'lus kwe] 'the Senate and People.' The most powerful factor is surely that of numbers and frequency. On the one hand, regular form-classes increase at the cost of smaller groups, and, on the other hand, irregular forms of very high frequency resist innovation. Irregular forms appear chiefly among the commonest words and phrases of a language.

23. 4. The regularizing trend of analogic change appears plainly in inflectional paradigms. The history of the regular plural-formation of English is a long series of extensions. The suffix [-ez, -z, -s] is the modern form of an Old English suffix [-as], as in *stan* [staːn] 'stone,' plural *stanas* ['staːnas] 'stones.' This suffix in Old English belonged only to the nominative and accusative cases of the plural; the genitive plural *stana* ['staːna] and the dative plural *stanum* ['staːnum] would both be represented today by the form *stone*. The replacement of this form by the nominative-accusative form *stones*, which is now used for the whole plural, regardless of syntactic position, is part of a larger process, the loss of case-inflection in the noun, which involved both phonetic and analogic changes.

The Old English nominative-accusative plural in *-as* occurred with only one type (the largest, to be sure) of masculine nouns. There were some classes of masculine nouns which formed the plural differently, as, ['sunu] 'son,' plural ['suna]; among these was a large class of *n*-plurals, such as ['steorra] 'star,' plural ['steorran]. Some nouns fluctuated: [feld] 'field,' plural ['felda] or ['feldas]. We do not know the origin of this fluctuation, but, once granted its existence, we can see in it a favoring condition for the spread of the [-as]-plural. A neologism like ['sunas] instead of older ['suna] 'sons' would perhaps have had no better chance of success than a modern *foots*, had it not been for the familiar fluctuation in cases like the word 'field.'

Neuter and feminine nouns in Old English had not the *s*-plural. Examples of neuter types are [word] 'word,' with homonymous plural, ['spere] 'spear,' plural ['speru], ['eːaje] 'eye,' plural ['eːagan]; feminine types, ['karu] 'care,' plural ['kara], ['tunge] 'tongue,' plural ['tungan], [boːk] 'book,' plural [beːk].

Even where the *s*-plural was traditional, sound-change led to divergent forms. Thus an early voicing of spirants between vowels led to the type *knife : knives*. Other irregularities of this sort have been overlaid by new-formations. In pre-English, [a] became [ɛ] in monosyllables and before [e] of a following syllable; after this change, [g] became [j] before a front vowel and in final position after a front vowel. The result was a set of alternations, as in the paradigm of 'day':

	Singular	Plural
nom.-acc.	[dɛj]	['dagas]
dat.	['dɛje]	['dagum]
gen.	['dɛjes]	['daga]

Later, there came a change of [g] to [w], whence the Middle English irregularity of *dei*, plural *dawes;* the latter form, as we have seen, was superseded by the regular new combination of *day* plus [-z].

The early Old English loss of [h] between vowels with contraction (§ 21.6), led to paradigms like that of 'shoe,' which were regular in Old English, but by subsequent phonetic change, would have led to highly irregular modern sets:

	Old English	Modern Phonetic Result
singular		
nom.-acc.	[sko:h]	*[šof]
dat.	[sko:]	[šuw]
gen.	[sko:s]	*[šos]
plural		
nom.-acc.	[sko:s]	*[šos]
dat.	[sko:m]	*[šuwm, šum]
gen.	[sko:]	[šuw]

Among the Old English paradigms of other types, that of 'foot' shows us an interesting redistribution of forms:

	Singular	Plural
nom.-acc.	[fo:t]	[fe:t]
dat.	[fe:t]	['fo:tum]
gen.	['fo:tes]	['fo:ta]

Here the form with [o:], modern *foot,* has been generalized in the singular, crowding out the old dative, and the form with [e:], modern *feet,* in the plural, crowding out the old dative and genitive forms.

In a few cases, two forms have survived with a lexical difference. Our words *shade* and *shadow* are reflexes of different forms of a single Old English paradigm:

	OLD ENGLISH	MODERN PHONETIC EQUIVALENT	
singular			
nominative	['skadu]	[šejd]	*shade*
other cases	['skadwe]	['šɛdow]	*shadow*
plural			
dative	['skadwum]	['šɛdow]	*shadow*
other cases	['skadwa]	['šɛdow]	*shadow*

Both forms, *shade* and *shadow*, have been generalized for the whole singular, and have served as underlying forms for new regular plurals, *shades, shadows;* the rivalry of the two resulting paradigms has ended in a lexical differentiation. The words *mead* and *meadow* arose in the same way, but in this case the fluctuation seems to be ending in the obsolescence of the form *mead*.

The word 'gate' had in Old English the nominative-accusative singular *geat* [jat], plural *gatu* ['gatu]. The old singular, which would give a modern **yat*, has died out; the modern form *gate* represents the old plural, and the new plural *gates* has been formed on the regular model.

Analogic creation is not limited to complex forms. A simple form may be created on the analogy of cases where a complex form and a simple form exist side by side. The Middle English noun *redels* 'riddle,' with homonymous plural, was subjected to analogic change of the pattern

PLURAL		SINGULAR
stones	:	*stone*
= *redels*	:	*x*,

whence the modern singular form *riddle*. This creation of shorter or underlying forms is called *back-formation*. Another example is Old English ['pise] 'pea,' plural ['pisan]; all the forms of the paradigm lead to modern *pease, peas* [pijz], and the singular *pea* is a back-formation. Similarly, Old French *cherise* 'cherry' was borrowed in Middle English as *cheris*, whence modern *cherries;* the singular *cherry* is an analogic creation.

23. 5. In word-formation, the most favorable ground for analogic forms is a derivative type which bears some clear-cut meaning. Thus, we form all manner of new agent-nouns in -*er*, on what is at present a normal grammatical analogy. This suffix was borrowed in pre-English time from Latin, and has replaced a number of native types. In Old English, the agent of ['huntian] 'to hunt' was ['hunta], which has been replaced by *hunter*. At a later time, *webster* was replaced by *weaver*, and survives only as a family-name. In *boot-black, chimney-sweep* old forms survive as compound-members. We not only form new agent-nouns, such as *camou-flager, debunker, charlestoner*, but also make back-formations, such as the verb *chauffe* [šowf] 'drive (someone) about in a motor-car' from *chauffeur* ['šowfṛ]. An analogy that permits of new formations is said to be "living."

The old suffix *-ster* in *webster* is an example of a type which perhaps never could have been described as "regular" or "living" and yet had its period of expansion. It seems to have denoted (as is still the case in Dutch) a female agent. The female meaning survives in *spinster*, originally 'spinneress.' Apparently, the female meaning was not obvious in all the words: the suffix became indifferent as to sex and appears in *tapster, huckster, teamster, maltster, webster* 'weaver,' *dunster* 'dunner, bailiff.' The action was not necessarily useful, witness *songster, rimester, trickster, game-ster, punster*. A non-human agent appears in *lobster*, which prob-ably represents Old English *loppestre*, originally 'jumper.' An inanimate object is *roadster*. An adjective, instead of verb or noun, underlies *youngster*. After the restriction to females was lost, words in *-ster* combined with *-ess: huckstress, songstress, seam-stress*. This last, by the shortening of vowels before clusters, be-came ['semstres]; the more regular rival form ['sijmstres] is ana-logic, with the vowel of the underlying *seam*. In cases like *-ster* we see a formation spreading from form to form without ever at-taining to the free expansion of "living" types.

Some formations become widely usable without pre-empting a domain of meaning. In English, the suffixes *-y, -ish, -ly*, which derive adjectives, have all remained quite "alive" through the historical period, spreading from word to word, and settling in various semantic patches. Thus, with the suffix *-y* (from Old Eng-lish *-ig*), some words appear in our Old English records (e.g. *mighty, misty, moody, bloody, speedy*), while others appear only later (e.g. *earthy, wealthy, hasty, hearty, fiery*). When the suffix is added to words of foreign origin, the date of the borrowing gives us a limit of age ("terminus post quem") for the new combination: *sugary, flowery, creamy*. At present, this suffix is expanding in certain zones of meaning, such as 'arch, affected': *summery* (e.g of clothes), *sporty, swanky, arty* ('pretendedly artistic'), *booky* ('pretendedly bookish'). In the same way, *-ish*, in some combinations a mere adjective-former (*boyish, girlish*), has staked a claim in the zone of 'undesirably, inappropriately resembling,' as in *mannish, womanish* (contrast *manly, womanly*), *childish* (contrast *childlike*). The starting-point of semantic specialization is to be sought in forms where the underlying word has the special value; thus, the unpleasant flavor of *-ish* comes from words like *loutish, boorish, swinish, hoggish*.

The shape of morphologic constituents is subject to analogic change, especially in the way of enlargement. In Latin, the set *argentum* [ar'gentum] 'silver' : *argentarius* [argen'ta:rius] 'silversmith' represents a regular type of derivation. In the history of French there was repeated losses of final phonemes; the modern forms are *argent* [arža^n] : *argentier* [arža^{n}tje]. The formula of derivation has become: add the suffix [-tje]. This suffix, accordingly, appears in words which (as the historian, quite irrelevantly, remarks) never contained a [t] in the critical position: French *ferblanc* [fer-bla^n] 'tin' (Latin type **ferrum blankum* 'white iron,' with the Germanic adjective *blank*) underlies *ferblantier* [ferbla^{n}tje] 'tinsmith'; *bijou* [bižu] 'jewel' (from Breton *bizun*) underlies *bijoutier* [bižutje] 'jeweler,' and so on.

In time, an affix may consist entirely of accretive elements, with no trace of its original shape. In Old English, verb-paradigms were derived from nouns on the pattern [wund] 'a wound': ['wundian] 'to wound,' and this is still the living type, as in *wound : to wound, radio : to radio*. In a few instances, however, the underlying noun was itself derived, by means of a suffix [-en-], from an adjective, as in the set [fɛst] 'firm, strong' : ['fɛsten] 'strong place, fortress' : ['fɛstenian] 'to make firm, to fortify,' Thanks to some fluctuation in frequency or meaning — such, perhaps, as a decline or specialization of the noun ['fɛsten] — the pair [fɛst] 'firm' : ['fɛstenian] 'to make firm' served as a model for new-formations on the scheme

$$fast : fasten = hard : x,$$

with the result of forms like *harden, sharpen, sweeten, fatten, gladden*, in which a suffix *-en* derives verbs from adjectives.

Less often, a relatively independent form is reduced to affixal status. Compound-members are occasionally reduced, by sound-change, to suffixes; thus, the suffix *-ly* (*manly*) is a weakened form of *like*, and the suffix *-dom* (*kingdom*) of the word *doom*. This happens especially when the independent word goes out of use, as in the case of *-hood* (*childhood*), which is a relic of an Old English word [ha:d] 'person, rank.' German *Messer* ['meser] 'knife' is the modern form, with analogic as well as phonetic shortening, of Old High German ['messi-rahs] originally 'food-knife,' in which the second member, [sahs] 'knife,' had been disfigured by Verner's change (§ 20.8) and the subsequent change of [z] to [r]. In German *Schuster* ['šu:ster] 'shoemaker' the unique suffix [-ster] reflects an old compound-member [su'tɛ:re] 'cobbler.' Merging of two words into one is excessively rare; the best-known instance is the origin of the future tense-forms in the Romance languages from phrases of infinitive plus 'have': Latin *amare habeo* [a'ma:re 'habeo:] 'I have to, am to love' > French *aimerai* [ɛmre] '(I) shall love'; Latin *amare habet* [a'ma:re 'habet] 'he has to, is to love' > French *aimera* [ɛmra] '(he) will love,' and so on. This development must have taken place under very unusual conditions; above all, we must remember that Latin and Romance have a complicated set of verb-inflections which served as a model for one-word tense-forms.

Back-formations in word-structure are by no means uncommon, though often hard to recognize. Many verbs in the foreign-learned vocabulary of English resemble Latin past participles; this is all the more striking since English has borrowed these words from French, and in French the Latin past participles have been obscured by sound-change or replaced by new-formations: Latin *agere* ['agere] 'to lead, carry on, do,' past participle *actus* ['aktus] 'led, done' : French *agir* [aži:r] 'to act,' participle (new-formation) *agi* [aži] 'acted' : English *to act;* Latin *affligere* [af-'fli:gere] 'to strike down, afflict,' participle *afflictus* [af'fliktus] 'stricken, afflicted' : French *affliger* [afliže], participle *affligé* [afliže] : English *to afflict;* Latin *separare* [se:pa'ra:re] 'to separate,' participle *separatus* [se:pa'ra:tus] : French *séparer* [separe], participle *séparé* [separe] : English *to separate.* The starting-point for this habit of English seems to have been back-formation from nouns in *-tion:* English verbs like *act, afflict, separate* are based on nouns like *action, affliction, separation,* from Latin *actionem, afflictionem, separationem* [akti'o:nem, afflikti'o:nem, se:para:ti'o:-nem] via French *action, affliction, séparation,* in modern pronunciation [aksjo^n. afliksjo^n, separasjo^n]. The immediate models must have been cases like *communion: to commune* (Old French *communion : comuner*); the general background was the English homonymy of adjective and verb in cases like *warm : to warm = separate : to separate.* This supposition is confirmed by the fact that the nouns in *-tion* appear in our records at an earlier time, on the whole, than the verbs in *-t.* Of the 108 pairs with initial A in the *New English Dictionary*, the noun appears earlier than the verb in 74 cases, as, *action* in 1330, but *to act* in 1384; *affliction*, in 1303, but *to afflict* in 1393. Moreover, we sometimes see the late rise of the verb with *-t:* in the case of *aspiration : to aspire* we have stuck to the Latin-French scheme, but round 1700 there appears the new-formation *to aspirate.* Modern formations of this sort are *evolute*, based on *evolution*, as a rival of the older *evolve*, and *elocute* based on *elocution.*

23. 6. The task of tracing analogy in word-composition has scarcely been undertaken. The present-day habits of word-composition in English produce the illusion that compounds arise by a simple juxtaposition of words. The reader need scarcely be told that the modern English pattern, in which the compound word equals the independent forms of the members, with modification only of word-stress, is the product of a long series of regularizing analogic changes. Thus, ['fowr-ˌhed] *forehead*, as a rival of ['fɑred], which has been irregularized by sound-change, is due to analogic re-formation:

> *fore, arm : fore-arm* ['fowr-ˌarm]
> = *fore, head : x.*

The relation of the compound to independent words often suffers displacement. Primitive Indo-European did not use verb-stems as compound-members; to this day, English lacks a verbal type, **to meat-eat*, which would match the noun and adjective types *meat-eater* and *meat-eating* (§ 14.3). Several Indo-European languages, however, have developed compounds with verbal members. In English we have a few irregular forms like *housekeep*, *dressmake*, *backbite*. From a compound noun like *whitewash* we derive, with a zero-element, a verb *to whitewash*, and from this an agent-noun *whitewasher*. The irregular type *to housekeep* is probably a back-formation on this model:

> *whitewasher : to whitewash*
> = *housekeeper : x.*

In a now classical investigation, Hermann Osthoff showed how forms of this kind arose in several of the Indo-European languages. In Old High German, abstract nouns like ['beta] 'prayer' were used, in the normal inherited fashion, as prior members of compounds: ['beta-ˌhuːs] 'prayer-house, house for prayer.' The morphologically connected verb ['betoːn] 'to pray' had a different suffixal vowel and did not interfere with the compound. During the Middle Ages, however, unstressed vowels were weakened to a uniform [e] and in part lost; hence in Middle High German (round the year 1200), in a set like ['beten] 'to pray' : ['bete] 'prayer' : ['bete-ˌhuːs] 'house for prayer,' the compound-member resembled the verb as much as it resembled the noun. If the noun lost in frequency or was specialized in meaning, the compound-member became equivalent to the verb-stem. Thus ['bete] 'prayer' lost in frequency — the modern language uses a different derivative, *Gebet* [geˈbeːt] 'prayer' — and, for the rest, was specialized in a meaning of 'contribution, tax.' As a result of this, compounds like *Bethaus* ['beːt-ˌhaws] 'house for praying,' *Bettag* ['beːt-ˌtaːk] 'day of prayer,' *Betschwester*, ['beːt-ˌšvester] 'praying-sister,' that is 'nun' or 'over-pious woman,' can be described only as containing the verb-stem [beːt-] of *beten* [beːten] 'to pray.' Accordingly, ever since the Middle Ages, new compounds of this sort have been formed with verbal prior members, as *Schreibtisch* ['šrajp-ˌtiš] 'writing-table,' from *schreiben* 'to write,' or *Lesebuch* ['leːze-ˌbuːx] 'reading-book' from *lesen* 'to read.'

The fluctuation between irregular compounds, such as ['fared] *forehead*, and analogically formed regular variants, such as ['fowr-ˌhed], serves as a model for new-formations which replace an obscure form by a compound-member. Thus, *inmost, northmost, utmost* (and, with regularization of the first member, *outmost*), with the word *most* as second member, are analogic formations which replace the Old English type ['innemest, 'norθmest, 'uːtemest]; the [-mest] in these words was a special form (with accretion) of the superlative suffix [-est]. Regularizing new-formations like this, which (as the historian finds) disagree with the earlier structure of the form, are sometimes called *popular etymologies*.

23. 7. Analogic innovation in the phrase is most easily seen when it affects the shape of single words. Conditioned sound-changes may produce different forms of a word according to its phonetic positions in the phrase. In the types of English which

lost [r] in final position and before consonants, but kept it before
vowels, there resulted sandhi-alternants of words like *water:* in
final position and before consonants this became ['wɔtə], but before a vowel in a close-knit phrase it kept its [r]: *the water is* ['wɔtər
iz], *the water of* ['wɔtər ov]. The final vowel of *water* was now like
that of a word like *idea* [aj'dijə], which had never had final [r].
This led to a new-formation:

$$water \text{ ['wɔtə]} \quad : \textit{ the water is } \text{['wɔtər iz]}$$
$$= idea \quad \text{[aj'dijə]} : x,$$

which resulted in the sandhi-form *the idea-r is* [aj'dijər iz].

In a language like modern English, which gives special phonetic
treatment to the beginning and end of a word, the phonemes in
these positions rarely fulfil the terms of an ordinary conditioned
sound-change, but are subject rather to conditioned changes of their
own. Only phrases with atonic words parallel the conditions which
exist within a word. Hence English sandhi-alternation is limited
largely to cases like the above (. . . *of*, . . . *is*) or to such as *don't*,
at you ['ɛču̇w], *did you* ['dijuw]. Moreover, the plain phonetic marking of most words, and in some positions even of ordinarily atonic
words, favors the survival or new-formation of variants that agree
with the absolute form: *do not, at you* ['ɛt juw], *did you* ['did juw].

In languages which give a less specialized treatment to word-
boundaries, sandhi-alternants arise in great numbers and give rise
to irregularities which are in turn leveled out by new-formations.
We saw in § 21.4 the origin of the initial-sandhi of Irish. In French,
the noun is on the whole free from sandhi-alternation: words like
pot [po] 'pot' or *pied* [pje] 'foot' are invariable in the phrase.
However, we need only look to phrase-like compounds (§ 14.2),
such as *pot-au-feu* [pɔt o fø] 'pot-on-the-fire,' that is 'broth,'
or *pied-à-terre* [pjet a tɛːr] 'foot-on-ground,' that is 'lodgings,'
to see that the apparent stability is due to analogic regularization.
Third-person singular verbs which were monosyllabic in the early
Middle Ages, have, by regular phonetic development, a final
[t] in sandhi before a vowel: Latin *est* > French *est* [ɛ] 'is,' but
Latin *est ille* > French *est-il* [ɛt i] 'is he?' On the other hand,
verb-forms of more than one syllable had not this [t]; Latin *amat*
'he loves' gives French *aime* [ɛm] 'loves' even before a vowel.
However, the pattern

$$[\varepsilon] : [\varepsilon t \ i] = [\varepsilon m] : x$$

resulted in a modern sandhi-form *aime-t-il* [ɛmt i] 'does he love?'

In the later Old English period, final [n] after an unstressed vowel was lost, except in sandhi before a vowel. Thus, *eten* 'to eat' became *ete*, *an hand* became *a hand*, but *an arm* remained. In the case of the article *a : an* the resulting alternation has survived; in early modern English one still said *my friend : mine enemy*. One must suppose that at the time of the loss of *-n*, the language did not distinguish word-boundaries in the manner of present-day English. The sandhi [n] was generalized in a few cases as a word-initial. Old English *efeta* ['eveta] 'lizard' appears in Middle English as *ewte* and *newte*, whence modern *newt*. A phrase like *an ewte* must have been pronounced [a'newte] and (doubtless under some special conditions of frequency or meaning) subjected to the new-formation

[a'naːme] 'a name' : ['naːme] 'name'
= [a'newte] 'a lizard' : *x,*

with the result that one said *newte*. Similarly, *eke-name* 'supplementary name' gave rise to a by-form with *n-*, modern *nickname;* *for then anes* is now *for the nonce*. On the other hand, an initial [n] was in some forms treated as a sandhi [n]. Thus, Old English *nafogar* ['navo-ˌgaːr], literally 'nave-lance,' Middle English *navegar*, has been replaced by *auger;* Old English ['nɛːdre] gives Middle English *naddere* and *addere*, whence modern *adder;* Old French *naperon*, borrowed as *napron*, has been replaced by *apron*.

After this loss of final [n], another sound-change led to the loss of certain final vowels, through which many hitherto medial [n]'s got into final position, as in *oxena > oxen*. These new final [n]'s came into final position too late to suffer the dropping; hence the language had now, beside the sandhi [n], which appeared only before vowels, also a stable final [n]. This led to some complicated relations:

| | OLD ENGLISH > | EARLY MIDDLE ENGLISH | |
		before vowel	otherwise
singular			
nominative	*oxa*	*ox*	*oxe*
other cases	*oxan*	*oxen*	*oxe*
plural			
nom.-acc.	*oxan*	*oxen*	*oxe*
dat.	*oxum*	*oxen*	*oxe*
gen.	*oxena*	*oxen*	*oxen*

This complicated habit was re-shaped into our present distribution of singular *ox*, plural *oxen*.

In most cases, a phrasal innovation results not in a new word-form, but in a new syntactic or lexical usage, such as the use of *like* as a conjunction (§ 23.2). In German we find such appositional groups as *ein Trunk Wasser* [ajn 'truŋk 'vaser] 'a drink of water,' where the related languages would lead us to expect the second noun in genitive case-form, *Wassers* 'of water.' The genitive case-ending in feminine and plural nouns has been reduced to zero by phonetic change: the genitive of *Milch* [milx] 'milk' (feminine noun) is homonymous with the nominative and accusative. The old locution *ein Trunk Wassers* has been replaced by the present one, which arose on the scheme

> *Milch trinken* 'to drink milk' : *ein Trunk Milch* 'a drink of milk'
> = *Wasser trinken* 'to drink water' : *x*.

This was favored, no doubt, by the existence of nouns whose genitive wavered between zero and -*es*, and by the circumstance that the genitive case was declining in frequency. It seems likely, in spite of the obvious difficulties, that further research will find many examples of analogic innovation in the phrase, both syntactic and lexical. Our philosophic prepossessions have led us too often to seek the motives of change in the individual word and in the meaning of the individual word.

23. 8. For many new-formations we are not able to give a proportional model. We believe that this is not always due to our inability to find the model sets, and that there is really a type of linguistic change which resembles analogic change, but goes on without model sets. These *adaptive* new-formations resemble an old form with some change in the direction of semantically related forms. For instance, of the two slang forms *actorine* 'actress' and *chorine* 'chorus-girl,' only the former can be described as the result of a proportional analogy (*Paul : Pauline = actor : x*). Now, *chorine* seems to be based in some way on *actorine*, but the set *chorus : chorine* is not parallel with *actor : actorine* either in form or in meaning. The set *Josephus : Josephine* [jow'sijfos, 'jowze-fijn] is uncommon, remote in meaning, and phonetically irregular. We can say only that many nouns have a suffix [-ijn], e.g. *chlorine, colleen;* that this suffix derives some women's names and

especially the noun *actorine;* and that the *-us* of *chorus* is plainly
suffixal, in view of the adjective *choral.* This general background
must have sufficed to make someone utter the form *chorine,* even
though there was no exact analogy for this form.

A new form (such as *chorine*), which is based on a traditional
form (*chorus, chorus-girl*), but departs from it in the direction of
a series of semantically related forms (*chlorine, colleen, Pauline,*
etc., including especially *actorine*), is said to originate by *adaptation.* Adaptation seems to be favored by more than one factor,
but all the factors taken together would not allow us to predict
the new form. Often, as in our example, the new form has a facetious connotation; this connotation is probably connected with
the unpredictable, far-fetched shape of the new word. This is true
of mock-learned words, like *scrumptious, rambunctious, absquat-
ulate.* It seems unlikely that more than one speaker hit upon
these forms: we suspect them of being individual creations, determined by the linguistic and practical peculiarities of some one
speaker. They must have agreed to some extent, however, with
the general habits of the community, since they were taken up
by other speakers.

Some adaptations are less far-fetched and merely produce a
new form which agrees better with semantically related forms.
English has borrowed many French words with a suffix *-ure,*
such as *measure, censure, fracture.* The Old French words *plaisir,
loisir, tresor,* which contain other suffixes, have in English been
adapted to the *-ure* type, for the [-žṛ] of *pleasure, leisure, treasure*
reflects an old [-zju:r]. Among our foreign-learned words, *egoism*
follows the French model, but *egotism* is an adaptive formation
in the direction of *despotism, nepotism.*

In the Romance languages, Latin *reddere* ['reddere] 'to give
back' has been largely replaced by a type **rendere,* as in Italian
rendere ['rɛndere], French *rendre* [rɑⁿdr], whence English *render.*
This **rendere* is an adaptation of *reddere* in the direction of the
series Latin *prehendere* [pre'hendere, 'prendere] 'to take' > Italian
prendere ['prɛndere], French *prendre* [prɑⁿdr]; Latin *attendere*
[at'tendere] 'to pay attention' > Italian *attendere* [at'tɛndere]
'to wait,' French *attendre* [atɑⁿdr] (and other compounds of Latin
tendere); Latin *vendere* ['we:ndere] 'to sell' > Italian *vendere*
['vendere], French *vendre* [vɑⁿdr]; here the word for 'take,' with its
close kinship of meaning, was doubtless the main factor.

Sometimes it is a single form which exercises the attraction. Beside the old word *gravis* 'heavy,' later Latin has also a form *grevis*, whose vowel seems to be due to the influence of *levis* 'light (in weight).' Formations of this sort are known as *blendings* or *contaminations*. We cannot always be sure that the attraction was exercised by only a single form; in our example, the word *brevis* 'short' may have helped toward the formation of *grevis*.

The paradigm of the word for 'foot,' Primitive Indo-European *[po:ds], genitive *[po'dos], Sanskrit [pa:t], genitive [pa'dah], appears in one ancient Greek dialect in the expected shape, ['po:s], genitive [po'dos], but in the Attic dialect has the unexpected nominative form ['pows]; this has been explained as a contamination with the word for 'tooth,' [o'dows], genitive [o'dontos], which is a phonetically normal reflex of a Primitive Indo-European type *[o'donts].

In the earlier stages of the Germanic languages, the personal pronouns must have been in a state of instability. The old form for 'ye' seems to have been a Primitive Germanic type *[ju:z, juz], which appears in Gothic as *jus* [ju:s] or [jus]. The other Germanic dialects reflect a Primitive Germanic type *[jiz]: Old Norse [e:r], Old English [je:], Old High German [ir]. This form has been explained as a contamination of *[juz] 'ye' with the word for 'we,' Primitive Germanic *[wi:z, wiz], reflected in Gothic [wi:s], Old Norse [ve:r], Old English [we:], Old High German [wir].

Similarly, in Gothic the accusative case of 'thou' is [θuk] and the dative case [θus]. These forms disagree with the other dialects, which reflect the Primitive Germanic types accusative *['θiki], Old Norse [θik], Old English [θek], Old High German [dih], and dative *[θiz], Old Norse [θe:r], Old English [θe:], Old High German [dir]. The Gothic forms have been explained as contaminations with the nominative *[θu:], Gothic, Old Norse, Old English [θu:], Old High German [du:]. For this, the word 'I,' which had the same vowel in all three forms, Gothic [ik, mik, mis], may have served as a kind of model, but there is no exact analogy covering the two paradigms, and we might equally well expect [mik, mis] to work in favor of *[θik, θis].

Numerals seem to have been contaminated in the history of various languages. In Primitive Indo-European, 'four' was *[kʷe'two:res], and 'five' *['penkʷe]; witness Sanskrit [ča'tva:rah, 'panča] or Lithuanian [ketu'ri, pen'ki]. In the Germanic languages both words begin with [f], which reflects a Primitive Indo-European [p], as in English *four, five;* and *five,* moreover, has an [f] for the [kʷ] of the second syllable, as in Gothic [fimf]. In Latin, on the other hand, both words begin with [kw]: *quattuor, quinque* ['kwattuor, 'kwi:nkwe]. All of these deviant forms could be explained as due to "distant assimilation"; it seems more probable, however, that the changes described under this and similar terms (§ 21.10) are in reality contaminative or adaptive. Ancient Greek [hep'ta] 'seven' and [ok'to:] 'eight' led in one dialect to a contaminative [op'to:] 'eight,' and in others to [hok'to:]. The words 'nine' and 'ten,' Primitive Indo-European *['newn̥, 'dekm̥], as in Sanskrit ['nava, 'daça], Latin *novem, decem,* both have initial [d] in Slavic and Baltic, as in Old Bulgarian [deveⁿtɪ, deseⁿtɪ].

Psychologists have ascertained that under laboratory conditions, the stimulus of hearing a word like 'four' often leads to the utterance of a word like 'five' — but this, after all, does not account for contamination. There is perhaps more relevance in the fact that contaminative "slips of the tongue" are not infrequent, e.g. "I'll just *grun* (*go* plus *run*) over and get it."

Innovations in syntax sometimes have a contaminative aspect. The type *I am friends with him* has been explained as due to contamination of *I am friendly with him* and *we are friends.* Irregularities such as the "attraction" of relative pronouns (§ 15.11) seem to be of this nature.

So-called popular etymologies (§ 23.6) are largely adaptive and contaminative. An irregular or semantically obscure form is replaced by a new form of more normal structure and some semantic content — though the latter is often far-fetched. Thus, an old *sham-fast* 'shame-fast,' that is, 'modest,' has given way to the regular, but semantically queer compound *shame-faced.* Old English *sam-blind,* containing an otherwise obsolete first member which meant 'half,' was replaced by the Elizabethan *sand-blind.* Old English *bryd-guma* ['bry:d-ₗguma] 'bride-man' was replaced by *bride-groom,* thanks to the obsolescence of *guma* 'man.' Foreign words are especially subject to this kind of adaptation. Old French *crevisse,* Middle English *crevise* has been replaced by *crayfish, craw-fish: mandragora* by *man-drake; asparagus* in older substandard speech by *sparrow-grass.* Our *gooseberry* seems to be a replacement of an older **groze-berry,* to judge by dialect forms such as *grozet, groser;* these forms reflect a borrowed French form akin to modern French *groseille* [grɔzeː j] 'currant; gooseberry.'

Probably forms like our symbolic words, nursery words, and short-names are created on general formal patterns, rather than on exact analogic models. It seems, however, that forms like *Bob, Dick* existed as common nouns, perhaps with symbolic connotation, before they were specialized as hypochoristic forms of *Robert, Richard.* It is a great mistake to think that one can account for the origin of forms like these by merely stating their connotation.

In some instances we know that a certain person invented a form. The most famous instance is *gas,* invented in the seventeenth century by the Dutch chemist van Helmont. In the passage where he introduces the word, van Helmont points out its resemblance to the word *chaos,* which, in Dutch pronunciation, is not far removed (though phonemically quite distinct) from *gas.* Moreover, van Helmont used also a technical term *blas,* a regular derivative, in Dutch, of the verb *blazen* 'to blow.'

It is evident that in such cases we cannot reconstruct the inventor's private and personal world of connotations; we can only guess at the general linguistic background. Charles Dodgson ("Lewis Carroll") in his famous poem, "The Jabberwocky" (in *Through the Looking-Glass*), uses a number of new-formations of this sort and, later in the book, explains the connotative significance they had for him. At least one of them, *chortle,* has come into wide use. More recent examples are the mercantile term *kodak,* invented by George Eastman, and *blurb,* a creation of Gelett Burgess.

CHAPTER 24

SEMANTIC CHANGE

24. 1. Innovations which change the lexical meaning rather than the grammatical function of a form, are classed as *change of meaning* or *semantic change*.

The contexts and phrasal combinations of a form in our older written records often show that it once had a different meaning. The King James translation of the Bible (1611) says, of the herbs and trees (*Genesis* 1, 29) *to you they shall be for meat.* Similarly, the Old English translation in this passage used the word *mete.* We infer that the word *meat* used to mean 'food,' and we may assure ourselves of this by looking into the foreign texts from which these English translations were made. Sometimes the ancients tell us meanings outright, chiefly in the form of glosses; thus, an Old English glossary uses the word *mete* to translate the Latin *cibus,* which we know to mean 'food.'

In other instances the comparison of related languages shows different meanings in forms that we feel justified in viewing as cognate. Thus, *chin* agrees in meaning with German *Kinn* and Dutch *kin,* but Gothic *kinnus* and the Scandinavian forms, from Old Norse *kinn* to the present, mean 'cheek.' In other Indo-European languages we find Greek ['genus] 'chin' agreeing with West Germanic, but Latin *gena* 'cheek' agreeing with Gothic and Scandinavian, while Sanskrit ['hanuh] 'jaw' shows us a third meaning. We conclude that the old meaning, whatever it was, has changed in some or all of these languages.

A third, but much less certain indication of semantic change, appears in the structural analysis of forms. Thus, *understand* had in Old English time the same meaning as now, but since the word is a compound of *stand* and *under,* we infer that at the time the compound was first formed (as an analogic new-formation) it must have meant 'stand under'; this gains in probability from the fact that *under* once meant also 'among,' for the cognates, German *unter* and Latin *inter,* have this meaning. Thus, *I understand these things* may have meant, at first, 'I stand among these things.' In other cases, a form whose structure in the present state of the language does not imply anything as to meaning, may have been semantically analyzable in an earlier stage. The word *ready* has the adjective-forming suffix -*y* added to a unique root, but the Old English form [je'rɛːde], which, but for an analogic re-formation of the suffix, can be viewed as the ancestor of *ready*, meant 'swift, suited, skilled' and was a derivative of the verb ['riːdan] 'to ride,' past tense [raːd] 'rode,' derived noun [raːd] 'a riding, a road.' We infer that when [je'rɛːde] was first formed, it meant 'suitable or prepared for riding.'

Inferences like these are sometimes wrong, because the make-up of a form may be of later date than its meaning. Thus, *crawfish* and *gooseberry*, adaptations of *crevise* and *groze-berry (§ 23.8), can tell us nothing about any older meanings.

24. 2. We can easily see today that a change in the meaning of a speech-form is merely the result of a change in the use of it and other, semantically related speech-forms. Earlier students, however, went at this problem as if the speech-form were a relatively permanent object to which the meaning was attached as a kind of changeable satellite. They hoped by studying the successive meanings of a single form, such as *meat* 'food' > 'flesh-food,' to find the reason for this change. This led them to classify semantic changes according to the logical relations that connect the successive meanings. They set up such classes as the following:

Narrowing:

Old English *mete* 'food' > *meat* 'edible flesh'

Old English *dēor* 'beast' > *deer* 'wild ruminant of a particular species'

Old English *hund* 'dog' > *hound* 'hunting-dog of a particular breed'

Widening:

Middle English *bridde* 'young birdling' > *bird*

Middle English *dogge* 'dog of a particular (ancient) breed' > *dog*

Latin *virtūs* 'quality of a man (*vir*), manliness' > French *vertu* (> English *virtue*) 'good quality'

Metaphor:

Primitive Germanic *['bitraz] 'biting' (derivative of *['biːtoː] 'I bite') > *bitter* 'harsh of taste'

Metonymy — the meanings are near each other in space or time:

Old English *cēace* 'jaw' > *cheek*

Old French *joue* 'cheek' > *jaw*

Synecdoche — the meanings are related as whole and part:

Primitive Germanic *['tu:naz] 'fence' (so still German *Zaun*) > *town*

pre-English *['stobo:] 'heated room' (compare German *Stube*, formerly 'heated room,' now 'living-room') > *stove*

Hyperbole — from stronger to weaker meaning:

pre-French *ex-tonāre 'to strike with thunder' > French *étonner* 'to astonish' (from Old French, English borrowed *astound, astonish*)

Litotes — from weaker to stronger meaning:

pre-English *['kwalljan] 'to torment' (so still German *quälen*) > Old English *cwellan* 'to kill'

Degeneration:

Old English *cnafa* 'boy, servant' > *knave*

Elevation:

Old English *cniht* 'boy, servant' (compare German *Knecht* 'servant') > *knight*.

Collections of examples arranged in classes like these are useful in showing us what changes are likely to occur. The meanings 'jaw,' 'cheek,' and 'chin,' which we found in the cognates of our word *chin*, are found to fluctuate in other cases, such as that of *cheek* from 'jaw' (Old English meaning) to the present meaning; *jaw*, from French *joue* 'cheek,' has changed in the opposite direction. Latin *maxilla* 'jaw' has shifted to 'cheek' in most modern dialects, as in Italian *mascella* [ma'šella] 'cheek.' We suspect that the word *chin* may have meant 'jaw' before it meant 'cheek' and 'chin.' In this case we have the confirmation of a few Old High German glosses which translate Latin *molae* and *maxillae* (plural forms in the sense 'jaw' or 'jaws') by the plural *kinne*. Old English ['weorθan] 'to become' and its cognates in the other Germanic languages (such as German *werden*, § 22.2) agree in form with Sanskrit ['vartate:] 'he turns,' Latin *vertō* 'I turn,' Old Bulgarian [vṛte:ti] 'to turn,' Lithuanian [ver'ču] 'I turn'; we accept this etymology because the Sanskrit word has a marginal meaning 'to become,' and because English *turn* shows a parallel development, as in *turn sour, turn traitor*.

24. 3. Viewed on this plane, a change of meaning may imply a connection between practical things and thereby throw light on the life of older times. English *fee* is the modern form of the paradigm of Old English *feoh*, which meant 'live-stock, cattle, property, money.' Among the Germanic cognates, only Gothic *faihu* ['fehu] means 'property'; all the others, such as German *Vieh* [fi:] or Swedish *fä* [fe:], have meanings like '(head of) cattle, (head of) live-stock.' The same is true of the cognates in the other Indo-European languages, such as Sanskrit ['paçu] or Latin *pecu;* but Latin has the derived words *pecūnia* 'money' and *pecūlium* 'savings, property.' This confirms our belief that live-stock served in ancient times as a medium of exchange.

English *hose* corresponds formally to Dutch *hoos* [ho:s], German *Hose* ['ho:ze], but these words, usually in plural form, mean not 'stockings' but 'trousers.' The Scandinavian forms, such as Old Norse *hosa*, mean 'stocking' or 'legging.' An ancient form, presumably West Germanic, came into Latin in the early centuries of our era, doubtless through the mediation of Roman soldiers, for the Romance languages have a type *hosa (as, Italian *uosa* ['wɔsa]) in the sense 'legging.' We conclude that in old Germanic our word meant a covering for the leg, either including the foot or ending at the ankle. Round his waist a man wore another garment, the *breeches* (Old English *brōc*). The English and Scandinavian terminology indicates no change, but the German development seems to indicate that on the Continent the *hose* were later joined at the top into a trouser-like garment.

In this way, a semantically peculiar etymology and cultural traces may confirm each other. The German word *Wand* [vant] denotes the wall of a room, but not a thick masonry wall; the latter is *Mauer* ['mawer], a loan from Latin. The German word sounds like a derivative of the verb *to wind*, German *winden* (past tense *wand*), but etymologists were at loss as to the connection of these meanings, until Meringer showed that the derivative noun must have applied at first to wattled walls, which were made of twisted withes covered with mud. In the same way, Primitive Germanic *['wajjuz] 'wall,' in Gothic *waddjus*, Old Norse *veggr*, Old English *wāg*, is now taken to have originated as a derivative of a verb that meant 'wind, twist.' We have seen that scholars try, by a combination of semantic and archaeologic data, to throw light on prehistoric conditions, such as those of the Primitive Indo-

European parent community (§ 18.14). The maxim "Words and Things" has been used as the title of a journal devoted to this aspect of etymology.

Just as formal features may arise from highly specific and variable factors (§ 23.8), so the meaning of a form may be due to situations that we cannot reconstruct and can know only if historical tradition is kind to us. The German *Kaiser* ['kajzer] 'emperor' and the Russian [tsar] are offshoots, by borrowing, of the Latin *caesar* ['kajsar], which was generalized from the name of a particular Roman, *Gaius Julius Caesar*. This name is said to be a derivative of the verb *caedō* 'I cut'; the man to whom it was first given was born by the aid of the surgical operation which, on account of this same tradition, is called the *caesarian* operation. Aside from this tradition, if we had not the historical knowledge about Caesar and the Roman Empire, we could not guess that the word for 'emperor' had begun as a family-name. The now obsolescent verb *burke* 'suppress' (as, *to burke opposition*) was derived from the name of one *Burke*, a murderer in Edinburgh who smothered his victims. The word *pander* comes from the name of *Pandarus;* in Chaucer's version of the ancient story of Troilus and Cressida, Pandarus acts as a go-between. *Buncombe* comes from the name of a county in North Carolina, thanks to the antics of a congressman. *Tawdry* comes from *St. Audrey;* at St. Audrey's fair one bought *tawdry lace*. Terms like *landau* and *sedan* come from the original place of manufacture. The word *dollar* is borrowed ultimately from German *Taler*, short for *Joachimstaler*, derived from *Joachimstal* ('Joachim's Dale'), a place in Bohemia where silver was minted in the sixteenth century. The Roman mint was in the temple of *Jūnō Monēta* 'Juno the Warner'; hence the Romans used the word *monēta* both for 'mint' and for 'coin, money.' English *mint* is a pre-English borrowing from this Latin word, and English *money* is a medieval borrowing from the Old French continuation of the Latin word.

The surface study of semantic change indicates that refined and abstract meanings largely grow out of more concrete meanings. Meanings of the type 'respond accurately to (things or speech)' develop again and again from meanings like 'be near to' or 'get hold of.' Thus, *understand*, as we saw, seems to have meant 'stand close to' or 'stand among.' German *verstehen* [fer'šte:en] 'understand' seems to have meant 'stand round' or 'stand before'; the

Old English equivalent *forstandan* appears both for 'understand' and for 'protect, defend.' Ancient Greek [e'pistamaj] 'I understand' is literally 'I stand upon,' and Sanskrit [ava'gaččhati] is both 'he goes down into' and 'he understands.' Italian *capire* [ka'pire] 'to understand' is an analogic new-formation based on Latin *capere* 'to seize, grasp.' Latin *comprehendere* 'to understand' means also 'to take hold of.' The Slavic word for 'understand, as in Russian [po'nat], is a compound of an old verb that meant 'seize, take.' A marginal meaning of 'understand' appears in our words *grasp, catch on, get* (as in *I don't get that*). Most of our abstract vocabulary consists of borrowings from Latin, through French or in gallicized form; the Latin originals can largely be traced to concrete meanings. Thus Latin *dēfinīre* 'to define' is literally 'to set bounds to' (*finis* 'end, boundary'). Our *eliminate* has in Latin only the concrete meaning 'put out of the house,' in accordance with its derivative character, since Latin *ēlīmināre* is structurally a synthetic compound of *ex* 'out of, out from' and *līmen* 'threshold.'

24. 4. All this, aside from its extra-linguistic interest, gives us some measure of probability by which we can judge of etymologic comparisons, but it does not tell us how the meaning of a linguistic form can change in the course of time. When we find a form used at one time in a meaning A and at a later time in a meaning B, what we see is evidently the result of at least two shifts, namely, an expansion of the form from use in situations of type A to use in situations of a wider type A-B, and then a partial obsolescence by which the form ceases to be used in situations which approximate the old type A, sc that finally the form is used only in situations of type B. In ordinary cases, the first process involves the obsolescence or restriction of some rival form that gets crowded out of use in the B-situations, and the second process involves the encroachment of some rival form into the A-situations. We can symbolize this diagrammatically as follows:

meaning:	'nourish-ment'	'edible thing'		'edible part of animal body'	'muscular part of animal body'
first stage:	*food*	*meat*		*flesh*	*flesh*
second stage:	*food*	*meat*	⟶	*meat*	*flesh*
third stage:	*food* ⟶	*food*		*meat*	*flesh*

In the normal case, therefore, we have to deal here with fluctuations of frequency like those of analogic change; the difference is only that the fluctuations result in lexical instead of grammatical displacements, and therefore largely elude the grasp of the linguist. The first student, probably, to see that semantic change consists of expansion and obsolescence, was Hermann Paul. Paul saw that the meaning of a form in the habit of any speaker, is merely the result of the utterances in which he has heard it. Sometimes, to be sure, we use a form in situations that fairly well cover its range of meaning, as in a definition ("a *town* is a large settlement of people") or in a very general statement ("vertebrate animals have a *head*"). In such cases a form appears in its *general* meaning. Ordinarily, however, a form in any one utterance represents a far more specific practical feature. When we say that *John Smith bumped his head*, the word *head* is used of one particular man's head. When a speaker in the neighborhood of a city says *I'm going to town*, the word *town* means this particular city. In such cases the form appears in an *occasional* meaning. In *eat an apple a day* the word *apple* has its general meaning; in some one utterance of the phrase *eat this apple*, the word *apple* has an occasional meaning: the apple, let us say, is a large baked apple. All marginal meanings are occasional, for — as Paul showed — marginal meanings differ from central meanings precisely by the fact that we respond to a marginal meaning only when some special circumstance makes the central meaning impossible (§ 9.8). Central meanings are occasional whenever the situation differs from the ideal situation that matches the whole extent of a form's meaning.

Accordingly, if a speaker has heard a form only in an occasional meaning or in a series of occasional meanings, he will utter the form only in similar situations: his habit may differ from that of other speakers. The word *meat* was used of all manner of dishes; there must have come a time when, owing to the encroachment of some other word (say, *food* or *dish*), many speakers had heard the word *meat* only (or very predominantly) in situations where the actual dish in question consisted of flesh; in their own utterances these speakers, accordingly, used the word *meat* only when flesh-food was involved. If a speaker has heard a form only in some marginal meaning, he will use this form with this same meaning as a central meaning — that is, he will use the form for a meaning in

which other speakers use it only under very special conditions —
like the city child who concluded that pigs were very properly
called *pigs*, on account of their unclean habits. In the later Middle
Ages, the German word *Kopf*, cognate with English *cup*, had the
central meaning 'cup, bowl, pot' and the marginal meaning 'head';
there must have come a time when many speakers had heard this
word only in its marginal meaning, for in modern German *Kopf*
means only 'head.'

24. 5. Paul's explanation of semantic change takes for granted
the occurrence of marginal meanings and of obsolescence, and
views these processes as adventures of individual speech-forms,
without reference to the rival forms which, in the one case, yield
ground to the form under consideration, and, in the other case,
encroach upon its domain. This view, nevertheless, represents a
great advance over the mere classification of differences of meaning. In particular, it enabled Paul to show in detail some of the
ways in which obsolescence breaks up a unitary domain of meaning
— a process which he called *isolation*.

Thus, beside the present central meaning of the word *meat*
'flesh-food,' we have today the strange marginal (apparently,
widened) uses in *meat and drink* and in *sweetmeats;* for dishes other
than flesh, the word *meat* went out of use, except in these two
expressions, which are detached from what is now the central
meaning of the word: we may say that these two expressions have
been *isolated* by the invasion of the intermediate semantic domain,
which is now covered by *food, dish*. In the same way, *knave* has
been shifted from 'boy, young man, servant' to 'scoundrel,' but
the card-player's use of *knave* as a name for the lowest of the three
picture-cards ('jack') is an isolated remnant of the older meaning.
The word *charge* is a loan from Old French *charger* which meant
originally 'to load a wagon.' Its present multiplicity of meanings
is evidently due to expansion into marginal spheres followed by
obsolescence of intermediate meanings. Thus, the agent-noun
charger is no longer used for 'load-bearer, beast of burden,' but
only in the special sense 'war-horse'; the meaning *charge* 'make a
swift attack (on)' is a back-formation from *charger* 'war-horse.'
The word *board* had in Old English apparently the same central
meaning as today, 'flat piece of wood,' and, in addition to this,
several specialized meanings. One of these, 'shield,' has died out
entirely. Another, 'side of a ship,' has led to some isolated forms,

such as *on board, aboard, to board* (a ship), and these have been extended to use in connection with other vehicles, such as railway cars. A third marginal meaning, 'table,' survives, again, in elevated turns of speech, such as *festive board.* Before its general obsolescence, however, *board* 'table' underwent a further transference to 'regular meals,' which is still current, as in *bed and board, board and lodging, to board (at a boarding-house),* and so on. This use of *board* is so widely isolated today from *board* 'plank' that we should perhaps speak of the two as homonymous words.

In Old Germanic the adjective *['hajlaz] meant 'unharmed, well, prosperous,' as *heil* still does in German; this meaning remains in our verb *to heal.* In modern English we have only a transferred meaning in *whole.* Derived from *['hajlaz] there was another adjective *['hajlagaz] which meant 'conducive to welfare, health, or prosperity.' This word seems to have been used in a religious or superstitious sense. It occurs in a Gothic inscription in runes, but as Bishop Ulfila did not use it in his Bible, we may suspect that it had heathen associations. In the other Germanic languages it appears, from the beginning of our records, only as an equivalent of Latin *sanctus* 'holy.' Thus, the semantic connection between *whole* and *holy* has been completely wiped out in English; even in German *heil* 'unharmed, prosperous' and *heilig* 'holy' lie on the border-line between distant semantic connection and mere homonymy of roots.

The Old English adjective *heard* 'hard' underlay two adverbs, *hearde* and *heardlice;* the former survives in its old relation, as *hard,* but the latter, *hardly,* has been isolated in the remotely transferred meaning of 'barely, scarcely,' through loss of intermediate meanings such as 'only with difficulty.'

Isolation may be furthered by the obsolescence of some construction. We find it hard to connect the meaning of *understand* with the meanings of *under* and *stand,* not only because the meaning 'stand close to' or 'stand among,' which must have been central at the time the compound was formed, has been obsolete since prehistoric time, but also because the construction of the compound, preposition plus verb, with stress on the latter, has died out except for traditional forms, which survive as irregularities, such as *undertake, undergo, underlie, overthrow, overcome, overtake, forgive, forget, forbid.* The words *straw* (Old English *strēaw*) and *to strew* (Old English *strewian*) were in prehistoric time morphologically connected; the Primitive Germanic types are *['strawwan] 'a strewing, that strewn,' and *['strawjo:] 'I strew.' At that time *strawberry* (Old English *strēaw-berige*) 'strewn-berry' must have described the strawberry-plant as it lies along the ground; as *straw* became specialized to 'dried stalk, dried stalks,' and the morphologic connection with *strew* disappeared, the prior member of *strawberry* was isolated, with a deviant meaning, as a homonym of *straw*.

Phonetic change may prompt or aid isolation. A clear case of this is *ready*, which has diverged too far from *ride* and *road;* other examples are *holiday* and *holy*, *sorry* and *sore*, *dear* and *dearth*, and especially, with old umlaut (§ 21.7) *whole* and *heal*, *dole* and *deal*. The word *lord* (Old English *hlāford*) was at the time of its formation 'loaf-ward,' doubtless in a sense like 'bread-giver'; *lady* (Old English *hlāfdige*) seems to have been 'bread-shaper.' The word *disease* was formerly 'lack of ease, un-ease'; in the present specialized meaning 'sickness' it is all the better isolated from *dis-* and *ease* through the deviant form of the prefix, with [z] for [s] after unstressed vowel (§ 21.4).

Another contributory factor is the intrusion of analogic new-formations. Usually these overrun the central meaning and leave only some marginal meanings to the old form. Thus, *sloth* 'laziness' was originally the quality-noun of *slow*, just as *truth* is still that of *true*, but the decline of the *-th* derivation of quality-nouns and the rise of *slowness*, formed by the now regular *-ness* derivation, has isolated *sloth*. An Old English compound **hūs-wīf* 'housewife' through various phonetic changes reached a form which survives today only in a transferred meaning as *hussy* ['hozij] 'rude, pert woman.' In the central meaning it was replaced by an analogic new composition of *hūs* and *wīf*. This, in its turn, through phonetic change reached a form *hussif* ['hozef] which survives, though now obsolescent, in the transferred meaning 'sewing-bag,' but has been crowded out, in the central meaning, by a still newer compounding, *housewife* ['haws-ˌwajf]. In medieval German, some adjectives with an umlaut vowel had derivative adverbs without umlaut: *schoene* ['šø:ne] 'beautiful,' but *schone* ['šo:ne] 'beautifully '; *feste* 'firm' but *faste* 'firmly.' In the modern period, these adverbs have been crowded out by regularly formed adverbs, homonymous with the adjective: today *schön* [šø:n] is both 'beautiful' and, as an adverb, 'beautifully,' and *fest* both 'firm, vigorous' and 'firmly, vigorously,' but the old adverbs have survived in remotely marginal uses, *schon* 'already' and 'never fear,' and *fast* 'almost.'

Finally, we may be able to recognize a change in the practical world as a factor in isolation. Thus, the isolation of German *Wand* 'wall' from *winden* 'to wind' is due to the disuse of wattled walls. Latin *penna* 'feather' (> Old French *penne*) was borrowed in Dutch and in English as a designation of the *pen* for writing. In French *plume* [plym] and German *Feder* ['fe:der], the vernacular word for 'feather' is used also for 'pen.' The disuse of the goose-quill pen has isolated these meanings.

24. 6. Paul's explanation of semantic change does not account for the rise of marginal meanings and for the obsolescence of forms in a part of their semantic domain. The same is true of so-called psychological explanations, such as Wundt's, which merely paraphrase the outcome of the change. Wundt defines the central meaning as the *dominant element* of meaning, and shows how the dominant element may shift when a form occurs in new typical contexts. Thus, when *meat* had been heard predominantly in situations where flesh-food was concerned, the dominant element became for more and more speakers, not 'food' but 'flesh-food.' This statement leaves the matter exactly where it was.

The obsolescence which plays a part in many semantic changes, need not present any characteristics other than those of ordinary loss of frequency; what little we know of fluctuations in this direction (Chapter 22) will apply here. The expansion of a form into new meanings, however, is a special case of rise in frequency, and a very difficult one, since, strictly speaking, almost any utterance of a form is prompted by a novel situation, and the degree of novelty is not subject to precise measurement. Older students accepted the rise of marginal meanings without seeking specific factors. Probably they took for granted the particular transferences which had occurred in languages familiar to them (*foot* of a mountain, *neck* of a bottle, and the like, § 9.8). Actually, languages differ in this respect, and it is precisely the spread of a form into a new meaning that concerns us in the study of semantic change.

The shift into a new meaning is intelligible when it merely reproduces a shift in the practical world. A form like *ship* or *hat* or *hose* designates a shifting series of objects because of changes in the practical world. If cattle were used as a medium of exchange, the word *fee* 'cattle' would naturally be used in the meaning 'money,' and if one wrote with a goose-feather, the word for 'feather' would naturally be used of this writing-implement. At this point, however, there has been no shift in the lexical structure of the language. This comes only when a learned loan-word *pen* is distinct from *feather*, or when *fee* on the one hand is no longer used of cattle and, on the other hand, loses ground in the domain of 'money' until it retains only the specialized value of 'sum of money paid for a service or privilege.'

The only type of semantic expansion that is relatively well understood, is what we may call the accidental type: some formal change — sound-change, analogic re-shaping, or borrowing — results in a locution which coincides with some old form of not too remote meaning. Thus, Primitive Germanic *['awzo:] denoted the 'ear' of a person or animal; it appears as Gothic ['awso:], Old Norse *eyra*, Old German *ōra* (> modern Dutch *oor* [o:r]), Old English ['e:are], and is cognate with Latin *auris*, Old Bulgarian [uxo], in the same meaning. Primitive Germanic *['ahuz] denoted the grain of a plant with the husk on it; it appears in Gothic *ahs*, Old Norse *ax*, Old German *ah* and, with an analogic nominative form due to oblique case-forms, Old German *ahir* (> modern Dutch *aar* [a:r]), Old English ['ɛhher] and ['e:ar], and is cognate with Latin *acus* 'husk of grain, chaff.' The loss of [h] and of unstressed vowels in English has made the two forms phonetically alike, and, since the meanings have some resemblance, *ear* of grain has become a marginal (transferred) meaning of *ear* of an animal. Since Old English [we:od] 'weed' and [wɛ:d] 'garment' have coincided through sound-change, the surviving use of the latter, in *widow's weeds*, is now a marginal meaning of the former. Of course, the degree of nearness of the meanings is not subject to precise measurement; the lexicographer or historian who knows the origins will insist on describing such forms as pairs of homonyms. Nevertheless, for many speakers, doubtless, a *corn* on the foot represents merely a marginal meaning of *corn* 'grain.' The latter is a continuation of an old native word; the former a borrowing from Old French *corn* (< Latin *cornū* 'horn,' cognate with English *horn*). In French, *allure* is an abstract noun derived from *aller* 'to walk, to go,' and means 'manner of walking, carriage,' and in a specialized meaning 'good manner of walking, good carriage.' In English we have borrowed this *al-*

lure; since it coincides formally with the verb *to allure* (a loan from Old French *aleurer*), we use it in the meaning 'charm.' It may be that *let* in *let or hindrance* and *a let ball* is for some speakers a queer marginal use of *let* 'permit,' and that even the Elizabethan *let* 'hinder' (§ 22.4) had this value; we have no standard for answering such questions.

Phonetic discrepancies in such cases may be removed by new-formation. Thus, the Scandinavian loan-word *būenn* 'equipped, ready' would give a modern English *[bawn]. This form was phonetically and in meaning so close to the reflex of Old English *bunden,* past participle of *bindan* 'to bind,' (> modern *bound* [bawnd], past participle of *bind*), that a new-formation *bound* [bawnd] replaced it; the addition of [-d] was probably favored by a habit of sandhi. The result is that *bound* in such phrases as *bound for England, bound to see it* figures as a marginal meaning of the past participle *bound.* Both the word *law* and its compound *by-law* are loan-words from Scandinavian. The first member of the latter was Old Norse [by:r] 'manor, town' — witness the older English forms *bir-law, bur-law* — but the re-shaping *by-law* turned it into a marginal use of the preposition and adverb *by.*

Beside the central meaning *please* 'to give pleasure or satisfaction,' we have the marginal meaning 'be willing' in *if you please.* This phrase meant in Middle English 'if it pleases you.' The obsolescence of the use of finite verbs without actors, and of the postponement of the finite verb in clauses, the near-obsolescence of the subjunctive (*if it please you*), and the analogic loss of case-distinction (nominative *ye* : dative-accusative *you*), have left *if you please* as an actor-action clause with *you* as the actor and an anomalous marginal use of *please.* The same factors, acting in phrases of the type *if you like,* seem to have led to a complete turn-about in the meaning of the verb *like,* which used to mean 'suit, please,' e.g. Old English [he: me: 'wel 'li:kaθ] 'he pleases me well, I like him.'

Partial obsolescence of a form may leave a queer marginal meaning. To the examples already given (e.g. *meat, board*) we may add a few where this feature has led to further shifts. The Latin-French loan-word *favor* had formerly in English two well-separated meanings. The more original one, 'kindly attitude, inclination,' with its offshoot, 'kindly action,' is still central; the other, 'cast of countenance,' is in general obsolete, but survives as a marginal meaning in *ill-favored* 'ugly.' In the aphoristic sentence *Kissing goes by favor*, our word had formerly this marginal value (that is, 'one prefers to kiss good-looking people'), but now has the central value ('is a matter of inclination'). Similarly, *prove, proof* had a central meaning 'test' which survives in the aphorism *The proof of the pudding is in the eating;* this was the meaning also in *The exception proves the rule*, but now that *prove, proof* have been shifted to the meaning '(give) conclusive evidence (for),' the latter phrase has become a paradox.

The old Indo-European and Germanic negative adverb *[ne] 'not' has left a trace in words like *no, not, never*, which reflect old phrasal combinations, but has been supplanted in independent use. Its loss in the various Germanic languages was due partly to sound-change and led to some peculiar semantic situations. In Norse it left a trace in a form which, owing to its original phrasal make-up, was not negative: *[ne 'wajt ek hwerr] 'not know I who,' that is, 'I don't know who,' resulted, by phonetic change, in Old Norse ['nøkurr, 'nekkwer] 'someone, anyone.' In other phonetic surroundings, in pre-Norse, *[ne] was entirely lost. Some forms which were habitually used with the negation must have got in this way two opposite meanings: thus, an *['ajnan] 'once' and a *[ne 'ajnan] 'not once, not' must have led to the same phonetic result. Actually, in Old Norse, various such expressions have survived in the negative value: *[ne 'ajnan] gives Old Norse *a* 'not'; *[ne 'ajnato:n] 'not one thing' gives Old Norse *at* 'not'; *[ne 'ajnaz ge] 'not even one' gives Old Norse *einge* 'no one'; *[ne 'ajnato:n ge] 'not even one thing' gives *etke, ekke* 'nothing'; *[ne 'ajwan ge] 'not at any time' gives *eige* 'not'; *[ne 'mannz ge] 'not even a man' gives *mannge* 'nobody.' In German, where *ne* has been replaced by *nicht* [nixt], originally 'not a whit,' the double meanings due to its loss in some phonetic surroundings, still appear in our records. At the end of the Middle Ages we find clauses of exception ('unless . . . ') with a subjunctive verb formed both with and without the adverb *ne, en, n* in apparently the same meaning:

with *ne: ez en mac mih nieman troesten, si en tuo z* 'there may no one console me, unless she do it'

without *ne: nieman kan hie fröude finden, si zergē* 'no one can find joy here, that does not vanish.'

The first example here is reasonable; the second contains a

whimsical use of the subjunctive that owes its existence only to the phonetic disappearance of *ne* in similar contexts. We observe in our examples also a plus-or-minus of *ne, en* in the main clause along with *nieman* 'nobody.' This, too, left an ambiguous type: both an old *dehein* 'any' and an old *ne dehein* 'not any' must have led, in certain phonetic contexts, to *dehein* 'any; not any.' Both these meanings of *dehein* appear in our older texts, as well as a *ne dehein* 'not any'; of the three possibilities, only *dehein* 'not any' (> *kein*) survives in modern standard German.

In French, certain words that are widely used with a verb and the negative adverb, have also a negative meaning when used without a verb. Thus, *pas* [pɑ] 'step' (< Latin *passum*) has the two uses in *je ne vais pas* [žə n ve pɑ] 'I don't go' (originally 'I go not a step') and in *pas mal* [pɑ mal] 'not badly, not so bad'; *personne* [pɛrsɔn] 'person' (< Latin *persōnam*) appears also in *je ne vois personne* [žə n vwɑ pɛrsɔn] 'I don't see anyone,' and in *personne* 'nobody'; *rien* [rjɛⁿ] (< Latin *rem* 'a thing') has lost ordinary noun values, and occurs in *je ne vois rien* [žə n vwɑ rjɛⁿ] 'I don't see anything' and in *rien* 'nothing.' This development has been described as *contagion* or *condensation*. It can be better understood if we suppose that, during the medieval period of high stress and vowel-weakening, French *ne* (< Latin *nōn*) was phonetically lost in certain contexts.

The reverse of this process is a loss of content. Latin forms like *cantō* 'I-sing,' *cantās* 'thou-singest,' *cantat* 'he-she-it-sings' (to which more specific mention of an actor was added by cross-reference, § 12.9), appear in French as *chante(s)* [šɑⁿt] 'sing(s),' used only with an actor, or, rarely, in completive speech, just like an English verb-form. This loss of the pronominal actor-meaning is evidently the result of an analogic change which replaced the type *cantat* 'he-sings' by a type *ille cantat* 'that-one sings' (> French *il chante* [i šɑⁿt] 'he sings'). This latter change has been explained, in the case of French, as a result of the homonymy, due to sound-change, of the various Latin inflections; however, in English and in German, forms like *sing, singest, singeth* have come to demand an actor, although there is no homonymy.

24. 7. Special factors like these will account for only a small proportion of the wealth of marginal meanings that faces us in every language. It remained for a modern scholar, H. Sperber, to point out that extensions of meaning are by no means to be taken for granted, and that the first step toward understanding them must be to find, if we can, the context in which the new meaning first appears. This will always be difficult, because it demands that the student observe very closely the meanings of the form in all older occurrences; it is especially hard to make sure of negative features, such as the absence, up to a certain date, of a certain shade of meaning. In most cases, moreover, the attempt is bound to fail because the records do not contain the critical locutions. Nevertheless, Sperber succeeded in finding the critical context for the extension of older German *kopf* 'cup, bowl, pot' to the meaning 'head': the new value first appears in our texts at the end of the Middle Ages, in battle-scenes, where the matter is one of smashing someone's head. An English example of the same sort is the extension of *bede* 'prayer' to the present meaning of *bead:* the extension is known to have occurred in connection with the use of the rosary, where one *counted one's bedes* (originally 'prayers,' then 'little spheres on a string').

In the ordinary case of semantic extension we must look for a context in which our form can be applied to both the old and the new meanings. The obsolescence of other contexts — in our examples, of German *kopf* applied to earthen vessels and of *bead* 'prayer' — will then leave the new value as an unambiguous central meaning. The reason for the extension, however, is another matter. We still ask why the medieval German poet should speak of a warrior smashing his enemy's 'bowl' or 'pot,' or the pious Englishman of counting 'prayers' rather than 'pearls.' Sperber supposes that intense emotion (that is, a powerful stimulus) leads to such transferences. Strong stimuli lead to the favoring of novel speech-forms at the cost of forms that have been heard in indifferent contexts (§ 22.8), but this general tendency cannot account for the rise of specific marginal meanings.

The methodical error which has held back this phase of our work, is our habit of putting the question in non-linguistic terms — in terms of meaning and not of form. When we say that the word *meat* has changed from the meaning 'food' to the meaning 'edible flesh,' we are merely stating the practical result of a linguistic process. In situations where both words were applicable, the word *meat* was favored at the cost of the word *flesh*, and, on the model of such cases, it came to be used also in situations where formerly the word *flesh* alone would have been applicable. In the same way, words like *food* and *dish* encroached upon the word *meat*. This second displacement may have resulted from the first because the ambiguity of *meat* 'food' and *meat* 'flesh-food' was troublesome in practical kitchen life. We may some day find out why *flesh* was disfavored in culinary situations.

Once we put the question into these terms, we see that a normal extension of meaning is the same process as an extension of grammatical function. When *meat*, for whatever reason, was being favored, and *flesh*, for whatever reason, was on the decline, there must have occurred proportional extensions of the pattern (§ 23.2):

leave the bones and bring the flesh : leave the bones and bring the meat
= *give us bread and flesh* : *x,*

resulting in a new phrase, *give us bread and meat*. The forms at the left, containing the word *flesh*, must have borne an unfavorable connotation which was absent from the forms at the right, with the word *meat*.

A semantic change, then, is a complex process. It involves favorings and disfavorings, and, as its crucial point, the extension of a favored form into practical applications which hitherto belonged to the disfavored form. This crucial extension can be observed only if we succeed in finding the locutions in which it was made, and in finding or reconstructing the model locutions in which both forms were used alternatively. Our records give us only an infinitesimal fraction of what was spoken, and this fraction consists nearly always of elevated speech, which avoids new locutions. In Sperber's example of German *kopf* 'pot' > 'head,' we know the context (head-smashing in battle) where the innovation was made; there remains the problem of finding the model. One might surmise, for instance, that the innovation was made by Germans who, from warfare and chivalry, were familiar with the Romance speaker's use of the type of Latin *testam, testum* 'potsherd, pot' > 'head,' which in French and Italian has crowded the type of Latin *caput* 'head' out of all but transferred meanings. We confront this complex problem in all semantic changes except the fortuitous ones like English *let, bound, ear*, which are due to some phonetic accident.

We can best understand the shift in modern cases, where the connotative values and the practical background are known. During the last generations the growth of cities has led to a lively trade in city lots and houses, "development" of outlying land into residence districts, and speculative building. At the same time, the prestige of the persons who live by these things has risen to the point where styles pass from them to the working man, who in language is imitative but has the force of numbers, and to the "educated" person, who enjoys a fictitious leadership. Now, the speculative builder has learned to appeal to every weakness, including the sentimentality, of the prospective buyer; he uses the speech-forms whose content will turn the hearer in the right direction. In many locutions *house* is the colorless, and *home* the sentimental word:

COLORLESS	SENTIMENTAL, PLEASANT CONNOTATION
Smith has a lovely house	: *Smith has a lovely home*
= *a lovely new eight-room house*	: *x.*

Thus, the salesman comes to use the word *home* of an empty shell that has never been inhabited, and the rest of us copy his style. It may be too, that, the word *house*, especially in the substandard sphere of the salesman, suffers from some ambiguity, on account of meanings such as 'commercial establishment' (*a reliable house*), 'hotel,' 'brothel,' 'audience' (*a half-empty house*).

The learned word *transpire* in its Latin-French use, meant 'to breathe or ooze (Latin *spīrāre*) through (Latin *trans*),' and thus, as in French *transpirer* [tra^{n}spire], 'to exhale, exude, perspire, ooze out,' and with a transfer of meaning, 'to become public (of news).' The old usage would be to say *of what really happened, very little transpired*. The ambiguous case is *it transpired that the president was out of town*. On the pattern

COLORLESS	ELEGANT-LEARNED
it happened that the president was out of town	: *it transpired that the president . . .*
= *what happened, remains a secret*	: *x,*

we now get the formerly impossible type *what transpired, remains a secret*, where *transpire* figures as an elegant synonym of *happen, occur*.

This parallelism of transference accounts for successive encroachments in a semantic sphere. As soon as some form like *terribly*, which means 'in a way that arouses fear,' has been extended into use as a stronger synonym of *very*, the road is clear for a similar transference of words like *awfully, frightfully, horribly*.

Even when the birth of the marginal meaning is recent, we shall not always be able to trace its origin. It may have arisen under some very special practical circumstances that are unknown to us, or, what comes to the same thing, it may be the successful coinage of some one speaker and owe its shape to his individual circumstances. One suspects that the queer slang use, a quarter of a century ago, of *twenty-three* for 'get out' arose in a chance situation of sportsmanship, gambling, crime, or some other rakish environment; within this sphere, it may have started as some one person's witticism. Since every practical situation is in reality unprecedented, the apt response of a good speaker may always border on semantic innovation. Both the wit and the poet often cross this border, and their innovations may become popular. To a large extent, however, these personal innovations are modeled on current forms. Poetic metaphor is largely an outgrowth of the transferred uses of ordinary speech. To quote a very well chosen example, when Wordsworth wrote

> *The gods approve*
> *The depth and not the tumult of the soul,*

he was only continuing the metaphoric use current in such expressions as *deep, ruffled,* or *stormy* feelings. By making a new transference on the model of these old ones, he revived the "picture." The picturesque saying that "language is a book of faded metaphors" is the reverse of the truth, for poetry is rather a blazoned book of language.

CHAPTER 25

CULTURAL BORROWING

25. 1. The child who is learning to speak may get most of his habits from some one person — say, his mother — but he will also hear other speakers and take some of his habits from them. Even the basic vocabulary and the grammatical features which he acquires at this time do not reproduce exactly the habits of any one older person. Throughout his life, the speaker continues to adopt features from his fellows, and these adoptions, though less fundamental, are very copious and come from all manner of sources. Some of them are incidents in large-scale levelings that affect the whole community.

Accordingly, the comparatist or historian, if he could discount all analogic-semantic changes, should still expect to find the phonetic correlations disturbed by the transfer of speech-forms from person to person or from group to group. The actual tradition, could we trace it, of the various features in the language of any one speaker, runs back through entirely diverse persons and communities. The historian can recognize this in cases of formal discrepancy. He sees, for instance, that forms which in older English contained a short [a] in certain phonetic surroundings, appear in Central-Western American English as [ɛ] in *man, hat, bath, gather, lather,* etc. This represents the basic tradition, even though the individual forms may have had very different adventures. Accordingly, when the speaker uses an [a] for the same old phoneme in the word *father* and in the more elegant variant of the word *rather*, the historian infers that somewhere along the line of transmission these forms must have come in from speakers of a different habit. The adoption of features which differ from those of the main tradition, is *linguistic borrowing*.

Within the sphere of borrowing, we distinguish between *dialect borrowing*, where the borrowed features come from within the same speech-area (as, *father, rather* with [a] in an [ɛ]-dialect), and *cultural borrowing*, where the borrowed features come from a different language. This distinction cannot always be carried out,

444

since there is no absolute distinction to be made between dialect boundaries and language boundaries (§ 3.8). In this chapter and the next we shall speak of borrowing from foreign languages, and in Chapter 27 of borrowing between the dialects of an area.

25. 2. Every speech-community learns from its neighbors. Objects, both natural and manufactured, pass from one community to the other, and so do patterns of action, such as technical procedures, warlike practices, religious rites, or fashions of individual conduct. This spread of things and habits is studied by ethnologists, who call it *cultural diffusion*. One can plot on a map the diffusion of a cultural feature, such as, say, the growing of maize in pre-Columbian North America. In general, the areas of diffusion of different cultural features do not coincide. Along with objects or practices, the speech-forms by which these are named often pass from people to people. For instance, an English-speaker, either bilingual or with some foreign knowledge of French, introducing a French article to his countrymen, will designate it by its French name, as: *rouge* [ru:ž], jabot [žabo], *chauffeur* [šofœ:r], *garage* [gara:ž], *camouflage* [kamufla:ž]. In most instances we cannot ascertain the moment of actual innovation: the speaker himself probably could not be sure whether he had ever before heard or used the foreign form in his native language. Several speakers may independently, none having heard the others, make the same introduction. In theory, of course, we must distinguish between this actual introduction and the ensuing repetitions by the same and other speakers; the new form embarks upon a career of fluctuation in frequency. The historian finds, however, that some of the later adventures of the borrowed form are due to its foreign character.

If the original introducer or a later user has good command of the foreign language, he may speak the foreign form in foreign phonetics, even in its native context. More often, however, he will save himself a twofold muscular adjustment, replacing some of the foreign speech-movements by speech-movements of the native language; for example, in an English sentence he will speak his French *rouge* with an English [r] in place of the French uvular trill, and an English [uw] in place of the French tense, non-diphthongal [u:]. This *phonetic substitution* will vary in degree for different speakers and on different occasions; speakers who have not learned to produce French phonemes are certain to make it.

The historian will class it as a type of adaptation (§ 23.8), in which the foreign form is altered to meet the fundamental phonetic habits of the language.

In phonetic substitution the speakers replace the foreign sounds by the phonemes of their language. In so far as the phonetic systems are parallel, this involves only the ignoring of minor differences. Thus, we replace the various [r] and [l] types of European languages by our [r] and [l], the French unaspirated stops by our aspirated, the French postdentals by our gingivals (as, say, in *tête-à-tête*), and long vowels by our diphthongal types [ij, uw, ej, ow]. When the phonetic systems are less alike, the substitutions may seem surprising to members of the lending community. Thus, the older Menomini speakers, who knew no English, reproduced *automobile* as [atamo:pen]: Menomini has only one, unvoiced series of stops, and no lateral or trill. Tagalog, having no [f]-type, replaced Spanish [f] by [p], as in [pi'jesta] from Spanish *fiesta* ['fjesta] 'celebration.'

In the case of ancient speech, phonetic substitutions may inform us as to the acoustic relation between the phonemes of two languages. The Latin name of the Greek nation, *Graeci* ['grajki:], later ['gre:ki:], was borrowed, early in the Christian era, into the Germanic languages, and appears here with an initial [k], as in Gothic *krēkōs*, Old English *crēcas*, Old High German *kriahha* 'Greeks.' Evidently the Latin voiced stop [g] was acoustically closer to the Germanic unvoiced stop [k] than to the Germanic phoneme which we transcribe as [g], say, in Old English *grēne* 'green'; presumably, at the time the old word for 'Greek' was borrowed, this Germanic [g] was a spirant. Latin [w] at this early time was reproduced by Germanic [w], as in Latin *vinum* ['wi:-num] 'wine' > Old English *win* [w:in], and similarly in Gothic and in German. In the early Middle Ages, the Latin [w] changed to a voiced spirant of the type [v]; accordingly, this Latin phoneme in loan-words of the missionary period, from the seventh century on, was no longer reproduced by Germanic [w], but by Germanic [f]. Thus, Latin *versus* ['versus] 'verse,' from older ['wersus], appears in Old English and in Old High German as *fers*. A third stage appears in modern time: German, having changed its old [w] to a spirant type, and English, having in another way acquired a phoneme of the [v]-type, now give a fairly accurate reproduction of Latin [v], as in French *vision* [vizjo^n] (from Latin *visionem* {wi:-

ʂi'o:nem]) > German [vi'zjo:n], English ['vižn̩].[1] In Bohemian, where every word is stressed on the first syllable, this accentuation is given to foreign words, such as ['akvarijum] 'aquarium,' ['konstelatse] 'constellation,' ['šofe:r] 'chauffeur.'

25. 3. If the borrowing people is relatively familiar with the lending language, or if the borrowed words are fairly numerous, then foreign sounds which are acoustically remote from any native phoneme, may be preserved in a more or less accurate rendering that violates the native phonetic system. In this respect, there are many local and social differences. Thus, the French nasalized vowels are very widely kept in English, even by people who do not speak French, as in French *salon* [salo^n] > English [sa'lo^n, 'sɛlo^n], French *rendez-vous* [rɑ^{n}de-vu] > English ['ra^{n}devuw], French *enveloppe* [ɑ^{n}v(ə)lɔp] > English *envelope* ['a^{n}velowp]. Some speakers, however, substitute vowel plus [ŋ], as in ['raŋdevuw], and others vowel plus [n], as in ['randevuw]. The Germans do the like; the Swedes always replace French nasalized vowels by vowel plus [ŋ]. In some forms English does not reproduce the nasalized vowel, as in French *chiffon* [šifo^n] > English ['šifɑn], and in the more urbane variant ['envlowp] *envelope*.

This adoption of foreign sounds may become quite fixed. In English the cluster [sk] is due to Scandinavian loan-words; the [sk] of Old English had changed in later Old English time to [š], as in Old English [sko:h] > modern *shoe*. This Scandinavian cluster occurs not only in borrowed words, such as *sky*, *skin*, *skirt* (beside native *shirt*), but also in new-formations, such as *scatter*, *scrawl*, *scream;* it has become an integral part of the phonetic system. The initials [v-, z-, ǰ-] came into English in French words, such as *very*, *zest*, *just;* all three are quite at home now, and the last two occur in new-formations, such as *zip*, *zoom*, *jab*, *jounce*. Thus, the phonetic system has been permanently altered by borrowing.

Where phonetic substitution has occurred, increased familiarity with the foreign language may lead to a newer, more correct version of a foreign form. Thus, the Menomini who knows a little English no longer says [atamo:pen] 'automobile,' but [atamo:pil], and the modern Tagalog speaker says [fi'jesta] 'celebration.' The old form of the borrowing may survive, however, in

---

[1] The discrepancies in this and similar examples are due to changes which the various languages have made since the time of borrowing.

special uses, such as derivatives: thus, even the modern Tagalog speaker says [kapijes'ta:han] 'day of a festival,' where the prefix, suffix, and accentuation are native, and in English the derived verb is always *envelope* [en'velop], with vowel plus [n] in the first syllable.

A similar adjustment may take place, at a longer interval of time, if the borrowing language has developed a new phoneme that does better justice to the foreign form. Thus, English *Greek*, German *Grieche* ['gri:xe] embody corrections made after these languages had developed a voiced stop [g]. Similarly, English *verse* is a revision of the old *fers;* German has stuck to the old form *Vers* [fe:rs]. In revisions of this sort, especially where literary terms are concerned, learned persons may exert some influence: thus, the replacement of the older form with [kr-] by the later form *Greek* was surely due to educated people.

For the most part, however, the influence of literate persons works also against a faithful rendering. In the first place, the literate person who knows nothing of the foreign language but has seen the written notation of the foreign form, interprets the latter in terms of native orthography. Thus, French forms like *puce, ruche, menu, Victor Hugo* [pys, ryš, məny, viktɔr ygo] would doubtless be reproduced in English with [ij] for French [y], were it not for the spelling with the letter *u*, which leads the literate English-speaker to pronounce [(j)uw], as in [pjuws, ruwš ,'menjuw, 'viktr̩ 'hjuwgow]. Spanish *Mexico*, older ['mešiko], modern ['mexiko], has [ks] in English because of literate people's interpretation of the symbol *x;* similarly, the older English rendering of *Don Quixote* (Spanish [don ki'xote]) is [dɑn 'kwiksɑt]. The latter has been revised, certainly under learned influence, to [dɑn ki'howtij], but the older version has been retained in the English derivative *quixotic* [kwik'sɑtik]. We reproduce initial [ts] in *tsar* or *tse-tse-fly*, but not in German forms like *Zeitgeist* ['tsajt-ˌgajst] > English ['zajtgajst], or *Zwieback* ['tsvi:bak] > English ['zwijbak], where the letter *z* suggests only [z]. Even where there is no phonetic difficulty, as in German *Dachshund* ['daks-ˌhunt], *Wagner* ['va:gner], *Wiener* ['vi:ner], the spelling leads to such reproductions as ['dɛš-ˌhawnd, 'wɛgnr̩, 'wijnr̩, 'wijnij].

This relation is further complicated by literate persons who know something of the foreign pronunciation and orthography. A speaker who knows the spelling *jabot* and the English form ['žɛbow] (for French [žabo]), may revise *tête-à-tête* ['tejteₜtejt] (from French [tɛ:t a tɛ:t]) to a *hyper-foreign* ['tejtetej], without the final [t]. The literate person who knows *parlez-vous français?* ['parlej 'vuw 'fraⁿsej?] (for French [parle vu fraⁿsɛ?]), may decide to join the *Alliance Française* [ali'jaⁿs 'fraⁿsej], although the Frenchman here has a final [z]: [aljaⁿs fraⁿsɛ:z].

25. 4. The borrowed word, aside from foreign sounds, often violates the phonetic pattern. Thus, a German initial [ts], even aside from the orthography, may be troublesome to many English-speakers. Generally, adaptation of the phonetic pattern takes place together with adaptation of morphologic structure. Thus, the final [ž] of *garage*, which violates the English pattern, is replaced by [j] and the accent shifted in the form ['garej], which conforms to the suffixal type of *cabbage, baggage, image*. Likewise, beside *chauffeur* [šow'fejr] with normal phonetic substitution, we have a more fully adapted ['šowfr̩].

The description of a language will thus recognize a layer of *foreign forms*, such as *salon* [sa'loⁿ], *rouge* [ruwž], *garage* [ga'raž], which deviate from the normal phonetics. In some languages a descriptive analysis will recognize, further, a layer of *semi-foreign* forms, which have been adapted up to a conventional point, but retain certain conventionally determined foreign characteristics. The foreign-learned vocabulary of English is of this type. Thus, a French *préciosité* [presiɔsite] was anglicized only to the point where it became *preciosity* [pre'sjɑsitij, pre'š(j)ɑsitij]; the unstressed prefix, the suffix *-ity* (with presuffixal stress), and the formally and semantically peculiar relation to *precious* ['prɛšos], do not lead to further adaptation. The English-speakers (a minority) who use the word at all, include it in a set of habits that deviates from the structure of our commonest words. This secondary layer of speech-habit owes its existence, historically, to old waves of borrowing, which will concern us in the sequel.

When the adaptation is completed, as in *chair* (anciently borrowed from Old French) or in ['šowfr̩] *chauffeur*, the foreign origin of the form has disappeared, and neither the speaker nor, consequently, an honest description can distinguish it from native forms. The historian, however, who is concerned with origins, will class it as a *loan-form*. Thus, *chair* and ['šowfr̩] *chauffeur*, in the present state of the language, are ordinary English words, but the historian, taking the past into view, classes them as *loan-words*.

At all stages, the assimilation of foreign words presents many problems. The phenomena of the type of phonetic dissimilation (§ 21.10), as in French *marbre* > English *marble*, are fairly frequent. We probably have to reckon here with highly variable factors, including adaptations based on the habits of individual speakers. Both during the progress toward the status of a loan-form, and after this status has been reached, the structure is likely to be unintelligible. The languages and, within a language, the groups of speakers that are familiar with foreign and semi-foreign forms, will tolerate this state of affairs; in other cases, a further adaptation, in the sense of popular etymology, may render the form structurally or lexically more intelligible, as in **groze* > **groze-berry* > *gooseberry; asparagus* > *sparrow-grass; crevise* > *crayfish* > *crawfish* (§ 23.8). The classical instance is the replacement, in medieval German, of Old French *arbaleste* 'cross-bow' by an adaptive new-formation *Armbrust* ['arm-₁brust], literally 'arm-breast.'

The borrowed form is subject to the phonetic changes that occur after its adoption. This factor is distinct from phonetic substitution and other adaptive changes. Thus, we must suppose that an Old French form like *vision* [vi'zjo:n] (reflecting a Latin [wi:si'o:nem]) was taken into medieval English with some slight amount of no longer traceable phonetic substitution, and that it gave rise to a successful adaptive variant, with stress on the first syllable. The further changes, however, which led to the modern English ['vižn̩] are merely the phonetic changes which have occurred in English since the time when this word was borrowed. These two factors, however, cannot always be distinguished. After a number of borrowings, there arose a fairly regular relation of adapted English forms to French originals; a new borrowing from French could be adapted on the model of the older loans. Thus, the discrepancy between French *préciosité* [presiɔsite] and English *preciosity* [pre'sjɑsitij, pre'šjɑsitij] is not due to sound-changes that occurred in English after the time of borrowing, but merely reflects a usual relation between French and English types — a relation which has set up in the English-speakers who know French a habit of adapting forms along certain lines.

25. 5. Where we can allow for this adaptive factor, the phonetic development of borrowed forms often shows us the phonetic form at the time of borrowing and accordingly the approximate date of various sound-changes. The name of *Caesar* appears in Greek in a spelling (with the letters *k, a, i*) which for earlier time we can interpret as ['kajsar] and for later as ['kɛːsar], and it appears in a similar spelling in Gothic, where the value of the digraph *ai* is uncertain and the form may have been, accordingly, either ['kajsar] or ['kɛːsar]. These forms assure us that at the time of these borrowings, Latin still spoke an initial [k] and had not yet gone far in the direction of modern forms like Italian *cesare* ['čeːzare] (§ 21.5). In West Germanic, the foreign word appears as Old High German *keisur*, Old Saxon *kēsur*, Old English *casere*, this last representing presumably something like ['kaːseːre]. These forms confirm the Latin [k]-pronunciation; moreover, they guarantee a Latin diphthong of the type [aj] for the first syllable, since the correspondence of southern German *ei*, northern [eː], and English [aː] is the ordinary reflex of a Primitive Germanic diphthong, as in *['stajnaz] 'stone' > Old High German *stein*, Old Saxon [steːn], Old English [staːn]. Thus, for the time of the early contact of Rome with Germanic peoples, we are assured of [kaj-] as the value of the first syllable of Latin *caesar*. On the other hand, the West Germanic forms show us that the various changes of the diphthong [aj], in Old Saxon to [eː] and in Old English to [aː] occurred after the early contact with the Romans. The vowel of the second syllable, and the addition of a third syllable in Old English, are surely due to some kind of an adaptation; the English form, especially, suggests that the Roman word was taken up as though it were *[kaj'soːrius] > pre-English *['kajsoːrjaz]. The word was borrowed from a Germanic language, doubtless from Gothic, by the Slavs; it appears in Old Bulgarian as [tseːsarĭ]. Now, in pre-Slavic time, as we know from the correspondences of native words, [aj] was monophthongized to [eː], and then a [k] before such an [eː] changed to [ts]. Thus, Primitive Indo-European *[kʷojnaː] 'penalty,' Avestan [kaenaː], Greek [poj'neː] appears in Old Bulgarian as [tseːna] 'price.' The Slavic borrowing, accordingly, in spite of its actual deviation, confirms our reconstruction of the old Germanic form, and, in addition to this, enables us to date the pre-Slavic changes of [kaj] to [tseː] after the time of early borrowing from Germanic, which, history tells us, occurred from round 250 to round 450 A.D. Moreover, the second and third syllables of the Slavic form show the same adaptation as the Old

English, to a Germanic type *['kajso:rjaz]; we may conclude that this adapted form existed also among the Goths, although our Gothic Bible, representing a more learned stratum of speech, has the correctly Latin *kaisar*.

Latin *strāta* (*via*) 'paved road' appears in Old Saxon as ['stra:ta], in Old High German as ['stra:ssa], and in Old English as [strɛ:t]. We infer that this term, like *caesar*, was borrowed before the emigration of the English. The correspondence of German [a:] English [ɛ]: reflects, in native words, a Primitive Germanic [e:], as in *['de:diz] 'deed,' Gothic [ga-'de:θs], Old Saxon [da:d], Old High German [ta:t], Old English [dɛ:d]; accordingly we conclude that at the time when Latin *strāta* was borrowed, West Germanic speakers had already made the change from [e:] to [a:], since they used this vowel-phoneme to reproduce the Latin [a:]. On the other hand, the Anglo-Frisian change of this [a:] toward a front vowel, Old English [ɛ:], must be later than the borrowing of the word *street;* this is confirmed by the Old Frisian form (of much later documentation, to be sure), namely *strete.* The medial [t] of the Germanic words shows us that, at the time of borrowing, Latin still said ['stra:ta] and not yet ['strada] (Italian *strada*). This contrasts with later borrowings, such as Old High German ['si:da] 'silk,' ['kri:da] 'chalk,' which have [d] in accordance with later Latin pronunciation ['se:da, 'kre:da] from earlier Latin ['se:ta, 'kre:ta] (§ 21.4). Finally, the [ss] of the High German form shows us that the South-German shift of Germanic medial [t] to affricate and sibilant types (§ 19.8) occurred after the adoption of the Latin *strāta.* In the same way, Latin ['te:gula] 'tile' appears in Old English as ['ti:gol] (whence the modern *tile*), but in Old High German as ['tsiagal] (whence modern German *Ziegel* ['tsi:gel]): the borrowing occurred before the South-German consonant-shift, and this is the case with a whole series of borrowings in the sphere of useful objects and techniques. In contrast with this, Latin words in the literary and scientific domains, which were borrowed presumably in the missionary period, from the seventh century onward, came too late for the South-German consonant-shift: Latin *templum* 'temple' appears in Old High German as ['tempal], Latin *tincta* 'colored stuff, ink' as ['tinkta], and Latin *tēgula* was borrowed over again as Old High German ['tegal] 'pot, retort' (> modern German *Tiegel* ['ti:gel]). The same re-borrowing of this last word appears in Old English ['tijele]; but here we have no striking sound-change to distinguish the two chronological layers of borrowing.

The South-German change of [t] to affricate and sibilant types shows us, in fact, a remarkable instance of dating by means of borrowed forms. A Primitive Germanic type *['moːtoː] is represented by the Gothic word ['moːta] which translates the Greek words for 'tax' and for 'toll-station' (e.g. in *Romans* 13, 7 and *Matthew* 9, 9–10); there is also a derivative ['moːtaːriːs] 'tax-gatherer, publican.' The Old English cognate [moːt] occurs once, in the meaning 'tribute money' (*Matthew* 22, 19); the Middle High German ['muosse] 'miller's fee' shows us the regular High German shift of [t] to a sibilant and an equally regular shift of [oː] to [uo]. Now, in the southeastern part of the German area we find also an Old High German ['muːta] 'toll' (> modern *Maut*) and the place-name ['muːtaːrun] (literally, 'at the toll-takers") of a town on the Danube (> modern *Mautern*). These forms not only lack the shift of [t] but also have an altogether unparalleled [uː] in place of Germanic [oː]. We have reason to believe that Gothic [oː] was close to [uː] and in later time perhaps coincided with it. History tells us that in the first half of the sixth century, Theodoric the Great, the Gothic emperor of Italy, extended his rule to the Danube. We conclude that the German word is a borrowing from Gothic, and, accordingly, that at the time of borrowing, Primitive Germanic [t] in Bavarian German had already changed toward a sibilant: the [t] of the Gothic word was reproduced by the German reflex of Primitive Germanic [d], as in Old High German [hluːt] 'loud' (> modern *laut*) from Primitive Germanic *['hluː-daz]; compare Old English [hluːd]. The spread of the Gothic ['moːta] or rather *['muːta] is confirmed by the borrowing into Primitive Slavic *['myto, 'mytarɪ], e.g. Old Bulgarian [myto] 'pay, gift,' [mytarɪ] 'publican.'

25. 6. Grammatically, the borrowed form is subjected to the system of the borrowing language, both as to syntax (*some rouge, this rouge*) and as to the indispensable inflections (*garages*) and the fully current, "living" constructions of composition (*rouge-pot*) and word-formation (*to rouge; she is rouging her face*). Less often, a simultaneous borrowing of several foreign forms saves this adaptation; thus, from Russian we get not only *bolshevik* but also the Russian plural *bolsheviki*, which we use alongside the English plural-derivation *bolsheviks*. On the other hand, native grammatical constructions which occur, at the time of borrowing, only in a few traditional forms, will scarcely be extended to cover the foreign word. After complete adaptation, the loan-word is subject to the same analogies as any similar native word. Thus, from the completely nativized ['šowfṛ] *chauffeur*, we have the back-formation *to chauffe* [šowf], as in *I had to chauffe my mother around all day.*

When many forms are borrowed from one language, the foreign forms may exhibit their own grammatical relations. Thus, the Latin-French semi-learned vocabulary of English has its own morphologic system (§ 9.9). The analogies of this system may lead to new-formations. Thus, *mutinous, mutiny, mutineer* are derived, in English, according to Latin-French morphology, from an old *mutine*, a loan from French *mutin;* French has not these derivatives. Similarly, *due* is a loan from French, but *duty, duteous, dutiable* (and, with a native English suffix, *dutiful*) probably had no French source, but were formed, with French-borrowed suffixes, in English. The back-formation of pseudo-French verbs in *-ate* (§ 23.5) is a case in point.

When an affix occurs in enough foreign words, it may be extended to new-formations with native material. Thus, the Latin-French suffix *-ible, -able*, as in *agreeable, excusable, variable*, has been extended to forms like *bearable, eatable, drinkable*, where the underlying verb is native. Other examples of French suffixes with native English underlying forms are *breakage, hindrance, murderous, bakery*. In Latin, nouns for 'a man occupied with such-and-such things' were derived from other nouns by means of a suffix *-āriu-*, as *monētārius* 'coiner; money-changer' from *monēta* 'mint; coin'; *gemmārius* 'jeweler' from *gemma* 'jewel'; *telōnārius* 'tax-gatherer, publican' from *telōnium* 'toll-house.' Many of these were borrowed into the old Germanic languages; thus, in Old English we have *myntere, tolnere*, and in Old High German *gimmāri*. Already in our earliest records, however, we find this Latin suffix extended to native Germanic underlying nouns. Latin *lāna* 'wool' : *lānārius* 'wool-carder' is matched in Gothic by *wulla* 'wool' : *wullareis* ['wulla:ri:s] 'wool-carder'; similarly, *bōka* 'book' : *bōkāreis* 'scribe,' *mōta* 'toll' : *mōtareis* 'toll-gatherer,' or, in Old English, [wɛjn] 'wagon' : ['wɛjnere] 'wagoner.' Cases like Old English [re:af] 'spoils, booty' : ['re:avere] 'robber,' where there was a morphologically related verb, ['re:avian] 'to despoil, rob,' led to new-formations on the model ['re:avian: 're:avere] even in cases where there was no underlying noun, such as ['rɛ:dan] 'to read' : ['rɛ:dere] 'reader' or ['wri:tan] 'to write' : ['wri:tere] 'writer.' Thus arose our suffix -er 'agent,' which appears in all the Germanic languages. Quite similarly, at a much later time, the same suffix in Spanish pairs like banco ['banko] 'bank' : banquero [ban'kero] 'banker,' was added to native words in Tagalog, as ['si:paʔ] 'football' : [si'pe:ro] 'football-player,' beside the native derivation [ma:ni'ni:paʔ] 'football-player.'

If many loans have been made from some one language, the foreign structure may even attract native words in the way of adaptation. In some German dialects, including the standard language, we find native words assimilated to Latin-French accentuation: Old High German ['forhana] 'brook-trout,' ['holuntar] 'elder, lilac,' ['wexxolter] 'juniper' are represented in modern standard German by Forelle [fo'rele], Holunder [ho'lunder], Wacholder [va'xolder].

25. 7. The speakers who introduce foreign things may call them by the native name of some related object. In adopting Christianity, the Germanic peoples kept some of the heathen religious terms: god, heaven, hell were merely transferred to the new religion. Needless to say, the leveling to which these terms owe their uniform selection in various Germanic languages, is only another instance of borrowing. The pagan term Easter is used in English and German; Dutch and Scandinavian adopted the Hebrew-Greek-Latin term pascha (Danish paaske, etc.).

If there is no closely equivalent native term, one may yet describe the foreign object in native words. Thus the Greek-Latin technical term baptize was not borrowed but paraphrased in older Germanic: Gothic said daupjan and (perhaps under Gothic influence) German taufen 'to dip, to duck'; Old English said ['full-jan], apparently from *['full-wi:hjan] 'to make fully sacred'; Old Norse said ['ski:rja] 'to make bright or pure.' This involves a semantic extension of the native term. American Indian languages resort to descriptive forms more often than to borrowing. Thus, they render whiskey as 'fire-water,' or railroad as 'fire-wagon.' Menomini uses [ri:tewɛw] 'he reads,' from English read, less often than the native description [wa:pahtam], literally 'he looks at it.' For electricity the Menomini says 'his glance' (meaning the Thunderer's) and telephoning is rendered as 'little-wire speech' rather than by [tɛlɛfoːnewɛw] 'he telephones'; a compound 'rubber-wagon' is commoner than the borrowed [atamoːpen]. Tools and kitchen-utensils are designated by native descriptive terms.

If the foreign term itself is descriptive, the borrower may re-produce the description; this occurs especially in the abstract domain. Many of our abstract technical terms are merely transla-tions of Latin and Greek descriptive terms. Thus, Greek [sun-'ejdeːsis] 'joint knowledge, consciousness, conscience' is a deriva-tive of the verb [ej'denaj] 'to know' with the preposition [sun] 'with.' The Romans translated this philosophical term by *con-scientia*, a compound of *scientia* 'knowledge' and *con-* 'with.' The Germanic languages, in turn, reproduced this. In Gothic ['miθ-wissiː] 'conscience' the first member means 'with' and the second is an abstract noun derived from the verb 'to know,' on the Greek model. In Old English [je-'wit] and Old High German [gi-'wissida] the prefix had the old meaning 'with'; in North-German and Scandinaviar. forms, such as Old Norse ['sam-vit], the prefix is the regular replacer of an old [ga-]. Finally, the Slavic languages translate the term by 'with' and 'knowledge,' as in Russian ['so-*vest*] 'conscience.' This process, called *loan-translation*, in-volves a semantic change: the native terms or the components which are united to create native terms, evidently undergo an extension of meaning. The more literate and elevated style in all the languages of Europe is full of semantic extensions of this sort, chiefly on ancient Greek models, with Latin, and often also French or German, as intermediaries. The Stoic philosophers viewed all deeper emotion as morbid and applied to it the term ['pathos] 'suffering, disease,' abstract noun of the verb ['paskhoː] 'I suffer' (aorist tense ['epathon] 'I suffered'). The Romans translated this by *passiō* 'suffering,' abstract of *patior* 'I suffer,' and it is in this meaning that we ordinarily use the borrowed *passion*. German writers, in the seventeenth century, imitated the Latin use, or that of French *passion*, in *Leidenschaft* 'passion,' abstract of *leiden* 'to suffer,' and the Slavic languages followed the same model, as, for instance, in Russian [stra*st*] 'passion,' abstract of [stra'da*t*] 'to suffer.' Ancient Greek [pro-'balloː] 'I throw (something) before (someone)' had also a transferred use of the middle-voice forms, [pro-'ballomaj] 'I accuse (someone) of (something).' The Latin usage of a similar compound may be a loan-translation: one said not only *canibus cibum ob-jicere* 'to throw food to the dogs,' but also *alicuī probra objicere* 'to reproach someone for his bad actions.' This was imitated in German: *er wirft den Hunden Futter vor* 'he throws food before the dogs,' and *er wirft mir meine Missetaten vor* 'he reproaches me for my misdeeds.' The use of terms like *call, calling* for 'professional occupation,' derives from a familiar notion of Christian theology. Our terms imitate the late Latin use in this sense of *vocātiō*, abstract noun of *vocāre* 'to call'; similarly, German *Beruf* 'calling, vocation, profession' is derived from *rufen* 'to call,' and Russian ['zvanije] 'calling, vocation' is the abstract of [zvat] 'to call.' A great deal of our grammatical terminology has gone through this process. With a very peculiar extension, the ancient Greek grammarians used the term ['pto:sis] 'a fall' at first for 'inflectional form' and then especially for 'case-form.' This was imitated in Latin where, *cāsus*, literally 'a fall,' was used in the same way (whence our borrowed *case*); this, in turn, is reproduced in the German *Fall* 'fall; case,' and in Slavic, where Russian [na'deš] 'case' is the learned-foreign (Old Bulgarian) variant of [pa'doš] 'a fall.' In English the loan-translations have been largely replaced, as in these examples, by Latin-French semi-learned borrowings; thus, the complex semantic sphere of Latin *commūnis*, now covered by the borrowed *common*, was in Old English imitated by extensions of the native word [je-'me:ne], of parallel formation, just as it still is in German by the native forms *gemein* and *gemeinsam*. In Russian, the loan-translations are often in Old Bulgarian form, because this language served as the medium of theological writing.

In a less elevated sphere, we have Gallicisms, such as *a marriage of convenience* or *it goes without saying*, or *I've told him I don't know how many times*, word-for-word imitations of French phrases. The term *superman* is a translation of the German term coined by Nietzsche. For 'conventionalized,' French and German use a derivative of the noun *style*, as, French *stylisé* [stilize]; one occasionally hears this imitated in English in the form *stylized*.

These transferences are sometimes so clumsily made that we may say they involve a misunderstanding of the imitated form. The ancient Greek grammarians called the case of the verbal goal (the "direct object") by the term [ajtia:ti'ke: 'pto:sis] 'the case pertaining to what is effected,' employing an adjective derived from [ajtia:'tos] 'effected,' with an ultimately underlying noun [aj'tia:] 'cause.' This term was chosen, evidently, on account of constructions like 'he built a house,' where 'house' in Indo-

European syntax has the position of a verbal goal. The word [aj'tia:], however, had also the transferred meaning 'fault, blame,' and the derived verb [ajti'aomaj] had come to mean 'I charge, accuse.' Accordingly, the Roman grammarians mistranslated the Greek grammatical term by *accūsātīvus*, derived from *accūsō* 'I accuse.' This unintelligible term, *accusative*, was in turn translated into Russian, where the name of the direct-object case is [*vi'nitel-noj*], derived from [*vi'nit*] 'to accuse.' The Menomini, having only one (unvoiced) series of stops, interpreted the English term *Swede* as *sweet*, and, by mistaken loan-translation, designate the Swedish lumber-workers by the term [saje:wenet] literally 'he who is sweet.' Having neither the types [l, r] nor a voiced [z], they interpreted the name of the town *Phlox* (Wisconsin) as *frogs* and translated it as [uma:hkahkow-mɛni:ka:n] 'frog-town.'

25. 8. Cultural loans show us what one nation has taught another. The recent borrowings of English from French are largely in the sphere of women's clothes, cosmetics, and luxuries. From German we get coarser articles of food (*frankfurter, wiener, hamburger, sauerkraut, pretzel, lager-beer*) and some philosophical and scientific terms (*zeitgeist, wanderlust, umlaut*); from Italian, musical terms (*piano, sonata, scherzo, virtuoso*). From India we have *pundit, thug, curry, calico;* from American Indian languages, *tomahawk, wampum, toboggan, moccasin.* English has given *roast beef* and *beefsteak* to other languages, (as, French *bifteck* [biftɛk], Russian [bif'šteks]); also some terms of elegant life, such as *club, high life, five-o'clock* (*tea*), *smoking* (for 'dinner-jacket'), *fashionable,* and, above all, terms of sport, such as *match, golf, football, baseball, rugby.* Cultural loans of this sort may spread over a vast territory, from language to language, along with articles of commerce. Words like *sugar, pepper, camphor, coffee, tea, tobacco* have spread all over the world. The ultimate source of *sugar* is probably Sanskrit ['çarkara:] 'gritty substance; brown sugar'; the various shapes of such words, such as French *sucre* [sykr], Italian *zucchero* ['tsukkero] (whence German *Zucker* ['tsuker]), Greek ['sakkharon] (whence Russian ['saxar]), are due to substitutions and adaptations which took place under the most varied conditions in the borrowing and lending languages; Spanish *azucar* [a'θukar], for instance, is a borrowing from an Arabic form with the definite article, [as sokkar] 'the sugar' — just as *algebra, alcohol, alchemy* contain the Arabic article [al] 'the.' It is this same factor of widespread cultural borrowing which interferes with our reconstruction of the Primitive Indo-European vocabulary, in cases like that of the word *hemp* (§ 18.14). Words like *axe*, *sack*, *silver* occur in various Indo-European languages, but with phonetic discrepancies that mark them as ancient loans, presumably from the Orient. The word *saddle* occurs in all the Germanic languages in a uniform type, Primitive Germanic *['sadulaz], but, as it contains the root of *sit* with Primitive Indo-European [d] (as in Latin *sedeō* 'I sit') unshifted, we must suppose *saddle* to have been borrowed into pre-Germanic, too late for the shift [d > t], from some other Indo-European language — presumably from some equestrian nation of the Southeast. The Slavic word for 'hundred,' Old Bulgarian [sʊto], phonetically marked as a loanword from a similar source, perhaps Iranian, belongs to the same geographic sphere. The early contact of the Germanic-speaking peoples with the Romans appears in a layer of cultural loan-words that antedates the emigration of the English: Latin *vīnum* > Old English [wiːn] > *wine;* Latin *strāta* (*via*) > Old English [streːt] > *street;* Latin *caupō* 'wine-dealer' is reflected in Old English ['keːapian] 'to buy' (German *kaufen*) and in modern *cheap*, *chapman;* Latin *mangō* 'slave-dealer, peddler' > Old English ['mangere] 'trader' (still in *fishmonger*); Latin *monēta* 'mint, coin' > Old English *mynet* 'coin.' Other words of this layer are *pound*, *inch, mile;* Old English [kirs] 'cherry,' ['persok] 'peach,' ['pisc] 'pea.' On the other hand, the Roman soldiers and merchants learned no less from the Germanic peoples. This is attested not only by Roman writers' occasional use of Germanic words, but, far more cogently, by the presence of very old Germanic loanwords in the Romance languages. Thus, an old Germanic *['wɛrroː] 'confusion, turmoil' (Old High German ['werra]) appears, with a usual substitution of [gw-] for Germanic [w-], as Latin *['gwerra] 'war' in Italian *guerra* ['gwɛrra], French *guerre* [gɛːr] (in English *war*, we have, as often, a borrowing back from French into English); Old Germanic *['wiːsoː] 'wise, manner' (Old English [wiːs]) appears as Latin *['gwiːsa] in Italian and Spanish *guisa*, French *guise* [giːz]; English *guise* is a loan from French, alongside the native *wise*. Germanic *['wantuz] 'mitten' (Dutch *want*, Swedish *vante*) appears as Latin *['gwantus] in Italian *guanto* 'glove,' French *gant* [gɑⁿ]; English *gauntlet* is a loan from French. Other Germanic words which passed into Latin in the early centuries of our era are *hose* (> Italian *uosa* 'legging'; cf. above, § 24.3), *soap* (> Latin *sāpō*), *['θwahljo:] 'towel' (> French *touaille*, whence, in turn, English *towel*), *roast* (>French *rôtir*, whence, in turn, English *roast*), *helmet* (> French *heaume*), *crib* (> French *crèche*), *flask* (> Italian *fiasca*), *harp* (> French *harpe*). An example of a loan-translation is Latin *compāniō* 'companion,' a synthetic compound of *con-* 'with, along' and *pānis* 'bread,' on the model of Germanic *[ga-'hlajbo:], Gothic [ga'hlajba] 'companion,' a characteristically Germanic formation containing the prefix *[ga-] 'along, with' and *['hlajbaz] 'bread' (> English *loaf*).

CHAPTER 26

INTIMATE BORROWING

26. 1. Cultural borrowing of speech-forms is ordinarily mutual; it is one-sided only to the extent that one nation has more to give than the other. Thus, in the missionary period, from the seventh century onward, Old English borrowed Latin terms relating to Christianity, such as *church, minister, angel, devil, apostle, bishop, priest, monk, nun, shrine, cowl, mass,* and imitated Latin semantics in the way of loan-translation, but Old English gave nothing, at this time, in return. The Scandinavian languages contain a range of commercial and nautical terms from Low German, which date from the trading supremacy of the Hanseatic cities in the late Middle Ages; similarly, Russian contains many nautical terms from Low German and Dutch.

In spite of cases like these, we can usually distinguish between ordinary cultural borrowing and the *intimate borrowing* which occurs when two languages are spoken in what is topographically and politically a single community. This situation arises for the most part by conquest, less often in the way of peaceful migration. Intimate borrowing is one-sided: we distinguish between the *upper* or *dominant* language, spoken by the conquering or otherwise more privileged group, and the *lower* language, spoken by the subject people, or, as in the United States, by humble immigrants. The borrowing goes predominantly from the upper language to the lower, and it very often extends to speech-forms that are not connected with cultural novelties.

We see an extreme type of intimate borrowing in the contact of immigrants' languages with English in the United States. English, the upper language, makes only the most obvious cultural loans from the languages of immigrants, as *spaghetti* from Italian, *delicatessen, hamburger,* and so on (or, by way of loan-translation, *liver-sausage*) from German. The immigrant, to begin with, makes far more cultural loans. In speaking his native language, he has occasion to designate by their English names any number of things which he has learned to know since coming

461

to America: *baseball, alderman, boss, ticket,* and so on. At the very least, he makes loan-translations, such as German *erste Papiere* 'first papers' (for naturalization). The cultural reason is less evident in cases like *policeman, conductor, street-car, depot, road, fence, saloon,* but we can say at least that the American varieties of these things are somewhat different from the European. In very many cases, however, not even this explanation will hold. Soon after the German gets here, we find him using in his German speech, a host of English forms, such as *coat, bottle, kick, change.* He will say, for instance, *ich hoffe, Sie werden's enjoyen* [ix 'hofe, zi: 'verden s en'tšojen] 'I hope you'll enjoy it,' or *ich hab' einen kalt gecatched* [ix ha:p ajnen 'kalt ge'ketšt] 'I've caught a cold.' He makes loan-translations, such as *ich gleich' das nicht* [ix 'glajx das 'nixt] 'I don't like that,' where, on the model of English *like,* a verb with the meaning 'be fond of' is derived from the adjective *gleich* 'equal, resemblant.' Some of these locutions, like this last, have become conventionally established in American immigrant German. The phonetic, grammatical, and lexical phases of these borrowings deserve far more study than they have received. The assignment of genders to English words in German or Scandinavian has proved a fruitful topic of observation.

The practical background of this process is evident. The upper language is spoken by the dominant and privileged group; many kinds of pressure drive the speaker of the lower language to use the upper language. Ridicule and serious disadvantages punish his imperfections. In speaking the lower language to his fellows, he may go so far as to take pride in garnishing it with borrowings from the dominant speech.

In most instances of intimate contact, the lower language is indigenous and the upper language is introduced by a body of conquerors. The latter are often in a minority; the borrowing rarely goes on at such headlong speed as in our American instance. Its speed seems to depend upon a number of factors. If the speakers of the lower language stay in touch with speech-fellows in an unconquered region, their language will change less rapidly. The fewer the invaders, the slower the pace of borrowing. Another retarding factor is cultural superiority, real or conventionally asserted, of the dominated people. Even among our immigrants, educated families may keep their language for generations with little admixture of English.

The same factors, apparently, but with some difference of weight, may finally lead to the *disuse* (extinction) of one or the other language. Numbers count for more here than in the matter of borrowing. Among immigrants in America, extinction, like borrowing, goes on at great speed. If the immigrant is linguistically isolated, if his cultural level is low, and, above all, if he marries a person of different speech, he may cease entirely to use his native language and even lose the power of speaking it intelligibly. English becomes his only language, though he may speak it very imperfectly; it becomes the native language of his children. They may speak it at first with foreign features, but outside contacts soon bring about a complete or nearly complete correction. In other cases the immigrant continues to speak his native language in the home; it is the native language of his children, but at school age, or even earlier, they cease using it, and English becomes their only adult language. Even if their English keeps some foreign coloring, they have little or no command of the parental language; bilingualism is not frequent. In the situation of conquest the process of extinction may be long delayed. One or more generations of bilingual speakers may intervene; then, at some point, there may come a generation which does not use the lower language in adult life and transmits only the upper language to its children.

The lower language may survive and the upper language die out. If the conquerors are not numerous, or, especially, if they do not bring their own women, this outcome is likely. In less extreme cases the conquerors continue, for generations, to speak their own language, but find it more and more necessary to use also that of the conquered. Once they form merely a bilingual upper class, the loss of the less useful upper language can easily take place; this was the end of Norman-French in England.

26. 2. The conflict of languages, then, may take many different turns. The whole territory may end by speaking the upper language: Latin, brought into Gaul round the beginning of the Christian era by the Roman conquerers, in a few centuries crowded out the Celtic speech of the Gauls. The whole territory may end by speaking the lower language: Norman-French, brought into England by the Conquest (1066), was crowded out by English in three hundred years. There may be a territorial distribution: when English was brought into Britain in the fifth century of our era, it crowded the native Celtic speech into the remoter parts of the island. In such cases there follows a geographic struggle along the border. In England, Cornish died out round the year 1800, and Welsh, until quite recently, was losing ground.

In all cases, however, *it is the lower language which borrows predominantly from the upper*. Accordingly, if the upper language survives, it remains as it was, except for a few cultural loans, such as it might take from any neighbor. The Romance languages contain only a few cultural loan-words from the languages that were spoken in their territory before the Roman conquest; English has only a few cultural loan-words from the Celtic languages of Britain, and American English only a few from American Indian languages or from the languages of nineteenth-century immigrants. In the case of conquest, the cultural loans which remain in the surviving upper language are chiefly place-names; witness, for example, American Indian place-names such as *Massachusetts, Wisconsin, Michigan, Illinois, Chicago, Milwaukee, Oshkosh, Sheboygan, Waukegan, Muskegon.* It is interesting to see that where English in North America has superseded Dutch, French, or Spanish as a colonial language, the latter has left much the same traces as any other lower language. Thus, from Dutch we have cultural loan-words like *cold-slaw, cookie, cruller, spree, scow, boss,* and, especially, place-names, such as *Schuylkill, Catskill, Harlem, the Bowery.* Place-names give valuable testimony of extinct languages. Thus, a broad band of Celtic place-names stretches across Europe from Bohemia to England; *Vienna, Paris, London* are Celtic names. Slavic place-names cover eastern Germany: *Berlin, Leipzig, Dresden, Breslau.*

On the other hand, if the lower language survives, it bears the marks of the struggle in the shape of copious borrowings. English, with its loan-words from Norman-French and its enormous layer of semi-learned (Latin-French) vocabulary, is the classical instance of this. The Battle of Hastings, in 1066, marks the beginning. The first appearances of French words in written records of English fall predominantly into the period from 1250 to 1400; this means probably that the actual borrowing in each case occurred some decades earlier. Round 1300 the upper-class Englishman, whatever his descent, was either bilingual or had at least a good foreign-speaker's command of French. The mass of the people spoke only English. In 1362 the use of English was prescribed for law-courts;

in the same year Parliament was opened in English. The conflict between the two languages, lasting, say, from 1100 to 1350, seems not to have affected the phonetic or grammatical structure of English, except in the sense that a few phonemic features, such as the initials [v-, z-, ǰ-], and many features of the morphologic system of French were kept in the borrowed forms. The lexical effect, however, was tremendous. English borrowed terms of government (*state, crown, reign, power, country, people, prince, duke, duchess, peer, court*), of law (*judge, jury, just, sue, plea, cause, accuse, crime, marry, prove, false, heir*), of warfare (*war, battle, arms, soldier, officer, navy, siege, danger, enemy, march, force, guard*), of religion and morals (*religion, virgin, angel, saint, preach, pray, rule, save, tempt, blame, order, nature, virtue, vice, science, grace, cruel, pity, mercy*), of hunting and sport (*leash, falcon, quarry, scent, track, sport, cards, dice, ace, suit, trump, partner*), many terms of general cultural import (*honor, glory, fine, noble, art, beauty, color, figure, paint, arch, tower, column, palace, castle*), and terms relating to the household, such as servants might learn from master and mistress (*chair, table, furniture, serve, soup, fruit, jelly, boil, fry, roast, toast*); in this last sphere we find the oft-cited contrast between the native English names of animals on the hoof (*ox, calf, swine, sheep*), and the French loan-word names for their flesh (*beef, veal, pork, mutton*). It is worth noting that our personal names are largely French, as *John, James, Frances, Helen,* including even those which ultimately are of Germanic origin, such as *Richard, Roger, Henry.*

26. 3. The presence of loan-words in a wider semantic sphere than that of cultural novelties enables us to recognize a surviving lower language, and this recognition throws light not only upon historical situations, but also, thanks to the evidence of the loan-words themselves, upon the linguistic features of an ancient time. Much of our information about older stages of Germanic speech comes from loan-words in languages that once were under the domination of Germanic-speaking tribes.

Finnish, Lappish, and Esthonian contain hundreds of words that are plainly Germanic in origin, such as, Finnish *kuningas* 'king,' *lammas* 'sheep,' *rengas* 'ring,' *niekla* 'needle,' *napakaira* 'auger,' *pelto* 'field' (§ 18.6). These loan-words occur not only in such semantic spheres as political institutions, weapons, tools, and garments, but also in such as animals, plants, parts of the body, minerals, abstract relations, and adjective qualities. Since the sound-changes which have occurred in Finnish differ from those which have occurred in the Germanic languages, these loan-words supplement the results of the comparative method, especially as the oldest of these borrowings must have been made round the beginning of the Christian era, centuries before our earliest written records of Germanic speech.

In all the Slavic languages we find a set of Germanic loan-words that must have been taken, accordingly, into pre-Slavic. There is an older layer which resembles the Germanic loan-words in Finnish, as, Old Bulgarian [kʊneⁿdzɪ] 'prince' < *['kuninga-], Old Bulgarian [xle:bʊ] 'grain, bread' < *['hlajba-] (Gothic *hlaifs* 'bread,' English *loaf*), Old Bohemian [neboze:z] 'auger' < *['naba-gajza-]. A later stratum, which includes cultural terms of Greco-Roman origin, shows some specifically Gothic traits; to this layer belong terms like Old Bulgarian [kotɪlʊ] 'kettle' < *['katila-], Old Bulgarian [myto] 'toll' < *['mo:ta], Old Bulgarian [tse:sarɪ] 'emperor' < *['kajso:rja-] (§ 25.5), Old Bulgarian [usereⁿdzɪ] 'ear-ring' < *['awsa-hringa-]. We infer that the earlier stratum is pre-Gothic and dates from the beginning of the Christian Era, and that the later stratum comes from the stage of Gothic that is represented in our written documents of the fourth century.

In what is known as the Great Migrations, Germanic tribes conquered various parts of the Roman Empire. At this time Latin already contained a number of old cultural loan-words from Germanic (§ 25.8); the new loans of the Migration Period can be distinguished, in part, either by their geographic distribution, or by formal characteristics that point to the dialect of the conquerors. Thus, the vowel of Italian *elmo* ['elmo] 'helmet' reflects an old [i], and the Germanic [e] of a word like *['helmaz] (Old English *helm*) appears as [i] only in Gothic; the Goths ruled Italy in the sixth century. On the other hand, a layer of Germanic words with a consonant-shift like that of South German, represents the Lombard invasion and rule. Thus, Italian *tattera* ['tattera] 'trash' is presumably a loan from Gothic, but *zazzera* ['tsattsera] 'long hair' represents the Lombard form of the same Germanic word. Italian *ricco* 'rich,' *elso* 'hilt,' *tuffare* 'to plunge' are similarly marked as loans from Lombard.

The most extensive borrowing in Romance from Germanic appears in French. The French borrowings from the Frankish rulers, beginning with the name of the country *France*, pervade the vocabulary. Examples are Frankish *[helm] 'helmet' > Old French *helme* (modern *heaume* [o:m]); Frankish *['falda-ₗsto:li] 'folding-stool' > Old French *faldestoel* (modern *fauteuil* [fotœ:j]); Frankish *[bru:n] 'brown' > French *brun;* Frankish *[bla:w] 'blue' > French *bleu;* Frankish *['hatjan] 'to hate' > French *haïr;* Frankish *['wajdano:n] 'to gain' > Old French *gaagnier* (modern *gagner;* English *gain* from French). This last example illustrates the fact that many of the French loan-words in English are ultimately of Germanic origin. Thus, English *ward* is a native form and represents Old English ['weardjan]; the cognate Frankish *['wardo:n] appears in French as *garder* [garde], whence English has borrowed *guard.*

It is not surprising that personal names in the Romance languages are largely of Germanic origin, as French *Louis, Charles, Henri, Robert, Roger, Richard,* or Spanish *Alfonso* (presumably < Gothic *['haθu-funs] 'eager for fray'), *Adolfo* (presumably < Gothic *['aθal-ulfs] 'wolf of the land'). The upper-class style of name-giving survives even when the upper language is otherwise extinct.

Repeated domination may swamp a language with loan-words. Albanese is said to contain a ground-stock of only a few hundred native words; all the rest are dominance-loans from Latin, Romance, Greek, Slavic, and Turkish. The European Gipsies speak an Indo-Aryan language: it seems that in their various abodes they have been sufficiently segregated to keep their language, but that this language figured always as a lower language and taker of loan-words. All the Gipsy dialects, in particular, contain loan-words from Greek. F. N. Finck defines German Gipsy simply as that dialect of the Gipsy language in which "any expression lacking in the vocabulary" is replaced by a German word, as ['flikerwa:wa] 'I patch' from German *flicken* 'to patch,' or ['štu:lo] 'chair' from German *Stuhl.* The inflectional system, however, is intact, and the phonetics apparently differ from those of German.

The model of the upper language may affect even the grammatical forms of the lower. The anglicisms, say, in the American German of immigrants, find many a parallel in the languages of dominated peoples; thus, Ladin is said to have largely the syntax of the neighboring German, though the morphemes are Latin. In English we have not only Latin-French affixes, as in *eatable, murderous,* (§ 25.6), but also a few foreign features of phonetic pattern, as in *zoom, jounce.* Non-distinctive traits of phonemes do not seem to be borrowed. When we observe the American of German parentage (whose English, at the same time, may show some German traits) using an American-English [l] or [r] in his German, we may account for this by saying that German is for him a foreign language.

With a change of political or cultural conditions, the speakers of the lower language may make an effort to cease and even to undo the borrowing. Thus, the Germans have waged a long and largely successful campaign against Latin-French loan-words, and the Slavic nations against German. In Bohemian one avoids even loan-translations; thus, [zana:ška] 'entry (as, in a ledger),' abstract of a verb meaning 'to carry in,' a loan-translation of German *Eintragung* 'a carrying in, an entry,' is being replaced by a genuinely native [za:pis] 'writing in, notation.'

26. 4. Beside the normal conflict, with the upper language, if it survives, remaining intact, and the lower language, if it survives, bearing off a mass of loan-words and loan-translations, or even syntactic habits, we find a number of cases where something else must have occurred. Theoretically, there would seem to be many possibilities of an eccentric outcome. Aside from the mystic version of the substratum theory (§ 21.9), it seems possible that a large population, having imperfectly acquired an upper language, might perpetuate its version and even crowd out the more original type spoken by the upper class. On the other hand, we do not know the limit to which a lower language may be altered and yet survive. Finally, it is conceivable that a conflict might end in the survival of a mixture so evenly balanced that the historian could not decide which phase to regard as the main stock of habit and which as the borrowed admixture. However, we do not know which of these or of other imaginable complications have actually occurred, and no one, apparently, has succeeded in explaining the concrete cases of aberrant mixture.

From the end of the eighth century on, Danish and Norwegian Vikings raided and settled in England; from 1013 to 1042 England was ruled by Danish kings. The Scandinavian elements in English, however, do not conform to the type which an upper language leaves behind. They are restricted to the intimate part of the vocabulary: *egg, sky, oar, skin, gate, bull, bait, skirt, fellow, husband. sister, law, wrong, loose, low, meek, weak, give, take, call, cast, hit.* The adverb and conjunction *though* is Scandinavian, and so are the pronoun forms *they, their, them;* the native form [m̩], as in *I saw 'em* (< Old English *him,* dative plural), is now treated as an unstressed variant of the loan-form *them.* Scandinavian place-names abound in northern England. We do not know what circumstances led to this peculiar result. The languages at the time of contact were in all likelihood mutually intelligible. Perhaps their relation as to number of speakers and as to dominance differed in different localities and shifted variously in the course of time.

Most instances of aberrant borrowing look as though an upper language had been affected by a lower. The clearest case is that of Chilean Spanish. In Chile, the prowess of the natives led to an unusually great influx of Spanish soldiers, who settled in the country and married native women. In contrast with the rest of Latin America, Chile has lost its Indian languages and speaks only Spanish, and this Spanish differs phonetically from the Spanish that is spoken (by the dominant upper class) in the rest of Spanish America. The differences run in the direction of the indigenous languages that were replaced by Spanish; it has been surmised that the children of the first mixed marriages acquired the phonetic imperfections of their mothers.

Some features of the normal type of the Romance languages have been explained as reflections of the languages that were superseded by Latin. It would have to be shown that the features in question actually date from the time when speakers of the earlier languages, having imperfectly acquired Latin, transmitted it in this shape to their children. If this were granted, we should have to suppose that the official and colonizing class of native Latin-speakers was not large enough to provide an ever-present model, such as would have led to the leveling out of these imperfections. Actually, the peculiar traits of the Romance languages appear at so late a date that this explanation seems improbable, unless one resorts to the mystical (atavistic) version of the substratum theory (§ 21.9).

Indo-Aryan speech must have been brought into India by a relatively small group of invaders and imposed, in a long progression of dominance, by a ruling caste. Some, at least, of the languages which were superseded must have been kin to the present-day non-Aryan linguistic stocks of India. The principal one

of these stocks, Dravidian, uses a domal series of stops [T, D, N]
alongside the dental [t, d, n]; among the Indo-European languages, only the Indo-Aryan have the two series, and in their history the domals have become more numerous in the course of time.
The Indo-Aryan languages exhibit also an ancient confusion of
[l] and [r] which has been explained as due to substrata that possessed only one or neither of these sounds. The noun-declension
of later Indo-Aryan shows a re-formation, by which the same
case-endings are added to distinct stems for the singular and plural,
as in Dravidian; this replaced the characteristic Indo-European
habit of different sets of case-endings, as the sole distinction between singular and plural, added to one and the same stem.

In Slavic, especially in Russian and Polish, the impersonal
and partitive constructions closely parallel the Finnish habit.
The languages of the Balkan peninsula show various resemblances,
although they represent four branches of Indo-European: Greek,
Albanese, Slavic (Bulgarian, Serbian), and Latin (Roumanian).
Thus, Albanese, Bulgarian, and Roumanian, all use a definite article that is placed after the noun; the Balkan languages generally
lack an infinitive. In other parts of the world, too, we find phonetic or grammatical features prevailing in unrelated languages.
This is the case with some phonetic features in the Caucasus,
which are common both to the several non-Indo-European stocks
and to Armenian and to the Iranian Ossete. On the Northwest
Coast of North America, phonetic and morphologic peculiarities
appear in similar extensions. Thus, Quilleute, Kwakiutl, and
Tsimshian all have different articles for common nouns and for
names, and distinguish between visibility and invisibility in de-
monstrative pronouns; the latter peculiarity appears also in the
neighboring Chinook and Salish dialects, but not in those of the
interior. The suggestion has been made that different tribes cap-
tured women from one another, who transmitted their speech,
with traces of their native idiom, to the next generation.

Where we can observe the historical process, we occasionally
find phonetic and grammatical habits passing from language to
language without actual dominance. In the modern period the
uvular-trill [r] has spread over large parts of western Europe as
a replacement of the tongue-tip [r]; today, in France and in the
Dutch-German area the former is citified and the latter rustic or
old-fashioned. At the end of the Middle Ages, large parts of the

English, Dutch, and German areas, including the socially favored dialects, diphthongized the long high vowels. The rise of the articles and of phrasal verb-forms consisting of 'have,' 'be,' or 'become' plus past participle, in perfectic and passive values, took place in both the Latin and the Germanic areas during the early Middle Ages.

26. 5. There remains a type of aberrant borrowing in which we have at least the assurance that an upper language has been modified, though the details of the process are no less obscure.

The English (now largely American) Gipsies have lost their language and speak a phonetically and grammatically normal variety of sub-standard English; among themselves, however, they use anywhere from a few dozen to several hundred words of the old Gipsy language. These words are spoken with English phonemes and English inflection and syntax. They are terms for the very commonest things, and include grammatical words, such as pronouns. They are used interchangeably with the English equivalents. Older recordings show great numbers of these words; apparently a long speech could be made almost entirely in Gipsy words with English phonetics and grammar. Modern examples are: ['mɛndij] 'I,' ['lɛdij] 'you,' [sɔ] 'all,' [kejk] 'not,' [pon] 'say,' ['grajr̩] 'horse,' [aj 'dow nt 'kam tu 'dik e 'muš e-'čumr̩n e 'gruvn̩] 'I don't like to see a man a-kissin' a cow.' Occasionally one hears a Gipsy inflection, such as ['rukjr̩], plural of [ruk] 'tree.' The phonetics and grammar of the Gipsy words mark them unmistakably as borrowings by native speakers of English from a foreign language. Presumably they passed from native speakers of the Gipsy language, or from bilinguals, into the English of their children or other persons for whom Gipsy was no longer a native language. It is remarkable, however, that speakers of the latter sort should have interlarded their English with borrowings from the senescent lower language. Under the general circumstances of segregation, these borrowings had perhaps a facetious value; certainly they had the merit of making one's speech unintelligible to outsiders. Americans of non-English parentage who do not speak their parents' language, sometimes, by way of jest, use words of this language, speaking them with English sounds and inflections. Thus, German-Americans will occasionally use forms like [šwits] 'to sweat' (from German *schwitzen*), or [klač] 'to gossip' (from German *klatschen*). This trick seems to be commonest among Jews, who live under a measure of segregation, and the borrowings, moreover, are to a large extent the very words which in German also are peculiarly Jewish, namely, semi-learned words of literary Hebrew origin, such as ['ganef] 'thief,' [gɔj] 'gentile,' [me'šuga] 'crazy,' [me'zuma] 'money,' or dialect-forms of Judeo-German, such as ['nebix] 'poor fellow' (< Middle High German ['n eb ix] 'may I not have the like'). It seems likely that the Gipsy forms in English represent merely an extension of this habit under conditions that made it especially useful.

Speakers of a lower language may make so little progress in learning the dominant speech, that the masters, in communicating with them resort to "baby-talk." This "baby-talk" is the masters' imitation of the subjects' incorrect speech. There is reason to believe that it is by no means an exact imitation, and that some of its features are based not upon the subjects' mistakes but upon grammatical relations that exist within the upper language itself. The subjects, in turn, deprived of the correct model, can do no better now than to acquire the simplified "baby-talk" version of the upper language. The result may be a conventionalized *jargon*. During the colonization of the last few centuries, Europeans have repeatedly given jargonized versions of their language to slaves and tributary peoples. Portuguese jargons are found at various places in Africa, India, and the Far East; French jargons exist in Mauritius and in Annam; a Spanish jargon was formerly spoken in the Philippines; English jargons are spoken in the western islands of the South Seas (here known as *Beach-la-Mar*), in Chinese ports (*Pidgin English*), and in Sierra Leone and Liberia. Unfortunately, these jargons have not been well recorded. Examples from Beach-la-Mar are:

What for you put diss belonga master in fire? Him cost plenty money and that fellow kai-kai him. 'Why did you put the master's dishes into the fire? They cost a lot of money and it has destroyed them' — spoken to a cook who had put silverware into the oven.

What for you wipe hands belonga you on clothes belonga esseppoon? 'Why did you wipe your hands on the napkin?'

Kai-kai he finish? 'Is dinner ready?'

You not like soup? He plenty good kai-kai. 'Don't you like the soup? It's very good.'

What man you give him stick? 'To whom did you give the stick?'

Me savey go. 'I can go there.'

In spite of the poor recording, we may perhaps reconstruct the creation of speech-forms like these. The basis is the foreigner's desperate attempt at English. Then comes the English-speaker's contemptuous imitation of this, which he tries in the hope of making himself understood. This stage is represented, for instance, by the lingo which the American, in slumming or when traveling abroad, substitutes for English, to make the foreigner understand. In our examples we notice, especially, that the English-speaker introduces such foreign words as he has managed to learn (*kai-kai* 'eat' from some Polynesian language), and that he does not discriminate between foreign languages (*savey* 'know,' from Spanish, figures in all English jargons). The third layer of alteration is due to the foreigner's imperfect reproduction of the English-speaker's simplified talk, and will differ according to the phonetic and grammatical habit of the foreigner's language. Even the poor orthography of our examples shows us substitution of [s] for [š] in *dish* and failure to use final [ŋ], in *belonga*, and initial [sp], in *esseppoon* for *spoon*.

A jargon may pass into general commercial use between persons of various nationality; we then call it a *lingua franca*, using a term which seems to have been applied to an Italian jargon in the eastern Mediterranean region in the early modern period. Pidgin English, for instance, is used quite generally in commerce between Chinese and Europeans of other than English speech. In Washington and Oregon, Indians of various tribes, as well as French and English-speaking traders, formerly used a lingua franca known as "Chinook Jargon," which was based, strangely enough, on a jargonized form of the Chinook language, with admixtures from other Indian languages and from English.

It is important to keep in view the fact, often neglected, that a jargon or a lingua franca is nobody's native language but only a compromise between a foreign speaker's version of a language and a native speaker's version of the foreign speaker's version, and so on, in which each party imperfectly reproduces the other's reproduction. In many cases the jargon or lingua franca dies out, like Chinook Jargon, without ever becoming native to any group of speakers.

In some cases, however, a subject group gives up its native language in favor of a jargon. This happens especially when the subject group is made up of persons from different speech-communities, who can communicate among themselves only by means of the jargon. This was the case, presumably, among Negro slaves in many parts of America. When the jargon has become the only language of the subject group, it is a *creolized language*. The creolized language has the status of an inferior dialect of the masters' speech. It is subject to constant leveling-out and improvement in the direction of the latter. The various types of "Negro dialect" which we observe in the United States show us some of the last stages of this leveling. With an improvement of social conditions, this leveling is accelerated; the result is a caste-dialect whose speakers, so far as linguistic factors are concerned, have no more difficulty than other sub-standard speakers in acquiring the standard language.

It is a question whether during this process the dialect that is being de-creolized may not influence the speech of the community — whether the creolized English of the southern slaves, for instance, may not have influenced local types of sub-standard or even of standard English. The Dutch of South Africa, known as *Afrikaans*, shows some features that remind one of creolized languages — such, for instance, as extreme inflectional simplification. Since it is spoken by the whole community, one would have to suppose that the Dutch settlers developed a jargonized form of Dutch in communication with native Africans, and that this jargon, through the medium of native servants (especially, of nurses) then influenced the language of the masters.

In the very unusual case where the subject group, after losing its native language or languages and speaking only a creolized language, is removed from the dominance of the model language, the creolized language escapes assimilation and embarks upon an independent career. A few such cases have been observed. Thus, the descendants of runaway slaves who settled on the island of San Thomé off the coast of West Africa, spoke a creolized Portuguese. A creolized Dutch was long spoken on the Virgin Islands. Two creolized forms of English are spoken in Suriname (Dutch Guiana). One of these, known as *Ningre Tongo* or *taki-taki*, is spoken by the descendants of slaves along the coast. The other, more divergent from ordinary types of English, is known as *Jew-Tongo;* it is spoken by the Bush Negroes on the Saramakka River, descendants of slaves who won their liberty in the eighteenth century by rebellion and flight. It owes its name to the fact that some of the slaves were owned by Portuguese Jews. The remarkable feature of Bush-Negro English is its extreme adaptation to the phonetics and structure of West African languages, and the retention of much West African vocabulary: if the slaves still spoke an African language, it is a puzzle why they should have abandoned it in favor of English jargon.

The following examples of Ningre-Tongo are taken from texts recorded by M. J. Herskovits:

['kom na 'ini:-sej. mi: sɛ 'gi: ju wan 'sani: fo: ju: de 'njam.] 'Come inside. I shall give you something to eat.'

[a 'taki: , 'gran 'taŋgi: fo: 'ju:] 'He said, "Thank you very much."'

[mi: 'njam mi: 'bɛre 'furu.] 'I have eaten my belly full.'

In the first of the following Bush-Negro English proverbs, kindly supplied by Professor Herskovits, the tones are indicated by numbers: [1]rising, [2]level, [3]falling, and by combinations of numbers, such as [13]rising then falling, [23]level then falling, and so on.

[fu[13] kri[21] ki[23] a[n1] taŋ[13] hɔŋ[2] wi[21]] 'full creek not stand uproot weeds,' that is, 'A full creek doesn't uproot any weeds' — said when a person boasts of what he is going to accomplish.

[ɛfi: ju: sei: ju: hɛdɛ, tɛ ju: baj hati:, pɛ ju: pɔti: ɛŋ] 'If you sell your head, then you buy hat, where you put him?' that is, 'If you sell your head to buy a hat, where will you put it?'

[ni:ki: mačaw faa ga[n] paw] 'Small axe fell great stick,' that is, 'A small axe can cut down a large tree.'

CHAPTER 27

DIALECT BORROWING

27. 1. The infant begins by acquiring the speech-habits of the people who take care of him. He gets most of his habits from some one person, usually from his mother, but he does not reproduce this person's speech exactly, because he takes some forms from other persons. It is a matter of dispute whether any permanent habits, in the normal case, arise as mere inaccuracies of imitation. Later on, the child acquires speech-forms from more people; children are especially imitative in their first contacts outside the immediate family circle. As time goes on, the range of imitated persons becomes wider; throughout his life, the speaker continues to adopt speech-habits from his fellows. At any moment, his language is a unique composite of habits acquired from various people.

Very often whole groups of speakers agree in adopting or favoring or disfavoring a speech-form. Within an age-group, an occupational group, or a neighborhood group, a turn of speech will pass from person to person. The borrowing of speech-habits within a community is largely one-sided; the speaker adopts new forms and favoritisms from some people more than from others. In any group, some persons receive more imitation than others; they are the leaders in power and prestige. Vaguely defined as they are, the different groups make similarly one-sided adoptions. Every person belongs to more than one minor speech-group; a group is influenced by the persons who, along some other line of division, belong to a dominant class. Among his occupational companions, for example, a speaker will imitate those whom he believes to have the highest "social" standing. To take the extreme case, when a speaker comes in contact with persons who enjoy much greater prestige, he eagerly imitates not only their general conduct, but also their speech. Here the direction of leveling is most plainly apparent. The humble person is not imitated; the lord or leader is a model to most of those who hear him. In conversation with him, the common man avoids giving offense or cause for ridicule; he suppresses such of his habits as might seem peculiar, and tries to

ingratiate himself by talking as he hears. Having conversed with
the great, he himself may become a model in his own group for
those who have not had that privilege. Every speaker is a mediator
between various groups.

The adjustments are largely minute and consist in the favoring
of speech-forms more often than in the adoption of wholly new ones.
A great deal of adjustment probably concerns non-distinctive
variants of sound. On the other hand, when rival forms enjoy
something like equality, the choice may be actually discussed: a
speaker deliberates whether he will say *it's I* or *it's me*, or speak
either, neither with [ij] or with [aj]. In our community, with its
tradition about the "correctness" of speech-forms, the speaker
asks "Which form is better?" instead of asking "With which
persons shall I agree in speech?" In the main, however, the process
does not rise to the level of discussion.

Every speaker, and, on a larger scale, every local or social group,
acts as an imitator and as a model — as an agent in the leveling
process. No person and no group acts always in one or the other
capacity, but the privileged castes and the central and dominating
communities act more often as models, and the humblest classes
and most remote localities more often as imitators.

27. 2. The important historical process in this leveling is the
growth of central speech-forms that spread over wider and wider
areas. Suppose, for instance, that in a locally differentiated area,
some one town, thanks to personalities that live in it or thanks
to a favorable topographic situation, becomes the seat of a recurrent religious rite or political gathering or market. The inhabitants of the villages round about now resort at intervals
to this central town. On these visits they learn to avoid the strikingly divergent forms of their domestic speech, replacing them
by forms that do not call forth misunderstanding or mockery.
These favored speech-forms will be such as are current in all or
most of the local groups; if no one form is predominant, the choice
will fall usually upon the form that is used in the central town.
When the villager goes home, he continues to use one or another
of these new locutions, and his neighbors will imitate it, both because they know its source and because the speaker who has visited
the central town has gained in prestige at home. At second, third,
and later hand, these locutions may pass to still more remote
persons and places. The central town becomes a *speech-center*,

whose forms of speech, when there is not too much weight against them, become the "better" forms for a whole area of the surrounding country.

As commerce and social organization improve, this process repeats itself on a larger and larger scale. Each center is imitated over a certain area. A new concentration of political power elevates some of these centers to a higher rank; the lesser centers themselves now imitate this main center, and continue to spread both its forms and their own over their petty spheres. This development took place in the Middle Ages in Europe. At the end of the medieval period, countries like England, France, and Germany contained a number of provincial speech-centers, though even by that time, in England and in France, the capital city was taking the rank of a supreme speech-center for the whole area. These levelings, where they occurred on a large scale, are reflected in the great isogloss-bundles that mark the conflict of cultural systems, such as the bundles which separate Low German and High German or Northern and Southern French. The lesser provincial and parochial levelings appear as minor isoglosses; thus, we saw that the boundaries of the petty states along the lower Rhine that were swamped by the French invasion of 1789 are reflected in lesser isogloss-bundles of today. All this would be plainer, were it not for the frequent shifting both of political boundaries and of the relative influence of centers. The most variable factor, however, is the difference between the speech-forms themselves, since some will spread more vigorously than others, either for semantic reasons or, less often, for reasons of formal structure.

A similarity of speech in a district of any size may date from the time when the speech-community first spread over this district. The word *house*, for example, spread over England with the entrance of the English language, at the time of the Saxon conquest. It then had the form [hu:s], and in the northern dialects which still speak so, the modern form may be a direct continuation of the old form.

In very many instances, however, we know that a uniformity does not date from the time of settlement. Thus, we know that the diphthong [aw] in *house, mouse*, etc., arose from older [u:] long after the settlement of England. In these cases, older students took for granted a uniform linguistic change over a large area, supposing, for instance, that a large part of the English area made a phonetic change of [u:] to [aw]. At present, we believe rather that the actual change occurred among a relatively small group of speakers, and that after this, the new form spread by linguistic borrowing over the large area. We are led to this opinion by the fact that isoglosses for parallel forms do not coincide. A divergence like that of the isoglosses of the vowels in *mouse* and *house* in the Netherlands (§ 19.4) fits into our classification of linguistic borrowing, but not into our classification of phonetic change. Some students see in this a reason for giving up our classifications, and insist that a "phonetic change" spreads in this irregular fashion. This statement, however, is inconsistent with the original application of the term "phonetic change" to phonemic parallelism in cognate speech-forms (§ 20.4). Accordingly, we should have to devise a new classification or else to find some way of reconciling the two kinds of phenomena that are included in the new use of the term "phonetic change" — and no one has even attempted to do either of these things. The method which distinguishes between a uniform *phonetic change* and the spread by *borrowing* of resultant variants, is the only formula that has so far been devised to fit the facts.

Even when a uniform feature could represent the type that was imported in the original settlement, we may find upon closer investigation that this feature has merely overlaid an older diversity. This may be disclosed by isolated relic forms (§ 19.5), or by the characteristic phenomenon of *hyper-forms*. Of these, Gamillscheg gives a beautiful example. In the Ladin of the Dolomite Mountains, Latin [wi-] has become [u-]: a Latin [wi'ki:num] 'neighbor,' for instance, appears as [užin]. In one corner of this district, however, the Rau Valley, this change apparently did not take place: Latin [wi-] is represented by [vi-], as in [vižin] 'neighbor.' However, there is a queer discrepancy. The Latin type [aw'kɛllum] 'bird,' which appears in Italian as [uč'čɛllo] and in the Ladin of the Dolomites as [učel], and did not have initial [wi-], has in the Rau valley the form [vičel] 'bird.' If the Rau valley had really preserved Latin [wi-] as [vi-], the form [vičel] 'bird' would be inexplicable. It can be understood only if we suppose that the Rau dialect, like the other Dolomite dialects, changed [wi-] to [u-], and afterwards took to borrowing the more urbane Italian [vi-] as a replacement for the native [u-]. In doing this, the Rau speakers went too far, and substituted [vi-] for [u-] even in the word *[učel] 'bird,' where Italian has [u-] and not [vi-].

An isogloss tells us only that there has occurred somewhere and at some time a sound-change, an analogic-semantic change, or a cultural loan, but the isogloss does not tell us where or when this change occurred. The form which resulted from the change was spread abroad and perhaps pushed back, we know not with what vicissitudes, in a process of dialect borrowing whose outcome is represented by the isogloss. The present area of a form may even fail to include the point at which this form originated. It is a very naïve error to mistake isoglosses for the limits of simple linguistic changes. The results of dialect geography tell us of linguistic borrowing.

27. 3. If the geographic domain of a linguistic form is due to borrowing, we face the problem of determining who made the original change. A cultural loan or an analogic-semantic innovation may be due to a single speaker; more often, doubtless, it is made independently by more than one. Perhaps the same is true of the non-distinctive deviations which ultimately lead to a sound-change, but this matter is more obscure, since the actual, linguistically observable change is here the result of a cumulation of minute variants. The speaker who favors or exaggerates some acoustic variant, as well as the speaker who adopts such a variant, has merely altered a non-distinctive feature. By the time a succession of such favorings has resulted in a change of phonemic structure, the borrowing process has doubtless long been at work. There must have been a time, for instance, when some parts of the American English speech-community favored the lower and less rounded variants of the vowel in words like *hot, cod, bother*. It is useless to ask what person or set of persons first favored these variants; we must suppose only that he or they enjoyed prestige within some group of speakers, and that this group, in turn, influenced other groups, and so on, in the manner of widening circles: the new variants were fortunate enough through some time and in repeated situations, to belong to the more dominant speakers and groups. This favoring went on until, over a large part of the area, and doubtless not everywhere at the same time, the vowel of *hot, cod, bother* coincided with that of *far, palm, father*. Only at this moment could an observer say that a sound-change had occurred; by this time, however, the distribution of the variants among speakers, groups, and localities, was a result of borrowing. The moment of the coincidence of the two former phonemes into one could not be determined; doubtless even one speaker might at one time make a difference and at another time speak the two alike. By the time a sound-change becomes observable, its effect has been distributed by the leveling process that goes on within each community.

The linguist's classification of changes into the three great types of phonetic change, analogic-semantic change, and borrowing, is a classification of facts which result from minute and complicated processes. The processes themselves largely escape our observation; we have only the assurance that a simple statement of their results will bear some relation to the factors that created these results.

Since every speaker acts as an intermediary between the groups to which he belongs, differences of speech within a dialect area are due merely to a lack of mediatory speakers. The influence of a speech-center will cause a speech-form to spread in any direction until, at some line of weakness in the density of communication, it ceases to find adopters. Different speech-forms, with different semantic values, different formal qualifications, and different rival forms to conquer, will spread at different speeds and over different distances. The advance of the new form may be stopped, moreover, by the advance of a rival form from a neighboring speech-center, or, perhaps, merely by the fact that a neighboring speech-center uses an unchanged form.

One other possible source of differentiation must be reckoned with: absorption of a foreign area, whose inhabitants speak their new language with peculiar traits. We have seen (§ 26.4) that this is entirely problematic, since no certain example has been found. For the most part, then, differentiation within a dialect area is merely a result of imperfect leveling.

27. 4. Increases in the area and intensity of unification are due to a number of factors which we sum up by saying that the economic and political units grow larger and that the means of communication improve. We know little about the details of this process of centralization, because our evidence consists almost entirely of written documents, and written documents are in this matter especially misleading; to begin with, they are in Europe mostly couched in Latin and not in the language of the country.

In the non-Latin (*vernacular*) records of the English and Dutch-German areas, we find at the outset, — that is, from the eighth century on, — provincial dialects. Internal evidence shows that even these have arisen through some degree of unification, but we do not know how much of this unification existed in actual speech. In the later Middle Ages we find beginnings of greater centralization. In the Dutch-German area, especially, we find three fairly uniform types of language: a Flemish ("Middle Dutch") type, a decidedly uniform North German ("Middle Low German") type in the Hanseatic area, and a South German ("Middle High German") type in the aristocratic literature of the southern states. The language of these documents is fairly uniform over wide geographic areas. In some respects, we can see how local peculiarities are excluded. The North German type is based predominantly on the speech of the city of Lübeck. The southern type strikes a kind of average between provincial dialects, excluding some of the localisms that appear in present-day dialect. In old Germanic the personal pronouns had separate forms for the dual and plural numbers; in general, the distinction was removed by an extension of the plural forms to the case where only two persons were involved, but in some regions the old dual forms were extended to plural use. In most of the German area the old plural forms, Middle High German *ir* 'ye' (dative *iu;* accusative *iuch*), survived, but certain districts, notably Bavaria and Austria, took the second alternative: the modern local dialects use the old dual form *ess* 'ye' (dative and accusative *enk*). Now, our Middle High German documents from the latter region scarcely ever show us these provincial forms, but write only the generally German *ir* 'ye.' On the other hand, careful study of a text will usually show in what part of southern Germany it originated, because many details had not been standardized. Poets' rimes, especially, conform, on the one hand, to certain conventions, but, on the other hand, betray each poet's provincial phonetics. It is remarkable that at the beginning of the modern period, in the fifteenth and early sixteenth centuries, this South German convention had broken down and our documents are again decidedly provincial, until the coming of the modern national standard language.

The modern standard languages, which prevail within the bounds of an entire nation, supersede the provincial types. These

standard languages become more and more uniform as time goes
on. In most instances they have grown out of the provincial type
that prevailed in the upper class of the urban center that became
the capital of the unified nation; modern standard English is based
on the London type, and modern standard French on that of
Paris. In other instances even the center of origin is obscure.
Modern standard German is not based on any one provincial dialect, but seems to have crystallized out of an official and commercial type of speech that developed in the eastern frontier region.
It was not created, but only helped toward supremacy, by Luther's
use in his Bible-translation. This origin is reflected in the fact
that the documents of standard German until well into the eighteenth century are far less uniform and show many more provincial traits than do those of English or French; the same can be
said of the standard language as it is spoken today.

The modern state, then, possesses a standard language, which
is used in all official discourse, in churches and schools, and in all
written notation. As soon as a speech-group attains or seeks
political independence, or even asserts its cultural peculiarity, it
works at setting up a standard language. Thus, the Serbo-Croa-
tians, emerging from Turkish rule, possessed no standard language;
a scholar, Vuk Stefanovich Karadjich (1787–1864) made one on
the basis of his local dialect, writing a grammar and lexicon. Bohemia, governed from German-speaking centers, had nevertheless
developed something like a standard language at the time of the
Reformation. The great reformer, Jan Hus (1369–1415), in particular, had devised an excellent system of spelling. In the seventeenth and eighteenth centuries this movement died down, but,
with the national revival at the end of this period, a new standard
language, based on the old, was created largely by the efforts of a
philologian, Josef Dobrowsky (1753–1829). Within the memory of
persons now living, the Lithuanian standard language, today
official and fully current in the confines of its nation, arose from
out of a welter of local dialects. Groups that have not gained
political independence, such as the Slovaks, the Catalans, and the
Frisians, have developed standard languages. The case of Norway
is especially interesting. For some centuries Norway belonged
politically to Denmark and used standard Danish as its national
language. The latter was similar enough to Norwegian speech-
forms to make this possible for persons who got school training.

The Norwegians modified their standard Danish in the direction of Norwegian speech-forms. This Dano-Norwegian *Riksmaal* ('national language') became the native speech of the educated upper class; for the uneducated majority, who spoke local dialects, it was almost a foreign language, even though after the political separation from Denmark in 1813, it was more and more assimilated to the general type of the native dialects. In the 1840's a language-student, Ivar Aasen (1813–1896) constructed a standard language on the basis of Norwegian local dialects and proposed its adoption in place of Dano-Norwegian. With many changes and variations, this new standard language, known as *Landsmaal* ('native language'), has been widely adopted, so that Norway has today two officially recognized standard languages. The advocates of the two are often in earnest conflict; the two standard languages, by concessions on either side, are growing more and more alike.

27. 5. The details of the rise of the great standard languages, such as standard English, are not known, because written sources do not give us a close enough picture. In its early stages, as a local dialect and later as a provincial type, the speech which later became a standard language, may have borrowed widely. Even after that, before its supremacy has been decided, it is subject to infiltration of outside forms. The native London development of Old English [y] is probably [i], as in *fill, kiss, sin, hill, bridge;* the [o] which appears in *bundle, thrush*, seems to represent a West-of-England type, and the [e] in *knell, merry* an eastern type. In *bury* ['berij] the spelling implies the western development, but the actual pronunciation has the eastern [e]; in *busy* ['bizij] the spelling is western, but the actual spoken form indigenous. The foreign [o] and [e] must have come at a very early time into the official London speech. The change of old [er] into [ar], as in *heart, parson, far, dark, 'varsity*, or *clerk* in British pronunciation (contrasting with the development in *earth, learn, person, university*, or *clerk* in American pronunciation) seems to have been provincial; the [ar]- forms filtered into upper-class London speech from the fourteenth century on. Chaucer uses *-th* as the third-person singular present-tense ending of verbs (*hath, giveth*, etc.); our [-ez, -z, -s] ending was provincial (northern) until well into the sixteenth century. Especially the East Midlands influenced London English during the early centuries of the latter's pre-eminence. In later times, the standard language borrows from other dialects only technical terms, such as *vat, vixen* (§ 19.1), or *laird, cairn* (from Scotch), or else facetiously, as in *hoss, cuss* as jesting-forms for *horse, curse;* here *bass* ('species of fish') for **berse,* (Old English *bears*) represents a more serious borrowing of earlier date.

The standard language influences the surrounding dialects at wider range and more pervasively as it gains in prestige. It affects especially provincial centers and, through them, their satellite dialects. This action is relatively slow. We have seen that a feature of the standard language may reach outlying dialects long after it has been superseded at home (§ 19.4). In the immediate surroundings of the capital, the standard language acts very strongly; the neighboring dialects may be so permeated with standard forms as to lose all their individuality. We are told that within thirty miles of London there is no speech-form that could be described as local dialect.

The standard language takes speakers from the provincial and local dialects. The humblest people make no pretense at acquiring it, but with the spread of prosperity and education, it becomes familiar to a larger and larger stratum. In western European countries today most people possess at least a good smattering of the standard language. The person who rises in the world speaks it as his adult language and transmits only it to his children: it comes to be the native dialect of a growing upper layer of the population.

Both in the gradual assimilation of lesser dialects and in the conversion of individuals and families to standard speech, the result is usually imperfect and is to be described as sub-standard or, in the favorable case, as provincially colored standard (§ 3.5). The evaluation of these types varies in different countries: in England they are counted inferior and their speakers are driven toward a more rigid standardization, but in the United States or in Germany, where the standard language belongs to no one local group, the standard is less rigid and a vaguely-defined range of varieties enjoys equal prestige. The English which the first settlers brought to America consisted, apparently, of provincialized types of the standard language and of sub-standard, rather than of local dialects. The characteristic features of sub-standard American English seem to be general features of dialectal and sub-standard British English, rather than importations from any special British local dialects.

27. 6. The study of written records tells us little about the centralization of speech and the rise of standard languages, not only because the conventions of writing develop to a large extent independently of actual speech, but also because they are more rapidly standardized and then actually influence the standardizing of speech. We have seen that even the early written notations of a language tend to use uniform graphs which soon become traditional (§ 17.7). The spellings of medieval manuscripts seem very diverse to the modern student, yet closer inspection shows that they are largely conventional. At the end of the Middle Ages, as the use of writing increases, the provincial types of orthography become more and more fixed. After the invention of printing and with the spread of literacy, the convention grows both more unified and more rigid; at last come grammars and dictionaries whose teachings supplement the example that everyone has before him in the shape of printed books. Schooling becomes more common, and insists upon conventional style.

This development conceals from us the actual centralization of the spoken language. The historian has to deal constantly with two opposite possibilities. The written convention, at bottom, reflects the forms that have prestige in actual speech; on the other hand, it conventionalizes much more rapidly and affects the prestige of rival spoken forms. The decisive events occur in the spoken language, yet the written style, once it has seized upon a form, retains it more exclusively, and may then weight the scales in its favor. We get a glimpse of the state of affairs in the spoken language from occasional aberrant spellings or from rimes. Thus, occasional spellings and rimes show us a rivalry in standard English between pronunciations with [aj] and with [ɔj] in words like *oil, boil, join;* the decisive victory, in the last two centuries, of the latter type is doubtless due to its agreement with the spelling; we may contrast the still unsettled fluctuation in similar matters where the spelling does not exert pressure, such as [a] versus [ɛ] in *father, rather, gather, command,* or [ɑ] versus [ɔ] in *dog, log, fog, doll.*

In syntax and vocabulary the message of the written record is unmistakable, and it exerts a tremendous effect upon the standard language. In Old English and to this day in sub-standard English, certain negative forms require a negative adverb with a finite verb: *I don't want none;* the habit of the standard language seems to have arisen first in writing, as an imitation of

Latin syntax. Everyone has had the experience of starting to speak a word and then realizing that he does not know how to say it, because he has seen it only in writing. Some words have become obsolete in actual speech and have then been restored, from written sources: thus, *sooth, guise, prowess, paramour, behest, caitiff, meed, affray* were revived by eighteenth-century poets.

We get a clearer notion of the influence of written notation in cases where it leads to actual changes in the language. Now and then a reviver of ancient forms misunderstands his text and produces a *ghost-word*. Thus, *anigh* 'near' and *idlesse* 'idleness' are pseudo-antique formations made by nineteenth-century poets. In Hamlet's famous speech, *bourne* means 'limit,' but moderns, misunderstanding this passage, use *bourne* in the sense of 'realm.' Chaucer's phrase *in derring do that longeth to a knight* 'in daring to do what is proper for a knight,' was misunderstood by Spenser, who took *derring-do* to be a compound meaning 'brave actions' and succeeded in introducing this ghost-form into our elevated language. Misinterpretation of an old letter has led to the ghost-form *ye* for *the* (§ 17.7).

It is not only archaic writings, however, that lead to change in actual speech. If there is any rivalry between speech-forms, the chances are weighted in favor of the form that is represented by the written convention; consequently, if the written convention deviates from the spoken form, people are likely to infer that there exists a preferable variant that matches the written form. Especially, it would seem, in the last centuries, with the spread of literacy and the great influx of dialect-speakers and sub-standard speakers into the ranks of standard-speakers, the influence of the written form has grown — for these speakers, unsure of themselves in what is, after all, a foreign dialect, look to the written convention for guidance. The school-teacher, coming usually from a humble class and unfamiliar with the actual upper-class style, is forced to the pretense of knowing it, and exerts authority over a rising generation of new standard-speakers. A great deal of *spelling-pronunciation* that has become prevalent in English and in French, is due to this source. In a standard language like the German, which belongs originally to no one class or district, this factor is even more deep-seated: the spoken standard is there largely derived from the written.

In standard English an old [sju:] developed to [šuw], as we see in the words *sure* [šuwr] and *sugar* ['šugṛ]. This change is reflected in occasional spellings since about 1600, such as *shuite* 'suit,' *shewtid* 'suited.' John Jones' *Practical Phonography* in 1701 prescribes the pronunciation with [š] for *assume, assure, censure, consume, ensue, insure, sue, suet, sugar.* The modern [s] or [sj] in some of these words is doubtless a result of spelling-pronunciation. The same is probably true of [t, d] or [tj, dj] in words like *tune, due,* which replaces an authentic [č, ǰ]; witness forms like *virtue* ['vṛčuw], *soldier* ['sowlǰṛ]. The British standard pronunciation ['inǰə] *India* is probably older than the American ['indja]. Since old final [mb, ŋg], as in *lamb, long* have lost the stop, it may be that the preservation of the stop in [nd], as in *hand,* is due to spelling-pronunciation; in the fifteenth, sixteenth, and seventeenth centuries we find occasional spellings like *blyne* 'blind,' *thousan, poun.* The old [t] in forms like *often, soften, fasten* is being constantly re-introduced by the lower reaches of standard-speakers.

The most cogent evidence appears where purely graphic devices lead to novel speech-forms. Written abbreviations like *prof., lab., ec.* lead to spoken forms [praf, lɛb, ek] in students' slang for *professor, laboratory, economics.* These serve as models for further innovations, such as [kwɔd] for *quadrangle,* [dorm] for *dormitory.* The forms [ej em, pij em] come from the A.M. and P.M. of railroad time-tables. Other examples are [juw es ej] for *United States of America,* [aj sij] for *Illinois Central (Railroad),* and [ej bij, ej em, em dij, pij ejč dij] for academic degrees whose full designations, *Bachelor of Arts, Master of Arts, Doctor of Medicine, Doctor of Philosophy,* are actually less current; the abbreviations, moreover, have the word-order of the original Latin terms. French has forms like [te ɛs ɛf] for *télégraphe sans fil* 'wireless telegraphy, radio'; in Russia many new republican institutions are known by names read off from graphic abbreviations, such as [komso'mol] for [kommuni'stičeskoj so'jus molo'doži] 'communistic union of young people,' or [ftsik] for [fseros'sijskoj tsen'tralnoj ispol'nitelnoj komi'tet] 'all-Russian central executive committee.'

The influence of written notation works through the standard language, but features that are thus introduced may in time seep down into other levels of speech. Needless to say, this influence can be described only in a superficial sense as conservative or regularizing: the loans from written notation deviate from the results of ordinary development.

27. 7. The full effect of borrowing from written documents can be seen in the cases where written notation is carried on in some speech-form that deviates widely from the actual language.

Among the Romans, the upper-class dialect of the first century B.C. — the Latin that we find in the writings of Caesar and Cicero — became established as the proper style for written notation and for formal discourse. As the centuries passed, the real language came to differ more and more from this convention, but, as literate people were few, the convention was not hard to maintain: whoever learned to write, learned, as part of the discipline, to use the forms of classical Latin. By the fifth century A.D., an ordinary speaker must have needed serious schooling before he could produce writings in the conventional form. In reading aloud and in formal speech, the custom apparently was to follow the written form, giving each letter the phonetic value that was suggested by the current forms of the language. Thus, a graph like *centum* 'hundred,' which in the classical period represented the form ['kentum], was now pronounced successively as ['kentum, 'čentum, 'tsɛntum] and the like, in accordance with the phonetic development of the actual language, which spoke, in the respective cases, say ['kentu, 'čentu, 'tsɛntu]. To this day, in reading Latin, the different nationalities follow this practice: the Italian reads Latin *centum* as ['čentum] because in his own language he writes *cento* and speaks ['čento]; the Frenchman reads it as [sɛntɔm] because in his own language he writes *cent* and speaks [sɑⁿ]; the German got his tradition of Latin-reading from a Romance tradition that used [ts] for *c* and accordingly reads Latin *centum* as ['tsentum]; in England one can still hear an "English" pronunciation of Latin, which says *centum* ['sentɔm], because it derives from a French tradition. These traditional pronunciations of Latin are now being superseded by a system which attempts to reconstruct the pronunciation of classical times.

This custom of carrying on written and formal or learned discourse in classical Latin passed, with Christianity, to non-Latin countries. Records in the actual Romance languages, or in Celtic or Germanic, begin round the year 700; they are scarce at first and become copious only in the twelfth and thirteenth centuries; until some time after the invention of printing, Latin books re=

main in the majority. Since Latin is still the official language of the Roman Catholic church, we may say that its use as a written and formal language persists to the present day.

As soon as classical Latin had begun to antiquate, persons who had not been sufficiently schooled, were sure to make mistakes in writing it. In the non-Latin countries this was true, of course, from the moment when Latin-writing was introduced. As to the thoroughness of the training, there were differences of time and place. The Latin written in Merovingian France, from the sixth to the eighth centuries, is decidedly unclassical, and reveals many characteristics of the authors' spoken language — the language whose later form we call French. In the ninth century, under Charles the Great, there came a revival of schooling: our texts return to a far more conventional Latin. Needless to say that in the Romance countries, and to some extent, perhaps, even in the others, errors in Latin-writing give us information about the actual language spoken by the authors. We have already seen that earlier scholars misconstrued this situation, mistaking changes in Latin-writing for linguistic change and drawing the moral that linguistic changes were due to ignorance and carelessness and represented a kind of decay (§ 1.4). Another error has proved more tenacious — namely, that of viewing the "medieval Latin" of our documents as an ordinary language. When we find a new form in these documents, there is only a remote possibility that this form represents an actual tradition of a classical Latin form; in by far the most instances, it is either a new-formation on the basis of classical Latin, or a latinization of some spoken form. Thus, the form *quiditas* 'whatness, characteristic quality' which appears in medieval Latin-writing, is roughly constructed on the analogies of classical Latin, and does not reflect any spoken form either of classical or of medieval times. The form *mansionaticum* 'place for a feudal lord to stop over night; domestic establishment' does not evidence the use of this form in classical Latin: it is merely a latinization of an actually spoken Old French *masnage* (or of its pre-French antecedent), which appears in later French as *mesnage*, modern *ménage* [mena:ž] 'household'; English *manage* is borrowed from a derived verb, French *ménager*. The latinization is correct, to be sure, in the sense that *masnage* is a morphologic combination whose elements, if we put them back into classical Latin form, would have combined as **mansiōnāticum.*

the medieval scribe hit upon the historically correct Latin equivalents, although, actually, classical Latin formed no such combination. When we read a perfect tense form *presit* 'he took' in Merovingian documents, we should do wrong to call this the ancestor of forms like Italian *prese* ['prese] 'he took,' or French *prit* [pri]; it is merely an error in Latin-writing, on the part of a scribe who was not familiar enough with the classical Latin form *prehendit* 'he took,' and wrote instead a pseudo-Latin form based on his spoken usage. This error tells us that the scribe's language already employed the new-formation of the type Latin **prensit*, which underlies the Romance forms and probably dates from a very early time, but it would be a grave methodic confusion to say that the Romance forms are derived from the "medieval Latin form." Again, when we find in Latin documents of German provenience a word *muta* 'toll,' it would be a naïve error to see in this "medieval Latin" word the source of Old High German *muta* 'toll' (§ 25.5); the writer merely used the German technical term in Latin-writing, because he knew no exact equivalent; one writer even speaks of *nullum teloneum neque quod lingua theodisca muta vocatur* 'no toll or what is in German called *muta*.' Moreover, we find the derivatives *mutarius, mutnarius* 'toll-taker' the latter with an analogic -*n*- that is peculiar to German morphology (modern *Mautner*). In sum, then, the medieval Latin-writer's deviations from classical Latin usage may throw light upon his actual speech, but dare not be confused with the antecedents of the latter, even in cases where the scribe succeeded in making a correct latinization.

27. 8. We find, now, that at all times, and especially with the modern spread of education, the Romance peoples introduced into their formal speech and then into ordinary levels, expressions from book-Latin in the phonetic form of the traditional reading-pronunciation. These borrowings from the written language are known as *learned words*, or, by the French term, as *mots savants* [mo sava^n]. After a book-Latin word came into current spoken use, it was subject, of course, to the normal changes which thereafter occurred in the language; however, these were sometimes followed by re-shaping in the direction of the bookish form. Many a Latin word appears in a Romance language both in its normally developed modern form, as a so-called *popular word*, and in a half-modernized Latin (or pseudo-Latin) form, as a learned word.

Latin *redemptionem* [redempti'o:nem] 'redemption' appears, by normal development, as modern French *rancon* [rɑⁿsoⁿ] 'ransom' (English *ransom* is a loan from Old French), but, as a borrowing from the written form, in modern French *rédemption* [redɑⁿpsjoⁿ] 'redemption.' At the time of bookish borrowings, the Frenchman, when reading Latin, used a pronunciation (based, as we have seen, upon the actual linguistic correspondences) which rendered a graph like *redemptionem* by a pronunciation, say, of [redɛmp'(t)sjo:-nɛm]: the differences between this and the present-day French [redɑⁿpsjoⁿ] are due to subsequent changes in the French language. Only some — perhaps only a minority — of the learned words actually went through this development, but on the model of those that did, one re-shapes any new ones that may be taken from the books; thus, if an educated Frenchman wanted to take up the Latin *procrastinationem* 'procrastination,' he would render it, in accordance with these models, as *procrastination* [prɔkrasti-nɑsjoⁿ].

Other examples of twofold development are: Latin *fabricam* ['fabrikam] 'factory' > French *forge* [fɔrž] 'forge,' learned *fabrique* [fabrik] 'factory'; Latin *fragile* ['fragile] 'fragile'> French *frêle* [frɛ:l] 'frail,' learned *fragile* [fražil] 'fragile'; Latin *securum* [se:'ku:rum] 'secure' > French *sûr* [sy:r] 'sure,' Latin *securitatem* [se:ku:ri'ta:tem] > French *sûreté* [syrte] 'sureness, guarantee,' learned *sécurité* [sekyrite] 'security.'

Sometimes the book-word got into the language early enough to undergo some sound-change which gives it a superficially normal look. Thus Latin *capitulum* [ka'pitulum] 'heading' was taken into French speech early enough to share in the development [ka > ča > ša], and appears in modern French as *chapitre* [ša-pitr] 'chapter.' The [r] for Latin [l] is due apparently to an adaptation of the type usually classed as aberrant sound-change (§ 21.10); doubtless quite a few such changes are really due to re-shapings of bookish words that presented an unusual aspect. In other cases, a bookish word borrowed after a sound-change, is still, by way of adaptation, put into a form that partly or wholly imitates the effects of this change. Thus, a Latin *discipulum* [dis'kipulum] 'disciple, pupil' would give by normal development a modern Italian *[de'šeppjo]; this does not exist, but the learned loan in Italian partly apes these vowel-changes; it is not *[di'šipulo], but *discepolo* [di'šepolo]. The number of learned and semi-learned forms in the western Romance languages is very large, especially as the standard languages have extended the analogy to the point where almost any Latin or Greco-Latin word can be modernized.

Among the French forms that were borrowed by English during the period after the Norman Conquest, there were many of these learned French borrowings from the Latin of books. The literate Englishman, familiar with both French and Latin, got into the habit of using Latin words in the form they had as French *mots savants*. We have seen how the Englishman made his own adaptations (§ 25.4). In later time, the English writer continued to use Latin words. In making these loans, we alter the Latin graph and pronounce it in accordance with a fairly well-fixed set of habits; these habits are composed of (1) the adaptations and phonetic renderings that were conventional in the French use of book-Latin words round the year 1200, (2) adaptations that have become conventional in the English usage of Latin-French forms, and (3) phonetic renderings due to English sound-changes that have occurred since the Norman time. Thus, the Latin *procrastinationem*, which is not current in French, is borrowed from Latin books into English as *procrastination* [pro₁krɛsti'nejšṇ], in accordance with the above set of analogies. Under (1) we have the fact that French borrows its Latin words not in nominative singular form (Latin *procrastinatio*), but in accusative or ablative form, with loss of ending: had the word been used, as a bookish loan, in the Old French of 1200 to 1300, it would have appeared as *procrastination* *[prokrastina'sjo:n], with phonetic changes which, like the selection of the case-form, are due ultimately, to the model of non-learned French words. The remaining deviations of the actual English form, namely [ɛ] for *a* in the second syllable, [ej] for *a* in the third, [š] for *ti* before vowel, and the weakening of the end of the word to [-ṇ], are modeled on the phonetic changes which have been undergone by words of similar structure that really were borrowed during the Norman period, such as Latin *nationem* > Old French [na'sjo:n] > English *nation* ['nejšṇ]. Finally, the shift of accent to pre-suffixal position copies an adaptation which English made in its actual loans from French. In the same way, when we borrow from Latin books the verb *procrastinare*, we render it as *procrastinate*, adding the suffix *-ate* in accordance with an adaptation that has become habitual in English (§ 23.5).

Both the Romance languages and English can borrow, in this way, not only actual Latin words, but even medieval scribal coinages, such as English *quiddity* from scholastic *quiditas*. We even invent new words on the general model of Latin morphology: *eventual*, *immoral*, *fragmentary* are examples of learned words whose models do not occur in Latin. Since the Romans borrowed words from Greek, we can do the same, altering the Greek word in accordance with the Roman's habit of latinization, plus the Frenchman's habit of gallicizing Latin book-words, plus the English habit of anglicizing French learned words. Ancient Greek [philoso'phia:] thus gives an English [fi'lɑsofij] *philosophy*. As in the case of Latin, we are free to coin Greek words: *telegraphy* represents, with the same modifications, a non-existent ancient Greek *[te:legra'phia:] 'distance-writing.'

Needless to say, we sometimes confuse the analogies. We render ancient Greek [th] in English, against the custom of the Romance languages, by [θ], as in [mu:tholo'gia:] > *mythology*. It is true that ancient Greek [th] has changed to [θ] in modern Greek, but the English habit is probably independent of this and due merely to the spelling. Moreover, medieval scribes, knowing *th* as an abstruse Greek graph and pronouncing it simply as *t* [t], occasionally put it into words that were not Greek at all. Thus, the name of the Goths, old Germanic *['goto:z], appears in medieval Latin-writing not only as *goti* but also as *gothi*, and it is from the latter graph that we get our pronunciation of *Goth*, *Gothic* with [θ]; the use of [θ] in *Lithuanian* is a modern instance of the same pseudo-learned pedantry. The same thing has happened in English to an ordinary Latin word, *auctorem* > French *autor* (modern *auteur* [otœ:r]) > Middle English *autor;* in English it was spelled *author* and finally got the spelling-pronunciation with [θ].

The habit of learned borrowing from the classical languages has spread to the other languages of Europe; in each one, the learned borrowing is accompanied by adaptations which reflect the circumstances of the contact, immediate or mediate, with the Romance-speaker's use of book-Latin. Thus, the German, who says *Nation* [na'tsjo:n], *Station* [šta'tsjo:n], could conceivably borrow a *Prokrastination* *[prokrastina'tsjo:n], — and similar habits exist in the other languages of Europe.

This whole history finds its parallel, including even the graphic

archaization of spoken forms (like the medieval scribe's *mansionaticum, presit*), in the use of Sanskrit in India. In the languages of India, graphic loans from Sanskrit are known as
tatsama ('like-to-it'). Like the *mots savants* of Europe, these
formations show us written notation exercising an influence upon
language.

EDITOR'S NOTES

CHAPTER 17 (pp. 281–296)

P. 282, cross-reference § 3.4. In any speech-community, an individual talks more to some people than to others. Between those who talk most to each other there is a high density of communication and often a greater similarity in speech. Lower densities of communication show a rough correlation with wider differences in speech.

P. 282, cross-reference § 2.1. The passage on p. 282 explains the difference between writing and language in essentially the same way as it is explained in § 2.1.

P. 283, cross-reference § 2.9. Drawings, paintings, and carvings have of course aesthetic, religious, and other functions; that of communication is relatively rare.

P. 289, cross-reference § 14.8 reads as follows: "In the Semitic languages the roots consist of an unpronounceable skeleton of three consonants; accordingly, every primary word adds to the root a morphologic element which consists of a vowel-scheme. Thus, in modern Egyptian Arabic, a root like [k-t-b] 'write' appears in words like [katab] 'he wrote,' [ka:tib] 'writing' (person), [kita:b] 'book'. . . ."

P. 296, cross-reference § 1 .6. Describes the Pāṇini grammar of Sanskrit (350 to 250 B.C.) which in Bloomfield's words, "presented to European eyes, for the first time, a complete and accurate description of a language, based not upon theory but upon observation."

Readings: Diringer, 1949 (a history of the alphabet); Gelb, 1952 (a study of writing); Karlgren, 1923 (on Chinese writing).[1]

Gleason, 1961, pp. 408–439; Hall, 1964, pp. 263–275; Hockett, 1958, pp. 539–549; and Lehmann, 1962, pp. 63–82 (all contain brief histories of writing and discussion of the interrelationships of writing and language).

CHAPTER 18 (pp. 297–320)

P. 297. The word 'primitive' in such names as 'Primitive Indo-European' and 'Primitive Malayo-Polynesian' is today replaced by the prefix "proto-,' as, e.g., in Proto-Indo-European and Proto-Malayo-Polynesian. 'Primitive' has been abandoned because it too often carries the false connotation that reconstructed ancestral languages somehow represent an earlier and cruder stage in the evolution of language.

P. 306. Cross-reference § 4.7 is to a more detailed listing of the Finno-Ugrian languages.

[1] Full citations of the books referred to are given in the Bibliography.

P. 309. The view that Hittite was so related to Proto-Indo-European as to make possible the reconstruction of a Proto-Indo-Hittite ancestral language has today been abandoned. Recently deciphered Greek texts provide Greek materials contemporary with Hittite, and so demonstrate that Hittite is in all likelihood descended, very early to be sure, from Proto-Indo-European.

P. 311, cross-reference § 3.3. Notes the difficulty (or in some instances the virtual impossibility) of defining a uniform speech-community. Although members of speech-communities speak in a more or less similar fashion, there are numerous differences in speech by virtue of geographic and social distance, age and generation, and differences in occupation, sex, and other factors.

P. 317, cross-reference § 3.6 reads as follows: "Within a dialect area, we can draw lines between places which differ as to any feature of language. Such lines are called isoglosses. If a village has some unique peculiarity of speech, the isogloss based on this peculiarity will be simply a line round this village. On the other hand, if some peculiarity extends over a large part of the dialect area, the isogloss of this feature will appear as a long line, dividing the dialect area into two sections." See Chapter 19 for examples.

Pp. 319–320. For a more detailed discussion of the ways in which linguistic reconstruction throws light upon non-linguistic conditions of earlier times, see *Selected Writings of Edward Sapir,* pp. 213–224, 389–462.

Readings: Gleason, 1961, pp. 440–479; Hall, 1964, pp. 300–313; Hockett, 1958, pp. 485–525; Lehmann, 1962, pp. 83–97, 137–146.

CHAPTER 19 (pp. 321–345)

P. 325. The New England dialect atlas has now been completed. Some of the publications that resulted from this research are listed in the readings below.

P. 326, cross-reference § 3.4. "Principles of density"—see note to p. 282, Chapter 17.

Readings: Gleason, 1961, pp. 398–407; Hall, 1964, pp. 239–259; Hockett, 1958, pp. 471–484; Lehmann, 1962, pp. 115–135.

On the New England dialect study: Kurath, 1939, 1949.

CHAPTER 20 (pp. 346–368)

P. 347, cross-reference § 1.7. Rasmus Christian Rask (1787–1832) and Jacob Grimm (1785–1863) were the first to discover and formulate phonetic correspondences between the Germanic languages and other Indo-European languages. Bloomfield's Chapter 1 contains an excellent brief account of the history of linguistic science in the nineteenth century.

P. 349, cross-reference § 13.8. The cross-reference is not necessary; the reduplication discussed is sufficiently defined and illustrated by the examples given on p. 349.

In the last paragraph on p. 349 Bloomfield points out that Grassman's correspondences, described in the preceding paragraph of p. 349, receive confirmation in the structure of Greek and Sanskrit, and in particular from a study of reduplication in these languages. Today this method of reconstructing linguistic history from structural irregularities found in a single language is called internal reconstruction. The method of internal reconstruction has, since 1933, been more precisely defined; see especially Hockett, 1958, pp. 461–470, and Lehmann, 1962, pp. 99–106.

P. 353, cross-reference § 1.9. August Leskien (1840–1916) was a student of the Baltic and Slavic languages who took a leading role in laying the foundations of historical methods of research.

Readings: Hall, 1964, pp. 295–299; Hockett, 1958, pp. 446–455; Lehmann, 1962, pp. 99–106.

CHAPTER 21 (pp. 369–391)

P. 371, cross-reference § 8.4. We find in all languages rules that restrict the positions in the utterance that phonemes may assume. "Habits of permitted finals" is one way of designating the rules that govern the occurrence of phonemes in the final position.

P. 371, cross-reference § 13.9. In nearly all languages there are morphemes that differ in phonemic make-up depending upon the combinations in which they appear. The differently constituted forms are called morphologic alternants. Thus, the English forms *deep* and *dep-* are morphologic alternants, the second found only in the combination *dep-th* and the first in all other combinations.

The second reference to § 13.9 on p. 371 directs attention to Samoan, which permits no final stem consonants at all. But it is evident from inflected forms that stems once had final consonants. Thus, the stem 'weep' is [tani] when it occurs without a suffix and [tanis-] when it occurs with the suffix [-ia] in [tanis-ia] 'wept.' This, incidentally, is another illustration of internal reconstruction; see note to p. 349, Chapter 20.

Pp. 371 f. The terms *sandhi* and *sandhi-form*. As we noted above, there are many languages in which the morphemes included in a word vary in phonemic make-up depending on the other morphemes in the same word. So also do words vary in phonemic shape depending on their position relative to each other and the phonemic shapes of adjacent words. The term *sandhi* refers to such alternations, and *sandhi-form* refers to the altered shape of a word or morpheme when such alternation is consequent upon combination with other words or morphemes.

P. 373, cross-reference § 13.9. See preceding two notes.

P. 374, cross-reference § 12.5. *Reminiscent sandhi* refers to sandhi alternations that preserve, in the sandhi-forms, older structural features of the language under study. It is clear, then, that reminiscent sandhi refers to what is today called internal reconstruction; see note to p. 349, Chapter 20.

P. 374, cross-reference § 6.7. A tongue-flip [t] is one made by a single rapid contact of the tip of the tongue against the gums or palate.

P. 374, cross-reference § 12.4. The data on Celtic sandhi alternations described in § 12.4 are not necessary to the discussion on p. 374.

P. 381, cross-reference § 11.7 reads as follows: "Some languages have the peculiar restriction, known as *vowel-harmony,* of tolerating only certain combinations of vowels in the successive syllables of a word. Thus, in Turkish, the vowels of a word are either all front vowels . . . or all back vowels. . . ."

P. 388, cross-reference § 9.7. Fixed formulas of speech, often also called stereotyped expressions, are phrases like *How are you?* that are not taken literally but simply as greetings. Such phrases, as the passage on p. 388 points out, are frequently reduced by excessive slurring.

P. 389, cross-reference § 8.7 reads as follows: "If we take a large body of speech, we can count out the relative frequencies of phonemes and of combinations of phonemes." Such counts, properly conducted, often reveal considerable differences between phonemes in frequency.

P. 390, cross-reference § 14.9. The section referred to is simply a more detailed discussion of the phenomenon here described.

Readings: Hall, 1964, pp. 314–318; Hockett, 1958, pp. 455–470; Lehmann, 1962, pp. 99–106.

For more detailed statements on internal reconstruction, see Hockett, 1958, pp. 461–470, and Lehmann, 1962, pp. 147–175.

Chapter 22 (pp. 392–403)

P. 402, cross-reference § 15.7 reads as follows: "The meaning of second-person substitutes [i.e., pronouns like the English *you* that refers to the person addressed] is limited in some languages by the circumstance that they are not used in deferential speech; instead the hearer is designated by some honorific term (*your Honor, your Excellency, your Majesty*)."

P. 403, cross-reference § 3.4. See note to p. 282, Chapter 17.

Readings: Hall, 1964, pp. 283–288; Hockett, 1958, pp. 446–451, 455–458; Lehmann, 1962, pp. 147–175.

Sapir, 1921, though an older book than Bloomfield's, contains an excellent and still pertinent discussion of linguistic change in the chapter on "drift," pp. 157–182.

Mention should also be made of glottochronology, a newly devised method for the measurement of linguistic change. See Hall, 1964, pp. 388–392; Hockett, 1958, pp. 526–535; Lehmann, 1962, pp. 107–113.

Chapter 23 (pp. 404–424)

P. 405, cross-reference § 16.6 Most speech-forms are regular, in the sense that the speaker who knows the constituents and the grammatical pattern can utter them without having heard them. A grammatical pattern is often called an analogy. A regular analogy permits a speaker to utter speech-forms which he has not heard; we say that he utters them on the analogy of similar forms which he has heard.

P. 416, cross-reference § 14.3 reads: "In English, we freely form compounds like *meat-eater* and *meat-eating,* but not verb-compounds like **to meat-eat. . . .*"

P. 418, cross-reference § 14.2. Phrase-like compounds in French are marked as compounds because French nouns do not display in phrases the kind of sandhi they display in compounds.

P. 423, cross-reference § 15.11. In languages with case-forms, the inflection of the relative pronoun is normally determined by its position in the clause. However, languages with complicated inflection now and then show *attraction* of the relative pronoun into an inflectional form that belongs properly to the antecedent, instead of that demanded by its position in the clause.

Readings: Hall, 1964, pp. 335–352; Hockett, 1958, pp. 425–438; Lehmann, 1962, pp. 177–182.

CHAPTER 24 (pp. 425–443)

P. 431, cross-reference § 9.8. Most linguistic forms have more than one meaning. Hermann Paul (1846–1921) was the first to distinguish central from marginal (or metaphoric) meanings (as defined on p. 431) and to indicate the possible significance of this distinction for the study of semantic change; see § 24.5.

P. 435, cross-reference § 9.8. We are likely to think that the transferred (or marginal) meanings of our language are inevitable. But transferred meanings occur in all languages, and transfers we may encounter in a language foreign to our own are not to be taken for granted.

P. 439, cross-reference § 12.9. The term cross-reference refers to a grammatical linkage between two forms joined in a sentence or phrase in which one contains a mention of the other. Thus, in the Latin phrase *puella cantat,* 'the girl sings,' *cantat* is literally 'she sings' and so contains a mention, by means of the implied pronoun, of *puella* 'girl.'

Readings: Hall, 1964, pp. 348–352; Lehmann, 1962, pp. 193–210.

CHAPTER 25 (pp. 444–460)

P. 445, cross-reference § 3.8 reads as follows: "The purely relative nature of this distinction appears more plainly in other cases. We speak of French and Italian, of Swedish and Norwegian, of Polish and Bohemian as separate languages, because these communities are politically separate and use different standard languages, but the differences of local speech-forms at the border are in all these cases relatively slight and no greater than the differences which we find within each of these speech-communities. The question comes down to this: what degree of difference between adjoining speech-forms justifies the name of a language border? Evidently, we cannot weigh differences as accurately as all this. In some cases, certainly, our habits of nomenclature will not apply to linguistic conditions. The local dialects justify no line between what we call German and what we call Dutch-Flemish: the Dutch-German speech area is linguistically a unit, and the cleavage is primarily political; it is linguistic only in the sense that the political units use different standard languages. In sum, the term *speech-community* has only a relative value. The possibility of communication between groups, or even between individuals, ranges all the way from zero up to the most delicate adjustment. It is evident that the intermediate degrees contribute very much to human welfare and progress."

P. 454, cross-reference § 9.9. Large borrowings from another language often introduce into the borrowing language combinations that follow the structure of the language from which they were borrowed.

Readings: Hall, 1964, pp. 319–322, 353–358; Hockett, 1958, pp. 402–424; Lehmann, 1962, pp. 211–231.

A recent and detailed study of borrowing (with an extensive bibliography): Weinreich, 1953.

CHAPTER 26 (pp. 461–475)

Readings: see references given for Chapter 25.

Interesting descriptions of a jargon (or pidgin) and a creolized language are found in Hall, 1943, 1953.

CHAPTER 27 (pp. 476–495)

P. 485, cross-reference § 3.5. Complex speech-communities develop a variety of languages, differentiated geographically and by social class. Bloomfield classifies these roughly as follows: literary standard (used in formal writing and speaking), colloquial standard (the speech of a privileged class), provincial standard (of privileged groups separated from the great cultural centers), sub-standard (spoken by less privileged groups; for example, "lower middle" class), and local dialects (spoken by the least privileged classes).

P. 490, cross-reference § 1.4. A reference to an earlier and mistaken notion that the speech-forms of books and upper-class conversation represent an older and purer form of the language, from which the vulgarisms of the common people branched off by a process of linguistic decay.

Readings: Hall, 1964, pp. 359–369.

BIBLIOGRAPHY

Diringer, David, 1949. *The Alphabet.* New York: Philosophical Library, Inc.

Gelb, Ignace J., 1952. *A Study of Writing: The Foundations of Grammatology.* Chicago: University of Chicago Press.

Gleason, H. A., Jr., 1961. *An Introduction to Descriptive Linguistics.* Revised Edition. New York: Holt, Rinehart and Winston, Inc.

Hall, Robert A., Jr., 1943. *Melanesian Pidgin English: Grammar, Texts, Vocabulary.* Baltimore: Linguistic Society of America.

Hall, Robert A., Jr., 1953. *Haitian Creole: Grammar, Texts, Vocabulary.* Menasha, Wis.: American Anthropological Association (Memoir 74).

Hall, Robert A., Jr., 1964. *Introductory Linguistics.* Philadelphia: Chilton Company—Book Division.

Hockett, Charles F., 1958. *A Course in Modern Linguistics.* New York: The Macmillan Company.

Karlgren, Bernhard, 1923. *Sound and Symbol in Chinese.* London: Oxford University Press.

Kurath, Hans, 1939. *Handbook of the Linguistic Geography of New England.* Providence, R.I.: Brown University Press.

Kurath, Hans, 1949. *A Word Geography of the Eastern United States.* Ann Arbor: University of Michigan Press (Studies in American English, No. 1).

Lehmann, Winfred P., 1962. *Historical Linguistics: An Introduction.* New York: Holt, Rinehart and Winston, Inc.

Sapir, Edward, 1921. *Language.* New York: Harcourt, Brace & World, Inc. (Reprinted in 1955: Harvest Books, No. HB-7).

Sapir, Edward, 1949. *Selected Writings of Edward Sapir.* Edited by David Mandelbaum. Berkeley: University of California Press.

Weinreich, Uriel, 1953. *Languages in Contact: Findings and Problems.* New York: Linguistic Circle of New York.

TABLE OF PHONETIC SYMBOLS[1]

The phonetic alphabet used in this book is a slightly modified form of the alphabet of the International Phonetic Association. The main principle of this alphabet is the use of a single letter for each phoneme (distinctive sound) of a language. The symbols are used very flexibly, and represent rather different sounds in the transcription of different languages, but the use is consistent within each language. Thus, [t] represents an English sound in *tin* [tin] and a somewhat different French sound in *tout* [tu] 'all.' Additional symbols are used only when a language distinguishes additional phonemes; symbols such as italic [*t*] or capital [T] are used in addition to [t] only for languages like Russian or Sanskrit which distinguish more than one phoneme of the general type of [t].

The following indications are to be read: "The symbol . . . represents the general type of the sound in. . . ."

[a] *palm* [pam]
[ɑ] *hot* [hɑt]; French *bas* [bɑ]
[ʌ] *son, sun* [sʌn]
[b] *big* [big]
[č] *chin* [čin]
[ç] Modern Greek ['eçi] 'has'
[d] *do* [duw]
[ð] *then* [ðen]
[e] *men* [men]; French *gai* [ge]
[ə] French *petit* [pəti]
[ɛ] *man* [mɛn]; French *dette* [dɛt]
[f] *few* [fjuw]
[g] *go* [gow]
[γ] Dutch *zeggen* ['zeγe]
[h] *how* [haw]
[i] *tin* [tin]; French *fini* [fini]
[ï] Turkish [kïz] 'girl'
[j] *yes* [jes]
[ǰ] *jig* [ǰig]

[1] [The symbols here listed differ in many respects from those used today. For discussion of modern phonetic transcription, the student is referred to Hall, 1964, pp. 36–75; Gleason, 1961, pp. 236–256; Hockett, 1958, pp. 62–83. It should further be noted that Bloomfield encloses his phonemic notations in brackets (he does not employ precise phonetic notations). Today it is a general practice to set phonetic transcriptions in brackets and to enclose phonemic transcriptions between slant lines. For example, the notation /p/ is to be read "the phoneme represented by p."—Editor.]

[k]   cook [kuk]
[l]   lip [lip]
[λ]   Italian figlio ['fiλo]
[m]   me [mij]
[n]   no [now]
[ŋ]   sing [siŋ]
[ɲ]   French signe [siɲ]
[o]   son, sun [son]; French beau [bo]
[ɔ]   saw [sɔ]; French homme [ɔm]
[ø]   French peu [pø]
[œ]   French peuple [pœpl]
[p]   pin [pin]
[r]   red [red]; French riz [ri]
[s]   say [sej]
[š]   show [šow]
[t]   tin [tin]; French tout [tu]
[θ]   thin [θin]
[u]   put [put]; French tout [tu]
[v]   veil [vejl]
[w]   woo [wuw]
[x]   German ach [ax]
[y]   French vu [vy]
[ɥ]   French lui [lɥi]
[z]   zoo [zuw]
[ž]   rouge [ruwž]
[ʔ]   Danish hus [huʔs]

Additional signs:

When a language distinguishes more than one phoneme within
any one of the above types, variant symbols are introduced; thus,
capitals denote the domal sounds of Sanskrit [т, ᴅ, ɴ], which are
distinct from dental [t, d, n], and capital [ɪ, ᴜ] denote opener
varieties, distinct from [i, u], as in Old Bulgarian; italic letters are
used for palatalized consonants, as in Russian [bit] 'to beat,' distinct from [bit] 'way of being.'

A small vertical stroke under a letter means that the sound forms
a syllable, as in button ['butn̩].

A small raised [ⁿ] after a letter means that the sound is nasalized,
as in French bon [boⁿ]. A small raised [ʷ] means that the preceding
sound is labialized.

The mark ['] means that the next syllable is accented, as be-

nighted [be'najted]. The signs [" ˇ ˌ] are used in the same way, wherever several varieties of accent are distinguished. Numbers [¹ ² ³ ⁴] indicate distinctions of pitch.

The colon means that the preceding sound is long, as in German *Kahn* [ka:n], contrasting with *kann* [kan].

Other marks of punctuation [. , ?] denote modulations in the sentence; [¿] is used for the modulation in *Who's there?* ['huw z 'ðejr¿], contrasting with *Are you there?* [ar ju 'ðejr?]

INDEX

Aasen, I., 484
abbreviation 288, 488
ablative 315
abnormal 378
abstract 429f., 456f.
accent 308f., 358f., 385, 450, *see* pitch, stress
accretion 414, 417
accusative 388, 392, 457f.
actor 297
adaptation 420–424, 426, 446, 449f., 458, 492f.
address 255f., 401f.
adjective 387f.
adult language 463, 485
adverb 433–435
affix 414, 454
affricate 342, 378
Africa 472
Afrikaans 474
agent 366, 412f., 454f.
Albanese 312, 315f., 467, 470
Alfred, King 281, 295
Algonquian 359f., 371, 381f., 396, 402
alliteration 296, 395
alphabet 290–294
alternation 370–376, 381f., 410f., 418f.
American English 325, 361, 366f., 374, 394, 396, 401, 444, 464, 471, 480, 484f., 488
American Indian 283, 404, 455f., 458, 464, 469, 473
analogic change 362–366, 376, 391, 393, 404–424, 426, 436, 439
analogy 454
anaptyxis 384
Anglo-Frisian 304, 311f., 452
Anglo-Saxon, *see* Old English
aorist 362–364, 456
aphoristic 438
apocope 382
apposition 420
Arabic 289, 294
Aramaic 289, 294
archaic 292, 331, 401–404, 487
Armenian 307, 312, 315f., 319f., 470
article 371f., 419, 458, 470f.
aspiration 348–351, 446
assimilation 373–381, 390, 423
assonance 395
Assyrian 288, 293, 320

atonic 364, 376, 382, 418
attraction 423
Avesta 295, 315, 389, 451
Aztec 287

Babylonian 288, 293
baby-talk 472
back formation 412–416, 432, 454
back vowel 376–381
Baltic 312–319, 400, 423
Batak 310
Beach la Mar 472f.
Bennicke, V., 325
Benrath Line 343
bilingual 290, 293f., 445, 463f., 471
blend 422, 424
Bohemian 291, 385, 447, 466, 468, 483
borrowing 298, 306f., 320–345, 361–367, 398, 412–416, 429, 445–495
Brant 295f.
breath 375
Breton 325, 414
British English 367, 396, 484f., 488
Bulgarian 290f., 306–308, 314f., 363, 371, 373, 383, 423, 427, 451, 453, 457, 459, 466, 470
Burgess, G., 424

Carroll, L., 424
case 297, 388, 392, 457
Catalan 483
category 388, 408
Celtic 307f., 312, 315f., 319, 386, 463f., 489
central meaning 402f., 431–437
centum languages 316
Champollion, J. F., 293
change 281–495
character 284–286, 294
Chaucer 281, 295, 429, 484, 487
Cherokee 288
child 386, 399, 403, 409, 432, 444, 476, 485
Chinese 296, 388
Chinese writing 284–288
Chinook 470, 473
chronology 309, 340, 368, 413, 416, 451–453
classifier 286–288
clause 407, 437f.
cluster 335, 367, 370–373, 383

507